FORGE OF THE GODS

THE LAST KNIGHT

By

ERIC FOGLE

Cover design by Jeremy Robinson

BREAKNECK BOOKS
PUBLISHING COMPANY

Published by Breakneck Books (USA)
www.breakneckbooks.com

First printing, February 2007

Printed in the United States of America.

Visit Eric Fogle on the World Wide Web at:
www.ericfogle.com

The first book of the Forge of the Gods series is dedicated to my wife, Kristy, who sparked my desire to pick up a pen and helped in every part of the process. She is also the one who gave me the resolve to never accept the word "no."

ACKNOWLEDGEMENTS

I have found the experience of writing a novel both exhilarating and mentally exhausting. In fact, writing with whatever talent I may or may not have, has been one of the hardest things I have ever done—I compare it to playing collegiate baseball and football.

With that said, I have been blessed with so many people who have helped in the process, that should I leave any out, I hope they will remind me later. Each one deserves a bow of deep appreciation for all their hard work.

First and foremost, I want to thank my wife, Kristy, for buying me a journal in which to jot down my ideas. It was so simple . . . but without that gift, I would never have taken my hobby to the next level.

I also would like to thank my mother-in-law, Nancy, who with a single discussion helped transform Forge of the Gods: *The Last Knight* from a single concept into a multitude of ideas.

I offer many thanks to Charity Hogge, my editor and friend, who read my novel in its roughest form, helping me take an unfinished manuscript and turn it into a piece of art. Without her aid, you would not be reading this.

My appreciation also goes out to Zak Salhab, Scott Bartholomew, Sakuri Hakari, and Seth Chase. Though I have never been able to sit them down and personally offer my thanks for their being my beta readers and hardest critics, they have my gratitude. They helped me refine ideas by calling into question my philosophy, world-building knowledge, and deities.

I wish to thank my publisher, Breakneck Books, for believing in my work. Simply put, if they did not embrace the religious undertones of the novel, there would be no book to read. Thank you for giving me the chance, guys!

Finally, I would like to offer my thanks to the readers. You are the ones giving this small-time author a chance. I hope that this epic tale both enchants and challenges you.

Extras

The world of Aryth, like all good fantasy worlds, is as vast as its characters are rich. To aid the reader in keeping track of this world and those who dwell within it, the author has created a website that both enhances the reading experience and provides wonderful detail beyond the scope of the first book in the Forge of the Gods series. At the website you'll find maps, journals, character charts, video and images that enrich the Forge of the Gods experience. Visit the author's website at: www.ericfogle.com.

PART I: DEATH OF A KING

~ PROLOGUE ~

20th Eternity (Eternal Timeline)

WHEN DISCUSSING reality, we can only describe it as experienced by humanity, and more importantly, as it is known to Heaven. Bound by its own laws, actuality is based upon the perception that any given thing that is—is real. However, perception is multi-faceted, since mortals are flawed creatures limited by their fragile existence. Thus when we break down reality, a distinction must be made between those things that are known to be real (Heaven) and those that are assumed to exist (Material Plane).

Let us examine Heaven in its entirety, then. It can be argued that the gods are pure existence. They are the functional equation that cannot be denied, a focal point that binds everything else—a circular algorithm of order and chaos, destruction and creation.

Assuming the gods are reality, it is only logical that Heaven is where all things begin and end. If Heaven is the center of creation for the rest of the multi-verse, it is also the destroying agent that governs reality, bound by its own certainties: what is created must be destroyed.

In Heaven, there exists a single rule of reality which has never been violated, a certainty that binds both immortal and mortal beings alike: time shall always move forward. Though this law is experienced most keenly by humanity, it still must be realized throughout eternal existence. In essence, even the gods age. This is a limitation; a flaw that goes against the certainty that the gods are the only beings that completely experience reality, for aging is a fact of reality that they cannot recognize.

From here we descend to the Material Plane (The Mortal Plane) of existence. Here time flows as mortals know it, an unpredictable equation of plausible possibilities that only the gods may view at any time in the sequence. From a heavenly perspective, the Divine Plane passes these events off as flutters of realized potential probability—those events that unfold dynamically on the Material Plane—only to be viewed by the gods as a truth of unreality. This is why on the Material Plane, change is permitted, evolution may happen, and the future corresponds directly to the present and the past. For it is only there, on *the Mortal Plane, that the gods are recognized and cherished by lesser minds that cannot comprehend the laws that bind them.*

An angel, Gabriel Truthbringer, contemplated these things as he strolled down a path made of pure order, reflecting on his existence and that of the gods. In his infinite wisdom, he could see how eternity rolled on—a metropolis of souls, angels, archons, and demons—all bound by that which he knew to be real and all very static.

Stasis isn't necessarily a bad thing, Gabriel thought. For he knew that on the Divine Plane death was impossible: a being either existed in a corporeal sense or was winked out of existence completely.

"Not a bad thing . . ." he murmured, to nothing in particular. He could not deny that he felt restless, as did most who resided in Heaven.

Gabriel looked up to see a maelstrom of cosmic energy swirling, bright blue flares scorching reality. He contemplated the difficulty one had telling time in this repository of the gods; he supposed that he had resided here since creation, or twenty eternities. He wondered how mortals perceived such things, considering their unreal existence changed so drastically in such short spans of time.

Why am I complaining about complacency? Gabriel looked thoughtfully at the energy, seeing both order and chaos at work. *In my lifetime, I have seen change. I have gone to war and destroyed entire sects of my race for Him. I have watched millennia go by and collected souls for Him. I have even seen the creation and destruction of another divine race . . . in His name. So why am I so restless?*

In that moment, Gabriel noticed that even the souls of the faithful looked stagnant. Not for the first time, he wished that he was not the High Seraphim of Starsgalt, or as mortals knew him, the Angel of Mercy. He wished that he could visit the Material Plane and become less than real for just a moment—to see the universe in all of its unpredictable glory.

Gabriel sighed and lowered his gaze. He had been so deep in thought that he had hardly noticed a colossal white building, supported by pillars of law, justice, and war, standing in front of him. To anyone in Heaven it was an awe-inspiring sight, even after so many eternities without change. And even though Gabriel had seen the magnificent residence of the All-Father, Starsgalt—the Halls of Law and Order—nearly every day since his coming into being, he admitted that the grand structure still awed him as well.

Gabriel let the power of the moment sink in and walked by a glowing statue of the All-Father before he strode with purpose up steps made of pure creation. He had come to the Halls for his daily routine of weeding existence, as it was his eternal duty to check in on the All-Father's followers and maintain the faith pool which kept all of Heaven in motion.

Just before the Angel of Mercy entered the great hall of the All-Father, he looked again to the cosmos and irritably muttered, "Why can't I appreciate this? I am the most powerful Seraphim in the entire Divine Plane, a demi-god, what more can I ask for?"

Gabriel silently cursed his blasphemous words. He couldn't argue with the fact that his faith and devotion had been rewarded by the All-Father several times over. In fact, time had been on his side. The Angel of Mercy had slowly climbed the ranks as a servant to God, using his ability to think beyond his immortal race's infallible limitations. Of course, such infinite wisdom had also propelled him to his current situation—monotony defined.

As he considered Heaven and his place within its hierarchy, a thunderous *crack!* split the heavens. Though Heaven did not truly consist of "ground," Gabriel watched in horror as the thunderous sound caused order to become organic—which then began quaking.

Boom! Another wave of thunder rocked the heavens, this one undoing the reality of one of the All-Father's pillars.

The effect was so impossible that time . . . began to warp.

For the first time, the Angel of Mercy looked around and did not understand reality. Rules he knew to be true were altered and absolutes became uncertain. Though he could see the limitless plausibility of time, at least fifty million new infinite probabilities erupted forth. It seemed to Gabriel that Heaven was being ripped asunder.

Another piercing *boom* tore through Heaven. The force of the shockwave again shook the ground and distorted the basic principles of law and order. Gabriel did his best to stay on his feet as the sky turned from flaring blue to deep crimson. He was sure that both the ground and the sky would soon erupt in blood.

In that moment, before reality was indeed realized, a miracle beyond the power of the gods occurred: time stood still.

Gabriel recognized it as a single thought conceived in his mind. In this brief moment, a mortal generation was created and destroyed (or approximately the amount of time it took to draw a single breath on the Divine Plane).

The Angel of mercy shivered violently and fell to his knees. The unbreakable law of Heaven was being violated! He could only gape as the sky turned purple and red, and black lighting forked out in countless directions, annulling whatever it touched. He told himself that the variation in time was insignificant, that many in Heaven wouldn't even notice that the first rule of reality had been desecrated. Yet it had.

Can it be that this will actually change *Heaven?* Gabriel thought as he tried to remain conscious, struggling to convince himself that the impossible was not really occurring.

He tried to stand but another *boom* erupted. This one ripped at the angel's being. He could feel it tearing him apart.

Gabriel clung to his infallible nature. He could not comprehend an event that was not even plausible on the Material Plane. In his infinite wisdom, he knew the rules of existence almost better than Starsgalt himself. Not even on the Plane of Mortals could one of the gods alter time and perform a miracle such as this!

Angel of Mercy thought reality ceased to exist. The moment of uncertainty caused his essence to unravel. His mind lost focus . . . his hands and feet begin to warp out of existence . . . that which was real distorted to the point of losing its base as reality.

Then, as suddenly as it had stopped, time exploded around Gabriel in normalcy. A rush of cosmic wind picked him up and threw him backwards into the All-Father's home. He thought that if an angel had bones, they would surely have all exploded.

In panic, Gabriel pushed himself to his feet and stumbled inside the Hall of Law. The sight that greeted him would haunt him for the rest of eternity—the All-Father was sitting with a look of disbelief etched on his perfect face. The expression marred the god's perfection, another impossibility of infinite proportions. Gabriel could only conclude that the All-Father was confused.

Thoughts of fear and disbelief rushed through Gabriel's mind. It was obvious that Starsgalt had felt the miracle and was too stunned to react.

"What is it?" a golden baritone of perfection poured into Gabriel's mind. It sounded . . . afraid.

He doesn't understand, Gabriel thought, awestruck into silence.

With a single thought, the All-Father sent out the call for a Great Convergence, where all the gods would be represented. In the time it had taken to send the thought, the All-Father was gone and the meeting had begun.

The aftermath left the angel speechless. The implications were preposterous. Another shiver ran through Gabriel's mind as a single thought lodged like an arrow in his heart: *is it possible we have just witnessed the birth of something greater than the gods . . .?*

1

1999 A.D. (After Devoid), Year of the Crescent Moon
(Mortal Timeline)

20th Eternity (Eternal Timeline)

AN OLTHARI walked past a twisted stump, one that had been sitting for countless years under a red sun—a sort of proof that life continues on even under extreme circumstances. The creature, a male version of its divinely immortal race, had traversed so many worlds that it had lost track of the countless probabilities it had seen. Now the creature was growing weary of such travels, and of his search. It seemed as though each new world was a blurry map in his mind, a mere silhouette of life's existence, ever-changing and ever moving forward.

The creature, called Thurm Stormrage by mortals, told himself that all of his inter-planar traveling was a necessary evil to track down the life-essence of his mate, a pursuit that had taken the better part of the past three eternities.

That he had been so close annoyed the immortal. An Olthari's infinite knowledge was supposed to be near infallible—almost perfection—especially in comparison to beings that existed on the Material Plane. There was no reason why his divinity should prove less than perfect! Yet, his opponent had always been one step ahead of him, leaving only hints for him to follow through the mist, to each new world.

This time, though, the mists held little interest for Thurm. He was growing exhausted with the pursuit and, more important, of his existence. Even now he questioned the purpose of living when the life-wave emitted by the Olthari race was weakening to the point of extinction. In fact, the longer his crusade lasted, the more uncertain he became as to whether or not his mate was still alive—her waning life-force ranged from a slow pulsing buzz to a

dull beat; and finally, to the nothingness to which his entire race had succumbed.

Such thoughts made him wonder if he truly was the last of a dying race.
And if extinction was truly upon them, how long could he could continue
as last of his kind? The olthari gazed to Heaven. The punishment of the
gods would soon fulfill itself, since he and possibly his mate were the last of
a race created by divine hands—now banished, hunted down, and exterminated by their creators. He still felt the divine call, which pained him worse
than even the thought of death. That his race was cursed until the end of
eternity made the longing for Heaven that much worse. They would never
be allowed to return home. It was a certainty he had accepted long ago.

Thurm, why do you torture your mind with such thoughts? The immortal wondered as he looked up at the sky. *I don't need to rush the inevitable, do I?*

In fact, Thurm knew exactly why he sullenly continued his being—some
part of him was still not ready to succumb to the nothingness. He told himself that it was still in his power to end his race's suffering, that there might
still be a way to stave off annihilation, even a chance at redemption. Most
of all, he wanted to believe that maybe one day he could go home. The
thought nearly made him cry.

For that reason alone Thurm tried to never gaze homeward. By looking
towards the red sky, he saw the life-essence of his entire race trapped by the
gods on a plane of non-existence. It was a dark reminder of the Olthari
race's betrayal of their masters. It had been a swift punishment for their
crime, carried out the moment it was conceived. After eight eternities wandering the Material Plane, Thurm could still remember the exact terms of
the curse . . .

His race had been sentenced to die a horribly slow death—damned to
walk the multi-verse, outside Heaven, until their lineage had completely
wasted away. At first, the gods had united in this curse by banishing them
from Heaven and decreeing that the Olthari should wander as immortal
mortals, unable to die except by unnatural death and unable to voluntarily
kill themselves.

When the Olthari race had adapted and resumed somewhat normal, albeit shattered, lives, Heaven again came together and decreed that the
wretched race suffer another, more diabolical curse—they destroyed the
Olthari's ability to reproduce, sterilizing and killing most of the females.
Additionally, the god Starsgalt demanded that the soul of a dead olthari
could neither ascend to Heaven nor be winked out of existence; all Olthari
souls were forever condemned to an infinite eternity in painful limbo.

And simply becoming extinct was not enough. The final sentence was
issued by the god Illuviel, who had demanded that no matter how far the
Olthari race traveled, and even in death, they would always long for
Heaven.

The finality of this curse weighed on Thurm's soul. Not a day passed that he did not consider his unhappy fate. It brought a dull ache to his heart, crushing any passing happiness.

Closing his eyes, he brushed aside his dark thoughts and focused inward, concentrating on the faint buzzing sound in his mind. He let the idea of multiple realities wash over him, a concept that allowed him to bend reality between the different levels of existence. After a long pause, the immortal drew his body into a godlike position and pictured reality how he wanted it to be. He then began to weave his own divine flows—an ability that had once been his race's greatest gift from the gods—his ability to walk through the various planes of existence by opening portals to any world imaginable.

Those days were long gone. Now, Thurm used his gift for a single purpose: to keep moving. The fact that he was cursed and dying meant that he could never get too close to anything. By staying uncommitted, he considered himself still truly immortal in one sense; he was powerful enough not to have a need for lesser beings. By remaining unattached and constantly moving, one of the last of the Olthari felt alive.

Not that it matters anymore, Thurm thought, considering the foolishness of his pursuit. The notion of an emotional attachment fluttered through his mind and offered his soul a quick reprieve. Maybe it was a good idea to meet members of other races. It was possible he could even make an attempt at friendship, a bond far more important than the olthari would ever admit. The idea of friendship allowed his mind to focus on the divine weave, intensifying his power.

With his will now wholly focused on a single thought, actuality faltered just before it tore wide open. Where there had been nothingness, a gaping ten-foot rip in the fabric of reality opened and shimmering, luminescent blue light poured forth. Thurm frowned and peered through. The light was all wrong.

This was not the world he had summoned.

Nor was it a world he recognized; a faint aura of evil permeated the air. In the distance, he saw a dull, lifeless sky, red as the planet on which he currently stood. However, unlike the burned-out nature of this planet (one of his favorites), a blurred swath of desolate wasteland greeted him. It looked like true chaos ate away at life.

Thurm contemplated the landscape with a grimace. This was not his portal . . . yet he was certain this was where Elissandera and her captor waited. Squinting into the gloomy distance, he decided to venture where his heart guided him. He assured himself that this was his only choice. If this was to be his last moment of life then it would be on his terms, searching for the one he loved.

With long even strides, he unhooked the great hammer strapped to his back by a giant harness, a massive weapon which stood two hands below his nine foot frame, and stepped through the portal.

Cosmic power swirled around the olthari as he moved through a pocket of nonexistence, the space in which inter-planar travel was possible. In a fraction of a second he stepped through a thin film of divinity and into the new world. The sickening feeling of winking out of existence then back wracked his body. He tried to look around but was blinded by white tracers that blurred his vision.

When his vision finally cleared, he was greeted with a horrific sight: this place was not a mortal probability. In a dark recess of his mind, Thurm realized that this world must be directly connected to the Divine Plane. He felt godly power exuding from everything. Though he tried to rationalize it, nothing could ever describe such an abomination of life; dark swirls of chaos tore at a shattered sky, giving off a deep purplish hue. His immortal eyes viewed a world devoid of any ordered thing; misshapen trees dotted the desolate landscape, doing their best to eke out an existence. Aside from this mockery, the scorched land was free of anything that even roughly resembled life.

The sight of true chaos made his skin crawl. Here the equation of the universe did not apply, time did not flow in mortal years, and balance was not achieved. By looking at the mottled husks of the trees, he knew that the equation was trying to right itself; however, only a travesty of creation prevailed.

A distant sound caught his attention.

Thurm gripped the shaft of his giant hammer as the wind blew the faint scream past him. The full power of the place came rushing upon him, intensifying his soul-bond with Elissandera. He was sure that she was located less than five miles to the east. It might be too late to save this world, but he knew she still lived . . . at least for the moment.

He cleared his mind and set out with resolve, shaking off his uneasiness. He told himself that he needed to be steady. His goal was in sight; he was here to find Elissandera and save her if he could or release her into eternity if he couldn't. He had decided long ago that if she needed to die, then he did, too—that if this was his fate, he would face the *thing* that had eluded him for so long. His resolve demanded that he die trying; for her he could not turn back.

Another faint scream swept across the desolate wasteland.

Thurm's hair rose. He felt Elissandera's soul-bond call out to him; this place seemed to magnify the essence of his people. For a moment he thought that he wasn't alone, an oddly satisfying feeling. An impossible thought tore through his defenses—could this be a parallel plane of existence to that of the divine?

A pocket plane for one of the gods, he thought sourly. If that was true then he had been summoned here for a reason, and whatever resided in this place would be unassailable by his powers. He could not win.

It is a fitting punishment that the same gods who created my race will also be the ones to end our existence, he thought sadly. It was likely that if this was a divine pocket, then there was a god toying with him, which was why his quest had lingered on so long. *I shall die proud,* he thought, standing straight and tall. *If one of the gods has summoned me here to end my life, then I will fight to the end.*

Thurm shook his head and banished such thoughts; he was thinking too far ahead. Whatever he faced was beyond his limited comprehension. His mind had been used against him, reminding him of old times and things long forgotten. He rubbed his perfect features and again set off toward the sound.

As Thurm prepared to take a step, his vision blurred and his skin started to crawl. The feeling was followed by a distortion of his physical features, which made him stumble forward in disorientation. He was about to succumb and fall to the ground when something called out and beckoned him, blinking him out of existence and back.

The summons nearly made him retch as he came crashing through the portal and staggered to the ground.

"So the destroyer has finally come!" boomed a sinister voice, its mocking tone filled with unpredictability and evil.

The olthari shook away the sparkling lights of his instantaneous transportation from his vision and looked around. It took him a moment to get his bearings, but he was sure that he was standing in front of a circular structure with random spires of ebony jutting up into the sky. Furthermore, he was greeted by an angel leaning against one of the columns, its features twisted into a perfect mask of chaos.

It took Thurm only a moment to realize his mistake. It had been so long . . . such a distant memory of what had been . . . that he could not have fathomed what stood before him.

The olthari stepped back and dropped to his knees in reverence and fear, recognizing not an angel but Illenthuul, the Dark God, and God of Chaos. What the greater god wanted with him was unimaginable. Thurm knew this god could do many things worse than kill him.

"I have come in search of my mate," Thurm said cautiously.

"So you have." Illenthuul warped behind him. *"However, the female is beyond your assistance, I'm afraid."*

"What have you done to her . . .?" Thurm screamed. With swift determination he leapt into the air and raised his great hammer, ready to strike down the god. He knew this would be his only chance.

With blinding speed Illenthuul nonchalantly reached out and grasped the olthari's wrist, stopping the immortal in place before shattering every bone.

The Dark God waited until Thurm was on the verge of unconsciousness before he let go.

"*Do not test my patience, little one,*" said Illenthuul, warping back to stand in front of a great dais that appeared. The god yawned and sat down, stretching out his legs.

"What . . . do you . . . want, my lord?" gasped Thurm, clutching his ruined arm.

"*That is better,*" Illenthuul said. "*What I want, is you, little one.*" Illenthuul grinned slyly, his eyes glowing crimson. "*My want is so great that I have hunted down your race, waging divine genocide on your entire species, until only you and your female remain.*"

"But . . . *why?*" Thurm croaked, crumpling to the ground.

"*I highly doubt you wish to hear all the nasty details.*" Illenthuul looked to the sky. "*The short version is that I had planned to use you as the great destroyer of Heaven.*"

"Never!" sobbed the miserable creature. "I will . . . never . . .!"

"*You already have,*" said Illenthuul. "*You have served me in the past and you will serve me now. In fact, your service is responsible for your race's extinction . . . and that I am here now and not in Heaven. But that is another story for another time. As I was saying, I require your presence in a very personal matter. I have a task for you.*"

"I will never serve you!" Thurm pushed himself up defiantly.

"*I had supposed not,*" said Illenthuul. "*The choice is yours; however, your female is now trapped between an eternity in my presence or a freedom that only I can offer.*"

Thurm's resolve faltered. "What do you mean? What freedom you could possibly offer her besides a quick death?"

The Dark God laughed. "*I have found a way to reopen the gates of Heaven, little one. And more important, I can restore the balance that has been missing for fifteen eternities.*"

"You are a liar!" Thurm erupted. How could he fall for such sinister trickery? "Your claim is impossible! *You* are the betrayer!"

"*Like I said, young one, I want only to restore Heaven to its full glory,*" Illenthuul responded. "*If you do this for me, I will save your entire species.*"

"You . . . do not have . . . the power." Thurm was too aghast to even consider this possibility.

"*Let* me *worry about my power,*" Illenthuul said. "*Here is your choice: You will serve me until the end of time, searching for the source of order that will allow me to conquer Heaven, or your race will face annihilation.*"

Illenthuul paused so his words sunk in. "*I will even offer you a chance to save whole mortal worlds—allowing you one year on every planet you visit to find the source. If you cannot find what I am looking for, Thurm, you will open portals into each world so that my armies can invade.*"

"And if your armies invade a world?"

"*Then I will scour the world clean of any life.*" Illenthuul smiled.

"What am I looking for?" the olthari asked in resignation.

"Not a single god knows." Illenthuul started to dissolve. Just before he dissolved, he added one more thing. *"But should you find it, little one, your job will be to protect it all costs."*

Moonlight streamed through the rusted bars of Lawlian Fortress's lowest dungeon cell. The stench of unwashed bodies, urine, and feces mixed with the moans of several inmates to give the dungeon a menacing presence. The high lord commanding the building had made sure that the populace could hear the cries of the criminals—a warning to all that law and justice would be served.

The strategy had been an effective one, for the Bre'Dmorian High Lord had been able to curb crime in the city of Brenly for over twenty years. That was, until a new sort of criminal had surfaced: a traitorous noble who slaughtered innocents in the name of Balzabuth, whom the Bre'Dmorians called the Angel of Murder.

Lord Edelin Hanson waved his hands into the dim moonlight and tried to figure out how he'd fallen so far. He knew that if the High Lightbringer had not forbidden capital punishment in Aresleighan courts, the High Lord would have killed him on principle. It all started with the fact that he had been beaten senseless several times in the last few nights. Though he had only been in the dungeon twelve days, his once fine clothes were torn, hanging in shreds from his fit body. The murderer looked wistfully to the ceiling of his cell and tried to picture the moon. He wondered what he would be doing now . . . if he was still free. He imagined that he would be dressed in the rich colors of Tares silk—the finest cloth in the world, which he had imported from the Far East—and once again relishing the screams of his victims.

It is a travesty that I will no longer be able to act upon God's will, Edelin thought sadly, hearing the soft creak of the nearby gallows. Death by hanging was a pittance compared to the utter chaos he had caused. He realized that this was the price he willingly paid to torture, mutilate, and finally murder such succulent specimens.

A smile crept across his tanned face. Not for the first time in his life, Edelin savored what a great time it had all been. In his twenty-three seasons of life, he had accumulated over one hundred murders, a small amount of death in comparison to what other servants of God had accumulated in the past decade, but not bad for a human. He could still see all the shallow graves that posterity would one would one day credit to him. A shiver of delight coursed through his body.

A whimper brought Edelin out of his reverie, and he looked around with disdain. He knew he was better than this. He wondered why those wretched heretics in the service of the Angel of Order, Starsgalt, stuffed him into this reeking hole. It was dark, and the stench was overpowering.

I deserve more than this for being such a devout follower of the One God, Balzabuth, Edelin thought, calculating a response to such moronic whining.

"Shut your damn mouth, filthy peasant!" He spat into the far corner of an adjacent cell that contained a young thief missing his right hand. The fallen noble assumed the young man had been caught filching, had his hand removed in gory fashion, and was then thrown into jail. Smugly, he made a mental note that the thief deserved such a fate, possibly even the gallows.

Standing up, the murderer moved towards the shadows of his cell. He hoped a guardsman was near. He needed to explain that he was still a noble in the small city of Brenly. Sure, he was awaiting trial and subsequent execution, but he hadn't truly committed a real crime! Each of his so-called transgressions had been in the service of Balzabuth, the One True God. He wanted to explain that he was simply a servant, an innocent.

Not seeing anyone nearby, the fallen noble kicked against the bars and yelled. However, only incessant whimpering greeted him. He wished that young thief would just shut up. He swore that if he met the young man in the afterlife, he would cut out the wretch's tongue and take the other hand as well. The thought calmed his murderous soul.

How can any mere human understand my artistry? Edelin wondered, falling back against the wall and gazing at the moonlight. Murder was artistry after all, a masterpiece that no one understood. To the ignorant heretic, it was a demented weave of gruesome pain and suffering. He, however, could see more—the depth, life, and cruelty that defined the divine attributes of God.

His eyelids fluttered as he inhaled the intoxicating power of fear. Why could no one understand his innocence? He deserved respect, something he could not expect from the Bre'Dmorians. One day, Balzabuth would come for their kind, and Edelin wondered how the King of Darkness would judge *them.* He realized they worshipped one of His servants, the Angel Starsgalt, who also followed the virtues of war. The Bre'Dmorians took life for the cause of justice. Edelin figured they were not so different than he, both honoring the murderous nature of God.

Edelin chuckled to himself. After a fair trial, a Bre'Dmorian lord would be his executioner. The murderer would be murdered.

The ironies of life never end. I will be murdered by an unbeliever to satiate God's hunger. The thought brought another wry smile to Edelin's face. It seemed only fitting that Balzabuth would murder him for his servitude. It would be a great honor, a position of elite standing among the One God's believers.

The sound of chewing—rats gnawing on the rotting corpse of a long-time inmate—interrupted Edelin's thoughts of grandeur. He despised rats.

In a sudden fit of rage, he picked up a small stone and threw it at the un-moving mass of human flesh. Though he could not see his target, squeaks and scurries led him to believe he'd found it.

Trying to calm his mind, Edelin closed his eyes and tried to recall a hap-pier period in his life. The first thought that came to mind was the sheer amount of resources the town had poured into his capture. Brenly was a poor town, modest by all standards, but Count Gustafson had spared no expense tracking him down. Edelin had even been part of the search party, leading Bre'Dmorian Templars in all directions, extending the manhunt for several months. For sure, a pleasurable thought.

Yet, it lacked a certain . . . *something*. Another memory surfaced; this one a conquest. He had manipulated the count's wife and daughters, seducing them into the service of the Dark King by poisoning their minds with pain and constant pleasures. He eventually had murdered all three, but not be-fore the once-fervent followers of Starsgalt had committed their souls to Balzabuth. He mused at this happy thought. It had been a shame to kill Count Gustafson's eldest daughter, Mara, for she had almost matched Ede-lin's own cruelty after her remarkable transformation.

The slight regret in the conquest memory urged the prisoner's mind on to a more recent endeavor—possibly his favorite—a murder done without the use of his hands. It involved the rotting corpse in the next cell who had been another simple thief, harshly punished for stabbing the local magis-trate. He could tell from their conversations that the man had not deserved to be in the bowels of this hellhole.

It was unfortunate for the young man that he had been placed next to Edelin, and even worse that Edelin had been so frustrated by his improper confinement. He suppressed a smile at the artistry used to poison the thief's mind, driving the man to insanity. In truth, it had not taken much, as the fear of death was already strong in the man. Still, Edelin savored the cor-ruption, drinking it like a fine wine, especially when the thief found a stick, ground it against the hard walls to make it sharp, and slit his own throat. It was the perfect murder.

Edelin again looked to a false sky and murmured a quick prayer. With such pleasant thoughts he could finally sleep.

Then a miracle occurred.

The dungeon became silence incarnate and darkness seeped from the walls, coalescing into a demonic mist. He could only stare in awe as it swirled around him, moving slowly up his body in a dark embrace.

Edelin dropped to his knees as tears of recognition streamed down his face. The Dark King had come to murder him in the night and take him to Heaven. He began to chant a recitation from the Dark Tome to expedite the process.

Within moments the darkness spread across the entire space of the cell; no light penetrated it. In less than two breaths, Edelin looked up into a pair of glowing purple eyes; a frighteningly beautiful head of obsidian was silhouetted against utter darkness.

"*Balzabuth,*" he whispered in awe, barely able to control his bodily functions in the presence of God.

"*I am not I AM,*" the voice resounded, perfection personified. It was almost too much for Edelin's mind to grasp. "*I am the messenger of His word!*"

"The messenger . . .?" Edelin tried to recall the Dark Tome's hierarchy of Heaven. He knew the holy artifact mentioned this messenger.

"*Come, mortal, and recognize Gadul, Angel of Hatred, First Demon Prince, and servant of I AM!*" Gadul announced.

"Have you come to . . .?" Edelin whispered reverently, his body still trembling.

"*I have not come to end your life,*" replied Gadul. "*I AM has dictated that His need for you has grown in this world. Moreover, He wishes to reward your servitude.*"

"Reward me for my service?" Edelin shivered. "What does God ask of me?"

"*He demands your subservience, mortal, and your devotion to His cause!*"

"I would do anything for Him," Edelin's voice broke with emotion.

Gadul devoured the essence of the faithful mortal soul in a moment of complete silence. "*Then He charges you with a holy crusade,*" he said. "*You are to seek out the source of good that plagues this world. Once found, it is your holy duty to destroy it! In return for your obedience, He will wipe away any memory of your name and face from those who would hunt you down or tell your tale. He will also grant you freedom and unimaginable power in the mortal world! There shall be murder on a scale never before heard of on Aryth.*"

"What *is* the source of good I seek?" cried Edelin fervently.

"*Seek miracles!*" Gadul replied, "*And, mortal, do whatever it takes . . .*"

The darkness became absolute and Gadul's form disappeared. Edelin swore he could feel the nothingness of such a destructive force caving in his will to survive. His mind wavered on insanity. Then the cell melted away and there was only the shining moon.

Edelin the Murderer was free.

The Bre'Dmorian Academy was arguably the greatest achievement of the past two thousand years. Unlike the rest of the City of Aresleigh, it had been constructed with divine magic, polished marble, and human architecture. It truly embodied the magnificence that was Starsgalt, God of Order. The building's central dome, a massive mural depicting Starsgalt's divinity, crowned at nearly one hundred and fifty feet in the air, a massive beacon to the world of the One True God's existence.

Lord Bowon Silvershield, a knight wearing a snow-white cape emblazoned with the golden crown of Arsgoth, walked between massive columns of gilded marble and stared intently at the mural. He was young, maybe twenty-one seasons, and his tall muscular frame carried a youthful face. By his insignia, he belonged to the lowest order of Bre'Dmorian Knighthood, a knight of the crown, referred to as a basic knight.

Those who knew Bowon understood that he was often deep in thought, his hazel eyes distant. Then again, he had always been a quiet man. Though most outsiders thought him dour, his quietude had nothing to do with his stern nature, the latter attributed to his upbringing as a peasant.

In fact, his life as a peasant had taught him many things—primarily that in a life of professional servitude, working in exchange for food and shelter, one quickly learned to speak only when asked a direct question. It was not uncommon that laborers turned to personal thought for comfort. Survival on the streets of Aresleigh required a silent compliance with orders, a vicious cycle of basic slavery.

As Bowon paused at the great Dome of Anduin, his thoughts took an unpleasant turn as he considered what had brought him down this path.

He remembered vividly how plague had gripped the poorest quarter of the city, Temapard Row. It had taken the lives of over seven hundred people before the duke had in the name of Starsgalt ordered whole neighborhoods showing signs of plague, including their inhabitants, to be burned until nothing was left but ash.

At one time the knight himself had been scheduled to burn with the rest of his people. It was in the last stages of the weeping sickness that God had miraculously intervened and purged the sickness from his body, and Bowon had truly been saved. The event had left him with pockmarks covering his torso, a reminder that God had saved him.

A tear trickled down his face.

He recalled looking out the window of the Bre'Dmorian Academy's hospital to see dark smoke rising into the afternoon sky. Even now there were moments when he secretly wished for death, as a part of him wanted to join his family that God had not seen fit to spare. He still heard his parents' screams as soldiers barricaded a section of city and flames licked at the plague victims.

Bowon knew that somewhere deep inside, he was still furious with God. However, he now realized that the duke and Starsgalt had done what was needed to save countless others—a difficult decision, but undeniably the correct choice.

The knight wiped his tears, acknowledging a moment of weakness.

That tragedy led me here, he thought grudgingly. On his tenth birthday he had come back to the Halls of the Hand, seeking resolution. At the time he had sought knowledge from an uncaring God, trying to understand why He allowed such a thing to happen. Mostly, Bowon wondered why only he had been spared, while the rest of the plague victims had been burned to death.

He'd asked an elderly cardinal that same question: "Why would a compassionate God of Law, Order, and Justice allow such tragedy, when He has the power to stop it?"

"Young man, what is your name?" the cardinal had inquired.

The young version of the knight bit on his lip before he finally answered, "Bowon of Foxworth Street, sir."

"Bowon, did your family own anything?" Cardinal Del Urelson had asked.

"We once owned a pig."

"Can you recognize that your father could make a decision about that pig, whether right or wrong, that the pig could not understand?"

"My papa would only kill the pigs if they were meant to eat!" the child Bowon had squeaked defiantly.

"That he did," the cardinal chuckled. "Your father knew the consequences of the matter at hand. With no food, you would have starved. He knew that it was necessary for the pig to be eaten, sacrificed to feed your family." The man paused thoughtfully. "It is like that with God. We are but pigs to Him, and what He does is far beyond our comprehension. He makes choices that we may view as wrong, but perhaps it is *we* who are limited in our view."

The lesson stuck with him. And, when he was ready, Cardinal Urelson had recruited Bowon into the Bre'Dmorian Academy and trained him in theology, history, and military matters. Though the young knight's role in God's grand scheme was as a military man, Bowon never forgot where he came from.

The horrific memory secured his faith in something greater, significantly beyond his limited understanding.

My limited understanding. Bowon mouthed the word "limited" as he strode with purpose toward a large antechamber. As he neared the chamber, a pair of young squires snapped to attention and barred his way.

"My lord," said the first squire respectfully, "what business do you have with Archbishop Urelson?"

Bowon announced himself and his need for spiritual guidance.

The second squire followed protocol and bowed his head to Bowon before he went through the ancient oak doors. The squire soon reappeared and invited the knight into another chamber.

Bowon smiled inwardly. He had hoped his relationship with the fragile holy man would gain him admittance, and so it had. Not many men, especially one so freshly inducted into the knighthood, could beg guidance from one of the most powerful priests in the Bre'Dmorian Order.

As Bowon walked through the doors and over to a large wooden table piled high with ancient texts, an old man looked up. The knight dropped to one knee and bowed his head, but not before seeing fondness in the old man's eyes. He knew his decision to talk to the Archbishop was a good one. In fact, he was about to impart some very startling news, news that would require the faith and service of the entire Bre'Dmorian Academy.

"Stand, Bowon. What guidance can this old man give you?" Archbishop Urelson asked in an informal tone, neatly stacking several ancient tomes.

The knight considered his words. "God has chosen me for a task of great magnitude, your holiness."

The Archbishop's eyes widened in surprise then sparkled merrily, almost knowingly. The robed elder closed his eyes and began to hum with power, trying to divine the nature of Starsgalt's desire. "God works in mysterious ways, child. I could feel His blessing on you so long ago; I feel it more so now."

Bowon's breath caught in his chest. If Archbishop Urelson, his friend and mentor, could feel the presence of God, then he was not going mad after all.

"What is it that The One asks of you, my son?" Archbishop Urelson asked and opened his eyes with a concerned expression.

"A servant of The One came to me during the last communion, your holiness," Bowon said slowly. "He told me that a spring of great chaos has entered the land and that I must seek it out at all costs. He said that this should take precedence over all other things."

"He has given you a holy crusade! That is why I cannot divine Him. What are you to seek?" the Archbishop asked.

"God did not specify, your holiness. He simply said 'find the source of corruption and look for miracles,'" Bowon responded. "Most important, I am to destroy the source at any cost."

The Archbishop looked up with understanding in his eyes. "You are one of the few champions of God since Anduin of Arlock," the words came out in reverence. "In His name, my son, you *must* find the source."

† † † † †

The hierarchy of creation breaks down into gods, angels, Olthari, and finally, dragons. This is not so much a pattern of power distribution but the timeline of when each race was created by the gods, assuming the gods have no creator. Though each god is the only "real" thing, each is chosen by lesser servants to be viewed as the One True God. This delegates all other gods, in the view of the faithful, false deities or mere angels.

Considering this hierarchy, the first divine race, angels, are not considered to be truly "created" at any one point in time. It is known only that they came to consciousness in the likeness of the gods and though they are a limited version of their respective deities, they are bound by a multitude of rules which do not affect their creators.

The first real creation of the gods, the Olthari, were to reside in Heaven as servants to the angelical race, partially-sentient beings bound by eternity's immortal rules of ascendance, time, and omniscience. It is guessed by the Olthari that they were created to serve as slaves to Heaven's denizens.

The final divine race created by the gods was the dragons—the only divine race created by Heaven to reside outside of Heaven—whose sole divine purpose was to collect information. Thus, their race was created to serve on the Mortal Plane of existence, and due to their dual lineage (divine and mortal) remain bound by the mortal timeline. Dragons age in mortal years.

That is not to say that dragons pass quickly away into nothingness; they have an exceptionally long lifespan, not reaching senility until their ten thousandth year, or three and one half eternities. However, there are those among dragonkind whom the gods choose to transcend age, becoming *Sinafthisar*, or Ancient Ones. These dragons are not fully divine but rise above the effects of age and are stripped of all the color they once displayed in mortal life. In terms of dragon longevity, Sinafthisar exceed fifteen thousand years old, are pure white, and are mostly divine.

The price a dragon pays for transforming into a state of Sinafthisar is a god-induced slumber of five hundred mortal years. This hibernation, the "Divine Purge," renders a dragon unable to care for itself and therefore open to all kinds of malicious predators. Additionally, being connected to the Divine Plane of existence had its drawbacks: dragons were no longer at the top of the food chain.

One night, when howling winds preceded a dark storm readying to release its fury upon the Dragonspine Mountains, a divinely inspired message stirred a slumbering silver dragon in its lair. The dragon, a female known by humans as Silverwing, looked up briefly before shifting her position and laying her head back down on her forelegs. In moments she was asleep again.

Though the dragon had not initially heeded the call of Illuviel, a second, more powerful message assailed her senses. She raised her gigantic head, her golden serpentine eyes opened, and two long ivory horns grazed the granite wall. She regarded the room quietly as her sight readjusted after several centuries of slumber. Not that she needed to be worried. If there was an intruder in her chamber, she did not need to see it; her peripheral senses would quickly locate the trespasser.

After several minutes of concentration and sensing nothing threatening in her chamber, she stretched her stiffened body out and moved back into a more comfortable position. She wondered how uncommon it was for a transcending dragon to awake spontaneously during a great purge.

The dragon yawned, guessing that she was one of the unlucky ones. Her biological clock told her that it had only been two centuries since she had last flown the skies of Aryth, over the kingdoms of man, elf, and dwarf. It should be easy enough to fall back asleep.

As she repositioned herself comfortably, she closed her eyes and thought of the greatest joy known to dragonkind: collecting information. It was the job of her mighty species to watch events and provide information to Illuviel, the All-Knowing One, the One True God of Heaven. As she saw it, there was no greater pleasure than watching events coalesce and deteriorate beyond the control of the unbelieving lesser races.

Not that she looked down on the lesser beings for being unbelievers. It was the purpose of each mortal being to follow his or her particular faith, however misguided it might be. Though most followed Illuviel's servants—Starsgalt, Illenthuul, Balzabuth, or even a direct subsidiary of God's faith, Raphael, better known as the Wizened One—subservience was subservience.

Such peaceful thoughts made the dragon slow her breathing. She was almost relaxed enough to cross back into slumber when another powerful wave of divinity crashed into her. This time it was full force and she recognized its source: for whatever reason, God was summoning her. More intriguing, the situation was urgent enough for Him to bombard her with powerful divinely inspired calls.

Silverwing stretched again, pushed herself up to her full height of twenty-six feet—several feet shy of the ceiling of the cavern—and unfurled her great wings. Though her lair was huge, the ancient wyrm was not able to fully stretch. She looked around the cavern and was disgruntled to notice all the cobwebs that had settled on her hoarded stacks of neatly piled manuscripts.

Satisfied that everything was still in place, she turned to regard herself, noticing that she was not yet Sinafthisar; each wing still shone metallic silver. She quickly assessed the rest of her body, raising her forelegs and turning to check her spine. The rest of her body was pure white. She wondered what could make God interrupt her Divine Purge.

She made a snorting noise that resembled a sigh.

Obviously great events are about to take place in the world, important enough for the Unsleeping One to wake me, and here I am worried about becoming Sinafthisar! The dragon chided herself sleepily. She was His most trusted servant in the whole Material Plane; why shouldn't He wake her if something significant was happening?

Silverwing decided that her reward for service could wait; by way of mortals, she still had plenty of time. She decided that, however inconvenient, at least God believed massive change was about to happen . . . and He needed her.

Maybe I will finally see something new! she thought.

With a deft movement, the dragon retracted her wings and moved towards the entrance of the ancient hall. As she exited the massive cave and looked out over a two hundred foot precipice, she unfurled her wings and sprang into the air with a great *whoosh*. Though not quite as agile as her twelve thousand two hundred year old frame had once been, her ancient silver wings remembered how to fly and beat furiously in the air.

Silverwing looked around as gusts of wind and sheets of rain pelted her. *It* has *been a long time,* she mused.

She chuckled—half snort, half gurgle—and soared on, considering all of the possibilities. *Maybe the humans have finally reproduced so much that the world is overrun with them! Maybe the rest of the races have ceased to exist, as I predicted.*

The silver dragon mulled over the countless probabilities she imagined would happen during her slumber. She was so deep in thought that she hardly noticed three hours pass as she flew from her home to Caer Crimmthan, the largest peak of the Dragonspine Mountains.

Having been to this place many times, Silverwing recognized the landscape and found the jutting mouth of a colossal cavern, in to which she glided. As her eyes adjusted to a dim orb of blue light, she noticed four other dragons perched in a semi-circle around a celestial form.

It looked almost like an angel.

She landed and was about to speak, when a silvery voice resonated in her mind. *"Trusted servants of the One, I am here to instruct you in a great crusade."* There was a short pause as all the dragons glanced amongst each other. *"God, in His infinite wisdom, has felt an unbalancing source of divinity unleashed upon the mortal world."*

What is it that we seek, my lord? The silver dragon thought. She was about to continue but the angel cut her thought off.

"The One wishes to test the wits of His faithful servants, Silverwing," the angel explained. *"He wishes to see how well you can gather the information He seeks without a true definition of what you are looking for."*

Silverwing heard her brethren silently questioning the angel. It seemed to her that each question only led to more cryptic answers.

In frustration, Silverwing let out a resounding roar meant to draw silence. *"And if we find this source, my lord . . .?"*

"Then you will destroy it!" the angel answered.

With that, the presence was gone

2

Variel 32nd, 2020 A.D., Year of the Sword (Mortal Timeline)

THE SOARING crystal spires of the Arcane Institute, the graceful ancient architecture of the Bre'Dmorian Citadel of the Hand, and the prosperity of a city accustomed to high mercantile traffic had made the Dukedom of Aresleigh the second-greatest city in Arsgoth. Over the past decade, the city had grown exponentially, rivaling Natalinople, the ancient capitol of the kingdom, in sheer size and grandeur.

All of Aresleigh breathlessly hoped that King Roderick II would take note of the grand city's large port and defensive positioning by announcing his new residence there. Fed by this hope, rumors spread throughout the region that it was only a matter of time before the king announced his move and named Aresleigh the new Arsgothian capitol. Beneath the whispers, the people of Aresleigh didn't expect much; however, it didn't hurt to prolong the rumor and remain in the speculative spotlight of the entire kingdom.

Aresleigh was split into two districts that skirted the Bay of Dawn, spanning outward from the coastline two miles to the east, and three miles from north to south. Though the port metropolis was six square miles, its seventy-five thousand inhabitants were spread throughout the inner and outer cities. The expansive population required countless miles of thick, mortared walls to protect it and was separated by three massive gatehouses, one for each direction in which a paved road left the illustrious city.

Aresleigh was truly the Jewel of the West.

The crisp morning air began to warm and beams of light pierced the clouds on the first day of fall. To an observer watching the eastern gatehouse—an imposing stone structure housing a pair of knights, four squires, and sixteen guardsmen to deal with incoming merchants—it was a normal day. And so it began as a normal day for a squire of the Bre'Dmorian Knighthood; the air became warm, the sun beat down as a long line of merchants filed down the King's Road, and the gate's custom officers processed incoming goods.

Areck of Brenly groaned as he watched an argument between three merchants become a heated discussion. It was a frequent early morning occurrence as people inched into the great city, a seamless mass of un-washed bodies all seeking mercantile business. Drawing his brows together in a tight frown, he slowly moved toward the trio thinking of better uses for his time.

Though he was in his ninth year of service to the Bre'Dmorian Academy, Areck spent each morning immersed in guard duty as a sub officer at the eastern gatehouse. The position granted him a measure of pride and respect. He wondered for a moment *why* he was proud of this duty as a customs officer, which was an honor among ninth-year students and highly sought after position within his class.

It isn't that guard duty is glorious, he thought. In fact, it wasn't glorious at all. All day long he watched merchants come through the gates from the outlying hamlets and thorps, trying to sell their wares and make a living.

Maybe the fact that this gate gets the most traffic makes it so desired by the others, he mused silently. Of the three outer gates, the eastern gate amassed the most people. Due to the high volume of passersby, Areck assumed that people who lived in the outlying areas of Aresleigh must accrue great wealth with all their trade.

The daily routine always made him think of an ever-rippling river of randomness. Then his more pragmatic side would point out that his days at the gatehouse tended to be lawful and orderly, except for the rare occasion when a capsized wagon or broken wheel slowed the steadily moving throng.

As Areck passed by several guardsmen confiscating contraband from a seedy-looking trader, the argument between the three merchants grew to shouting. It frustrated him, having to deal with arguments, since most broke out over trivial matters.

Deciding that patience was a virtue, Areck stood for a moment and watched the merchants argue. Satisfied that he understood what was going on, he began to assess the situation, which involved a bucking mule and a pair of carts. He could see from the ripped bags of flour what had tran-spired: the mule had kicked the flour cart and tipped it into a second cart carrying a load of sweet cakes. Not only had both carts tipped, but several bags of flour had exploded, ruining both merchants' inventory.

No wonder they aren't pleased, he thought grimly, sweeping his finger across some of the gooey remains.

A colorful expletive taking the One's name in vain, aimed at the lineage of one of the merchants, brought Areck's head up. Quickly, he stepped between the men and raised his hand. It was one thing to be angry; it was another to curse in God's name. He was greeted with silence.

Areck looked at his commanding officer, a rotund knight-captain of middle years, for reassurance. To his surprise, Lord Bowon Silvershield extended his arm in Areck's direction, nodded, and held Areck's would-be reinforcement back. He guessed that his commander must have been hoping to see a good fight erupt and now that his hope was dashed, was leaving him to rectify the situation.

The young squire groaned as one of the merchants broke the silence with another curse. He knew he had to act before the bad situation turned ugly.

"Gentlemen!" Areck said.

"If ye *fed* that dern beastie, then it wouldn'a been buckin' in the first place!" said a beady-eyed man Areck recognized as the miller Sanderson.

"Bah! Ye no good cheat!" screamed a peasant, his fist shaking righteously in the air. "If *ye* hadn'a been crowding the streets so bleedin' much, ye wouldn'a spooked my poor Betsy! 'Tis yer broken cart wheels 'ere that done all this damage!"

"Why, I'm the finest miller in these parts!" Sanderson retorted. "I'm thinkin' ye don' understand who yer speakin' to!"

"You blathering idiots," the baker said in frustration, "I don't care about *your* malnourished mule or *your* ruined flour. *My* concern is that these sweet cakes were meant for Lord and Lady Ebony!"

Areck studied the three men, trying to decide a course of action.

"Now if you will both stop your arguing for five minutes," the baker said shrilly, "you can each explain how you plan to pay for my wares, which are ruined."

The others looked at the baker incredulously then simultaneously turned to the squire to mete out justice.

"Milord, me flour was ruined by '*dis* man," the miller pointed to the peasant. "'Tis no fault o' mine, and I expect to be paid!"

"Milord, you's a sensible man," the peasant said. "You's a witness. Dis 'ere man be followin' my poor Betsy too dern close. 'Tis 'is own fault 'is flour was destroyed! Just look at me cart!" The man was near tears.

"Squire, these men are obviously drunkards. He," said the more eloquent merchant, who spit a wad of tobacco to the ground and pointed at the miller, "might have been following too closely." The baker then pointed at the peasant. "And, this man's cart may be ruined. However, what *I* am delivering is of the utmost importance to Lord Ebony. I demand compensation!"

Areck raised his hand for silence. "Do the three of you respect the laws of the merchants' guild?" he asked.

Each man bobbed his head quickly; to refuse the guild's laws was to drop a noose around one's neck.

"Good," Areck looked each man in the eye. "I happened to be watching when the three of you entered the city and will offer an objective opinion." Areck paused and looked at both the peasant and the miller. "You, sir, know the etiquette when bringing your animals into such a crowded city. Our laws firmly state that all loss pertaining to livestock are the responsibility of the owner."

The miller smiled until Areck continued. "However, Miller Sanderson, you were following much too closely and you're lucky this mule didn't aim for . . . more *precious* cargo."

The miller opened his mouth, but Areck held up his hand for silence. He turned to face the baker. "You were also traveling too close, sir. If you follow the by-laws of our city, you know that it is your duty to both cover your wares and keep your own cart more than one full length behind another. Thus I determine that the fault in this matter belongs to each of you."

"But, my lord, you cannot . . .!" The baker and miller began to argue, disgruntled scowls on their aged faces.

"As I have already said, it is the law to keep your livestock under control, to keep a proper distance, and to keep all fresh wares covered. As an officer of this gate, I *could* charge all three of you the clean-up cost, a ten-silver penalty for following too close, and another penalty for not following proper etiquette when entering the city," Areck said, letting the threat hang.

Mouths snapped shut.

"Each of you has lost valuable supplies this morning," Areck said. "And I *know* none of you want to argue my decision, am I correct?"

Areck could tell the baker had misjudged the situation and was wishing that he had never asked for a knightly sentence. There was an uncertain look on the peasant's dirt-stained face. It was well known that by asking for a customs officer's aid the men were bound by whatever decision was made, even if that decision was profitable for no one.

"Since the greatest faith comes from loss," Areck began confidently, "and since there seems to be loss on all sides, I wish to offer a benefit to each of you."

All three men were practical merchants and dropped their gaze to the ground, knowing well that the day's loss would be less than compounded gate penalties.

"Sir," Areck said, nodding towards the baker, "I am of the opinion that to produce your goods you need a reliable supplier of flour?" The baker nodded solemnly. "Would I also be correct in assuming that you come to

Aresleigh each morning to deliver your goods to more than just Lord Ebony? If so, is it possible that you seek a means of transportation both to and from your place of business?"

"Yes, my lord," replied the baker. "Miller White died last summer and I have no constant supplier. And, as you can see by my being here, my search for a good laborer to haul the product has been less than fruitful."

"You, sir," Areck pointed to the peasant who owned the mule. "When you come through these gates each dawn your cart is barren. There isn't an abundance of work for laborers this time of year, am I correct?" The peasant bobbed his head excitedly. "This man needs a man with a strong back, able to pick up resources each dawn, bring them to his bakery, then deliver fresh wares back into the market."

Miller Sanderson began to protest then gave the idea some thought. The squire had managed to keep the baker supplied with flour, possibly give the contract to the miller, while ensuring that it was logistically possible to get supplies to and from the market each day.

"Milord, I see where ye's goin' with dis fine suggestion," the miller piped in. "I would definitely be willin' to assist 'dis fine gentleman 'ere by supplyin' him 'igh quality flour at the lowest possible prices. Not to mention, I also need me a laborer to 'aul flour into the city."

"I dunno what ta say! Me Betsy be da finest pack animal in 'ere Aresleigh!" The peasant was overcome with emotion, his skinny frame bobbing with excitement. "I had come ta sell 'er off today, times bein' so rough 'dese last months. If dese 'ere gentlemen will 'ave me, I can haul deir supplies for 'em!"

And people say that suffering has no part in the eyes of God. Areck chuckled to himself, remembering the old adage. *Only in suffering can we see the greatest miracles . . .*

The insistent drumming of words broke him out of his reverie. "My lord?"

"My lord, are you all right?" The three merchants looked concerned.

Areck nodded his head in embarrassment. He silently scolded himself for daydreaming on the job.

"My lord," the baker began, "We spoke while you were . . . uh . . . locked in thought. With your permission, your words are agreeable and we wish to clean up so that we may discuss the matter fully."

"I wish you a good afternoon, gentlemen," Areck said, saluting. "May Starsgalt's blessing continue to shine on each of you."

With a curt nod, Areck bowed and returned to the gatehouse. When he looked back, the merchants had cleaned what mess there was, moved their carts to the side, and were walking toward the Twisted Oak Inn.

Areck smiled at a job well done. It was just one of the many small miracles he saw each day.

Lord Silvershield was still sitting when Areck approached him. Areck guessed that his commander wanted to see how he dealt with the situation. Though he could not be sure, Areck thought his elder knight had an uncommon smile of pride—a thought he quickly shook away. A squire's superior did not encourage unnecessary actions or manipulation to appease peasants. Areck remembered his professors lecturing on how to keep strict order at a gatehouse, especially during the morning, so traffic could flow along efficiently.

Lord Silvershield stood and approached his squire. He slapped Areck on the back and laughed. "I cannot think of a young man more deserving than you, lad. You have an ingenious mind!"

Areck frowned uncertainly. He didn't understand what his superior found so funny about the situation.

"You have served under my badge for five years now and you continue to amaze me," Lord Silvershield said, still chuckling. The knight-captain had been with Areck long enough to understand his squire's modest nature.

Areck nodded, not knowing if this was a reprimand or a critique of his decision-making.

"Stop looking so dour, Areck," the knight-captain said. "Every day I watch you sort through issues such as this. I am continually astounded that a man with the tongue of a noble remains in the service of the Academy, as you do."

Areck gawked at his commanding officer. What would the other squires think if they heard such talk? The thought made his face redden in a fit of embarrassment. Lord Silvershield chuckled again.

"The point is, you will make a fine knight, lad," Lord Silvershield said with a beaming smile. "It is to your credit that you do not always turn to steel to mete out justice. Compassion will one day make you a great leader. It is because of your sense of justice and honor that I will be proud to sponsor you next year."

Areck tried to contain his excitement. A sponsorship into the knighthood! The young squire knew many who did not think he belonged in the Bre'Dmorian ranks, and Areck was comforted by the support of his mentor.

He was jarred from his excitement by an avuncular blow to his right shoulder. "Well, lad, enough of this old man's ramblings; it's time to get back to work. Those three set us back quite a bit this morning," Lord Silvershield said as he strode away.

Areck looked out the gates, saw the milling throng of people trying to enter the city, and knew Knight-Captain Silvershield was right. His interference with the merchants had held up the entire line. Areck frowned in concentration as he followed the commander through the gates and began issuing commands.

As the eldest squire assigned to the eastern gates, Areck was responsible for the small force of squires and guardsmen that manned the colossal entryway. Lords Silvershield and Umberton determined the daily routine and let their sub officers run the show. It was beneath a knight of the crown to directly partake in such affairs. Therefore it was no surprise that Lord Silvershield walked past several more arguing merchants into the gatehouse, and sat down to play chess with his counterpart.

"Derrick! Choal!" Areck shouted towards a pair of guardsmen surrounded by a group of people pushing their way to the front of the line. "Calm those people down! We'll be accommodating their needs within the hour.

"Squires Wolfer and Krys, get out there and reform those lines!" Areck called, pointing to a second group of unruly peasants. "The rest of you, help me sort through the people who have been waiting patiently; it's time we get these masses moving again!"

The squires and guardsmen snapped to attention and waded into the frenzy of people. Upon seeing Bre'Dmorian colors, the crowd eased a bit.

Areck guessed that it would take the rest of the day to reform the throng of peasants into proper lines. Putting his head down, Areck of Brenly went to work.

† † † † †

It was mid-afternoon when Areck first noticed the plume of dust approaching from the east. Though he could not see the source, he guessed it was a fast approaching rider.

They must be traveling at a full gallop to create such a cloud, Areck thought, his eyes following the King's Road, which connected Aresleigh to Natalinople.

Areck guessed that the rider was still several minutes away. He pulled a man-at-arms aside and asked that he alert Lord Silvershield to the situation. Whoever was in such a hurry would require a commander's approval for quick process. The guardsman bolted inside the gatehouse where the two knights sat at their game of chess. In the meantime, Areck turned back to a woman bent with age, bearing mugroot—a vile component consistently used by the Arcane Institute.

As Areck pulled the soft leather cover from the cart, a sulfurous smell wafted out so strong it made his eyes water. Areck flung the cover back over the product without further investigation. He had heard the rumors, that the herb's oily residue wouldn't come off the body for days, making the unlucky victim smell like rotten eggs. Deciding that there were no illegal wares in the cart, Areck hurried the old woman through the gates and into the city, hoping never to smell that noxious scent again.

He turned to find Lord Silvershield and Lord Umberton exiting the officer's quarters, looking to the east.

The rider drew close enough to exhibit the royal colors: dark blue livery trimmed with silver, a golden dragon emblazoned on both tunic and cape. The royal courier reigned in an exhausted black thoroughbred and maneuvered through the throng of people. The man's cloak was heavy with dust, his once elegant clothing bedraggled and dirty.

The crowd parted to allow the rider free passage to the gatehouse. The courier nodded curtly in appreciation and spurred his mount forward with graceful haste. It seemed to the squire that the man's haggard face held an unhappy story. Areck recognized the noble bearing of the courier's origin: his dark brown hair, chiseled features, and hawkish nose indicated that the man was Almassian.

The courier's steed bore King Roderick's personal mark. There could be no doubt about whence he came.

The rider brought his horse to a halt and scanned the faces at the gate, locking eyes with Lord Silvershield. "My lord, I apologize for my abruptness, but I come with urgent news for Duke Hawkwind."

"What news is that?" asked Lord Silvershield.

"I have a message of extreme urgency," answered the man, pulling a small parchment from his tunic and handing it to Bowon. "Please, my lord, I cannot reveal the nature of my visit, but that writ is marked with the royal seal."

Lord Silvershield studied the seal for a moment and gestured to Areck. "Allow me to quicken your journey, then, by offering the service of my personal squire, Areck of Brenly. He will guide you swiftly through the city and to the ducal palace."

Areck understood the order, nodded to his commander, and strode off toward the small stables near the gatehouse. He grabbed a bridled stallion, pulled his leg up, and prepared to maneuver the crowded streets of Aresleigh.

He silently vowed to see this man to the palace with all possible haste. He did not question the critical news that had prompted the man's rush across Arsgoth, though he couldn't help but speculate.

† † † † †

As Areck led the courier along the King's Road, gilded with marble and gold, traffic began to thicken. He groaned inwardly, realizing that going west had been a poor decision. It was a common misconception among newcomers entering the city that the larger road was more accessible during the day. In truth, the King's Road veered west then north into a large open plaza of vendors, laborers, and other mercantile businesses, often filled with several hundred people.

Seeing no alternative, Areck decided to try a side alley, a shortcut that would increase the distance of their ride but would reduce the amount of time it took to reach the inner city. He just hoped that it would be better then maneuvering through a throng of commoners. The courier rode behind him, eyes alight with wonder.

"This city is a grand sight!" the messenger said in awe. "Natalinople doesn't hold such magic as this!"

Areck nodded as he led them down several other side streets—letting the courier take it all in and ask questions about the city—before he turned down another alley that put the riders in plain view of the inner city walls. Within moments the pair exited the alley and entered a large square adjacent to the inner gatehouse.

Areck felt a slight tickle as arcane magic surrounded them. Though he could not see the magical flow, he sensed the aura of creation that exuded from the inner city. The feeling always made him shudder.

"I still get shivers when I gaze upon the inner city," Areck said when he saw his companion's mouth agape. A brief speculation of Heaven's grandeur passed through Areck's mind. He wondered how much greater God's Halls of Law and Order must be compared to the inner city, which was one of the greatest things he had ever seen. "Have you never visited Aresleigh, sir?"

"My name is Arawnn," replied the messenger, "and, yes, this is my first trip inside the duchy. Too bad it is under such dire circumstances. This looks like a city unaccustomed to tragedy."

Areck pondered the cryptic message as the courier's smile faded into grimness. He tried to place himself in the man's position and decided that maybe the look was not so much from bad news as from sleep deprivation. He decided to show a gesture of honor by offering the man a chance for some small talk.

"You look tired, Messenger Arawnn, and ready for conversation," Areck said thoughtfully. "When you have conducted your business with the duke, come find me; I have never been to Natalinople and would be happy to possibly show you around and barter some stories."

"I just might take you up on that, Squire, if I'm not forced back out on the road," the courier replied with a slight nod.

As the riders neared the inner gatehouse, a knight-captain greeted them. Areck watched the messenger offer the royal seal. The knight-captain took the seal and examined it, studied the squire, and waved them in with a dismissive gesture.

The pair passed through the grand gatehouse and into an open area that looked like another market. The marble-tiled road became marble slabs, inlaid with the golden lion of the ducal house.

Areck gave the courier a moment to soak it all in; the crystal spires of the Arcane Institute soared to the southwest and the massive marble domes of the Bre'Dmorian Academy were barely visible to the northeast. Before the messenger could speak, Areck spurred his mount down a street lined with inns and temples. When they reached the palace, he heard the courier gasp.

Though he always noticed the ducal palace when entering and exiting the city each day, it had never really impressed him, lacking the arcane possibility or divine majesty of other sights. Yet Areck had to respect a man-made achievement when it was due. What had once been Aresleigh Keep, a small coastal fortress, was now a fortified palace, reconstructed with modern architecture and finished with rare dwarven craftsmanship and stone.

The achievement spoke volumes about the nobleman who ruled the city; Duke Edelin Hawkwind was a boisterous man who had inherited his uncle's title due to the old duke's sudden death. In only nine years, the new duke had changed the port into a thriving metropolis, brought economic power into the region, and quintupled the population. With so much change and prosperity, the duke had become exceedingly popular with the locals who poured into the grand city. The sudden population explosion had forced the duke to expand the original city walls by reducing the old city to rubble and rebuilding a rich inner city, a working class outer city, and a new, better version of Aresleigh.

Areck had tried to find fault in the noble's strategy but finally conceded that Duke Hawkwind had to be a remarkable man to achieve so much. The sheer effort that went into the rebuilding of the city, and Hawkwind Palace, must have been tremendous. It made him wonder if there was magic bound into the stone. According to rumors, the duke had specifically instructed that his palace be erected *without* priestly aid from the Bre'Dmorians or wizardly aid from the Arcane Institute. But one had to wonder.

Perhaps it is pride, Areck thought, wondering why a man would try to produce something perfect without assistance from a higher power.

Areck dismounted and stroked his stallion's muzzle before passing the reigns over to a young stable boy. The squire led the goggling courier up a flight of marble stairs to stand before a pair of elite guardsmen whose polished armor gleaming in the sun.

The guardsmen, looking straight ahead, dropped their halberds to block the duo's path. Areck snapped to attention, embarrassed that he had broken protocol. The courier followed suit.

After a moment the doors opened and an elderly man dressed in brocaded green silk with a dark blue sash across his chest stepped out to greet them. Areck recognized the nobleman as Lord Faldorn Caldey, a frontier baron who now served as the lord chamberlain of the duke's household. The chamberlain was a polite man with little patience for either the faith-driven Bre'Dmorians or the political scheming of upper nobility. Areck assumed that Lord Caldey didn't believe in the One God, yet despite this major shortcoming the man had a reputation of being honorable, stern, and precise in his job.

A sudden thought struck Areck: the lord chamberlain had been awaiting their arrival. This meant that Lord Silvershield had sent Areck not to ensure the messenger received a quick passage but to buy time to send runners to the palace. The realization made Areck's skin crawl, as though his honor had been sullied. He decided that, though it was quite un-knightly, he would ask his lord about this.

Why must I assess everything? Areck reprimanded himself, trying to keep his expression blank. *These are blasphemous thoughts. Lord Silvershield has his reasons and it's not my job to question them.*

Areck watched as the messenger introduced them and explained their purpose. It looked like the chamberlain would ask Areck to leave when the nobleman touched his ear momentarily, seemed to talk to himself, then nodded his head in what could only be understanding.

"This way, gentlemen," Lord Caldey said, turning on his heel as he walked into the palace. The guards raised their halberds to allow the men to pass.

Areck had never been inside the palace before, and its majestic splendor overwhelmed him. When he realized he was gaping at the thick marble columns, rich tapestries, and the polished floor that mapped all of Aresleigh, he attempted to close his mouth. He turned to see the messenger caught up in the same wonderment.

A small cough interrupted Areck's awe. "Gentlemen, I was under the impression that you were in a hurry." the chamberlain emphasized the last word. "If you will follow me, I will lead you to the duke."

The pair followed the chamberlain down a corridor that ended abruptly at a gigantic, elaborate door. With a small gesture, the chamberlain held up his hand for them to wait and entered by himself.

Most likely dwarven, Areck thought, ascertaining that the intricate designs on the door couldn't have been made by man. The squire made a quick mental note: once he arrived back in the Citadel of the Hand, he would do some research on dwarven craftsmanship.

Areck was so deep in thought that he didn't notice the chamberlain open the door. Nor did he see the man beckon them both forward. It wasn't until another discreet cough was put forth that the wide-eyed squire looked up.

"Young man," said Lord Caldey, looking at Areck, "it is not my place to discipline you, but if you do not consider a meeting with Duke Hawkwind an important enough honor, I will be forced to speak to your knight-commander."

Areck's face reddened at the reprimand. *I am embarrassing myself,* he thought furiously, apologizing to the elder noble. He should be honored to meet a man who worked so well in The One's name, a man who had redefined how a truly dignified nobleman should act.

"Your Grace, per your request, may I present the messenger, Arawnn of Almassia, and his escort, Squire Areck of Brenly," the lord chamberlain bowed deeply to the duke.

Duke Edelin Hawkwind was a middle-aged man with a hawk nose, black hair, and the sharpest eyes Areck had ever seen. He looked up from his desk, rolled a pair of scattered maps, and placed them in round containers before carefully placing his quill into an inkwell. With a powerful air of authority the duke pushed himself away from his desk and strode toward the three men.

"Thank you, Lord Caldey, I think I can handle these two." The duke smiled. "Please give the guardsman a break; let them take the rest of the afternoon off."

"Your grace?" Caldey asked, his bushy eyebrows rising in alarm.

"Whatever Messenger Arawnn brings is for my ears only," replied the duke. "Besides, there is a Squire of the Hand in my room, should any mishaps occur." Lord Hawkwind turned his dark eyes upon Areck. "You are trained in the arts of war, are you not?"

As the duke's gaze penetrated Areck, the squire felt a sweeping aura of divinity emanating from the man. It was strong enough to incite Areck's unfortunate reaction of nausea in the presence of the divine. For a moment Areck was speechless. He had been prepared to deliver the messenger to the duke and go back to his duties. However, Duke Hawkwind was asking him to stay—and if he could wield a weapon. He almost didn't know what to say.

"Yes . . . er, yes, your grace, I am a master with both the long sword and stave," Areck responded. He regarded the duke with a new respect building in his heart, realizing that God had entered this noble's life. Areck figured that he would never again meet a non-knight of such greatness, one that left him so breathless and nervous.

"As you wish, your grace," Lord Caldey sighed, eyeing Areck with skepticism. "If you should need my assistance, do not hesitate to call out." The lord chamberlain left the room and barked orders at the guards.

"Such a good man," the duke remarked. "Baron Caldey has been like a father to me since Duke Eleran passed away." There was a fleeting sadness in the duke's expression. "Look at me . . . going on forty-four seasons and still affected by such memories." Hawkwind wandered over to a table holding several bottles of liquor. With a slow hand, the duke studied several flasks of wine before settling on a pungent apple brandy, and poured himself a cup. He then turned to face the pair of waiting men.

"Messenger Arawnn, you look parched," the duke said, filling a second glass for the courier. "Take this and collect your thoughts, sir; when you're ready, I wish to hear your story."

Areck again wondered why the duke had not dismissed him. It was not his place to stand before royalty like this, and certainly not to hear private information. Areck lowered his gaze, moved silently toward the exit, and stood just to the right of the door.

Though he had no idea why the duke had not released him, as a senior member of royalty Duke Hawkwind was to be treated like a knight-commander. The same rules applied: it was not Areck's place to question. His own speculation about the duke's motives made Areck's face glow with shame. He was here for a reason and would remain silent until the duke called upon him, doing his best to ignore the conversation.

The messenger accepted the cup of brandy and downed the fiery liquor in one gulp. He knelt uneasily before the duke and spoke the words that would forever change the face of the Arsgoth: "Your grace, I regret to inform you that King Roderick II has been killed on a hunting expedition in the Moonwood Forest."

Areck nearly bit through his tongue. A chilling wave of nausea coursed through his bones.

The king was dead.

3

SILENCE FOLLOWED Arawnn's announcement as both the duke and Areck let the information sink in.

Finally, the courier held out his cup for more brandy. When Duke Hawkwind solemnly poured the messenger another cup, Arawnn continued, "With this knowledge in mind, my lord, I have more urgent matters to discuss. As you know, King Roderick left no heir sitting upon the Dragon Throne. To make matters worse, dark rumors have already begun to fly in the royal court concerning those nobles present during the king's death."

"What rumors are those?" the duke asked.

"There can be no doubt that several of those nobles within the king's hunting party have been loyal to other factions in the past." Arawnn began with caution.

"Were any nobles injured?" Hawkwind asked, his eyes clouded in thought.

"One, your lordship," Arawnn replied. "The only noble actually in the presence of the king was Duke Valimont Windson of Thames."

"Was he questioned?" Duke Hawkwind continued.

The courier nodded. "The Duke of Thames has been put to the question several times and has revealed little information regarding events. His story is that he was knocked unconscious when the crossbow bolt impacted the king."

"Was Duke Windson still in Natalinople when you left?" Duke Hawkwind asked.

"Nay, my lord," responded the courier. "His retainers announced that he left in fear of his life."

The duke frowned at the statement. "I'm sure Duke Windson left for good reason, sir, and I would advise you remember your station. The Duke of Thames has served this kingdom for well over fifteen years. However, his departure is going to make matters more complicated, especially when this news reaches the general population. How has the royal court reacted to this situation?"

Arawnn took a moment to consider his words. "I fear the lords and ladies of the court have already begun to send out missives to those nobles for whom they serve. For this reason Lord Constable Highman has sent me here," explained Arawnn.

Duke Hawkwind nodded and considered the news. "He made the right choice. If those nobles with rightful claims to the throne start amassing power, especially before a Council of Lineage can be drawn, there might be civil war."

Areck listened to the exchange with dread. He could hardly comprehend what he was hearing. The royal bloodline that had lasted for nearly three hundred years was over.

"I am afraid I will need your services again, Messenger Arawnn," Duke Hawkwind said, bringing his dark eyes to the courier. "A great event is about to unfold in our kingdom, and we must move with haste to prevent any fractures. The last thing this kingdom needs is squabbling nobles, especially ones willing to risk open warfare."

"What would you have me do, your grace?" Arawnn asked.

"I wish you to move without delay, sir," Duke Hawkwind responded. "If we can call a Council of Lineage here in Aresleigh, we might be able to prevent dire consequences. I must emphasize how important it is that the meeting occurs *here*."

"Shall I leave tonight?" the courier asked wearily.

Duke Hawkwind looked at the man with understanding. "The night is yours to do as you please, Arawnn of Almassia. However, upon the morrow you will be granted a new mount, some fresh clothes, and an escort to ride with you all the way to Natalinople. Once there, you will give my seal and a missive to Steward Landon and Lord Constable Highman; hopefully they will begin the process of calling the nobility here."

"Are there any other instructions, your lordship?"

Areck felt bile rise in his chest and his breath came in shallow gasps. His vision began to blur as the first stages of hyperventilation hit him.

"Only to enjoy your night of leisure, young man. You have certainly earned it," Duke Hawkwind replied.

"Thank you, your grace," Arawnn said with a bow. "I appreciate your offer to rest, as this squire was nice enough—" The messenger's voice was cut off by the sounds of Areck retching.

Duke Hawkwind and Arawnn moved toward Areck with haste, concern etched on their faces. "Easy, young man," the duke said as he knelt next to the gasping squire.

"I'm sorry for embarrassing myself in front of you, Lord Hawkwind," Areck said, trying to calm his breath. "I . . . I was not expecting such dire news. May Starsgalt protect the king's soul."

Duke Hawkwind guided Areck onto his back and instructed him to extend his arms parallel to the body. He gave orders for Arawnn to alert Lord Caldey that the squire had become ill and would need some mint tea. When the messenger left the room, the duke whispered, "I bet you are wondering why I have kept you here, lad. It is because you have a part to play in all this. You are the only one I can fully trust to be expedient, formal, and honor-bound to keep this information *to himself*."

Realization struck Areck. It was almost as if God was leading him down a chosen path of virtue. Looking up at Duke Hawkwind, Areck nodded with determination.

"Good, Squire, I am glad you understand," the duke said. "Once you have received some tea, you must personally take word to the High Lightbringer and deliver a sealed parchment that I have yet to write. It is very important we act with haste; all of us may be in jeopardy. Do you understand?"

Again Areck nodded.

"If you are recovered enough to stand, I will begin lettering a writ to bypass anyone outside of the High Lightbringer," Lord Hawkwind said. "You are my word now, Squire Areck, and your service to the crown shall not go unnoticed."

"Thank you for your concern, my lord," Areck said, trying to sound improved. "My nerves are already feeling much better. I will wait here while you prepare the documents."

The duke stood and sat in a gilded chair at his desk, moving several dark markers around a large map. Without looking down the man took a piece of parchment, pulled out his quill, and began writing in a noble's hand.

As Areck watched the duke's pen making strong swift marks, he began to think of the implications. Duke Hawkwind had kept him around for precisely this reason: to act as an open conduit to the High Lightbringer. By protocol, a squire should never carry important information to a high ranking official. Areck cringed with the realization that his carrying the message to the Bre'Dmorian Academy would be an insulting gesture to a man of Lord Lightbringer's station.

Areck tried to calm his mind. This was different; he would carry news that would shake the very foundation of Arsgoth. In his opinion, the duke was correct in thinking that only a Bre'Dmorian could transport such information safely.

Areck could only hope that Lord Lightbringer would not question him—he was already nervous in the presence of God's Chosen Voice—such dire news would only make his emotions worse.

A rustle drew Areck's thoughts back to the duke and his preparations. Lord Hawkwind was rolling four separate pieces of parchment and stamping them each with his personal seal—a hawk with a rose in each claw.

"You feel better, Squire?" Duke Hawkwind asked with distracted concern.

"Yes, your grace. I thank you for your concern in my moment of weakness," Areck replied, ashamed of showing such emotion in front of the noble.

"Not to worry, young man. The news is unsettling to me as well. It is good to see that the young men of the Academy care so much for their realm. I know when it is your time to serve in battle, you will honorably defend the kingdom."

Duke Hawkwind looked down and considered the pieces of parchment. "Now that the wax has cooled, you must take these two writs. This," he raised the first scroll stamped with the royal seal, "is a royal writ of passage. It will allow you to travel freely in the city and will expire after tonight."

The noble lord raised a second parchment, this one with a blue ribbon attached. "This is to be given to the High Lightbringer. No one else is to see this parchment. It is not to be opened by anyone else, upon penalty of treason. Do you understand, Squire Areck?"

Areck nodded and the duke handed both scrolls to the young squire who took them gingerly.

"You have my honor-bound oath, my lord. I will seek Lord Lightbringer within the hour, and unless someone pries my dead fingers from these," Areck held the parchments up, studying the wax seals, "no one else will lay eyes upon them."

With that, Areck stepped a foot back and knelt before the duke. In knightly custom, he waited five seconds in the posture of fealty before he stood and walked out of the room.

Areck didn't notice the duke's chuckle. Nor did he notice that as he left the room, Lord Hawkwind sat back down in his chair and began inking several black dots on his map near the Dragonspine Mountains.

As Areck wandered out of the palace, he pondered the importance of accepting the duke's task. He remembered reading of such political strife happening in the smaller kingdoms to the east—with no heir to the throne, the nobles of the realm would jockey for positioning. This always led to unholy alliances, back-stabbing, and civil war, until one became strong enough to rule the country. Duke Hawkwind was obviously trying to avoid such violent controversy and dissuade the tragic influx of scheming.

When Areck finally reached the stables, the duke's captain of the guard was giving a small regiment of men specific orders for their nightly routine. Next to the guard captain stood Arawnn and a young stable hand intently waiting for the captain to finish. It was obvious from the captain's stiff posture and clipped speech that the man was not accustomed to so much attention during this part of his day.

Lord Caldey appeared and handed the captain and Arawnn each a pair of sealed documents, whispered a few instructions in the courier's ear, and walked back inside the palace.

Areck clenched his jaw. Just by looking at the signs, he could tell the guard captain was hoping the incursion would wander elsewhere and let him go about his usual business. Areck considered leaving them to discuss matters; however, when he looked at the sky, he recognized that without some aid there would be no time to report to Lord Silvershield before sundown.

Deciding a direct approach was best, Areck strolled over to the captain and held out Duke Hawkwind's writ. The captain frowned, took the document, and began to read.

After a moment the captain nodded thoughtfully and turned back to regard Arawnn. Once the guard captain finished evaluating the situation, he called over a stable boy and began to discuss stallions bred for speed, asking what stock the duke had available.

The pair eventually settled on a mount suited for great speed and known for its endurance before turning back to both Areck and Arawnn.

"I will have Frostalf saddled up and ready," the guard captain stated, nodding at Arawnn. "With so far to travel, I am giving you Duke Hawkwind's fastest thoroughbred. If you can wait just a moment, I will make sure your mount is ready for your travels."

"My thanks, Captain, but I will not need the stallion tonight," Arawnn said, inclining his head in a slight bow to the captain. "However, if, on the morrow, Frostalf can be taken to the Citadel of the Hand with enough provisions for a week's travel, I would appreciate it."

"It shall be as you request, my lord." The captain saluted the royal courier. "Your mount will be stocked, delivered, and ready to ride by then."

"May Starsgalt shine on you, Captain," Arawnn extended his hand in the customary Almassian salute and turned around. Had the courier not been so nimble, he would have run into Areck.

"Squire!" Arawnn exclaimed, trying to catch his balance. "Are you ready?"

Areck looked at the royal courier but did not respond. Instead he glared at the captain, annoyed that the man had all but ignored him.

"My lord, how I can assist you this afternoon?" the captain said, tensing under Areck's gaze. "I . . . I do not suppose you also wish to discuss fine thoroughbreds?"

Despite his anger, Areck smiled at the joke. "You have seen my orders, Captain, and I am not here to procure a mount. It is time for me to report to Lord Silvershield, first knight-captain of the eastern gatehouse. However, events have unfolded that will take me to another part of the city. I wonder if you can spare a man to tell Lord Silvershield that I will not be able to make it back to my post."

The captain relaxed and looked around in a conspiratorial way. "Events vital enough for the duke to offer up his personal stock of horse and for a squire to ask the assistance of a man-at-arms must be important indeed."

"Sir, even if there were events going on, I would not betray Duke Hawkwind with idle conversation," Areck replied stiffly.

The startled captain gaped at the squire and stammered a reply. "My lord, I did not mean to imply that I should be so lucky as to be informed of important business. I will have a man sent this instant. Is there anything else I should relay?"

Areck's face flushed. He had not meant to sound harsh, but the man had asked for him to betray private information. His nerves were raw and he had not comprehended that the captain had spoken in jest.

"Thank you, Captain," Areck said, "but no. I just want you to inform my commander that I shall not be back to the gatehouse this day."

The captain saluted the squire and barked quick orders to the closest man-at-arms. When he looked satisfied that his man understood the instructions, he turned back towards Areck. "Squire, is there anything else you require?"

Areck shook his head and lowered his gaze. Rather than offering his hand and offending the man further, Areck thanked him and strode off towards the stables. He noticed after a moment that Arawnn was walking next to him. He stopped and regarded the royal courier, his brows drawn with wonderment.

"My orders state that I am to escort you to the Academy of the Hand," Arawnn explained emphatically.

Areck relaxed. "Lord Arawnn, the duke never mentioned your assistance, but I would gladly accept your company towards the Academy. I apologize for not recognizing your role while we conducted our business."

"That is unimportant, my friend. However, I do have a request. I know it is not necessarily your way, but I prefer my unofficial title rather than so much formality," Arawnn said.

Areck frowned at the comment—he was not used to breaking such protocol—but with a shrug turned and made his way toward another stable hand. He politely asked for the boy to retrieve his mount. In other circumstances, he would have just left the horse; however, the Bre'Dmorian Academy's stable master was an old man of a dour nature who would not be pleased if the young squire did not bring the stallion back to its rightful home, even if only for a night.

When the pair reached the proper stable, a young man brought Areck's dark stallion outside, followed by Arawnn's lighter thoroughbred. Areck noticed that the courier's horse had already been stripped of gear and given a lighter riding saddle.

"I see the captain moves with ample speed," Arawnn said, a touch of surprise in his voice.

"It looks that way," Areck smiled. "I think I might have smudged his honor though, by not catching on to his joke."

"You don't say?" Arawnn chuckled. "I think it is a rule that every knight is quite dour, Areck." The comment made Areck blanch. He was about to respond when Arawnn continued, "However, regardless of your iron tongue, I still wish to take you up on the offer you made earlier. I have never seen such splendid city and wish to see what it has to *offer*, if you understand my meaning."

Areck flushed at Arawnn's words. The royal messenger referred to drinking and wenching, something Aresleigh was well known for in her days of glory. That it was something the Academy also looked down upon made him flinch. By the Anduinic Code's ethos, men were not allowed to marry until their tenth year of acceptance into the knighthood. Once married, a knight would be would expected to have children and carry upon their noble line. However, until that time, they were to save themselves for their future mate by staying away from drinking, a vile habit which inhibited decision-making and altered the senses.

"From your look, you are about to say no! However, I believe you said that you would barter stories with me. And, if I can only barter when being shown around town, that is not my fault. Thus, would rejecting my offer not be a matter of honor, Squire?" Arawnn asked with a devilish grin.

"But . . . I . . . I," Areck floundered. The royal messenger had made a good point, one that a knight could not argue. With a sigh, Areck regained his composure. "It is an honor to be taken up on my offer, sir. Once dusk has fallen, I shall be available to partake in such tasteless endeavors."

Arawnn roared in laughter and slapped the young squire on the back. "We are going to have a wonderful time! In fact, this is already more fun than most noble parties back home."

The royal courier was still laughing as he walked away. Areck let out another sigh and followed Arawnn, his stallion behind him.

From the palace Areck saw both the Citadel of the Hand to the southeast and the Arcane Institute to the southwest. The entire noble district of Aresleigh was laid out in neat rows of lordly estates, temple districts, powerful merchant families, and a central courtyard with wide marble streets. Each of these streets eventually ran into one of three magnificent buildings which dominated the inner city, coalesced into a main road, then exited through a gatehouse. For one who had never been to the inner city, it was a daunting sight that took months to get used to. However, once familiar with the general location of Hawkwind Palace, the Citadel of the Hand, and the Arcane Institute, it was easy to find a gatehouse and make one's way out.

As the pair made their way through the marble streets of several more prominent merchant holdings, the sun sank into the horizon. The towering Dome of Anduin was awe-inspiring in the gathering dusk, affecting both men as they came into view of the Citadel of the Hand. The Citadel was something special; though Duke Hawkwind had spent a fortune in precious stones, abundant produce, and port tariffs to pay the dwarves of Hammerstone Citadel to craft the inner city, nothing could compare to the powerful godly magic used upon the Bre'Dmorian Academy.

Areck felt God's presence each time he neared the Citadel; he basked in the warmth of being a warrior of Starsgalt. He felt the great care and astuteness of the building, knowing that it had never been taken, never fallen into ruin, and represented the glory of Starsgalt. Trying to fully explain it was impossible; simply put it, was a monument of faith, law, and wisdom to the whole world.

This was where the High Lightbringer, the Hand of God, Lord of the Bre'Dmorian knighthood, held his seat of power. Here the bulk of Starsgalt's holy warriors were concentrated, and here the One True God's powers were centered. Although there was an Academy of the Hand in each of Arsgoth's other dukedoms—Lord Consulate Galryn, better known as the High Lord of the Knights of the Ring, resided in Thames, while the Lord Marshal Olrith, the High Lord of the Knights of the Crown, resided in Calimond—neither compared to the sheer size and grandeur of The Citadel in Aresleigh.

With the capacity to hold over three thousand men, the Bre'Dmorian Academy contained many elder knights, scholars, and lightbringers when they were in the city. It also housed five hundred squires that sought to join the actual ranks of the knighthood. To gaze from the outside, common men could not see the inner parade grounds, the countless sparring areas, the great hall, the main cathedral, countless barracks, or the several academic centers for various subjects.

It was here that Areck would serve a minimum of ten years in service to the Knights of Bre'Dmor. Though only fifty students were accepted on an annual basis per academy, the lengthy tenure was required by any student who studied in the service of Starsgalt. Upon graduation, thus receiving the basic title of knight, a young man usually set forth to explore the repositories of the One God's knowledge and the rest of the world. It was not uncommon for knights to become advisors to powerful noble families, or even priests singing the virtues of faith. However, no matter which path was chosen, a typical knight was driven by the burning desire to become a Lightbringer and spread the word of Starsgalt.

Thus had Anduin of Ardoc, First High Lightbringer and the first Champion of God, forged his code of ethos. As stated in the Tome of Anduin, the commandments were deemed the Anduinic Code: Honor thy God first, defend thy knightly covenant second, and protect thy realm Arsgoth from chaos under all circumstances. Though much more complicated than those basic principles, the Code of Anduin had been a beacon of chivalry to the men serving the One God for over two thousand years. It stated that the Bre'Dmorians were beyond politics, beyond even kings and queens, and certainly beyond minor disputes of nobility. Finally, it stated that not only were they protectors to the world, but they were to be a shining beacon of purity and faith in God.

As Areck approached the Citadel of the Hand, he noted the young squires standing diligently on guard duty. He had been there several years before, standing duty with the rest of the sixth year squires, most ranging in age from seventeen to twenty-two winters.

They look uncomfortable, he thought, alighting on his own odd memory. When his thoughts cleared, Areck recognized one of the squires standing guard as one who had continually come to him for guidance concerning the theology behind the Tome of Anduin, God's written word.

"Kendall," Areck said and approached the young man, who tried to stare intently forward, "who is the officer on duty?"

The young man's eyes darted around to be sure that no knights were present. "Sir, it is against the Code to talk while on duty!" he whispered. "However, I believe Lord Millbert is the ranking officer tonight."

Areck couldn't help but remember his own nervousness when others had tried to talk to him during guard duty. He offered a quick arm clasp to Kendall and guided Arawnn inside a massive door.

When the pair entered, they nearly ran into Lord Connor Millbert, a handsome crusader who was discussing the hierarchy of Bre'Dmor with several Templars. With a grunt of annoyance, the crusader ceased his conversation and turned to the two young men.

Areck knew he had interrupted his elder knight and cringed under Crusader Millbert's gaze. He had always respected the crusader, appreciating the man most for teaching him the art of sword technique and strategy. The elder knight had been his mentor during the annual dueling events, which Areck had won in four out of the last five years.

As fierce as the elder knight could be, his symmetrical features held a hint of softness. In truth, the crusader was a kind man of middle years, with long black hair that was peppered with streaks of gray and tied at the nape of his neck. A carefully trimmed goatee framed a face that was marred by several scars gained in the service of God.

Areck bowed to Lord Millbert and pulled the royal courier away to a respectful distance. When he was satisfied that he was no longer impugning the crusader's honor, he lowered his eyes and waited.

After finishing with the Templars, Lord Millbert concluded his business and dismissed the lower ranking knights. "Squire Areck, why are you in the citadel and not out with Lord Silvershield monitoring traffic?" He glanced at the royal courier and back to the squire, taking stock of the situation.

"I have come from the duke, my lord," Areck said and handed over the royal writ of passage. "It is news of great importance, meant for Lord Lightbringer's ears alone, by pain of death."

The crusader read the writ of passage and looked at the squire. Areck could see a touch of alarm in Lord Millbert's eyes. Areck could not be sure, but it looked like the crusader held a degree of anger at the fact his squire was being used as a courier, even if it was for the Duke of Aresleigh.

"Areck, will you please follow me?" When both men started forward, Lord Millbert held out his hand. "This is a meeting of knights, Messenger Arawnn, and though you are welcome to take shelter with us tonight, you are not allowed to follow."

Arawnn nodded in understanding, grasped Areck's arm and whispered that they would discuss plans later.

After Arawnn had left, Lord Millbert beckoned Areck to follow him and led them to the citadel's main cathedral with a grim expression.

Areck recognized the chamber—a place where younger knights spent their evenings in communion—something that illuminated a piece of God's wisdom and lent credence to the term "faith." Because of its open forum, this usually left the main cathedral dotted with knights who did not mind praising Starsgalt in front of the public. Those who prayed in the open believed that a man could not be locked away from the world if he wished greater understanding.

This, of course, was very different than most of the elder Bre'Dmorian knights, who considered serving Starsgalt in seclusion the only way to enlightenment.

This created a minor chasm in the knighthood. The older knights wished to spend their time in their private chambers, reflecting pious doctrine, while the younger knights fervently believed that the world should know of God by setting an example to the faithful.

† † † † †

It was in the latter statement which Taryon Griffonsword, known now as Lord Taryon Lightbringer, believed. He had concluded long ago that Starsgalt had given man the means to learn about the relationship God expected and the free will to decide if that relationship was correct. He even lectured on the subject—that God had created the Voice of God, the High Light-bringer, to further extend His influence into the world.

As the High Lightbringer, Taryon believed it was his job to stay away from private prayer sessions, abstain from petty politics, and not be swayed by trivial differences. He assumed that to exemplify faith in the All-Father, a leader must be willing to kneel in subservience to God, in front of all who would watch, unafraid of heretics who would question the One God's loving embrace.

This was why the world considered Taryon a truly great religious leader, unafraid of faith and honor, a leader who knew that through his mistakes God changed the world.

He could still remember his last days as First Crusader and the event that led to his promotion to High Lightbringer almost thirty winters ago. In those days, he had been a young man of thirty-eight years and the personal attendant to Lord Thoman Lightbringer. Taryon had served his liege for well over ten years—happy with serving and helping the elder High Light-bringer in several military campaigns. In those days he had borne the brunt of the Bre'Dmorian Knighthood's rule without actually having had the stress of the title.

Then one day it all came to an end and a new era started: lord Thoman's heart failed and he died in his sleep. The death had been shattering to Taryon, exemplified by how hard those first ten winters had been under him. Now he was a legend himself among the elder knights

Lord Taryon recalled his first order twenty-five years prior. He had sent two legions of knights, soldiers, and men-at-arms on a holy crusade into the Great Devoid. Of those twelve thousand men, only four thousand had returned from the north, many with ruined minds and bodies. The fading memory still stung his pride. Somewhere deep inside, he knew that his forces had awoken the armies of whatever godforsaken lord ruled that place. The aftermath of the crusade was a decade that had seen the ferryll pour forth from the Devoid, destroying land, blighting mountains, and quickening the pace at which the Dead Lands advanced. It had taken the full might of Arsgoth's seven legions and the entire Bre'Dmorian Knight-hood to finally push the ferryll back into the dark mists of the Swamp of Corruption, a seething bog that surrounded the Devoid.

The crusades evolved Lord Taryon into the man he was now. He became a man who believed in showing rather than talking to the world, in action rather than debate, and most of all, in spreading the glory of The One True God through the world by being open about devotion.

Areck felt the High Lightbringer's heavenly presence wash over him, followed by his customary nausea and shame. The place bubbled with so much raw power that even Lord Millbert seemed to notice.

Such true faith, Areck thought, trying to clear the silver streaks that blurred his vision. The pain always brought confusion. As long as he could remember, he'd had trouble with sickness in the temples of God. The greater the divine power, the more trouble he had. The clerics who taught him philosophy and theology claimed that it was a lack of faith that brought the uncomfortable feelings; Areck didn't know what to think.

One day I will be worthy, Areck thought. *I can feel His warmth and love. One day soon I will understand His lesson and know faith without pain.*

Areck's hands trembled as the communion ended, bringing the power in the room to a head. He clenched his teeth as a stabbing pain shot through his body.

It will be over soon, Areck tried to focus. *It is another lesson in humility. I should be inspired at the sight of Lord Lightbringer kneeling in reverence to the All-Father.*

As the room grew still and divine essence dissipated, the High Lightbringer rose to his feet, picked up an adamantine dagger, and laced its leather sheath in place. With finely tuned patience, Lord Taryon buckled a belt and turned to face the two men who waited for him.

"Crusader Millbert," Lord Taryon said, nodding to the elder of the men. "What brings you to our glorious cathedral this fine eventide?"

Lord Millbert gave a slight bow. "My Lord Lightbringer, I apologize for interrupting your eventide prayers. Squire Areck has a writ that is to be delivered directly to you. I would have brought the message myself, but he has given his word to ensure it reached you by his own person." With the briefest of smiles, Lord Millbert nodded in Areck's direction.

"Stand, Squire," Lord Taryon said, gazing at the young man. "If I am not mistaken, this is your ninth year of study?"

"Yes, my lord," Areck said meekly, knowing where this was going.

"Though this is not a reprimand, son, but I am sure you are aware that giving your word before taking the Oath of Anduin is not permitted." Lord Taryon placed his hand on Areck's shoulder and looked into the young man's eyes. "However, I do appreciate your situation and sincerity. Now, what has Duke Hawkwind deemed so important that he requests an Oath from a squire?"

Areck quickly drew the duke's note from his tunic and passed it with a shaking hand over to Lord Lightbringer. He watched as the Lord of the Bre'Dmorians pulled the dagger from his belt and with a slice opened the document.

As the head of the Bre'Dmorian Order, Lord Lightbringer did not need to dismiss himself from the two men in the room. With his head bowed, he silently read the parchment and wandered around the chamber while both men waited for orders. When his eyes finally reached the end, the High Lightbringer's face looked ashen from shock, turned crimson from anger and righteous fury, and then settled into a hardened grimace saved for the bleakest of times.

Lord Taryon mumbled something and sank into a chair near the large alter. The High Lightbringer betrayed as much emotion as he ever would; his silence was a bad sign. Areck could tell by his look of consternation that the lord commander was strategizing his next move. Areck guessed that the Lord Taryon was considering the ramifications of the duke's words and with how much haste the knighthood should respond. If push came to shove, where would the Bre'Dmorian Order stand in a Council of Lineage?

"Lord Millbert, we need messengers sent to Lord Marshal Olrith and Lord Consulate Galyrn," the High Lightbringer spoke. "Also, gather the ranking officers and have them meet in the Hall of War in two hours!"

4

"YOUR HOLINESS, is there a cause for such haste?" Lord Millbert asked, surprised by the sudden interest. When Lord Taryon looked up, his brows drawn together, the crusader added, "I do not presume to question your authority, most holy lord, but it will take several hours to get the senior officers together."

Lord Taryon frowned, and then handed the parchment to Millbert, allowing the crusader to read the note:

Lord Lightbringer,

I apologize for not coming myself in this matter of great importance. Please understand that I know what I am about to discuss demands my personal attention. However, with the arrival of Courier Arawnn, the nobles of Aresleigh will have already grown suspicions regarding the information he carries. I beg your indulgence in this situation, as it must be contained until it is announced to the people.

It is my duty to impart the sad news at hand. As of ten days ago, our lord King Roderick II died from grievous wounds suffered on his yearly hunting trip. As you know, there is no heir to the throne. In an attempt to control the situation, I wish to send Lord Arawnn back to Natilinople in hopes that the Lord Constable will call a Council of Lineage here in Aresleigh.

Though the Bre'Dmorian Order does not involve itself in the trivial matters of nobility, I think it is time to state the obvious; Aresleigh has become the second most powerful city in Arsgoth. It is my family that has bled for the crown and it is my family that should rule the kingdom. In this, I seek your approval. However, I may be overstating myself and the council may not come to pass.

I am sure you are aware of the seedy implications that the powerful noble families, including the Duke of Thames, will embrace. I also think we both wish to avoid civil war. Still, you should know that one rumor has it that Duke Valimont is the assassin.

With this information in mind, there is no one in the city outside of the knighthood whom I can trust. Please dispatch a small unit of Knights to escort the courier back to Stormwind Keep. Once there, it would be wise to send no more than two through the Dragonspine Mountains and on to Natalinople, as this is a mission of utmost speed.

I thank you for your support in this matter.

    Edelin Hawkwind

    Duke of Aresleigh

Lord Millbert set the note down, his face a mask of fury.

"The duke thinks he can give an order to the knighthood and dictate our actions!" Lord Millbert said with contempt. "You are not actually planning on following through this, are you, your grace?"

"Calm yourself, Lord Millbert." Once again, Lord Lightbringer had a range of emotions written on his wizened brow. "I am sure the duke did not mean to demand anything of us, only to ask."

"My Lord Lightbringer . . .!" the crusader retorted. "I mean no disrespect to our younger men; but why would the duke send a mere *squire* to pass along information so important, especially when he *orders* us to act?"

"I do see his point, Connor," said Lord Taryon quietly. "If the duke would have come to me personally, the criers would have spread word faster than we like. Furthermore, his words have merit. Maybe this is a sign from Starsgalt. I do not pretend to understand the precise will of God or why the duke wishes to involve us in his actions, but the man does seem confident that there is trouble brewing."

"It goes against the Anduinic Code, your holiness!" Lord Millbert burst out. "We are above this and he knows it!"

"Do not presume to decipher the Code, Crusader Millbert!" Lord Taryon said, leveling his gaze upon his subordinate. "If this situation is not handled with care, there could be civil war. And *that* is also against the Code."

Lord Millbert lowered his gaze and flushed. "We are going to send a small contingent of knights with the courier, then?"

Lord Taryon looked thoughtful. If he sent a detachment of men with the royal courier, Duke Hawkwind would have directly given an order to the knighthood. It might be viewed that the High Lightbringer was obeying that order, compromising the bipartisan status of the Bre'Dmorian Knighthood. However, if Lord Lightbringer refused to give assistance to the duke at such a crucial moment, the kingdom might assume that the order had lost its faith in the infrastructure that it served.

The duke is a respected man, Lord Taryon thought, strategizing options. *The question is, will there be war? If the nobles start to squabble for the scraps of kingship, it will not matter, and either way the situation will escalate. This may be a way to not overtly act in our politics, but to have a say nonetheless—and it will save lives.*

"Yes, Lord Millbert, I will send a detachment of men with the royal courier. Please carry out my orders and gather the men," Lord Taryon said. "God is giving us an opportunity to silently help our kingdom with a just cause. Plus, if the kingdom falls into war . . . that can only mean anarchy and a lack of faith in Him."

"As you wish, your holiness." Lord Millbert bowed and retreated with Areck close behind him.

As Areck neared the door, the High Lightbringer noticed the young man. "Squire, I require your presence. You witnessed the royal courier giving his dissertation on King Roderick's death?"

Areck lowered his eyes. "I did, Lord Lightbringer."

"I am going to ask you some questions about the information you overheard, Areck. I wish to know the character of the man who relayed the information."

"Of course, your holiness," Areck said. He recited the day's events.

By asking Areck to explain his version of events, the High Lightbringer was indulging in risky business. Lord Taryon knew that young men often lacked the experience needed to judge character. However, he also knew that Areck was not a normal student. Each of the squire's commanders had reported amazement at the young man's resourcefulness in battle, quick study in theology, and desire to assist his brethren. They were also vocal about the boy's zealous promotion of the All-Father. It was unusual, but not unheard of, that a squire every decade or so would shine very brightly in the eyes of God. Lord Taryon knew the young man to be honorable beyond reproach in comparison to his fellow squires. He also knew that Areck, of all the men, would remember minor details about the situation. He wondered if there was a chance that Starsgalt had sent a sign in Areck, a messenger in what could fast become uncertain times.

As Areck related the day's events, Lord Taryon contemplated his course of action. The first step was to discuss the matter with Duke Hawkwind, explaining proper etiquette for approaching a fellow seat of power. He would also announce his intentions that, for the moment, the knighthood would back the Duke of Aresleigh.

The next question was, how trustworthy was this royal courier? Areck seemed to think the man was a good-hearted soul. This did not mean Arawnn had no other ties of allegiance or his own political agenda. Since the royal courier was being sent back to Natalinople by the duke, the man could not be exchanged for a more suitable messenger, one picked by the High Lightbringer.

What kind of detachment will I send? Lord Taryon wondered, listening to Areck's description of the courier's personality. *It should be a company built for speed. However, I need to set an example for the good duke.*

That would be the hard part, as the High Lightbringer agreed with Duke Hawkwind on the matter at hand. Still, Lord Taryon needed to find a balance and uphold his honor. Because the duke had broken protocol in more ways than one, it would be a tough compromise.

How am I going to uphold the decree of the duke, keep my honor, and accomplish this task? Lord Taryon shut his eyes.

When Areck finished his story, Lord Lightbringer studied the young man standing before him. As the he stared at the squire an idea came to him, one that held little danger to his knights while accomplishing his goals. Lord Taryon considered the possibilities and decided the company should consist of three knights and nine hand-picked squires. He would create this small company of twelve men, which would be led by one of his lowest ranking knight-captains. This would allow the High Lightbringer to save face, treating the issue as a training exercise for the nine lucky squires. It also respected the duke's request of a small company of men to escort the royal courier to Stormwind Keep.

The High Lightbringer could also address another issue, a nagging inquiry several months old. Deep in thought, he pulled several folded reports from one of the many pouches strapped across his body and scanned the messages: requests from the eastern town of Brenly, asking for Bre'Dmorian aid against constant raids.

Lord Taryon smiled. His solution illustrated his power over the situation by committing untrained forces to the duke. Thirty years as High Lightbringer had taught him patience. It also made him used to considering every angle of a situation. The theory had helped him maneuver undesirable events that tested even a highly skilled man of faith.

Lord Taryon considered the role of such a unit. It must be able to ride with the courier to Stormwind Keep unnoticed by noble scouts. The company's armored forms would dissuade most highwaymen from attempting anything illegal.

If I plan this correctly, the company will reach Stormwind within five days, Lord Taryon thought, satisfied with his reasoning. *At that point, two knights can break away from the company and escort the courier to Natalinople.*

Lord Taryon smiled grimly at the thought of ordering the training company back to Brenly—it would be a great opportunity for his young men to strategize and investigate the disturbances in the area, while giving assistance to Count Gustafson and his plague issues. It would be an excellent opportunity to put the younger men in a position to test their faith.

"Squire, you have done very well tonight," the High Lightbringer said. "The rest of the night is yours. My advice is that you meet for evening prayers then join the younger knights in celebration. I have heard rumors that a few are heading to the observatory to stare into the heavens. Maybe you will see a dragon's tail soaring through the sky."

"My Lord Lightbringer, I have offered my companionship to another this night."

The High Lightbringer arched a bushy brow.

Areck realized that the companion in question sounded like a female and flushed a deep red. "I did not mean to imply . . . I mean . . . Messenger Arawnn has requested a tour of the city and that I escort him. If your holiness would allow, I would like to keep my word."

The High Lightbringer's eyes gleamed with mirth. "Squire, you may enjoy doing whatever is within God's boundaries. Come morning I will be commissioning a journey to Stormwind Keep, one of which you will be part of," Lord Taryon said. "Just be sure you arrive at the stables by dawn, as your knight commander will be inspecting his line and issuing his orders."

As Areck began to leave, Lord Taryon added, "It is an honor to be selected for this assignment, Areck. One I think you deserve."

"I thank you, High Lightbringer! May I be so bold as to ask my commander's name?" Areck asked with shining eyes.

It looks like the boy can hardly contain his excitement. Lord Taryon smiled. He paused and measured his answer. There were many good choices, but he was looking for an older knight who had field experience with squires. As Lord Taryon considered several men, he looked at Areck and was struck by an answer.

One man in particular, Lord Bowon Silvershield, a portly knight-captain of middling years, who drank too much and was known as a womanizer, stood out. At one time Bowon had been a consulate, but his poor choices had caused Lord Taryon to demote him several times, to the lowest rank a senior knight could hold. Yet Lord Bowon's men loved him and Taryon had discussed many things with the jovial knight. The High Lightbringer knew the man had a keen mind and was more than capable of leading such a small foray. Bowon also had teaching experience and might even uncover what was happening in Brenly.

If nothing else, it will keep him away from drinking, Lord Lightbringer mused. It was almost shameful what had happened to the man. Taryon still remembered the days when Lord Silvershield had been blessed by God.

"Actually, you know the commander quite well, Squire," Lord Taryon stated. "The company will be led by Knight-Captain Silvershield. Now, Areck, I think it is past time for your evening prayers. Enjoy your eventide with the courier. It will be your last in Aresleigh for many weeks," Lord Taryon finished.

With a swift bow Areck took the last statement as his dismissal, spun on his heel, and walked out of the room.

As a ninth year student, Areck's entire class had moved to the fourth floor of the eastern wing of the citadel. For those who resided within the Academy's grounds accommodations were simple. Each floor's commanding officer was stationed near the multiple stairways, known by squires as "the hub." As the hallways spread outward, the further a room was from the hub, the simpler in design and the smaller in scale it was. The farthest quarters held few accouterments and were reserved for the lowest ranking squires, while honor students resided near the entrance.

Areck tried to recall his first days at the Academy. The first two winters in service to the Bre'Dmorians were by far the toughest for young boys, called "tyros." Many would be homesick and unaccustomed to the winters of Western Arsgoth. For this reason, tyros were stationed in the heart of the citadel, until they were promoted on their fifth year of service to Initiates of the Hand. It wasn't until his sixth year that a squire resided with fewer than four people in his room. In his eighth year, an initiate finally earned private chambers, allowing further development of his spirituality.

As Areck made his way towards the eastern hub, assessing the honor that had been bestowed upon him, he walked right into a woman!

The impact of their bodies brought forth a feminine grunt as she bounced backwards in a silent protest. Though she wore the white tabard of Gabriel, The Angel of Mercy and had highly polished chain mail, her hood was pulled down far enough to partially conceal her long blond hair and penetrating blue eyes.

When Areck looked up, the woman had caught her balance and was intently staring at him. He realized she was waiting for an apology. Areck gaped, dumbfounded and speechless, at what he considered to be the most beautiful creature he had ever seen. Though he had read about the Hospitaler Order, an all-female knighthood that resided in the southern Barony of Shalwen's Grove, he had never met a member. This did not sway his awe-inspired judgment; female clerics were allies of Starsgalt and thus must be special to God.

"I believe a simple 'Excuse me' would do, young man," the lady's voice was like a soft breeze waving across the beach.

"I . . . I . . . I am sorry, my lady," Areck stuttered before dropping his gaze from her beautiful face. He had never been so embarrassed and exhilarated in his life. "If you will excuse my clumsiness, I apologize."

With a shy smile she reached for Areck's hand. "It is as much your fault as it was mine. I wasn't paying much attention, either. My name is Elyana Healhand, Lady Prelate of Gabriel," the lady cleric said.

"I am pleased to make your acquaintance, my lady. I am Squire Areck of Brenly," Areck said. "I have never seen a Cleric of Gabriel before . . . I mean, one this far north. May I help you find something?"

"I was just coming from the library, Squire Areck," Elyana responded with a yawn. "I do thank your for your offer, but it was a long journey from Shalwen's Grove."

Areck was about to wish her luck when Elyana asked, "I do not suppose you can point me to the eastern halls? The Citadel of Hand is so large in comparison to our own, I get lost each time I come here." She chuckled and motioned to the hub.

"Lady Elyana, for nearly knocking you off your feet, I would be honored to escort you," Areck responded with a shy smile. "Albeit I, too, still get lost at times, I am sure we could find the way eventually."

"Oh no, young man!" she said, throwing her hands up to mockingly fend him off. "You looked quite preoccupied in your task. I think verbal directions will suffice."

Embarrassed, Areck turned red, something that in his opinion had happened all too often that day. As he pointed out landmarks within the citadel and the proper directions to get to the guest quarters, Elyana smiled. When Areck finished, the cleric repeated the directions back to him verbatim. A slight tingling tugged at Areck's senses. He guessed the cleric must be of significant power within her sisterhood. For the first time in his young life, Areck stepped back and appraised a woman, not as a squire in reverence to a cleric or a knight, but as a man does a woman.

Is this desire? It is an odd sensation and one that is forbidden to the young. He contemplated the thought. *How do these thoughts force themselves into my mind?* Areck shook his head to clear such blasphemous thoughts and the woman frowned in concern.

"Are you well, young man?" She placed her hand on his chest.

He jerked away from her contact. He noticed Elyana's shocked expression as she snatched her hand back and yelped. Even though he was wearing a chain hauberk, her touch was like a dull fire that caressed the whole of his body.

"I am fine, Lady Elyana, really!" Areck stepped backward, his eyes dropping in shame. "I am not used to someone listening so attentively to me, able to repeat my words perfectly. If there is nothing else I must be going . . . to prepare . . . for eventide prayers."

Elyana did not move. She glanced curiously from her hand to the young squire. Though there was no malice in her gaze, Areck felt her blue eyes judging him. A surge of divine magic filled the room, making his stomach turn and vision waver.

"My lady, if I offended you, I am sorry," he said, backing away from the cleric and trying to clear his mind. "But I would appreciate it if you would cease casting whatever divine spell you are calling upon."

The power subsided. Elyana's beautiful face creased with a frown. "I would not cast a spell on you, Squire Areck."

"I can feel your divine power, my lady; you radiate it," he responded grimly.

"Are you accusing me of a *lie*?" she asked incredulously, her voice taking on a quiver of anger. "I said I did not cast anything on you, young man!"

Why does she keep calling me a "young man" and not referring to me with the proper protocol? He thought. It was very odd for the circumstances. *What is wrong with me? Focus your thoughts, Areck! You have just offended a powerful member of the clergy with that comment!*

"I did not mean to accuse you, Lady Elyana," Areck said. "I acutely feel divine magic; it makes me sick often enough. One of the side-effects is that it makes my tongue and mind act out of hand. If you would accept another apology, I have embarrassed both myself and my knighthood enough this day."

Elyana visibly relaxed. Areck thanked Starsgalt that he was given a sharp tongue and quick mind. He could tell the cleric was visibly shaken and whatever had happened, she was somehow involved. He couldn't take the chance of accusing her of lying because she was a Cleric of Gabriel. Regardless of her age, Elyana's authority was absolute and his word would be invalid, even if something strange was afoot.

Areck stepped back to offer an appropriate amount of distance between them, enough as not to seem insincere but far enough away to keep whatever was going on at bay.

Elyana did not notice. She gazed intently at her hand, deep in thought. When she finally looked up, she noticed the distance Areck had taken. With proper etiquette, she accepted his apology and thanked him for assisting her with directions.

Trying to conceal her interest in the young man, Lady Elyana watched Areck bow deeply and apologize again for running into her, allowing her to dismiss him. Without another word, the squire turned away and with quick strides made his way towards the hub. He never looked back to see Elyana watching him with a highly intrigued look on her face.

She had in fact tried to cast a simple divination spell on him to discern his divine aura. Though Elyana had cast the spell a thousand times since she had come to the Bre'Dmorian Academy, a strange feeling told her that this young man would one day be worth watching. She had become so adept at the spell that she could do it without making sound or gestures. Still, that squire, a man not more than twenty-five winters, had not only felt the spell but destroyed her weavings.

With a speculative eye Elyana watched Squire Areck make his way up the hub. *It isn't a wise idea to let odd circumstances distract me,* she thought.

It was time to leave the Academy. Elyana had been in the library for more than a week, and if she ever wanted to return to the Academy without attracting undue attention, she knew she had better not press her luck. With a last look at the young man climbing the stairs, she re-concealed her face and made her way out of the Citadel of the Hand the same way she had made her way in. The route was safe and would take her back through the Twisting Oak Inn, where her partner would be waiting.

5

ARECK CLIMBED the hub in silence. He was feeling quite sick from his meeting with Lady Elyana. If the divine magic had not ceased when it did, the amount of power flowing through the room might have made him vomit.

He still remembered the rules he had taught himself during his third year of service. It started with a basic principal: conceal the sickness. Since then, he had added control, acceptance, and tolerance to the equation. Still, it was very hard to be one with his creator when such blasphemy coursed through his veins. Not to mention that the more Areck came in contact with divine magic, the more nauseated he became. The only difference from his childhood was that he could now completely hide that fact from others. It had been a long time since his councilors had made him sit in the presence of God for what they saw as his obvious lack of faith.

The only thing those lessons did for me was make me more sick! he thought, confused by his weakness of character. *Of course, it made me realize that the more I cry out, the longer the punishment of God lasts.*

Areck told himself that he was a man of faith and prayed for salvation every night. He followed the doctrine of the All-Father without question, sacrificing endlessly for God because God knew best. In his heart, Areck recognized that God was testing him with the pain—a lesson that would be taught each and every night until he overcame his lack of conviction. The squire accepted all of this as fact and told himself that this was all part of his relationship with God.

But Areck had not been prepared when the divine curse accosted him this time. It was easy to control his emotions when he knew it was coming. It was another thing to be blindsided by a burst of divine magic. The question in his mind was why the cleric had lied about it. A true servant of Starsgalt could not lie; to do so would require atonement, in which a knight would either fast or pray for spiritual penance by asking forgiveness. Though Areck was not a man of magic, he was sure Elyana had done *something*, and so she was lying.

Is it so absurd that a cleric lied? I have lied for nine years by concealing my curse. Then again, why would God's chosen not tell me the truth? Or am I wrong . . .?

Areck tried to clear his mind. Although he could not cast spells, he had seen powerful priests work minor miracles with the assistance of God. It was the look in her eyes, the inquisitive glance she had given him at his re-action to her touch. She was definitely powerful. And she most definitely was not evil, as evil couldn't walk under the gaze of Starsgalt . . . at least not in his home. Still, he was positive that she had cast a spell on him, even if she had not spoken a word nor made any hand gestures.

As he exited the hub, Areck again tried to clear his thoughts but they continued to wander back to the mysteriously beautiful woman. *Maybe I should go find her. She will be in bed by now;* he reprimanded himself for several indecent tangents that popped into his mind. *It has to be the circumstances.* He sighed. *Or am I intrigued by her? She is so unusual.*

Areck had heard stories from some of the knights about their wives: tales of beauty, faith, friendship, and . . . he turned red at the thought of the more intimate moments. He had to admit that the prospect of a woman was fascinating. His personal commander, Lord Silvershield, always told such interesting stories, even if the old knight-captain was known as a womanizing brute.

Lord Silvershield had many female companions. In fact, now that Areck thought about it, numerous highly prized noble females pawed all over the rotund knight. He smiled as he started down the hallway to the fifth door that opened into his domicile.

Areck entered the room and went over to a wooden cabinet that held his personal belongings, including several fine tunics. Though he rarely dressed for such occasions, he owned one white tunic for each completed season within the Academy and one that was a gift from Lord Silvershield for finishing top in his class—a dark blue vest made of fine northern wool and braided with golden linen. He had only worn the blue tunic once, for the annual Ball of Roses at the winter festival; he was a warrior at heart, and preferred leather and chain armor over the cloth livery of nobility.

It was not uncommon for knights to wear some kind of armor most of the day, be it padded, leather, or hardened armor. In fact, it was quite cus-tomary to do routine tasks such as morning workouts, daily chores, and study, while prepared to take on chaotic adversaries.

Tonight, however, Areck was prepared to wear his best clothes and lead Arawnn through the city as promised. He sighed at the thought. It was only a matter of time before he led the courier into a tavern or inn and the tightly crowded bar erupted by throwing ale, which the more raucous of taverns practiced nightly. His tunic would be ruined.

"Why do I feel the need to give my word before I have taken the Oath of Anduin?" he asked the open cabinet, laying the tunic, breeches, and his best knee high boots on the bed.

Because I am young, he guessed.

It was a fact that Areck was quick to give his word on matters. It made him feel important to think that one day soon his word would mean something. Yet it was hard not to recognize such a weakness. He knew he was not supposed to make issues so important, since the young could hardly comprehend what was appropriate and honorable.

Then again, squires could get away with many minor infractions of the faith. However, if basic rules were broken continuously, punishments became more severe. That was the point—for the smarter ones, it only took once.

Areck still remembered watching a trio of squires sneak out of the Academy and into the city proper. After the third time of being caught, their knight commander sent them to clean pig-sties for three weeks in the rain and sleet. Though the penalty was harsh, it only took one boy to break under the effort before the rest had learned their lesson. Such punishments were the reason it was nearly impossible to be kicked out of the Academy. Unless a young man broke one of the three founding oaths of Anduin: show faith in God, guard thy brethren, and protect the kingdom from chaos, they were in for life.

For Areck, the lessons of making hasty decisions were learned when people took him up on the offers he made. Thus, Areck found himself in the situation he was in now. Because Arawnn had called him on his word, there was no choice; he had to go.

An idea came to him: what if Arawnn *couldn't* find him? The royal courier could not possibly know the Citadel very well. If the squire descended a level and went in to one of the chapels in the western wing, he would be worshipping Starsgalt by prayer and honoring his word to Arawnn. It would not be his fault if the courier did not know his way around. No one could say that he wasn't honoring his word in this matter either, could they? He would be dressed in his finest clothes, apparently ready and willing for the night on the town.

"A good idea." He whistled. "Maybe I should stop talking to the air and get ready."

Smiling to himself, Areck pulled off the last of his armor. The leather smelled of oil and sweat, yet it was his, given to him by the Marquis of Couth for a rendered service. Though the senior noble rarely visited Aresleigh or the Bre'Dmorian Academy anymore, Areck had never forgotten the old man, mainly because he had served as the High Scholar in the

Hall of Philosophy. The man was a shining example of the graciousness Starsgalt taught his followers: compassionate, understanding, and tolerant of other viewpoints. Mostly, it was he who had secured Areck's faith in Starsgalt, despite the pain of being in the divine presence.

Though it was uncommon for a Bre'Dmorian to wear anything less than heavy armor—mainly banded, scale, or a suit of field plate—Areck had vigilantly cared for the lighter armor and hired expert tailors fit it to his maturing body. By learning to fight in lighter armor, Areck had become an anomaly among his brethren; he was also effective in the cumbersome burden of plate mail or that of leather and chain. It really depended on what kind of foe he was fighting.

For two thousand years, plate-wearing knights had dominated the battlefields against the enemies of Arsgoth. However, the Marquis of Couth was a strategist in ancient warfare and had pointed out flaws in the cumbersome armor, the first being that once a warrior lost his feet, he usually lost his life. The marquis argued that against an opponent wearing burdensome plate, a lightly armored fighter would have room to plan precise strikes. He said that sometimes it took a nimble mind to beat an enemy, that there was weakness in everything, it only took maneuverability to exploit it. The man's opinion did not stop plated armor from being the predominant type among knights throughout the world. It allowed warriors to stay with the mentality that by barricading oneself inside heavier armor, a combatant could feel secure that stronger was always better.

Areck pulled off a shiny gauntlet and dropped it into a neat stack of armor. He then picked up the dark blue vest and eyed it warily. The clothes were fit for a lesser noble of the realm.

A night outside of the Academy might not be all that bad, Areck thought, considering the amount of time he had spent in study. *It isn't like I have spent much personal time outside the Halls . . . well, other than following Lord Silvershield around the underbelly of the city.*

The solid impact of a shutting door brought Areck out of his reverie. He glanced towards the entrance to his room and tugged on trousers. He reprimanded himself for daydreaming. If he did not hurry, he might as well seek out Arawnn and just deal with his sinful venture into the city.

With moderate haste, Areck sat down and pulled on a pair of soft leather boots. When he was satisfied, he glanced at the mirror, posed, and than grabbed a plain white cloak. As he walked from the room, he snatched a small dagger and buckled it to his left hip.

He considered pulling the hood of his cloak up to conceal his face. *I am already pushing the limits of the Code,* Areck thought. *If I conceal my face, I will only look more suspicious. Someone might even take me for a thief!* The thought was more than he could handle. He decided that his honor would not be sullied with such rumors.

Areck opened the door and peeked down the hall. He was surprised that it was empty. He guessed that most squires would be in nightly prayers or studying, with the exception of men heading off to guard duty or coming back from a day of chores. If his guess was correct, most squires would be in the cathedral where he had first encountered Lord Lightbringer that day.

"Thank Starsgalt!" Areck muttered. His heart raced with fear of being caught, as it would be very awkward if any his peers were to witness his sneaking around.

Areck made his way down the hall and back to the hub, descending two flights of stairs in short order. When he exited the stairwell, Areck glanced down another empty corridor and made his way towards the war room, a large chamber in the middle of the second floor. At this time of night it was usually empty; however, Areck was surprised to see a pair of knights standing guard. Areck heard voices rising angrily inside the chamber but could not discern what was being said. He told himself that it did not matter what was being said and it was none of his concern.

With purpose, Areck lowered his gaze and walked passed the guardsmen, nodding to each one before making his way to the far end of the hallway. He then worked his way through several groups of fifth year students heatedly discussing the application of the Book of Anduin. The group of younger squires was so engrossed in the conversation that they hardly noticed him pass by.

Areck smiled. It was an interesting subject that posed several legitimate questions. He wanted to tell his peers that in philosophy, every message was highly subjective to the perspective of each individual. In fact, he had been having discussions with a scholar named Vandallan, whom he considered a friend, about the hypocritical view of the world. The man consistently challenged him by questioning why Areck thought his faith was the only answer.

Areck had tried to explain that in religion, belief in God was a choice; a price one paid to the service of God. More so, for a mere man to have a relationship with God, pride needed to be released and trust in His word, the Book of Anduin, was required. To Areck's mind, his explanation made sense. But Vandallan always returned to a single argument: everything was affected by perspective, culture, and symptomatic comfort. Areck hated how each conversation ended: "Why can't *you* be the misguided one, in both your judgmental belief structure and the proper way of service God?"

Areck knew his thoughts made him different, and in his own mind, sub par in comparison to other squires. He was too logical to follow along blindly into the night. His subconscious mind demanded that objectivity was the only way for a man to answer his innermost questions about God.

Though Areck could feel Starsgalt in everything, the sickness never left him. Because of this, his mindset led to his suffering. There was only one way to bring about redemption: acceptance that some things weren't meant to be answered. He spent hours trying to commune with Starsgalt and he wished for salvation more than anything, but still his mind begged for answers. This was the problem Areck of Brenly grappled with: he sought answers to the questions each professor claimed had no answer.

It had taken Areck nine seasons of prayer to realize he might never feel the warmth of God's most sacred gift, divine sight. He had never received a divinely inspired vision, which was quite uncommon for even the lowest ranking squires. His limitation only made him pray more.

As Areck rounded the corner, a small chapel he used frequently came into view. He had spent many long hours in the private chapel and it felt comfortable to him, empty as it was. Following a familiar pattern, he entered the small room, removed his cloak then knelt at the base of the shrine. With practiced hands, he mixed rosemary oil and holy water in a small bowl. After a moment he pulled a small flint from his pocket and lit several candles surrounding the memorial. He then lit the base of a Starsgaltian statue and placed several candles around it. Aromatic smoke began to rise.

Satisfied with the layout, Areck inhaled and felt calm roll through his soul. The wispy strands of gray smoke brought the clarity of mind it took to commune with the divine. It had been used for well over a thousand years to summon more precise visions, though custom dictated that the concoction was beyond a squire. Areck so wished to be normal, he had long ago decided that the potential reward was worth the sacrifice.

Closing his eyes, Areck began the first part of contacting the Divine Plane by clearing his mind. It only took a moment before he purged enough of his frivolous thoughts so that he could begin the Anduinic chant. He felt the familiar sickness associated with divine magic enter his stomach. Although his senses barely registered the pain his spirit yearned for a time when Starsgalt would answer his call and deem him cleansed.

Areck's mind began to drift away and he felt a loving presence enter the room. His subconscious grew nauseated with the raw power and he guessed that a lesser servant of God had come to investigate the call. His senses registered the electric feeling and goose bumps ran down his spine.

Intuitively, Areck praised the fact that God cared enough to answer such an unworthy servant. With an iron will, he suppressed the sickness and let his mind slip further into the trance, trying to solidify the connection. Tonight he gave thanks to Starsgalt for allowing him the chance to be included in the day's activities. He asked God to forgive those sins that he was yet to commit. When he was done giving thanks for a blessed life, Areck prayed for his company's safety in what would be a long journey, and for King Roderick II to find his way to Heaven.

Areck was about to add several more prayers when a whisper glided across his face and the churning in his stomach intensified. He could feel something, possibly an angel, enter the room. It listened to his thoughts, brushing his skin with its presence. Its touch sent tingles through his arms, making his eyes water in pain. He had never felt love like this before, so powerfully pure! His heart soared with joy—an angel was making contact with him!—it made him feel like he was truly a knight. For the first time in his young life, Areck's prayer was answered. The event caused a tear of pride to roll down his face!

Understand. A perfect thought bloomed in his mind.

White light flared in his mind and the tingling in his body intensified. It came to a crescendo, leaving him trembling with pain and joy. He realized at once that he was not ready to understand what he was being shown. Worse, it was against The Code to cease a vision once started. It would be the greatest dishonor, one that would strip a knight of rank and pride, to ask for a vision and then deny it. He tried to comprehend the indecipherable words to no avail. He wanted it to stop, but realized that his only choice was to endure the pain.

With that, Areck of Brenly let to divine vision take him.

† † † † †

The light dimmed, leaving him with a view of mountains. His vision blurred and he saw a trio of peaks, which Areck theorized were the Three Sentinels. Then he was hovering above Stormwind Keep, an impregnable city-fortress built into the mountain itself, controlling the only pass between Aresleigh and Natalinople. He saw Stormwind's mighty walls manned with soldiers, each carrying a longbow, poised stoically and watching merchants.

He sped in his vision past Stormwind Keep and into the Pass of Storms, its long winding road leading out of the Dragonspine Mountains and towards Natalinople.

Again, Areck's vision blurred. This time he saw the glint of metal from a battlefield with a pair of dead knights . . . or at least one seemed to be a knight. Movement caught his eye; one was still moving, crawling away from the battlefield, grievously wounded.

There was another bright flash of light.

Areck looked around just in time to see a third figure approaching, bearing the cloak of a Bre'Dmorian knight, emblazoned with a pair of crisscrossing long swords encompassed by a golden crown. The man drew an ungainly sword and walked over to defend his fallen comrade— wait, that was not correct—the wounded man was crawling *away* from the knight, who was now darkened by a demonic shadow.

Areck tried to call out, but no sound came from his lips.

The wounded man rolled over to defend himself with a shortsword. Fear ripped through Areck's mind as he glimpsed the wounded man's face. Though it was heavily distorted, the visage belonged to Arawnn!

With a deft motion, the Bre'Dmorian slammed his sword into the chest of the courier and turned around . . .

"Are you well, Areck?" a voice cut into his mind. "Areck . . .?"

The voice sounded concerned. Though Areck recognized it, the voice was distant, tugging at the corner of his thoughts. The vision swirled and the mist thickened. He was no longer soaring over the mountain pass.

"Areck, are you awake or dreaming?" the voice was insistent. It dragged him back before he could finish.

Areck felt like he was being sucked down by a whirlpool. He was not finished! The knight's face, he had not seen it! He desperately tried to fight off the beckoning sound, but the voice was overpowering, repeatedly calling his name.

Everything went dark.

"What in Starsgalt's name is wrong with you, Squire?" the voiced asked.

Slowly, Areck's mind became conscious and his eyelids fluttered before they squinted up at the ceiling. This was highly unusual; he was no longer kneeling but lying on his back. The vision had been exceptionally intense, especially for his first time. He accepted the pain the divine presence inflicted upon him to see the end, but someone had dishonored him by ending the communion prematurely.

Areck opened his eyes and gazed into the concerned visage of the royal courier. The young man was sitting with a dampened cloak in his hands and a relieved look on his face.

Righteous anger boiled in Areck. He had been rudely interrupted and humiliated, in front of one who was not even his brethren.

"Why did you do that?" Areck whispered hoarsely. "Do you not know the Code? No one outside the Bre'Dmorian Academy may interrupt a communion. You have humiliated me in the eyes of Starsgalt!"

The look on Arawnn's face almost made Areck apologize. "I . . . I watched you enter the chapel," Arawnn stumbled for words. "Lord Millbert mentioned you would be here. For more thirty minutes I have wandered around and observed your customs. I even talked with several knights before making my way here.

"It wasn't until I heard you cry out that I entered the chamber," Arawnn continued, "where I found you collapsed on the floor. I thought maybe you were injured."

"It was not your place to interrupt a communion, *even* on my behalf," Areck said. "It is a knight's duty to sacrifice in the name of Starsgalt. Sometimes meaning is unknown to us and suffering is the road that must be traveled."

"You are not a knight yet," Arawnn said. "And though it is true I do not know your customs, my orders *do* include you as an escort to Stormwind Keep. To have you fall into the Waking Death is not something that would benefit the cause. Anyway, you look ready to keep your word in the matter of showing me a night on the city! You certainly are dressed for the occasion." Arawnn gestured, trying to relieve the tension.

Areck glared at the young man before him. He could tell that there was no malice in the heart of Arawnn of Almassia. The courier had come to his aid, heedless of the situation or the consequences. The man had risked Areck's ire to make sure the squire was not injured. And Areck had to admit that he had never witnessed a communion that ended with a disciple crying out and collapsing. Although Areck would never forget the humiliation, God was plainly teaching him a lesson of mercy and forgiveness.

Areck took a deep breath. This man had not meant to interrupt the communion, therefore it was hard to fault him for reacting the way he did. "My anger is misguided, sir. In my weakness, I cried out. Were I a stronger man, I would have accepted Starsgalt's gift with joy rather than pain. It is my own fault that you acted the way you did. However, I would ask that if the situation repeats itself, please do not interrupt."

Areck left no room for argument. He wanted to make sure that it was apparent he was offering an apology but that Arawnn should respect his wishes.

The courier nodded in understanding. Satisfied with the response, Areck knelt down to the shrine and offered a quick prayer of thanks before dousing the candles. After he had finished pouring the contents of the cask on the small fire, Areck stood up and turned towards Arawnn.

He was about to say something witty when two thoughts came to him. First, he had left his quarters in the hopes of losing Arawnn for the night yet here the man was; it seemed rather odd. Second, the vision had ended with Arawnn's death. The question in Areck's mind was, did the vision have a singular possibility, or did it show the actual event as viewed by Starsgalt? If it was divine sight, meaning predestination by God, then Arawnn was going to die and nothing could change that fact. However, if the vision was a single possibility amongst a plethora of probabilities, God could be trying to offer assistance, especially dealing with a traitorous knight.

Areck did he best to process the information before judging the meaning of his contact. Was it his place to tell Arawnn of his doom, or should he pray that another vision would clarify events? If he told Arawnn in order to prevent the man's death, and the meaning behind the vision was to warn of the betrayer, then telling Arawnn might alter the outcome.

What if I am wrong and have misjudged my first communion? Areck thought. *Even if I am wrong and told Arawnn what could happen to him, if God already saw it, can it be changed? What if God is offering me a chance to save him?*

Areck shook his head in bewilderment. This was beyond him. He trusted his intuition but was not ready to gamble with the life of another person for something that was not clear.

"Are you going to stand there all night, Squire?" Arawnn broke the silence with a quick smile.

Areck looked about and smiled at the royal courier. Arawnn must be uncomfortable inside the Citadel of the Hand. Those who had not spent a great deal of time within the Bre'Dmorian Academy often felt confined by its closeness. Not to mention, so many Bre'Dmorians in such close proximity made many people feel like they were being scrutinized.

"I am sorry, sir, my mind is wandering tonight. Things have moved so fast, which is uncommon for the Bre'Dmorian Order. How about I lead the way out and we discuss what's in store?" Areck waved his hand towards the exit.

With a hoot and clap on the back, Arawnn strode eagerly towards the hub.

Areck grimaced. He knew this was going to be an interesting night, especially with the terrible knowledge he now held.

Maybe it is my job to let him have some fun before he is to die. Areck considered the statement. *Even if I cannot save the man, at least I can show him a good time.*

With that, Areck followed Arawnn down the hall.

6

ARECK AND Arawnn made their way down the hub in relative silence. As the pair prepared to leave the building, a hand grabbed Areck's shoulder.

"Squire, I have been searching for you!" a jovial voice announced.

Areck turned around to see the not-so-lean Lord Silvershield smiling at him, still dressed in a polished suit of scaled-plate mail. Though his superior looked full of merriment, Areck knew the man was a fearsome foe in the cumbersome armor, which conformed to his wide chest and equally large stomach.

"My lord," Areck responded with a nod of his head.

"I have just come from a council with the High Lightbringer, Areck!" Lord Silvershield said. "I will be leading a company of men on a training exercise as an escort for our young friend here. Furthermore, Lord Lightbringer wishes that nine squires accompany me in this task. You are to be one of them!"

Areck opened his mouth for a reply, but was cut off.

"I already have each squire picked out, lad, as well as the meeting time. We will be at the stables, geared up and ready to leave at dawn," the commander said. With a wink to Arawnn he added, "By the way, you will be leading them, Areck."

"Me?" Areck gulped. "My lord, I do not think I heard you correctly."

The rotund knight could only chuckle. His squire was often in the middle of each day's action yet oblivious to his abilities as a leader. Lord Silvershield saw a bright young commander in the making. He had kept Areck under his command since the boy's last knight had released him.

"This is a training campaign, Squire. You have been my right hand for many years and are very capable of the responsibility. I did not think you would have a problem with this order. Am I wrong?"

"No, Lord Silvershield," Areck replied crisply, excitement in his voice. "I am honored to serve as a junior officer on this campaign!"

Lord Silvershield placed both hands on Areck's shoulders and for once looked serious. "The High Lightbringer informed me that you would be joining Arawnn here in the city?"

Arawnn stepped forward, interpreting Lord Silvershield's serious nature as a reprimand to his guide. "My lord, I asked Areck's indulgence for the night. It is my fault that he will be placed in a less than honorable situation, but I give my word to keep him out of harm's way."

Areck glanced sideways and saw an amused look on the face of Lord Silvershield, though he suspected the knight was likely annoyed at the interruption and breach of protocol.

We will discuss the proper etiquette later, Areck thought, deciding that he needed to show patience with Arawnn. He wondered if the man thought such rules were stupid.

"Not that you aren't a fearsome fighter, Lord Arawnn, but I highly doubt Areck will need your protection," Lord Silvershield replied, a toothy grin splitting his face. "Still, it is good to see a young man step in and take the punishment for another. This is a lesson many among our own order have forgotten."

"As to *you* . . ." Silvershield turned his attention back to Areck.

"My lord, I do not plan on indulging myself in any sin tonight. I will only be there to guide this man around."

"Bah! I am not reprimanding either of you, so get those scowls off your faces!" the knight-captain snorted. "If you will let me finish . . .?" He glanced at both young men. "Good. As I was saying, since you will be touring the city tonight, I have some advice on the better establishments for different pleasures."

Lord Silvershield described for twenty minutes the best drinking holes, the finest inns, and places in Aresleigh where a man could indulge his curiosity with discretion. The smile on his face broadened when he noticed Arawnn paying close attention to the whereabouts of each place, whereas Areck was quite red at the thought of being drunk and doing what was being suggested.

"Lad, there is nothing wrong with having some fun outside of the Code." Bowon said with a small frown, pulling Areck within earshot so no one would overhear such blasphemous words. "I can see the look on your face. You are aghast at the mention of some of the places I suggest. Let me tell you a story of a young man much like yourself: full of honor and pride. He was the type of man that refused such sinful actions. Then he was given a great task, one that was beyond his abilities—one in which he failed. When God turned from that man, he learned that it was his job to live life to the fullest; that to fear the Almighty's wrath made him weaker, not stronger. Do not make that same mistake."

Lord Bowon sighed at the fact that he was lecturing his squire. He could see that Areck was nodding to be agreeable but had no concept of was being said. He reprimanded himself for interfering; the boy embodied what Starsgalt intended in the world. He knew an old man's philosophy had no place in a humanity that was lost in their religion; sometimes reason was forgotten in the face of faith and honor.

"Take Arawnn to a good place, Squire, and enjoy everything," Lord Silvershield announced. "I promise that we will not see the comfort of a city for several weeks once we set out."

"Thank you, my lord," Arawnn said smiling. "I will drag him to at least two of your recommendations."

"Aye, thank you, my lord," Areck echoed, looking relieved by the change of subject. "I have an interesting night in store, one where I will probably be protecting *him!*" Areck pointed at Arawnn, giving him an amused shrug.

"I shall see you at dawn, then," Bowon said. He clasped each young man's arm, spun around, and made his way towards his own room.

The two young men exchanged glances as they watched the large knight walk away.

"I really like that man." Arawnn broke the silence as Lord Silvershield rounded a corner. "He is so unlike the rest of you knights, so . . . cheerful in his demeanor," Arawnn chuckled.

"Aye, he is a good man, Arawnn, even if he wanders down the wrong path at times," Areck replied. In fact, he could feel great divinity within Lord Silvershield, suppressed by years of sinful action. It was hard to understand how someone, whom rumor suggested to be a vagabond and heretic, could be so firmly enveloped in Starsgalt's glory.

Arawnn nodded, opened the door and motioned outside. "If we are going to be back by dawn, we had better get going."

Areck groaned and followed the courier past the courtyard and on to Veres Street, which would lead them towards an inner gatehouse. He was overwhelmed with how busy the night was.

Several carriages rattled down the paved roadway towards the inner city's most prominent theatre, the Galleon's Stage. Though he was not accustomed to a noble's night life, Areck knew that such people preferred drinking when a troupe came to town. It looked like this was such a night.

Areck had once seen a play, long ago, depicting the cycle of life. It had been an interesting story about growth and decay. He remembered it mostly because Lord Silvershield had enjoyed a small cask of brandy, some smokeweed, and of course a debate with Areck, long into the night.

It was worth it, Areck thought, recollecting a conversation which spanned the entirety of the universe. *It is too bad that common people cannot afford such things. Not that they could understand such complicated metaphors, anyway.*

"So, Squire Areck, some of the places Lord Silvershield recommended sound quite intriguing. Where shall we start?" Arawnn asked, looking toward the palace, trying to get his bearings.

"I guess that depends on what you wish to do," Areck responded. "I have been inside three of the places Lord Silvershield mentioned and can give my own input on each, if you'd like."

"*You* have been inside a tavern, Squire?" Arawnn said, with an incredulous smirk on his face.

"I did not say I had partaken in anything sinful," Areck raised his hands in mock surprise. "There *are* other alternatives to drinking, fighting, and wenching."

"Granted," Arawnn said, laughing. "I cannot think of much off hand, but I am sure you are right, there are other fancies to be had in such places. How about you tell me what you have in mind, and I'll tell you what I wish to see?" Arawnn asked, still chuckling.

Areck nodded and walked to the middle of the courtyard. He pointed north, towards a gathering of buildings. "Down this street is the Silver Horn Inn. It is one of the places that the younger noblemen of the city prefer. They have good ale from all over the region, but they are pricy compared to the rest of the city. Although I shun looks, the Silver Horn attracts many shapely young daughters looking for wealth."

"Aye, wealth and power always seem to attract each other," Arawnn said. "My job has taken me to too many cities, and there is always a place where the two can meet. I find nobles quite boorish, though. Either they get too drunk and their mock honor is easily offended, or they alienate anyone not of their lineage. Let's not visit that establishment till last."

"I haven't even told you of the others yet."

"Anything will be better than dealing with scheming nobles and wealthy women looking to marry, that I promise you," Arawnn said.

Areck had no knowledge of such things so he just chuckled and continued on to the next option. "Over there is the Foaming Tankard Tavern, a dwarven-owned establishment. I am not sure if you have had dwarven ale but from all accounts, it has no equal. I have frequented this place several times; there are bards of renown, good food, and several booths to conduct private business."

"Hmm. I have never seen a dwarf." Arawnn looked interested. "What kind of crowd are we talking about?"

Although the dwarves of Hammerstone Citadel were not regular inhabitants of the city, some had been commissioned by Duke Hawkwind in the expansion of Aresleigh. Those that remained were now allies of sorts, trading their highly valued time for precious metals, gems, and intimate crafting projects that human hands could not produce.

"Well this dwarf, Druegar Smithbound, is a wealthy landowner here in Aresleigh," Areck explained. "To answer your question, the Foaming Tankard draws many ruffians! In fact, the motto of the tavern is, 'Most fights start here!' Oh, I should also mention that there are very few options for . . . womanly company. Druegar doesn't believe in mixing women with beer." Areck further explained what would be expected if they walked into the Tankard looking for a night of fun and drinking.

Arawnn's shoulders sagged. "What is the last establishment on your list? I do not wish to be hasty when it comes to drinking and fighting."

Areck nodded and continued. "The Twisting Oak Inn is adjacent to the eastern gatehouse. We passed it on our way to see the duke. It is not as rowdy as the Foaming Tankard, but lacks high quality food, beer, and nobility. It is an open establishment visited by many merchants, army enlistees, and some of the less notable bards."

Areck knew the establishment well, as he had been visiting it with Lord Silvershield most of his young life. Though the Oak's reputation did not extend to seedy, it kept secrets well. This reputation was helped by the fact that less than honorable folk stayed away from an area patrolled by so many knights. It was also the reason why his commander chose to meet his countless informants in the private rooms the inn offered.

"Go on." Arawnn looked thoughtful.

"Well, you said you wished to drink and meet young maidens," Areck said. "With so many merchants flowing through its doors, the Twisting Oak has a reputation for attracting in pretty serving girls, as well as courtesans from all over the city."

Arawnn smiled. "There is an old saying in Almassia, Squire:' There would be no reason to drink if not for feasting and fornicating.' So yes, I am looking for a place that can provide more drink and women than a good bar-room brawl."

Arawnn slapped Areck on the back and moved off. "Since our course is decided, let us be on our way. I have to admit that a mug of artesian ale sounds exceptionally good after all the talking I have had to endure today!"

Areck smirked. The poor fellow did not seem to recognize the irony of the proclamation; though he bemoaned having to listen, Arawnn never seemed to run out of things to say.

I guess that is typical of most nobility, Areck thought, hurrying after the cheerful young courier who had the single purpose of getting drunk with female companionship on his mind.

Unlike the inner city, the outer city was exceptionally quiet. Other than vendors stacking their wares on various carts or hauling recently arrived cargo to their warehouses, the streets were empty. It was not unusual that when the nobles were bustling, commoners were drinking, and vice versa.

As they passed several vendors packing up fresh produce, Areck noticed a group of whores lounging near a burned-out oil lamp. He averted his eyes from the lewd gestures the prostitutes were making toward several drunk men who seemed to be enjoying the attention. It disgusted him that such women would be in high demand, especially with so many enforcement agents so close.

Areck had never liked the profession of prostitution; it went against the Anduinic Code. It was hard to have honor and faith when a prostitute sold her soul for coin. He guessed that the Bre'Dmorians allowed such atrocious acts because it curbed violence, allowing the lower class to drink itself into a night of bar room brawling before finding the cheapest lover one could afford. He almost felt sorry for them. The Bre'Dmorian Knighthood did nothing to stop violence against such women, treating them as though they did not exist. Areck guessed it was easier to frown upon the problem than arrest everyone suspected of dishonorable conduct.

Just another blasphemous thought, he supposed. *The Academy does not have the unlimited resources it would take to stop the problem.*

Soft music interrupted his thoughts. He tried to suppress a smile; it seemed they had picked a good night to visit the Twisting Oak. Areck noticed the bustling throng of people entering the establishment, and those who were already drunk outside.

"They have bards!" Arawnn said.

Since Areck wasn't planning to partake in drinking or socializing, he had secretly hoped that the night would be filled with bardic stories. "You are truly a master judge of things," Areck said, pointing out the obvious nature of Arawnn's comment.

Arawnn laughed. "Let us hope they are a good lot tonight. It always helps to meet the fairer sex when they are preoccupied with a good story."

Areck could only shake his head. "I have been here on many occasions. If the entertainment resembles that of my experience, I would think your chances of success hinge solely on your solemn nature."

Arawnn looked questioningly at the squire.

"Did I mention that they almost always sing of Anduin of Ardoc, the first virtuous knight?" Areck said, trying not to smile at his joke. "Of course, this is just my opinion, but I would think a lot of laughter and flirtation during such a story would only enrage the companion you are seeking. I could be wrong, though."

For once the courier was speechless. Rather than waiting for his friend to slap him on the back and walk off, Areck decided to have a little fun.

"Well do not stand there, sir, let's go listen . . .!" Areck clapped Arawnn on the back, laughed, and walked off towards the inn.

† † † † †

Arawnn strode after him. Though the squire had unexpectedly won the last round of quips, Arawnn had to admit Areck's mind was astute, even if the man was restricted by the tyranny of the church. Not that it mattered; tonight was all about having fun. This would be his last evening in civilized lands for many weeks. He knew that once he reached Natalinople, the lord constable would immediately send him off to the Duchies of Thames and Calimond, to confirm the king's demise.

It was worth the price, though, to be part of something special. The events that would unfold, and how they came to pass, would rely on him.

Arawnn considered why he had chosen the position of a royal courier. He had come from the small kingdom of Almassia and was the third son in a small township ruled by his father, Baron Cedric. Because he was a third son there was no possibility of claiming a noble title, and thus no chance to ever be involved in the goings-on of the world. That was why he had chosen an existence that kept him on the road, acting as messenger for the royal court of Arsgoth. It was an important job that afforded him a wealthy estate in Natalinople and a title of Arsgothian lordship. He knew the career suited him well: he met many people, was friends with none, yet trusted by all.

Arawnn had always told himself that he could not afford friendship— that he was on the road to often and that the risk of being killed in the line of duty was too high. He held life in high regard, cherishing good ale and attractive young ladies. Yet, now he was involved in important events and on his way to becoming friends with a man who was considerably different than himself.

Arawnn smiled, considering how Areck seemed torn between the buttoned up squire he wanted to be and the man he truly was. With a final gaze at his conflicted companion's back, he climbed up the wooden stairs and plunged into the Twisting Oak.

It was hard to see anything with so many people walking around the commons. Arawnn stood in perhaps the largest inn room he had ever seen, with two stages on opposite sides of the building and several long tables meant for feasting. By the look of the people, Arawnn guessed that he was in the midst of a caravan from northern Arsgoth, mixed with several local merchants and various commoners. Each table was laden with a roasted pig, a keg of ale, and an assortment of produce. The heady aroma of roasting pork made Arawnn's stomach rumble. Though Duke Hawkwind had been kind enough to offer brandy, a custom of thanks and luck to each courier who arrived, Arawnn had not had a well-prepared meal in days. He pushed through a thick group of people, stepped up on a booth meant for private customers, and scanned the room for his companion.

It only took a moment for Arawnn to spot Areck procuring one of the smaller tables near the northern stage. Satisfied, he stepped down from his perch and decided to slice off a hunk of roasted pig. As he grabbed a knife, Areck turned and motioned him to come take a seat.

Arawnn shrugged. It was not that he didn't carry coins enough to eat— he always carried a small pouch of gold and silver each time he left the capitol. He just couldn't help but act roguishly at times; it seemed to attract young ladies who would be eager to assess his charms.

With a sigh, Arawnn realized that with an honor-bound squire in his company, he would have to shelve his tricks. Deciding patience would be the wiser option; Arawnn dropped the knife, inhaled the savory smell of meat, and pretended to be knocked off balance by a young serving maid walking by. He gave the woman just enough time to gather herself before he acted out his part, which was to seem offended at being run into.

"I am sorry, sir" she stammered, blushing at his scrutiny. "I had not meant to jostle you."

"My lady, it was no fault of yours," Arawnn said, bowing. "I was admiring the scent of food and was not paying attention. My friend and I have not had a good meal in weeks. Do you think you could bring us a few slices, perhaps from the haunch?" Arawnn smiled at the young server and winked. He leaned in and whispered in her ear. "I would be *very* appreciative."

"You must not have been here before, good sir?" She looked at him curiously.

Arawnn shook his head.

She giggled and said, "This is the night one of the local lords, Lord Barbury, comes into our establishment. His is the caravan you see there. To show his appreciation, he purchases three roast pigs and allows any man to take his share."

Arawnn groaned inwardly, but chuckled. He was glad that he had not stolen any of the meat; it would have only made him look like a fool in front of the entire tavern.

I should say thank you and walk away, he mused.

Seeing his disappointment the serving maid added with a shy smile, "If you'd like, though, I'd be happy to bring you both full plates and some ale as well."

For the first time Arawnn noticed the woman's green eyes. She was quite pretty—a slender frame, flowing dark brown hair, and an angular face. He glanced over at Areck to see how his companion was faring.

"I would be honored to receive such service, my lady, but I think we should start with names. I am Arawnn of Almassia and my dour friend over there is Areck. We are mercenaries who have not yet earned our last

names," he chuckled, raising his hand in a gentlemanly salute. "I am pleased
to make your acquaintance."

When Areck looked back to see Arawnn conversing with a pretty young
serving wench, he sighed with annoyance. *I should have stayed with him,* he
reprimanded himself, realizing that by entering the room and picking out a
seat, he had left Arawnn to get into trouble.

Now, the royal courier was pointing him out to a giggling young lady,
which made him duck his head and nearly fall off his stool. As he caught his
balance and looked up, Areck turned red at the humiliation. He tried in vain
to conceal his face, hoping that no one would recognize him as a Squire of
the Hand. Knowing that his efforts would be in vain, he dropped his gaze
to the table, trying unsuccessfully to melt into the oaken post he was leaning against.

After several moments of Areck staring down at the table, he again
looked up. This time the courier was walking toward him with a pair of
mugs in each of his hands, followed by the serving wench carrying two
heaping plates of roasted meat, cheese, and bread. His friend looked full of
mischief and mirth.

Such a good-hearted fellow, Areck thought, reflecting on the vision he'd had
only an hour ago. He told himself that even though the courier was becoming his friend, according to the Code, he could not allow himself to alter
history. Plus, he was honor-bound to decipher the vision before he informed Arawnn of the matter.

The possibility of sacrificing his friend to catch a traitor did not sit well
in Areck's heart. *Yet what,* he wondered, *can be done about it?* Before he could
further ponder such possibilities, a laughing Arawnn reached the table followed by the wench, who laid both platters in front of them.

"Well, are you going to thank Kristina for her kindness, my friend?"
Arawnn broke through his thoughts.

Areck reddened at his rudeness. The Code demanded he treat peasants
as equals. *I should have been paying more attention,* Areck thought, *rather than trying to hide my embarrassment from customers.*

Not really knowing how to handle a woman, Areck called upon what he
had heard from fellow knights: he stepped away from his chair, dropped to
one knee, and took her small hand. He was sure the maneuver looked quite
ridiculous, but it was the only way he knew how to act. "If you will let me,
my lady, I would like to apologize for my rudeness. I am honored that you
would bring such plentiful rations to our table."

She gave a quick curtsy and glanced towards the bar but saw no one looking in her direction. "Please get off the ground before the barkeep sees my lack of work."

Kristina's reply made Areck hurry to his feet, realizing that his actions might draw attention to himself, and more important, get the young lady in trouble.

She giggled at the gesture and looked at Arawnn. "For a mercenary he has the manners of one of those knight-men. If only more men had such an earnest look about them!"

With a wink Arawnn gave a mock bow. "You mean like this?" Deftly, he reached out and pinched her rear.

Kristina gave a slight jump and squeaked—doing her best to look somewhat affronted. "I best get back to work before Elijah gets it in his head to make me wash platters! He doesn't like it much when we talk with the customers." The woman then winked at Arawnn, patted his face gently, and whispered something in his ear. The effect made the royal courier cough up his ale. She curtsied again toward Areck and flounced towards a large table of men who were being very vocal about needing large pitchers of ale before the show started.

With a wistful expression, Arawnn's eyes followed her; whatever she said had certainly increased his interest. "She is a magnificent creature, is she not?" Arawnn said, finally bringing his attention back to the squire.

Areck followed the courier's gaze, a smile splitting his face. Though Kristina was a beautiful woman, nothing could compare to the majesty of Elyana.

"I have been to many taverns, balls, and inns in my travels, Areck. The funny thing is, I think she might be the most beautiful peasant I have ever seen—outside of those twins I met in Kyelund," Arawnn chuckled.

Areck could only shake his head at the comment. It did not seem like a good way to conduct affairs: judging a woman by her looks, social standing, or the money the wealthy so often flaunted. He wanted to tell his friend that beauty was never a true reflection of a person's inner value, since that was lost in a lifetime. In other circumstances he might have explained Starsgalt's teachings—that a person's value lay in their heart, with deeds of compassion, love, and acceptance. But most people already knew such things but refused to accept them as facts.

Who am I to tell another man how to love? Areck thought. *This man will most likely never return to Aresleigh. Why not look for something to appeal to the eye, given a lifestyle such as his? Actually, I can think of several reasons not to,* he concluded. *However, the choice isn't mine to make.*

Areck decided that he would guide his friend around the town without offering advice unless it was asked for. With a quick glance around the room to make sure no one was paying any attention to him, Areck pulled a knife from his belt, stuck a piece of meat, and began to devour the food in front of him.

7

THE TWISTING Oak was not as grand as some of the more costly inns, yet it was known for bringing in quality entertainment considering the coin spent. On previous occasions Areck had seen jugglers, sword artists, storytellers, and bards who sang of times long forgotten or the great empires to the far-east. His personal preference had always been tales re-telling Arsgoth's history, sometimes discussing the valor and heroes of the Bre'Dmorian Knighthood.

It wasn't until someone dressed in dark green hose, a silk jacket, and long flowing cape stepped onto the stage that Areck felt the first tingle of divine magic and finally looked up from his meal. What greeted him was a young man who had a trimmed beard, stark grey eyes, a green hat that sported a dragon's talon, and a pair of silver pins attached to either side of his cape—which declared the man a professional troubadour of some renown. Areck could only stare; he had met several younger entertainers just getting into the business, but none had bore the markings of a professional bard, nor accumulated enough recognition to earn a single pin.

The man must be a master lyricist, Areck thought, wondering how a man of such stature ended up in the Twisting Oak Inn. *Maybe he belongs to Song & Stories!* The thought excited him. The Song & Stories guild was an elite conglomeration of similarly minded bards, usually seeking to pass on their knowledge and resources to like-minded agents. The rumors said agents of Song & Stories were common in Aresleigh yet they were not openly discussed, as the kingdom would exercise its right to tax those who gathered for profit on knowledge.

The young man seemed to feel the squire's stare and turned to regard his audience. With a slight nod, he glanced at Areck and locked eyes momentarily before gazing at the rest of the hall.

Areck got the distinct impression the man was looking for something specific—or someone—a theory that intensified when his stomach started to clench. He could almost feel the man's divinity reaching out. And then, as abruptly as it started, the divine magic ceased. Areck took a deep breath and looked up, noticing the man's gaze had stopped at a point near himself. As a Bre'Dmorian, Areck's eyes instinctively followed the gaze of the professional entertainer past several tables, the overhang of a balcony, and into the shadows of the far wall.

Unfortunately, when a large man bumped into Areck, he was forced to drop his eyes and allow the man to pass or be pushed from his seat. When he looked back up, he saw only the shadow of a slender figure making its way towards the far end of the stage.

A woman, Areck thought. By the way she was sneaking in the crowd, Areck concluded that she was attempting to remain hidden. As he craned his neck to get a better view of her, the woman came out of the shadows. However, before he saw her face, another sharp tingling sensation ran through his fingers and an intense stabbing pain filled his head.

Countless possibilities ran through his mind. Areck looked away from the shadowed woman and scanned the room—his curse was never wrong; someone with significant divine presence besides the troubadour was in the tavern.

Maybe Lord Silvershield has sent a messenger to deliver new orders! He thought, as a cool shiver of excitement coursed through his body.

"Expecting someone?" Arawnn asked dryly.

With an annoyed sigh, Areck sat back down. "I think one of my order has entered the room. Maybe the commander has sent someone to retrieve us."

"Is this a common practice among you Bre'Dmorians?" Arawnn asked.

"What do you mean?"

"Well, it is obvious that you didn't wish to come here tonight, Squire," Arawnn said, "but I wasn't expecting you to look for someone to save you from my presence."

Areck frowned. "You have my word, Arawnn, that someone exuding divine power has entered the room. I know this because God has granted me the ability to sense the presence of divine practitioners."

The skepticism on Arawnn's face was enough to make Areck cease trying to explain. It was obvious that the man did not believe his story.

"You are a squire so I know that you cannot lie, but since that bard came on stage, you have been scouring the room. What do you expect to find with this . . . ability?" Arawnn asked, finally breaking the awkward moment.

"Honestly, I don't know. Like I already said, I believe it signifies that one of the knighthood is in this room. Yet, it feels odd; even though I first noticed the divine aura when that bard stepped on the stage, I don't think he's the one causing this particular feeling. It wasn't until I noticed the man's gaze stop on a shadowed female that I felt the sensation intensify."

"Did you see her face?"

"No. Why?"

"I was just curious," the cheerful nature of the courier returned. "I was following your gaze and saw the woman you speak of . . . a gorgeous creature!"

"Did you not hear what I just said?" Areck asked in exasperation.

"I heard you, Areck." Arawnn smiled. "However, the night is young and unless you know who it is, there are other options to be had!"

Areck grumbled at the courier's comment, but did not argue. Instead, he ignored the remark and continued on with his line of thinking. "My senses are limited in here. Maybe we should walk around a bit? If someone is looking for us, it might help to move towards the doors."

"If someone is looking for us, then to move would only lengthen the process. My advice is we stay here."

Areck knew the courier was right. A Bre'Dmorian messenger would find them if they were needed, and if not, at least he now knew there were more Bre'Dmorians than Lord Silvershield and himself who visited the Twisting Oak.

With his nerves calmed, Areck turned his attention back towards the woman but she was no longer in sight. With a frown he turned towards Arawnn and asked about the "gorgeous creature." Areck was surprised with the amount of detail the courier remembered. From the description, he gathered that the woman had flowing blonde hair, finely chiseled features, and a regal bearing. He guessed that was why she was sneaking around; she was of noble birth, come to see her favorite bard in a common inn.

Areck was about to comment on the assumption when the master bard commanded the attention of the room. The audience quieted and the bustling ceased, leaving only the whispers of serving maids to be heard.

"Hear ye! Hear ye! Ye who have not heard this story must listen now! From the depths of the Forsaken Lands comes the story of Anduin of Ardoc. Bear witness to the last ride of the First Lightbringer and the birth of thy kingdom!"

There was no greater story than hearing a lament of the First Knight, a story meant for the halls of high ranking nobles, possibly even the king. Though Areck had played a joke on his friend, the Twisted Oak was definitely not the kind of place to play such high-minded ballads. Yet, here was a master bard about to begin the solemn tale regarding the history of the kingdom and the knightly order which protected it. It made the tingling in his hands intensify.

The man's beautiful tenor was deep enough to gather the emotions that Anduin of Ardoc must have felt when Hell first opened and the ferryll had flown like an obsidian river out of the Great Devoid. The evil race of demonic creatures—who had destroyed the northwestern portion of Aryth and burnt the Ten Kingdoms of Kal'un'Dell to the ground—had then turned their eyes to the south. They had killed hundreds of thousands in the invasion.

When all hope was lost, a young officer, Anduin of Ardoc, was given apocalyptic visions by Starsgalt, the One True God of mankind. Guided by the god-granted vision, Anduin allowed Starsgalt to lead him deep into the greatest peaks of the Dragonspine Mountains, where he was anointed the First Lightbringer, Champion of Law and Order. As Anduin walked down the mountain the land begin to shake, and the chaos that had spread through the lands begin to tremble. For God had armed Anduin of Ardoc with holy fire and the Band of Sunlight, a small bracelet embedded with unearthly jewels that shone brightly in the face of non-existence.

With God's power at his disposal, Anduin had used the Band of Sunlight to unify the broken lands against the invasion. His first decree was to create others like himself, those who would accept the holy fervor of Starsgalt as a way of life. The decision had turned the tide of war, and Anduin Lightbringer began a crusade against the demons, using the holy fire to slice through the chaos that surrounded them.

History would tell that victory came swiftly and that the world had recovered. However, so many died against the ferryll that the men burning the bodies lost count and the historical record held no number for the amount of dead. Areck's friend Vandallan speculated that the corpses were piled so high that they topped oak trees before being burned with purging holy fire.

Thus Anduin created the Bre'Dmorians, which in the old tongue meant Guardians of Law and Order, to protect Arsgoth from chaos. It was his last sacrifice before he was divinely inspired to venture into the Great Devoid to seal the rip in Hell.

Areck loved this story; it was exciting, factual, and tragic. The war to drive the ferryll back into Hell had consumed Anduin. Not that he disagreed with the sacrifice, but it concerned him that God would demand a purge which forced mankind into following Him. The bard didn't say it, but in those days the Bre'Dmorians had burned those unable to see the redemption Starsgalt offered.

"Thus, my friends, time never forgets such things, tales of valor and tragedy! It is just a moving current that carries on, with little regard for mortals! Thus ends the first tale of Anduin of Ardoc!"

Areck was not surprised that the bard had masterfully spun the ancient tale, expertly stirring emotions within the room. Areck himself had been drawn in by the verses, moved in ways he had never imagined; a greater sense of what he represented coursed through his mind. But for the presence of divine magic, he might have truly enjoyed the tale. When he looked around, the rest of the tavern was spellbound.

With some regret Areck focused his mind. If the commander had indeed sent someone to seek them out, Areck could not dismiss his responsibilities. His oath superseded everything. It was his duty to find the cleric in this building, and preferably to get orders that demanded he escort Arawnn back to his quarters. From there they both would prepare for the ride to Stormwind Keep.

Trying to be as quiet as one could in such a close quarters, Areck pushed his muscular form back from the table and excused himself. Although Arawnn gave an annoyed scowl, he did not say anything because the bard was beginning the second act in the tale of Anduin.

To pacify his friend, Areck broke his oath by drinking his mug of beer, pointed to Arawnn's now empty pint, and motioned that he was going to get another round. Arawnn's frown evaporated and his attention returned to the stage. Areck smiled at the courier's dramatic facial expressions.

Shouldering his way past burly merchants with pock-marked faces and the reek of too much drink, Areck snaked through the tables surrounding the stage. For no reason other than to satisfy his own curiosity, he decided to start his search in the shadows where he had noticed the lithe female picking her way through the crowd. He reminded himself that his task was to find the cleric, not to answer his own interest. He remembered an old adage commonly used in the Academy: "Curiosity is not a virtue of the faithful. It leads only to revelations that are unattainable." He wondered how true that saying was—curiosity had been the downfall of many heroic knights; however, it also led men to the rise above the doctrines of Starsgalt, often creating tales that were still sung.

When Areck reached the outer circle of attendees, he made his way to the overhang, still sure that there was a divine presence in the room. He was tempted to move directly to the bar, as logic demanded, but he needed to answer his question before he left the inn. He knew that if the cleric found him before he finished, he was sure his orders would be very clear and he would have to leave immediately.

Who is to say that the cleric is not in this direction anyway? Areck concluded. *Nowhere in the Code does it say that I cannot look for the messenger throughout the whole of the bar. If I happen to stumble upon the woman first, well, so much the better.*

He sighed in chagrin, having already partaken in several breaches of his own ethos. He told himself that his thoughts were sound and that the cleric might actually *be* in the other direction. If anything, he figured that he might as well hope for the best and just seek the answer; otherwise it would nag him well into the ride of the next day.

Seeing his destination, Areck ducked into the narrow lane that separated the crowd from the wall.

Areck's sense of direction and general knowledge of the inn helped him move down the approximate path of the woman he was seeking. Due to the crowd's density, he guessed that she would not wish to fight for line of sight, rather making her way to the stage where she might find a better vantage point.

Fortunately, Areck was a tall man, standing half a head over most of the crowd, and it was easy to see the small pockets of empty space that formed when large gatherings of people coalesced into one spot. But he still did not see her.

Once again, Areck lowered his shoulder into the crowd, excusing himself as he bumped an elderly woman aside and made his way towards the stage. The press of bodies made it difficult to slide farther up since most did not wish to let him pass. The irritable grumbles of the crowd did not dissuade him, though, and he pushed through, finally making it to the third row. He could now easily view the stage, the crowd opposite his location, and Arawnn staring thoughtfully at the words hanging in the air.

Areck craned his neck, but did not see her. With a grunt of disapproval he decided to move again, this time working his way towards the northern side of the dining hall.

As he began to slide past the large fellow next to him, a hand reached out and a middle-aged woman spoke, "I am not one for anger, young man, but there are more people here than just you. Either move into the crowd or out of it. You are disrupting Master Rahk's tale."

Areck spun around to see the woman scowling up at him. He could tell that she was heated, and although Areck stared in her surprise, the woman poked him in chest!

He wanted to tell her of his indignation—that he was a Bre'Dmorian Squire, and that he could pass as he wished. However, the thoughts brought a deep color to Areck's cheeks.

I am being disrespectful, he thought. *I owe this woman an apology.*

"I apologize, madam," Areck began. "A friend of mine has passed this way, and I was searching for her. I will wait, however, to make my way . . ." He caught the sight of a familiar form in the front row making her way out of the crowd, which seemed to be almost parting for her.

Giving a short bow, Areck took an angle of pursuit toward the woman. He decided that winding his way through the crowd would be the only way to cut her off. If she made it through the crowd and to the door, he would have to let her go.

What am I going to say? He silently screamed, angry that such a question had not crossed his thoughts until now. *I have never solicited an unwanted conver-*

sation with a female before, especially not a noble. If I reach for and take her unaware,
surely I will look the fool. What if she reacts poorly?

Areck hesitated, considering not speaking to her at all. There was no
reason he should be seeking her in the first place, so why make more of a
fool of himself? If he could just glimpse her eyes, he could mark her in his
mind and satisfy the urge that had welled up inside him.

With some resolve he made a decision and reached for the woman's
arm. She abruptly stopped and turned back to the stage, her lowered hood
keeping most of her face in shadow. Areck had to spin away or run the
poor woman over. Though his reflexes were good, his quick reaction was
not enough to prevent impact. With a soft grunt the woman reached out
and sought support from Areck lest she fall to the floor.

Areck regained enough composure to notice that he was leaning against
the wall and the pressure of the crowd was forcing the woman against his
torso. He also noticed that the woman was funneling an immense amount
of divine aura through her body—causing an almost excruciating pain.

"How dare you follow me so close? You drunken oaf!" she said, not
looking at her assailant. She tried to remove an arm that had been pinned
against the wall by the Areck's body.

Areck turned crimson in embarrassment. He could hear the tremor of
anger in her melodic voice, one that sounded vaguely familiar. He stared at
the ground and did not see that the woman's cowl had been pulled back
enough to reveal her familiar face.

"I shall *not* ask again," she said, brushing herself off as if she had been
soiled by the contact. "I do not look the part of a harlot, do I? And I certainly never asked for your company! Why the blazes are you so following
so close?"

Areck's heart raced as he tried to stammer out a reply. "I meant only to
make my way out of the crowd, my lady. You stopped so suddenly and—
please forgive me—I was not paying attention. I am very sorry!" His voice
cracked with nervous tension.

Silence finally brought Areck's gaze up to see the incredulous face of Elyana staring back at him. He was shocked to see that she was no longer
dressed in armor but wore a flowing emerald dress covered by a long gray
cloak. Furthermore, her hair was drawn up in a bun and she looked the part
of any noble: face lightly painted, nails lacquered, and she now bore a very
regal demeanor.

It wasn't until she pulled her hood up and began to back away that
Areck figured out she was waiting for him to make a move. He noted the
concern in her eyes, and her movement was slow and deliberate, as if going
slowly might not break the shock of the moment.

The woman's rattled look gave her away. She was no noble of this
realm, let alone a cleric. Yet there was something in her eyes . . . something

exquisitely and mysteriously curious. Areck had to admit he was curious as well and even though justice had to be served, he wanted to talk to her.

"I think we should talk," he finally sputtered.

"There is nothing to talk about. I do not know how you came to be within arm's reach of me, maybe fate, but I do know that my time is limited," she said, her face shrouded by the shadows of the hood. She backed away from him, nearing the open door and her escape. He considered his options. He had not anticipated a fight.

Swiftly, Areck stepped through Elyana's outstretched arms and before she could react, maneuvered her towards the wall. His move made her either backpedal and be cut off or turn and flee, causing unwanted attention.

Areck felt her body stiffen, but she never moved away. Satisfied that she was not going to bolt, he bent down and whispered in her ear. "It is a crime that some of my order would consider deserving of death, my lady."

Her mouth dropped open and she allowed herself to be directed to the wall. She sighed and pulled her hood back down to regard him.

"It is Areck?" Elyana asked, continuing when he nodded. "I do not know what you are talking about, sir. I would be grateful if you would move out of the way, since I have more pressing issues to attend to."

"You know of what I am speaking, my lady," Areck explained, taking several steps back. "It is obvious that you are some kind of magic user, one who has a connection to the One God. Although I do not understand this, I know you are not a Cleric of Gabriel."

"You are a Bre'Dmorian, why do you lie?" She changed the subject. "Isn't being deceitful a quick way to the dungeon? We both know there is no death penalty for impersonating a cleric, and what I am is no consequence to you; only know that I am your superior!"

Areck's mouth tightened into a dark scowl. *She knows some of our customs it seems*, he thought. *It was stupid of me to try and force my hand by using our laws; she has spent time learning about the knighthood.*

"Indeed it is. However, if I am not mistaken, the Book of Anduin says that sometimes one must take extreme measurers to ensure that law and justice are served. Still . . . you are right; we should take this to the local authorities. I think the duke could deal with a common thief more appropriately than a Bre'Dmorian Knight." Areck turned to go fetch a local warden.

As he was about to pull away, the woman's fierce voice stopped him. Oddly, it was tinged with real emotion. "How *dare* you call me a thief . . .?"

"Am I wrong? Why don't you tell me why you are impersonating people, and I will not get the authorities." He would allow her to take this conversation in the direction he wanted.

"If you were not so rude, I was about to recommend that we sit somewhere, drink some wine, and discuss this," she said. "Do you remember my name, at least?"

"I doubt it is real, but if I am not mistaken, it is Lady Elyana."

"Well, at least the young men of the Academy have enough respect for a noble lady to remember her name, even if they lack manners," she pursed her lips. "I suppose you are going to lead us to a table?"

"My friend is holding our table," Areck pointed to where Arawnn was seated, still waiting for the round that had been promised. "I recommend dropping the pretense that you are any kind of true noblewoman; it doesn't stand up to close scrutiny."

She grimaced before pushing past him in the direction he had pointed. Areck had to admit that she was good; her composure gave credence to the assertion that she was nobly born. However, as he watched her walk away, he could tell by her lithe movements that she was an imposter. There was no mistaking a woman born of nobility when one watched them glide.

It did not matter that she was lying, as he had never meant to take her to the authorities in the first place. Instead he found himself more intrigued by the woman, especially with the powerful divine radiation she was giving off. With a slight smile he thought, *what an interesting night*, and plowed ahead after her.

8

IN THE walled city of Aresleigh, many alternatives were used, some seedier than others, to come into the city. Of those who used these routes—most of whom were practitioners of illegal trade: slavers, opiate dealers, assassins, and other illegal contraband merchants—most used the dwarven mines of Kurin's Deep which ran beneath the poorer districts of the city and up into the warehouse district.

Long ago, the ancient dwarves of the legion had used their reinforced tunnels to build a mighty merchant empire, trading with the humans above them for weapons, armor, and highly prized Neferium, a mysterious ore that came from the death of angels, and once hardened was harder and lighter than any known substance on the Mortal Plane. This of course begged the question that, if such a statement were true, since there were several deep veins of the ore, hundreds of thousands of angels must have perished at some point in the distant past.

Because of these tunnels, organized crime flourished in every part of the duchy, run by a wealthy conglomerate of merchants who used their legal trading services to cover for the specialized products that the nobility often desired. For whatever reason, both the duke and his Bre'Dmorian counterparts chose to ignore the problem.

On this night, a man in black leather armor worked his way through the underground caverns of Kurin's Deep, a portion that had been inactive for the better part of one thousand years. The man did not wonder what happened to the dwarves, though. Nor did he care about illegal trade or angels; to this man there was no God, and it wouldn't matter if there was. He was not a highly educated man, as history mattered little in his profession. He relied more on his acute sense of practicality and deftness of mind. He had heard it said more than once that intelligence was not what one knew, but what information one could apply. The man considered the thought for a moment. Maybe that was why he had such a hard time accepting God as any kind of savior: God had certainly never looked down upon the razor thin road this man had traveled. Then again, even if God was looking, such thoughts were for scholars, which the man was not.

The man's practical nature was the reason he had stayed alive so long; an exception in his profession, since few assassins escaped Bre'Dmorian justice for more than a few years. That's what made him special—he was an atheist and an assassin—and more important, he was still alive. That is not to say that he hadn't killed his share of holy men, because he had, or had never enjoyed it, because he did. Bre'Dmorians were not the kind of people that ended up being his mark, and killing people that were not his marks never sat well in his stomach.

It was necessary, though, to sometimes kill innocents when they got in the way. This reputation, to kill whoever got in his way, was the reason why the services of Var Surestrike did not come cheaply. In the Kingdom of Arsgoth he was known as a killer without remorse, one with no concern for those who tried to stop him, and who always killed everyone whom he was paid to.

His latest assignment had been his greatest achievement so far: assassinating the King of Arsgoth in a discreet manner. He had been paid handsomely in advance, by an unknown benefactor, making the deal even sweeter. It was good that his employer had not shown his face; it was none of Var's concern who the figure was, as long as gold continued to flow. Now, he was back to turn in proof of his deed and possibly collect a bonus.

Since the king had been such an easy mark, he had given his contractor the additional benefit of framing the Duke of Thames, Lord Valimont, for the murder. Var hoped his employer would appreciate the extra time and effort it took to set such things in motion.

Var recalled how easy it had been to steal Duke Valimont's crossbow and setup his plan of attack, relying on the man's prideful nature to not reveal the theft until after the fact. The next morning Var laid his trap. He had waited for both men to ride far enough out of earshot before he knocked the duke unconscious with a blunted bolt to the temple and shot the king in the heart. Neither man had seen the blow, as Var's dark armor had allowed him to walk in the shadows, unseen by all but the most astute observers.

Var reached into one of his many pouches and pulled out a small device that he had purchased from a powerful wizard, a square box with a quicksilver hand floating in the middle of a viscous liquid. In theory he could think of any destination he needed to reach and the quicksilver finger would twirl in the direction he needed to travel. It was one of the many secrets he held which secured his prized reputation of always knowing where to find his mark. This time, however, he needed it to find his way through these damn tunnels. He knew the entrance to the chamber was near, but in the dark his eyes were easily fooled.

As Var held the compass out, the quicksilver hand swung to the southeast, to a solid wall. He raised his eyes in surprise and mumbled a curse. Although he did not make mistakes often, he guessed there was always a chance that he had missed the correct junction.

"Wasting time is wasting money," he grumbled at the grimy surface of the wall.

Why do I have to travel underground? Var thought, reminding himself that he hated such confined places. *I know that secrecy is important, but I hate this place!*

The thought made him grimace. His employer had demanded that he use this particular entrance into the city and it was not likely the man would change his mind. Then again, Var had been paid enough to keep his complaints to himself.

With a frown, Var begin to backtrack down the dark length of the tunnel. However, as he spun away from the wall, the quicksilver arrow reversed itself and pointed the way he had come. Puzzled, he swung back around and walked a different direction, again the pendulum swung towards the stone wall.

"He must be using illusions," Var said to the darkness, placing the compass back in his pouch.

Var moved within a hand's length of the wall, studying details. He recognized that his statement was correct. Although it was very realistic to the untrained eye, cast by a powerful wizard who knew his craft well, subtle imperfections stood out. With a determined move, Var placed his hands on a section of chipped stone, the only portion clinging with subterranean moss, and walked through. In a fraction of a second, he stood in a dimly lit tunnel leading upward. The overwhelming stench of human bodies assailed his senses, meaning that the tunnel's draft had also been concealed by the illusion. It also meant that he was nearing the meeting place of the lord who had sought his services.

Var wound his way upwards, through narrow passageways lit by burning sconces, until he finally reached a dead end. Remembering instructions, he felt for a small crack within the mossy wall, trying to find the lever that would open another secret passage. With a faint click the door rotated, allowing Var to pass into a small chamber lined with several suits of plated armor.

Var hesitated at the sight of the shining warriors on each side of the room. He knew they were magical guardians and would kill any uninvited intruder. With silent resolve he stepped into the middle of the room.

Nothing happened. Var let out a deep sigh of relief and strode across the room and into another small tunnel which ended at an ornately carved door.

Var felt a shiver run down his spine, knowing this was the place he was seeking. Although he had never seen its like, the evil aura and demonic carvings on the door made it clear that the chamber was the holy place of some dark god. It made him think of darkness, something so dark it that drank in the light and suppressed all memories of things that cherished life. Something reached out from beyond the door and caressed his inner flame, stoking his murderous tendencies.

Var shook his head and tried to clear his mind. He pushed through the heavy doors, which squealed sharply in protest.

"Do you know what this place is, Var Surestrike?" a deep, bitter voice echoed from the shadows of the room.

It surprised him that someone had been waiting for him to enter. Out of the corner of his eye, Var watched as a dark mist spilled into the room and began to roll towards him. With the solid movements of a killer, Var took a step back and held his ground, his face a stern mask of concentration.

There is nothing to worry about, he told himself. *I have seen this before, another cheap illusion used to control my actions.*

"Do not look so alarmed, assassin. If I wished you dead, you would have been a corpse upon passing through my magical wards." The sinister voice chuckled.

"I have come to collect my bounty!" Var said.

"Do not presume you are owed anything!"

The shadows parted and a tall man stepped swiftly toward him. Var was quick; years of training allowed him to circumvent the deadly blows of those he chased. In that moment, Var's reflexes saved his life, as a steel gauntlet snaked out of the robes and grazed his head, stunning him momentarily. His senses picked out another blow speeding towards his chest but blurred vision made it hard to react. Var used his tactical knowledge to assess the fact that there was no way to dodge such a strike, so he prepared his body to receive it.

The blow was intense.

Though it caught him full in the chest and threw him across the room, Var absorbed the impact with another grunt, tucked his shoulder, and rolled into a crouching position. Not understanding what had provoked the attack, he instinctively unsheathed a pair shortswords. He then prepared to kill his employer, telling himself that he would need to be fast; the man was obviously channeling magic to hit him with such force.

With little concern for his life, Var stepped towards the man, his usual steely demeanor as a death dealer intact. He had never killed a sorcerer before; it was something he had always hoped to stay away from, as the magic-inclined tended to have powerful allies. But this was something that could not be avoided.

"You are fortunate that the Master has spared you, assassin!" the voice gloated. "I would have killed a lesser man for the pleasure of murdering the weak! However, you have earned yourself a second chance."

"And you have earned yourself death," Var said through clenched teeth.

"Ah, the assassin is unafraid," the man said, pulling a longsword that Var recognized as Bre'Dmorian. However, the man did not advance but circled Var in a defensive stance.

This is no Bre'Dmorian, he thought, lashing out with several quick blows, testing his opponent. Although he had killed several of the holy men, he knew that they were not associated with such evil as this.

"You are not interested in a second contract?" the man asked as he parried the blows, feinting, looking for a weakness.

"Why would I accept the offer of a man who tried to kill me?" Var spat.

The man only laughed at the question and assumed a more offensive posture, striking out in several different combinations. Var felt a surge of dread run through his body and knew that the man was toying with him. He had faced many challengers, lawful and unlawful, and in all that time none were such self-assured foes.

"The Master will not allow me to kill you! At least . . . not yet," the man stepped back and lowered the tip of his weapon to the ground, showing parlay. "Because you are so resourceful, he is willing to give you another opportunity to prove yourself. However, his kindness does have boundaries, should you not be willing to listen."

Var hesitated. Though he wished to kill the man for striking him, he was at a crossroads. On one hand, there was no doubt that he would die if he did not at least listen. On the other, he really wanted to bath in this man's blood. For every assassin there came a time when life no longer held meaning and a man no longer feared death. Was he at that point?

"I can see the hatred in your eyes, assassin," the man stated, letting his guard down, inviting a killing blow. "You are trying to decide if you wish to die tonight or listen to my proposition. If it makes a difference, I would rather eradicate your kind from the face of Arsgoth, but the Master still has a use for you."

"What is in it for me?" Var asked, stalling for time as he decided which road he wished to travel.

"There is the chance that you will be allowed to live, of course," the shadowed man responded. "Not to mention the Master will double his offer; two thousand gold crowns, which should be enough for one of your kind to retire into luxury."

"And if I take this job, what is there to keep you from killing me later?" Var asked.

"Oh, I promise you that I will come for you myself when this is all done, Var," the man sneered, his hood pulling back just enough to show an aged face and glowing black eyes.

Var considered the words. The shrouded man had just admitted that he would eventually come to kill him. However, if Var chose patience, he would be granted a once in a lifetime opportunity—to use this extra time to seek out the man's identity and take the offensive. Var knew that if the robed figure was a Bre'Dmorian Knight, he would be easy to track down. If not, well, how many men carried around such a sword? With much resolve, Var took a few steps back, sheathed both shortswords, and offered his hands in submissive gesture.

"I see you have chosen life," the man stepped forward, sliding his sword back into its intricate scabbard. "That is good. Now, let us begin with business. You were asked to kill King Roderick II, the Sentinel of Arsgoth, with efficiently. However, the Master had not expected you to be so careless."

"What are you *talking* about?" Var asked incredulously. "The king died in confusion! No one could have known it was linked to your agenda."

"It is not the death of the king that has given us this new opportunity," the man drawled with a half chuckle, his dark eyes flaring. "You are a professional and I trust that you left no trace. What *does* concern him is the fact that a royal courier beat you back to the city. Because of your lack of haste, the Master has been forced to improvise, speeding things along by many years and in some cases, ruining his plans altogether!"

"I was forced to kill another messenger to make sure the proper information was being relayed to the capital. I could not be seen leaving the city after the King of Arsgoth was murdered . . . at least not so close to my arrival," Var said. Nowhere in his contract had it been declared that upon completion, he was to return with all haste back to the Aresleigh. "You are lucky that the Master knows all, Var," the man said, "and that our plans will be carried out regardless. The death of King Roderick is only the beginning to a fitting end to this age."

Var contemplated a quick death at the hands of the man when a revelation hit him: *Whatever the reason, my employer still needs me.*

"What plans?" Var finally asked.

"It is about time you asked," the man said, pulling a sealed parchment from the folds of his cloak and holding it out to the assassin. "We both know you have other means to enter and exit each city within the kingdom. That should make your next mark easy prey."

"Who is it this time?" Var asked, reaching for the document.

"I told you that our plans our in motion. However, they need a *push* in the right direction," the man explained. "The Master wishes to usurp the power in Arsgoth for his own. To do this, the most powerful noble houses must be driven into a series of events that will start a war."

"The Duke of Aresleigh, then . . .?" Var tapped his chin.

"No. The name of your mark, manner in which he needs to die, and the exact route which he will travel, are in the letter. We do not wish anyone so powerful killed this time. Your target is a royal courier who will be leaving Aresleigh at dawn. His death will pull the thread that unravels the entire realm, as the nobility will turn on each other like wolves. It will also place our Bre'Dmorian friends in a very precarious situation."

"How do you plan on accomplishing all of that off of a meaningless courier's death?" Var scowled.

"We will indict Duke Valimont with these false documents, which order the messenger's death," the robed man said, holding out another sealed document bearing the official seal of Thames. "No one, and I mean *no one*, can know who is responsible until they find these documents . . . which you will plant."

Do I really want to start a civil war? Var asked himself. Although he was a killer and often played into the political scheming of the nobility, this was a different scenario.

"With the evidence pointing at the Duke Thames and the rumors you planted in Natalinople about his involvement in the murder of the king, the rest of the realm will have no choice but to unite against him," the man continued. "The result will allow the Master to destroy one of the houses that stand in his way."

"So I am to kill a man, a lowly courier of no importance, and begin civil war?" Var asked with a suspicious gleam. This was sounding worse by the minute.

Ignoring the question, the man continued. "I have secured you a Bre'Dmorian assistant, one who will be traveling with the courier towards Natalinople. You will make contact with him somewhere to the north and set up the proper place of death." the man retreated into the shadows. "One more thing, assassin," the robed figure paused. "After you have done the deed, I want you to kill the Bre'Dmorian traitor."

As the man began to vanish, Var heard a menacing laugh. "We will be watching you, Var . . ."

Areck followed Elyana through the crowd, wondering what questions he should ask. Although he could charge her with the impersonation of a Cleric of Gabriel, it was not the crime he was interested in. He was more interested in who she was and why she gave off such a powerful divine presence.

Why is another faith's clergy wandering around the Academy unescorted? And why is she pretending to be a Hospitaler? he asked himself thoughtfully, concluding that it was her regal demeanor, rather than her beauty, that attracted him. *What if I become tongue-tied in her presence?* He told himself that sexual attraction was beneath him, hoping to push such thoughts from his mind. It did not work.

As Elyana strode imperiously towards the courier, Areck attempted to judge her attitude, which reminded him of their first meeting. If she really was a noblewoman, she would be feeling an angry impatience, a common attitude of nobles who dealt with subordinates.

Pulling back a chair for Elyana, Areck waited for the woman to sit before he looked around the room and took a seat.

"Nice to see you brought back a serving wench," Arawnn said, an appraising look in his eye. "Yet I am a bit saddened by the fact neither of you are carrying ale!"

Areck almost fell off his stool at the comment, and Elyana stiffed and turned red. In other circumstances, he might have reprimanded Arawnn for the lack of etiquette, but amazingly, Arawnn's insult had shaken Elyana. However, Areck knew the key to this conversation would be in keeping her off guard and stopping her from gaining a foothold of power in the exchange. It was an ancient strategy used by many scholars when debating.

"Why you imperious, self-inflated . . ." she stammered incredulously. "How dare you presume to call me a serving wench?" She poked a finger in Arawnn's chest, almost cursing in indignation.

"I think what Lady Elyana is trying to say is that she is not in the wenching profession." Areck could not help but chuckle at his friend being prodded by the beautiful, and very angry, woman. Even funnier was the fact that Arawnn looked off guard himself, glancing about to make sure no bodyguards were coming to toss him out of the tavern.

Areck was about to say something when he noticed Arawnn wink at him. He saw the man mouth, "You can thank me later."

Areck nearly choked at the realization. His friend was using a ploy! The man had purposefully insulted Elyana to get a reaction out of her, removing any possibility that she might dominate the conversation. By all means, Areck needed to make a mental note conceding that, if nothing else, his royal friend knew this style of woman.

Elyana scowled. "And I meant every—"

Arawnn cut her off. "I meant no offense, Lady Elyana, I was merely noting that beauty such as yours usually merits a job where men can admire you . . . I mean, *it*," Arawnn made a slight mock bow as a sign of apology.

Areck saw Elyana's mouth tighten. He knew another verbal assault was coming, as her eyes began to blaze. However, she took a deep breath and lowered her gaze, chagrined. "You know how to raise a lady's blood, sir," she said stiffly. "My advice is that you add thinking before speaking to your repertoire! That way you might avoid noble ladies and their dangerous paths."

Arawnn broke into a good-hearted laugh, put his arm around the young squire, and smiled at Elyana. "This is the man you need to stay around if you need any thinking, my beautiful lady," Arawnn said. "It just occurred to me that the two of you have been interrupted by me for long enough. Do you have any particular taste, my lady?"

"Do I *what?*" Elyana stood up.

"I was talking about ale," Arawnn chuckled. "Since Areck did not bring us back any, I was planning to talk to that tasty young morsel over there," Arawnn said, gazed at his serving maid, who winked at him once then went back to business, "and procure us some wine."

Elyana considered her response, and then smugly picked several of the most expensive wines in house, settling on a fifty year vintage of apple wine from northern Almassia.

Arawnn shrugged and sauntered his way past several friendly serving maids until he finally reached his chosen lady. He put his arm around her and moved towards the barkeep; whispering quips that made her giggle and nod her head.

"You have expensive tastes, my lady," Areck commented, watching his friend move gracefully across the floor, wench in hand. He wondered if the man noticed the barkeep's angry glare at the loss of his beautiful serving girl.

Areck's concern was short lived. Arawnn pulled a fat money pouch from his jacket and tossed it on the table. The barkeep's frustration evaporated and was replaced with a greedy gleam. The serving girl looked at the pouch with an open mouth then reared back and punched the courier in the arm, making Arawnn grimace in mock pain.

Areck found it odd that the women stopped with a single punch—and instead of true anger, she looked as if she had gained a curious respect for the courier. Then again, the server now knew that Arawnn was wealthy, a thing that most men tried to hide.

"Well, he deserves it. Did you see the way he was looking at me?" Elyana said with distaste, watching the courier rub his arm, causing the serving girl to give him a more personal rub.

"How does a Bre'Dmorian squire fall in with such vermin?" she continued with a shudder as she watched Arawnn pinch the girl's bottom.

"I have not 'fallen in' with anyone," Areck exclaimed, cheerfully noting the disdain on Elyana's face. He decided that this was as good of time as any to breach the main subject, and with little preamble, began. "Why is it that you impersonate one of the Hospitalers?" he asked, noticing her stiffen at the unexpected question.

"I am here on personal business that serves a higher power." Elyana explained that she had been given visions to seek out elder lore regarding the knighthood. She also explained that her quest required the utmost privacy.

"So you were sent to infiltrate us by a false religion?" Areck asked incredulously. It explained why she was permeating such divine power.

"I was sent for reasons you could not understand," she said.

"That does not answer my question."

She smiled back at him, lightly tapping her painted nails on the table. "You did not ask for a complicated explanation of my history. The question was, 'Why am I impersonating one of Lord Gabriel's Clerics?'"

She is trying to manipulate me, he thought, *trying to get me to leave this path of questioning.*

Areck changed tactics.

"Are you a noble of Arsgoth?" he asked, smelling possible dissent within a kingdom that was heading towards conflict.

"Actually I am a noble, but the exact definition is a matter of interpretation," she responded with a sigh, once again dodging the question.

Areck spent the better part of an hour asking various questions about her heritage, lineage, and background. He was about to ask what her reason was for being in the city when Arawnn cheerfully slapped him on the back and set down a dull black bottle of Almassian wine. Areck decided to use the alcohol to his advantage—he had already downed some beer for Arawnn's sake; why not use the wine to loosen Elyana's tongue?

Areck had never before been allowed to imbibe any quantity of alcohol, but he reasoned was that he had trained all his life and the rigorous lifestyle would allow his body a fair tolerance to the poison. He had to admit he had been outmaneuvered, but the wine might slow her quick mind enough for Areck to get his questions answered.

"It is about time you brought us some wine, heathen," Elyana exclaimed, goading Arawnn back into another round of insults.

Areck let the two verbally duel for several minutes, intervening only when Arawnn started to look worse for wear.

"Arawnn, if you are quite done giving Lady Elyana the opportunity to dismantle your ancestry, I would appreciate some more time alone . . . so that we may continue speaking of private matters," Areck said, trying to hide his amusement.

Nodding his head in defeat, Arawnn offered his arm to his young companion, who, as they staggered off, grabbed it with a gleeful look. It was obvious that the royal courier had seen many drinks whilst winning over his companion at the bar.

"At least the buffoon has a quick mind," Elyana pointed out, watching Arawnn slam several silver coins in front of the barkeep and buy a round of ale for everyone in the vicinity, bringing cheers from those at the bar. "That one's future is uncertain," she whispered to herself.

"Excuse me?" Areck asked with a frown.

"I was just saying that you have asked me several questions and I still know nothing about you," she said, pouring wine for them both. "Your actions are surrounded by uncertainty."

"We are not here to discuss me," he rubbed his chin warily, taking the proffered glass of wine and letting his prior thought fade.

She only smiled, took a deep swallow of her wine, and proceeded to ask about his heritage, seeking details about his past. Had Areck not found Elyana so overwhelming, he might have noticed that both of her hands had slipped under the table and with deft movements she wove the intricate hand gestures of an arcane spell.

When Elyana had first met Areck in the Bre'Dmorian Academy, her divine spells had not agreed with him and he'd shaken off her spell. This time she relied on more powerful magic, the arcane, which combined hand gestures and reagents to invoke her desired answers. Though she had not come to Aresleigh for any reason besides information, Areck intrigued her. In fact, she felt the familiar weave of divine presence within the young man. That was why she had allowed him to capture her, hoping that with patience she could regain the upper hand and deflect the topic back in the direction she wished it to go.

Not that her prodding had helped much. So far he had answered each of her questions with one of his own, which she then deflected to another topic. She asked him another question, waiting for her spell to complete itself by branching out and testing the strings of fate which surrounded all mortal races. She did not know what to expect. From all appearances, the young man was as normal as any other Bre'Dmorian squire she had ever met, but she could not help but feel drawn to him.

With a last flick of her fingers, the spell came together and sped eerily beneath the table—wrapping itself around Areck's legs, spreading slowly upwards. To her satisfaction, Areck did not appear to feel the spell nor resist it. Satisfied that her spell was working, Elyana turned away another question regarding her identity, stalling for time so her spell could finish.

As the spell's aura enveloped Areck's head, he shivered and began looking around the room as though searching for something.

Elyana was speechless. She tried to utter something, anything . . . but nothing came out. She could hardly comprehend what had happened—the moment her young squire had felt the spell, it had vanished. No mere man could shake off an arcane divination spell unless he was either prepared for it magically or sealed away from the tapestry of time.

"I am assuming your astonished look means you felt it as well?" he asked quizzically, shaking his head with a quick chuckle.

"It felt as if something entered the room." She lied and tried an experiment which would involve her casting a clerical spell. "I do not feel it anymore, though."

She was about to draw upon her innate ability when he spoke.

"Whatever you are about to do, I can feel it," Areck said. "You are a divine magic caster. I felt it in the Academy, and I can feel you pulsing with it now."

Elyana let the spell's pulse slip away. Her instinct had been right! The boy could feel divine magic, which is why he was able to resist it. Her lips pursed in thought. How had he been able cut the tether of her arcane spell?

"What does this feeling tell you?" she asked.

"I do not wish to talk about it."

"You would not have mentioned it if you did not wish to discuss it, Areck. Now what does this feeling tell you? Can you actually *feel* the spell's weave being constructed?" she asked again.

After a moment of silence, Areck clarified that since childhood he had been able to sense powerful divinity, including her divine magic. He explained that the feeling was not a good one, as it made him sick.

"If we had met under different circumstances, I think I could have helped you," she interrupted, pouring another glass of wine.

Areck nodded. He understood their current circumstances meant that he could never accept her help, even if she had been willing to give it.

Areck silently saluted Elyana. Although the wine had stained her cheeks pink, the woman's mind was still keen enough to take control of the situation. With only a brief thought of why he accepted a third glass of wine, Areck realized that his mind was becoming numb and that Elyana had quite possibly gotten the better of him.

He had not expected to find an intricate portrait behind such a beautiful face. When he looked into her eyes, he knew that he would allow her to go free without procuring any information. He mulled over the feeling of failure as he sipped the wine.

"I think . . . that . . . thish coveshatien ish . . ." As he put the cup down Areck begin to notice his speech slurring and the room began to spin. Understanding cut him to the core. He had studied the effects of various poisons and was mostly aware of their effects. "I wassss aboot to . . . let . . ."

He struggled to get the words out as the poison known as *dagweed* coursed through his mind, numbing coherent thought.

To all appearances, the poison created the illusion of a severely drunken stupor and even created a headache in the morning. It was often used by thieves when marks were drinking heavily in public.

Areck's mind raced to find a crack in the poison, fighting with all his willpower to stop its effects which included loss of speech, movement, and equilibrium. After a minute, his body succumbed to the toxins and the world faded away. He tried desperately to grab onto her arm.

Elyana easily broke the weak grasp and moved into his lap.

"I know you would have let me leave on my own accord, young one," she purred, "but who is to say that you wouldn't have followed me? I do apologize for the headache in the morning." A painted nail circled his face. "You are truly an amazing young man and I wish I had more time to talk. However, I need to be on my way. *Alone.*"

To make the act seem real, Elyana gave Areck a quick kiss on the cheek, which many of the surrounding patrons cheered. With a coy smile she pushed herself off, pulled her hood up, and once again started for the doorway.

She only got a few steps away when a strong hand grabbed her from behind.

The shock of the touch made her stagger into another man. She regained her balance and turned around to see that Areck, stumbling and nearly blind with dagweed, had followed her before finally passing out. She had no idea how he had taken a single step, drugged as he was. The important thing was that she knew he was no normal man and he merited special interest.

"I know you can hear me, Areck," she whispered into his ear. "We will meet again, I promise you. Know that you have piqued my interest and that I shall ever be watching."

Against her better judgment, Elyana asked the man she had run into for help dragging the unconscious Areck back to the table. With a last thoughtful look, Elyana neared the door, took a deep breath, and sauntered into the night air of Aresleigh.

9

AS DAWN approached, the aroma of freshly baked bread wafted from the lower levels of the Twisting Oak Inn. Each morning the owner of the inn, Gimbal Inntrader, made it his duty to awake before dawn, stoke the furnaces, and begin the baking of his famous sweet bread, a western society favorite. The cherubic innkeeper knew business was good—he saw countless patrons who had become too inebriated the night before start make their way home.

With a smile, Gimbal opened a draft chute and allowed the smell of delicious round rolls, Almassian spices, and sausage to wake his blurry-eyed guests. He figured that since they had passed out in his inn, offering an early breakfast would be another great opportunity to make some coin. This was the morning ritual in Aresleigh: merchants drank all night and then passed out. All woke just in time to either wander back to their homes or eat a filling meal in his inn before beginning another day of bartering in the streets.

It was just before sunrise when the bustle of mercantile traffic woke Areck from dreams filled with a beautiful woman dodging questions and plotting his ultimate demise. With sluggish movements he rolled over, putting his cheek in a puddle of drool. Disgusted, he sat upright, wiping his face. Trying to get his bearings, he ran his hand through his hair, feeling several pressure lines zigzagging across his face. When he rubbed his eyes, a dull pain shot through his skull and he collapsed in nausea. His stomach growled.

As his vision swam, Areck gradually pieced together his thoughts and brought the spinning room back into focus. The aromatic smell of food filled the room, replacing his initial thoughts of sickness with hunger. Slowly he sat back up and looked around.

To Areck's amazement, he was not in his personal chambers at the Academy. Rather, he was in a room which contained furniture and a small window that allowed the dim light of the brightening sky to leak in. At first glance, nothing looked out of the ordinary. However, when he looked to the right, he noticed a second bed filled with two figures wrapped around each other and snoring loudly.

Areck grimaced. The young courier had won the beautiful serving maid over during the night and had procured a room. As Areck looked down, he noticed several piles of garments littering the room and flushed at their implied meaning. Several memories flooded his senses . . . he vividly remembered passionate moans. Once again his stomach rolled and he fell back on the bed.

What would his superiors think? To all appearances he had filled his belly with too much wine and had passed out. They would think that he was unable to make it back to the Academy, for Starsgalt's sake! To make matters worse, he had been in the room during a couple's most private moments. How could he possibly explain his actions?

A soft moan and a gentle touch made Areck jump off the bed and roll across the floor in a panic. A slender face regarded him with wide eyes as wild thoughts flew through his mind. How in Starsgalt had he not noticed her lying beneath the covers, half curled around him? With his hand outstretched in defense, he backed towards the door. His mind raced frantically, trying to recall *why* the woman was in his bed! Unfortunately, one of the drug's side effects was a lapse in memory.

Is she here on my behalf . . .? The thought trailed off in a plethora of possibilities. *What have I done? There are only a few reasons why women hide themselves in a man's bed.*

Horror pushed away all thoughts of sickness and fear gripped his heart. If he had taken the young lady outside of union, especially as a squire, there would be nothing to stop the Academy from sending him into the cold, bereft of all possessions.

The girl regarded Areck with a look of determination as she pursed her lips, pushed the covers away, and stood on her knees, revealing her perfect nakedness.

Areck realized that her action was meant to call him back to bed, to whatever they had been doing before. He averted his eyes and put a hand up to conceal her nudity. There was no mistaking that she was there for him, and that he had participated. His heart raced as his mind devoured the possibilities.

I have just thrown away my entire career! There is no way to explain this!

The thought of losing ten years of military service, and his shattered honor, induced waves of despair in Areck's soul.

His mind raced.

Would it be better to tell them that he had knowingly allowed a criminal to escape justice because he wished to talk with her, or that he had solicited sex from another? He could try and explain that his poor judgment had led to being drugged by the woman. Although it would make him look inept, there was a possibility that the Council might understand such a mistake, allowing him to clarify the entire evening.

Arawnn's voice cut through the morning chill. "What in hell's name are you doing, Areck?" He yawned, rubbing a hand down his face.

The royal courier became alarmed when he took in the scene of the still-naked woman darting under the covers and Areck pinned up against the wall, hand outstretched to block his vision. However, Arawnn chuckled when he realized that the woman posed no threat. The laughter was loud enough to bring another head above the covers.

When Areck finally regained some composure he dropped his eyes and regarded the laughing couple. He could tell that his own partner was moving, but he dare not glimpse her nakedness again, less he further his own embarrassment.

"Do the three of you have no decency?" Areck managed, doing his best not to look at either woman.

"After your little drunken escapade with Lady Elyana, you would lecture *me* of modesty?" Arawnn said, tears of laughter rolling down his cheeks.

"There is more to that story . . ." Areck began, stopping when he realized how stupid he must be look, pinned against the door.

"I hope you understand that we were *forced* to rent this room for you," Arawnn responded, "because you were so drunk that we couldn't move you."

"I think I was drugged," Areck said, no longer caring if he offended anyone.

"Oh, without a doubt, my friend!" Another burst of laughter lit Arawnn's face. "We call alcohol the drug of choice, here. At least we now know that you cannot handle firewater without consequences."

He does not believe me!

The sound of feet on the floor brought Areck's attention back to the young woman sitting on his bed, lacing up rugged leather sandals. She no longer paid him any mind and tears slid down her face. Areck could tell that his reaction had offended the young lady. He had acted like she was beneath him, when in reality he was no longer pure enough for her.

The woman's gaze lifted and she noticed that everyone staring at her. With a curt nod at the squire she turned to Arawnn and rubbed her eyes. "I would like to take my leave," she said, dipping into a small curtsy, "unless *you* have need of me, my lord!"

Arawnn regarded her with a warm smile and politely refused her offer. He then pulled a silver piece and placed it in her hand. The action made Areck's heart sink even further. The monetary gesture assured that the woman was a servant, most likely a prostitute.

"This is all?" asked the woman. "We agreed upon a gold piece!"

"Your part was not fulfilled; exactly what do want payment for?" Arawnn asked.

"I did what I could!" the woman responded defensively. "He is impotent or has some . . . *problems*, because he was unconscious the entire night. And now that he has woken, it appears he does not care for me at all."

Arawnn frowned at Areck but conceded the woman's point, handing her a single gold coin. With a snort she snatched the gold, looked at Areck, and stormed out of the room.

Understanding settled on Areck: his friend had purchased him a whore. Without much thought, Areck pulled a dagger from his hip, completely oblivious to the fact that he was still fully clothed.

"Tell me the truth, Arawnn," Areck said. "What happened between that woman and I?"

Arawnn's body stiffened as his gaze moved from the dagger to meet Areck's questioning stare. His companion had pulled the covers over her head and was hiding.

"I hired that woman to spend the night with you, my friend," Arawnn said nervously. "I felt remorse for losing you an opportunity with Lady Elyana, and wanted to make it up to you." Arawnn explained that he had hired the prostitute as a friendly gesture, hoping she would compensate for the loss of Elyana.

"I am not interested in your intentions, Arawnn!" Areck's voice began to crack with anger. "Now answer the question. What happened last night?"

It dawned on Areck that his pure intentions with the noblewoman had been perceived as anything but! Worse, he had hired a woman to perform indecent acts with him.

"Areck, my friend," Arawnn said, allowing his cautious grin to become a light chuckle. "Nothing happened between you and that woman last night. Can't you see that not one piece of your clothing has been removed?"

The courier was acting like he didn't understand what all the fuss was about. Areck guessed that Arawnn thought it strange that any man should be so upset over one night spent with a woman. After all, Areck wasn't paying for it!

With force, Areck shoved his dagger back into its sheath and took a deep sigh. "If nothing happened, then why did you pay her?"

"It wasn't her fault that you couldn't . . . perform," Arawnn said, grinning from ear to ear. "Besides, she at least tried to seduce you. You were so drunk that it took all three of us just to get you up here, and onto the bed! How does your head feel, by the way?"

With adrenaline subsiding, Areck's skull pulsed with pain. "Fine . . . I feel fine," Areck breathed as he sat on to the bed. "I just need to lie down for a second."

"You'll need more than that, I'm afraid. It might be a good idea to . . ." Arawnn was cut off by the ringing of the nearby Starsgaltian Cathedral's bell, chiming in the dawn hour.

Dong!

Areck leapt out of his bed and made sure all of his clothes were in place. "Get yourself dressed, Arawnn, we need to go. *Now!*" In nearly ten years at the Academy, Areck had never been late for anything until this moment, when it became obvious that his bad situation had just gotten worse! By all accounts, dawn had broken.

Dong!

Areck was so engrossed in thought that he did not notice Arawnn's mistress remove herself from the covers. When he looked up, the woman was slipping a garment over her bare breasts. He glanced at her face in embarrassment to see if she had noticed and was met by a wink.

"I will wait for you in the hall," Areck could barely speak. This entire situation was quite overwhelming. "Please hurry," he blurted, closing the door behind him.

Moments later, Arawnn emerged with a bright glow in his eyes.

"What a night, huh, Squire? Sorry you missed most of it," Arawnn patted Areck stiffly on the shoulder. "You have a great city here—such lovely women and good drink. This next week is going to make you wish you hadn't missed out."

"But I was not . . ." Areck began to protest but found it useless. "We have little time."

Areck hurried through the inn and to the stables. As much as his head hurt, he could only imagine what punishment awaited him once the knighthood found out about last night's fiasco. Even if they believed that he had been drugged and unconscious the entire night, he had ignored his duty and allowed a criminal to outsmart him. Truly, the pain in his head was the least of his worries.

Lord Bowon Silvershield was the first to arrive at the Academy's stables, in his usual early morning, partially drunken stupor. Although he was known for his excessive drinking, several squires—who were now running after him—had decided to test the theory by knocking on the commander's door. The result was that Bowon had answered, still half asleep, with direct orders to take in the morning air with a run.

As the small company of jogging squires passed a darkened smithy, Lord Silvershield ordered another pack of squires who had just come into his sight to search for the stable master and ready the warhorses.

His scale armor jingling with each irritated stride, the knight-captain crossed the final stretch of paved road and stepped into the moist sod where the Academy housed its finer warhorses. He had always loved the smell of the stables and inhaled deeply as he entered into the first set of stalls in search of his own bonded mount, Legion. It was easy for the knight-captain to sense his trusted mount. And though the charger had been decommissioned for many years, the bond between them was still strong. In truth, the only thing he still thanked God for was that he had been given Legion.

"My lord," the distant voice of the stable master nearly brought him out of his bad mood. At least those young men were not badgering him anymore, looking accusingly at his improper behavior. He hated that.

"Stable Master Del, have you readied our mounts?" Bowon asked.

"Of course, Lord Silvershield," responded Del, walking to where Legion's head had popped over the gating and was nuzzling its friend's shoulder. "Your orders were to ready twelve mounts for a variety of different skill levels."

"Yes, yes, Del." Bowon waved the old man to silence. "Would you see that each squire has met their mount? I am going to take Legion for a quick gallop around the courtyard to limber him up a bit."

"You will be taking him with you them, my lord?" The stable master asked. When Bowon shook his head in confirmation, the man continued, "Very good, then, my lord. So you know, I believe the only squires to arrive are those on their morning jog. Should I give your orders to Lords Vinion and Malketh instead?"

Lord Silvershield frowned and walked out to the courtyard, looking towards the coming dawn. Eight of his nine squires were still limbering themselves up. He barked nine hand-picked names and got eight replies. Nowhere in the line of young men was Bowon's personal squire and friend, Areck of Brenly.

"Areck is late," he mused.

With the patience of a military commander, Bowon issued a silent command. Instantly his men halted and formed a line, which he inspected. Happy that his orders had been followed to perfection, Bowon paused at the oldest squire.

"Before you prepare your mount, I want you to go to Squire Areck's room and knock once. If there is no reply, return here and start preparing for the journey. Am I understood, Squire Redmon?"

Not waiting for Redmon to nod, Silvershield turned and ordered the rest of the company to head to their various stables in search of their mounts.

It wasn't until the young men saluted and set off that Lord Silvershield called Del over to make sure Squire Redmon's mount was ready when the boy returned. Satisfied, he nodded to himself and entered Legion's stall.

Areck was ten paces ahead of Arawnn as they raced towards the gates of the Academy. The trick would be to draw as little attention as possible, relying on secrecy to enter the building. However, as the pair slowed to a hurried walk, several guards noticed the weary-looking men and offered a good morning tide. By protocol Areck was forced to return the gesture.

Areck knew there would not be time to cleanse the stench of the tavern smoke from his body, nor the whisper of perfume from his mind. Even as he said his greetings and the sun leaked past the building and cast a golden path towards their destination, his mind kept focusing on a dire future.

Areck looked over at the sweating Arawnn and realized that the courier's life would never be as complicated as his own, especially in these circumstances. The man could simply tell the truth and, although the company would look down on him for it, never suffer the consequences. In fact, Arawnn's debauchery was almost understandable due to his lifestyle of incessant travel and the stress that he endured.

The sudden knowledge that his life was held in the hands of Arawnn, who had tried to purchase him a prostitute, caused Areck to stop in midstride.

"You must not . . ." Areck's words trailed off. He realized that he had started the conversation with a direct order. Calming his mind, he decided to start over. "I will have plenty of explaining to do when we finally meet Lord Silvershield," Areck began with a pleading look in his eyes. "Will you please not tell stories about last night? I wish to come to my commander on my own terms, especially if I am to be stripped of all rank and thrown out of the Academy."

"As you wish, my friend," Arawnn replied with a mockingly modest tone. "Although you do realize that the night will not be nearly as exciting without them?"

Areck accepted that as the best answer he could hope for.

"There is little time before the company will leave without me," Areck said. "However, they cannot leave without you. Please take as long on you like on your way to the stables. If I am lucky I will meet you there shortly."

The walk back to the Bre'Dmorian Academy entrance was uneventful, in the sense that knights high enough in rank to be curious of his attire did not greet him. That was not to say that more than a few low ranking knights

did not murmur in disapproving tones at what they assumed to be a dishonorable night amongst city folk. Areck remained impassive, prepared to
face the consequences from his superiors.

As he hurried up the hub in silence, Areck tried to collect his thoughts.
If Arawnn took his time, there still was a chance Areck might make it to the
Westinghouse Stables before Lord Silvershield moved out. His hopes were
dashed when he remembered that in any case he would still have to answer
questions regarding his tardiness and appearance.

When Areck reached his floor, he crept down the hallway. Walking in-
cognito made his chest tight and his hands shake with nervousness.

Areck was just about to open his door, when out of nowhere, a voice
cut through the dense silence. With stoic calm, Areck turned to face a
squire one year younger them himself.

"Lord Silvershield has sent me to fetch you, Squire Areck," Redmon
said with a thick accent.

Areck's heart sank. If Lord Silvershield had sent the young man to retrieve him, the commander would want answers before the campaign got
underway. He tried to keep his composure by squaring his shoulders in de-
fiance.

"Please let Lord Silvershield know that prayers took longer than expected and that I will be down shortly," Areck said, immediately regretting
the words.

What have I done? he thought to himself. *Is it not enough that I have soiled everything the knighthood holds dear, now I must lie about it? Starsgalt please forgive me,*
he prayed silently.

Areck saw the confusion in Redmon's face. He smelled of smoke. However, it was not another squire's place to comment, so the young man nodded to Areck and trotted back down the hub.

Though Areck felt soiled by the lie, he let out a sigh of relief. He would
eventually have to come clean about his sinful situation but not yet, not
until the company was well outside of Aresleigh, and it would be too late to
be removed from the mission.

When Redmon was beyond his vision, Areck made sure no one else was
looking and entered his room. There was little time to spare, so he dampened a wool cloth and wiped his face. He then grabbed a small vial of
scented oil, which he used on the rare occasion of visiting a noble. After
dabbing oil on his neck and wrists Areck inhaled, deciding that he smelled
much better than before.

Still moving with haste, Areck undressed and pieced together his suit of
light armor. He heard feet shuffling past his quarters as he tied the hauberk
in place and slipped on his greaves. Finally, he pulled a pair of reinforced
leather boots over his heel and laced them. Not worrying about whether his

straps and buckles were secure, Areck grabbed his weapon belt, riding gloves, and tabard.

With a last glance around the room Areck shuffled outside and down the hub, offering another prayer to Starsgalt.

As he raced into the courtyard, he could see the mounted party gathering outside in two neat columns, a single mount readied and rider-less. He barely noticed Arawnn deep in an animated discussion with the trio of knightly officers.

Putting his head down, Areck marched towards his stallion, which caused the entire company to regard him. When he looked up, Areck saw the look on both Knight-Captain Vinion's and Knight-Captain Malketh's faces, indicating that the pair wished to leave him behind for Lord Millbert to deal with. It seemed, however, that Arawnn was arguing on his behalf. Finally Lord Silvershield raised his hand for silence and rode his mount forward with a grim smile.

"I see you finally grace us with you presence, Squire Areck." Lord Silvershield announced.

"My . . . my . . . my lord," Areck stuttered under the scrutiny. "I was—"

"I did not ask for excuses, Squire! My advice is that you saddle up and remain in silence. Be thankful I do not remove you from this campaign."

Lord Silvershield spun his warhorse around and addressed the rest of the company. "Understand that tardiness is a breech of protocol," he said. "Areck has just volunteered to dig latrines wherever we fortify our position."

Areck was relieved that his knightly mentor had held his place within the company. Any other commander would have sent him back to the barracks followed by six weeks of duty in the midden heap.

As Areck mounted a black charger in full armor, Lord Silvershield brought his horse along side him. The old man gave a quick wink, and grumbling, took off down the line.

The small company of Bre'Dmorians looked regal in their armor, the sun glinting off polished mail. Areck thought they all looked ready to begin a long career in the service of the Bre'Dmorian Knighthood.

With a final salute to his men, Lord Silvershield ordered a leisurely pace towards the northern gatehouse, where military personnel usually exited the crowded city.

And so the men marched off, not knowing that a traitor was in their midst or that the man they were to protect was about to be murdered.

PART II: HISTORY IS CHANGED

10

THE ANGEL Gabriel Truthbringer walked in Starsgalt's gardens in silence, contemplating the cascading events that had unfolded since time had stopped. The Great Convergence, a gathering of the all the gods, had determined that the event was a miraculous anomaly of time, space, and the everlasting nature of Heaven. Still, it unsettled the angel that the gods referred to time's failure as "unknown." After all, the entirety of Heaven was built upon the foundation that each god was omniscient.

If they are referring to something as the unknown, does that mean they are no longer all-knowing? Gabriel wondered. He knew that the gods were bound by their infallibility; nothing was beyond their immeasurable power.

This functional theory allowed mortals to believe their dreams were plausible and allowed the gods to flaunt power by granting miracles. It was an understanding which relied on the acceptance that reality was only as real as one believed, in turn bound by the unknown that the gods controlled. No god would admit something was beyond his or her supremacy.

A single feather, so white it shimmered, fell from the Gabriel's outstretched wings, fluttering as though fearful to leave the confines of the angel's body. With infinite speed he snatched it from the air, bringing it to his face. He had existed for eternity (Gods and angels do not count time, but view ten eternities of existence as "eternity") and knew that even a small thing, something as insignificant as a feather, could signify chaos. If he had let it land in a pool of pure energy, there was a minute probability that the feather would cause ripples in the fabric of reality, creating an endless stream of multiplying possibilities, until existence itself was nullified.

With all that is going on, why take the chance?

However, Gabriel was not sure the current situation was connected to a breach in reality. He was not sure *what* to think. For the gods to talk about the unknown meant something was terribly wrong.

The angel gazed up at the swirling cosmos. *The gods created this, therefore Heaven is real beyond a doubt,* he thought. He knew *his* knowledge was absolute. *We are infallible; it must be absolute . . . !*

Gabriel cursed as an errant stream of creation shot across eternity. He was a being of pure order and creation. Though unusual, the stream reminded him that the gods were the creators of everything, including time—that they moved at will, parallel through the mortal timeline, able to look down on any point within history, past, present, or future. It was how the gods shaped the chaos of the multi-verse, channeling it into thought, which inversely created mortal reality. This reality did not truly exist, however; Heaven was the *only* true constant, existing beyond reality's boundaries of time, death, and life.

So what happened is impossible, the angel's infinite logic screamed.

"For the gods to admit to not knowing something . . ." he whispered. He should not think such things. The implications were unspeakable, bordering on the blasphemy, heretical! The plausibility that his own existence might be false made him indignant and angry.

"This has to be Illenthuul's doing," he grumbled, showing an emotion that strangely resembled mortal irritation.

The Dark God, as Illenthuul was commonly known, had not existed upon the Heavenly Plane for time untold, being confined to his prison: the Infernal Plane of Hell. However, Gabriel could not accuse the Greater God of subterfuge, considering that Illenthuul had been allowed back into Heaven, if only for a moment, to participate in the Great Convergence.

Not to mention, Gabriel thought, *the Dark God looks worried, his ever-changing form is constant, and he has announced his willingness to share information.*

The thought made Gabriel purse his divine lips at the irony. Every concept offered more questions. That the God of Chaos offered any knowledge at all meant that even Illenthuul was under the impression that something beyond his all-knowing gaze existed.

The impossibilities brought Gabriel back to the moment; it had been five mortal years since time stopped and again all of Heaven sat in a Great Convergence, their second since time had stopped. Though he had not been at the first Convergence, Gabriel thought that the gods had argued about the severity of the issue. To be more precise, the damning miracle had caused apocalyptical events to rage on in Heaven. At what first seemed like a simple but perception-altering event, the stoppage of time, continued to produce adverse effects.

The newest threat to existence was that no god could pierce the veil of mortal time. It seemed that all knowledge of the future had disappeared, as if a thick mist blocked their divine sight, leaving only the past and the probable present to decipher the problem. Even Illuviel, God of Knowledge, was left to guess that the condemning source existed outside of Heaven, somewhere in another plane of existence.

To their credit, each god had chosen champions to seek out information—millions of them, tens of millions, even. The gods had called upon all resources in all realms of reality, throughout every mortal and immortal world, to find the source. Yet for all their efforts, none of the gods could comprehend such a powerful force, nor could they offer insight as to what was sought. Because of this fact, the gods agreed that whatever *it* was, it not only threatened themselves, but all of existence.

Even Gabriel, the High Seraphim of Starsgalt, had been asked to play a part. His job was to call a Great Convergence at the Forge of Creation once every five mortal years, so the gods could relay new information.

Not that it is working, Gabriel thought. *This is just the first of five sessions and they are already fighting!*

The angel sighed. He would not be surprised if the gods parted ways with open animosity and suspicion between them. It was possible that many wouldn't speak until the next meeting, and perhaps even open war would occur, which offered him something to worry about outside of the strange singularity.

"If they cannot find a solution soon," he said to no one, "Heaven could be destroyed!"

The thought of his existence ending struck Gabriel with force. Maybe it was time for him to do his own investigation, leaving the gods to bicker over unknown facts that were quite possibly beyond them. He would need to contact his mortal emissaries, most of which he attempted to conceal from Lord Starsgalt in hopes of hoarding the power of the "faithful" souls for himself.

Gabriel pondered his first action. One advantage of being an angel was that he could walk the Material Plane without a significant drain on his power. If a god decided to walk the Mortal Plane, the imperfection of such an existence would render him less than all-powerful—a perception the greater gods would not tolerate—which was why most sent angelic minions to do their lesser tasks.

As the angel flexed his giant wings, preparing to open a portal into the Mortal Realm, another feather shook loose and began its descent.

This one did not look healthy. It did not shimmer with immortal essence, instead exhibiting a dull, listless aura of decay. The strange feather distracted the angel. He ceased his summoning, dropped to a knee, and picked up the fallen feather.

Gabriel twisted around to look at his wings, not comprehending the significance of such a surprise. With trembling fingers he analyzed the anom-

aly, drawing upon his vast knowledge of existence. Slowly, he began to understand what was making him feel uncomfortable. He was not drawn away
from the others by their bickering, but rather the fact that they looked
changed.

The realization made Gabriel nauseous. He wondered if the gods had
figured it out.

For all of his esteemed knowledge and wisdom, Gabriel had not considered that maybe time had *not* stopped. *What if we are looking at this all wrong?*
he thought. *Would it not seem that time has stopped to those who exist here in
Heaven, when it merely has* slowed?

Each new thought brought greater revelation. It was not that time
stopped *per se.* The gods would still be able to view the future, if time had
stopped and remained constant. Gabriel wondered how his new hypothesis
was even possible, but continued on anyway.

If time didn't stop then what happened? he mused. *Did the event merge the contin-
uum . . .?*

What if we are only assuming *that time as we know it is the truth?* He thought,
trying to grasp such alien ideas. He looked once again at the decaying
feather and fear burned through his immortal soul.

*What if such alterations to time were not perceptible by divine beings? What if eternal
time has slowed down so much that a new reality poured forth, one where we are now
caught up in the mortal timeline!*

The angel finally understood. Heaven was caught up in time. Whatever
had transpired had bound Heaven to mortal reality.

Heaven's clock was now ticking . . . and they were all dying!

11

21st Eternity (Heavenly Timeline)

2004 A. D. (After Devoid), Year of the Eagle (Mortal Timeline)

EARLY MORNING fog blanketed the stone valley as mist drizzled down upon a beleaguered rider who had been traveling through the Ironstone Mountains, a tectonic range that stretched from the northern tip of Rathadon to the southern coasts of Almassia, for weeks. Needless to say it was a tough ride in even the most pleasant of seasons. Now that autumn had begun to wane and winter was setting in, it made the trek all the worse.

The rider, a Bre'Dmorian Knight, wondered when the first winter storm would unleash itself on the mountain pass, a common occurrence during this time of year. The thought made the knight shudder. He might not be able to escape this place before that happened, which was akin to slowly freezing to death.

The knight searched the fog bank looking for alternatives. However, it was so dense that it was impossible to see farther than twenty paces ahead, making the unpaved road disappear into nothingness. Again he shivered, this time pulling his cape closer an attempt to block out the early morning chill.

Lord Bowon Silvershield grumbled a curse. It had been many weeks since he had eaten a hot meal or even sipped the warm tea he so enjoyed. The cold made his bones ache and was multiplied by the fact that he had spent too much time on horseback. He could only imagine how his warhorse felt.

The thought of his weary steed made Bowon stretch out a gauntleted hand and stroke the charger's silky black mane. He had not been able to feed his warhorse a proper meal of oats for several days and needed to remind the beast that his trip was almost over. The charger simply grunted in approval, nodding several times before indicating they had come to yet another fork in the road.

"This place is a maze!" Bowon exclaimed, his greens eyes squinting into the thick fog. It seemed like he had been on this same stretch of road for more than a week . . . and maybe they had. The knight no longer knew what to think. It seemed as if time and all the life that encompassed it had stopped.

"Maybe it is time that I admit I'm lost," Bowon said, knowing that without the sun or moon there would be no chance of finding the proper direction through the valley. He told himself that because of the fog, which refused to rise above the mountains even a well trained astrologer would be lost in these dreary days. It lessen the sting some.

Lowering his gaze, Bowon shivered and issued several new commands to his mount. His trained warhorse reacted with a confident "nay" before veering right. The knight understood that allowing his horse to choose their path was a dangerous move, but what other choice did he have? At least he knew his steed could navigate the hidden road.

Of course, with no concrete destination, Bowon thought, *we are relying upon the luck of the draw as to where we end up.*

As his charger lurched forward, Bowon let his thoughts wander, remembering all the deeds that had led him to this point. For the last five years he had crusaded in the name of God, searching for a source of great chaos that threatened the land. During that time, he had met with one failure after another as each lead proved to be false. To make matters worse, God still refused to clarify what Bowon was searching for, maintaining that miracles and chaos defined the nature of the source. Thus, he had spent these last several years tracking down rumors, traveling between kingdoms and seeking out ancient texts, which only led him to *more* rumors.

Is it coincidence that each rumor has taken me to different regions? He thought. *Though I have learned new ways of life and historical facts, why won't God tell me what to look for?*

Bowon stiffened. His thoughts bordered on blasphemy; he should be ashamed of himself! He had never felt as lost as he did now. Nothing was working the way he planned; he was trapped in this fog, the ancient books revealed nothing, and in his despair, he blamed God.

I am traveling blind, The knight thought, conceding that he knew not where the strands of fate were taking him. *I refuse to say such things. I do have a goal: to seek out the source. I just don't know where to find it, or what exactly it is.*

Bowon considered it ironic that his inability to find the source was what had led him here, to this pass, in which he was lost. He had been told to seek a local legend, a blind prophet named Malacheye, a hermit who supposedly lived somewhere in *this* mountain pass. In truth, he now realized he had made a mistake by coming this far alone, that his pride and fresh tracks had led him astray. He had followed the tracks into the stone valley that he was now wandering. Then the thick blanket of fog had toppled down upon him and all sight had been cut off.

I let thoughts of arrogance cloud my judgment, Bowon fumed. *If only I had stayed true to the Code!* He had persuaded himself that nothing was more important than the will of God. Because of this, his heart had swelled at the thought of Starsgalt's choosing him to serve in such a holy quest. Such thoughts had allowed him to travel down a dangerous path. He had aligned with a man of evil repute in search of information, dismissed his guide, and still thought he was following God's will!

The knight thought of the years he spent buried in the libraries of Arsgoth's trio of academies.

"That is where I should have stayed," he said to the stallion. "If only I could take it all back!" It was not that any of the things he had done bothered him, as much as they were all for naught—a waste of valuable time he didn't have to spare.

Bowon's war-horse stopped in mid stride.

Looking down he noticed that its ears were perked at an odd angle, hearing something the knight could not. A quick survey of the shrouded land, still deep within the fog's embrace, revealed nothing so the knight spoke another quick command. The charger grunted and shook its head. With an irritated sigh, Bowon hopped down from his mount and grabbed the reins. Though the warhorse looked tired, other than the flaring of its nostrils, the knight could see nothing wrong. The stallion grunted, nuzzling into the large warrior.

"Are you finally lost then, my old friend?" Bowon asked, surprised at the unexpected attention from his mount. The two had been together for over seven years, since before he had set out from Aresleigh on this crusade. "Or are you just hungry?"

"Your horse is not lost," said a voice from behind the thick mist. "He has led you to me."

Bowon spun around, drawing steel and unclasping his cape in a single movement.

The figure in front of him did not pose much of a threat: an old man sitting on the ground, shakily holding an oak staff. The man looked wild indeed, his clothes in tatters and his gray hair a tangled frenzy that pointed every direction.

Yet it was none of those attributes that made the knight uneasy. It was the fact that the man's black, sightless eyes were following him with a mournful expression.

"Are you the prophet Malacheye?" Bowon asked cautiously, hoping that after a week's journey, he had finally stumbled upon the hermit.

The old man did not answer the question, simply offering a gap-toothed grin.

Bowon recognized the man's telltale description and so slid his sword back into its jeweled scabbard. He raised his hands in supplication and began to ask another question but was cut off.

"I have been waiting for you, child," Malacheye said. " And though it has taken you several years to find me, I knew you would finally come."

"You are mistaken, sir," Bowon replied with a confused expression. "This is the first we have ever—"

"It is unimportant that we have never met, child, because I know *you*." The man turned and waved the knight to follow him into the parting fog.

"Why should I follow you?"

"Because I know what you seek," Malacheye said. "For all these years, you have wandered lost in a fog much like this. If you come with me, I shall help you find what you seek."

Bowon hesitated, unsure of what to do. The old man waited for him to follow, but the knight was frozen in place. "Who are you?" The question lingered, as Bowon tried to think of a solution to this eerie predicament.

"Unimportant," Malacheye whispered. "Know only that I have the information you so desperately desire."

"Prove to me, sir." The knight stood frozen. "Prove to me that the legends concerning you are true! Tell me one piece of my future."

"The future is not to be revealed so casually, youngling," the prophet responded. "It is not something you wish to know."

"I am not afraid of my death," Bowon stated, thinking he knew what the prophet would tell him. "Now if I am to follow you, tell me a piece of my future."

Malacheye turned and his dark orbs no longer seemed empty. Something glittered in the darkness. "As you wish, child," the prophet said. "In five years, you will be taught a lesson of divine magnitude and it will start you down a misguided path. Yet, this path, *which you will take*, will only spiral you down into misery. When that cycle is complete, you will betray the only thing you love, and when you do, the Bre'Dmorian Order will fall."

Bowon stood in shock, while Malacheye moved into the mist.

The dragon Silverwing soared above the Lightmist Mountains, peering down at rugged grey rock still frosted with ice. After five years of scouring the small Kingdom of Rathadon, a relatively new monarchy, for an unknown source of imbalance, she was becoming desperate. More important, Illuviel, The One God, was tiring at her lack of information.

Silverwing flexed her mighty wings and circled a giant outcropping of jagged rock. She told herself that this was all in the service of God. However, she could feel things changing. Illuviel, whatever his goals, had began to awaken any dragon he could contact, most of which were still undergoing the Divine Purge.

It was not uncommon that Illuviel chose to record history with multiple agents, which proved He worked in mysterious ways. Yet, Silverwing had not expected God to wake thousands of her kind to scour the whole of the world. She considered her mission—to seek out miracles, gather information, and destroy the unknown source—perfect for solo research. As the eldest champion awake, she deserved such respect.

It is almost insulting, the dragon sighed. She felt betrayed that God had not been clearer, expecting her to follow His hints. The problem was that none of His hints made any sense! If she did not know better, Silverwing would have thought that the One God did not know what He was after.

She cleared her mind of the blasphemous thought, which furthered her ire, and scolded herself for doubting Illuviel's divine sight. It just did not make any sense: why was God being so silent in affirming the source of His desire? And now *this*!

Was God questioning her intellectual abilities? *That is absurd! There is no reason why God should doubt my ability to gather His information,* she thought. *In fact, there is no reason why He is doing* any *of this! What help can the others possibly be to me?*

So far, Silverwing had encountered dozens of her kind roaming the vast continent of Jelindia, many willing to share what little information they could . . . which was nothing. She grumbled and told herself that their lack of knowledge just proved her hypothesis correct: she should be the only dragon working on this crusade!

As she circled the outcrop, Silverwing spotted a massive cavern that darkened the side of the mountain. The sight of the cavern made her anxious, a strange emotion for such a long-lived race. She closed her eyes and held her breath, trying to stop the frantic beating of her heart. After several ineffective moments, she let her keen senses reach out, looking for the thing she knew resided in such a place. It only took a moment for fear to wash over her.

This is a bad idea, she thought, beating her wings in a slow rhythmic motion, allowing herself to hover. She considered reversing her course, hoping that she could change God's mind. She was about to turn back when another wave of divine fear washed over her, strong enough to make her wings falter—strong enough that she knew the thing she sought was somehow calling her.

Catching a current of air to stabilize her flight, the dragon realized she was frightened. She craned her neck towards the sky, her limbs feeling heavy and sluggish.

"My Lord God, are you certain that you wish me to do this?" Her voice boomed. She received only silence. "Illuviel, Master of All Knowledge, please speak to me! I know there are great events about to unfold, Master, but to awaken the Shadow Dragons . . . it could induce the end of this world!"

Again she was met by smothering silence. The ancient Shadow Dragons were Sinafthisar, who had turned from God during the creation of the Mortal Plane. They were so powerful that Heaven refused to destroy them, instead placing a great curse upon the entire sect.

With a shudder, Silverwing knew that this particular Shadow Dragon, Vulsevandat, would be especially displeased at having his slumber interrupted. To make matters worse, she was waking him on God's behalf, who was hoping that such an ancient wyrm might hold answers. She realized that it was fear of the Shadow that had led to her questioning Illuviel, The One True God.

The thought of waking the Shadow clouded Silverwing's mind with trepidation. It was not worth the sacrifice, as legends pertaining to these monsters were painstakingly clear: not *all* of dragonkind were creatures of knowledge. In truth, she knew that there were those among dragonkind who wished nothing more than to destroy Heaven. Since that was out of the question, such dragons often obliterated lesser races and killed their own kind. Most of these Shadow Dragons were hunted by roaming armies of humans and killed or grew so old that they never left their lairs. Which posed the question: how may Shadows were actually in existence?

"A question for another time," she told herself. "Now, if I wish to survive this encounter, I must focus!"

Silverwing tried to recall the history of Vulsevandat. Though existence of such a beast was considered folklore, as the mighty Shadow had not been seen for over eleven thousand years, some tales still existed. Legend said that Vulsevandat was the mightiest Sinafthisar in existence, first born of Heaven, and older than the mortal timeline itself. Those same texts described the wyrm as a killer of anything it pleased, quite capable of mad fits.

If he is anything like the last Shadow, then I will be attacked on sight, Silverwing thought, preparing several arcane defenses.

Though it was forbidden to kill her own kind in cold blood, if it came down to it and she had no choice, she would fight back with lethal force. Of course, she realized that if a battle ensued her life would end. If Vulsevandat meant to kill her, whether she was a Champion of Illuviel or not, there was no way to stop him. Dying at the hands of such a vile beast angered her. She was a faithful servant of God, His proclaimed champion, why had He wasted her on such a menial task?

"Because Vulsevandat *might* respect my age enough to listen," she growled to no one, "at least, before he incinerates me."

With a deft motion, Silverwing folded her wings, closed her eyes, and spun into a tight dive, speeding towards the ground like an arrow. It was a maneuver that helped release her fear. If she did not react in time, she would perish on the ground, and God could find Himself a new champion. If she was quick enough, however, she could catch an updraft, catapulting herself into an aerial display.

The ground fast approached, rock clusters opening like a razor-edged maw in anticipation of its prey. At the last moment, the dragon's wings spread wide and she rolled her body to catch the wind. The strain on her joints caused bittersweet agony to shoot through her system as she used the air currents to slingshot herself through the air with tremendous force. When she opened her eyes, Silverwing noticed that she was still airborne, and that her daredevil antics had succeeded.

It seems I am to survive, she thought. She had lived for nearly twelve thousand years, recording history and gathering information; it seemed today began another chapter in that saga.

Making another circle of the area, Silverwing again hovered over the rock spire and picked out what she was searching for: a jutting rock, which looked a lot like a tusk and signified the entrance to a massive hall. If her memory was correct, this was Neth'uul Stenuuk, or Hall of Stone, an ancient dwarven kingdom destroyed in the Purge of Ancient Souls. If her history was correct, she could assume that Vulsevandat had resided here for no more than fourteen hundred years, since the last time humans tried to secure the region in the Year of the Lightbringers.

Silverwing found an open spot and landed on a crumbling road, moss covered statues of gold, silver, and Neferium lining each side. Next to each statue stood makeshift pillars made from the skulls of the lesser races; the stench of death and decay clogged her senses. As a reactionary measure, she recast a series of powerful defensive spells which she hoped would annul the Shadow's breath weapon, should he use it. Of course, there was a chance that Vulsevandat would see the wards as offensive and annihilate her anyway.

With a sigh, the dragon tried to calm her nerves, moving almost in slow motion as she neared the mouth of the cave. After several steps she snapped her eyes shut, fear creating hallucinations in her mind, and stopped. Using every ounce of her willpower, the dragon forced her massive talons to again move forward and eventually reached a greasy film that covered her thick scales, some kind of ward to keep out lesser species. The film clung to her scaled body like a glistening sheen of sweat, making her shiver. When she opened her eyes, Silverwing was greeted with utter darkness, having to rely on her acute senses to maneuver.

It took only a moment for her eyes to adjust, easily picking up the huge form wrapped peacefully around a massive column. She could feel her heart clench in fear, body frozen. Struggling to move, she willed herself onto an obsidian platform, built long ago so incoming arbiters could show proper respect.

A great eye opened.

Silverwing crouched in shock. She had not said anything, nor had she made much sound entering, and still Vulsevandat knew she was here!

The silver dragon envisioned her death: slow, painful, and ashamed at having failed God. Yet, the Shadow did not move.

"Why have you woken me from slumber, bonded scum?" Vulsevandat boomed.

"My lord, I come on behalf of the One God, Illuviel," she replied, her voice tense with horror. "He has assigned me a holy crusade . . ."

"I care nothing of the petty affairs of your god!" Vulsevandat's voice exploded. "Nor do I care about your search! Tell me why the mighty Vulsevandat should not incinerate you?"

"Because I serve a greater power, my lord!" she tried to explain. "Surely you must . . ."

"I *must* do nothing," his voice was like thunder. "*You* serve nothing! You *are* nothing! And now, I will prove it."

She could see the Shadow Dragon's head lift, heard the intake of breath. She could feel the bone-numbing sensation of heat, so hot that it seared nerve endings. Before the blast struck, she heard his voice dripping with venom.

"It is time for you to see the truth!"

The gate shimmered into being, its blazing blue aura crackling with the unbridled energy of a rip in reality.

The olthari, Thurm Stormrage stepped to the gate and paused. As he looked back at the dying world, which had once been like all the others, teeming with sentient life and oblivious to its impending eradication, grief washed over him. He had been given a chance to save this world, along with his cursed race, by finding the unknown source of order. Yet, for the last five mortal years he had failed miserably. Thus, Thurm had become the "Destroyer of Worlds," a prologue to Illenthuul's purge, which was sweeping the entire multi-verse.

Thurm knew that The Dark God was single-minded in his pursuit to find the source. With each failure, Illenthuul destroyed a world and a portion of the Olthari souls trapped in oblivion, angered at His lack of knowledge. The olthari knew that Illenthuul wished to conquer Heaven, not destroy it, by using the unknown power against his fellow gods. This entire thing was about the source, always about the source.

He lowered his head in shame, knowing that he was an accomplice in this atrocity. He could still hear the anguish of his people, crying out in terror as the god destroyed their souls. The olthari could not allow his emotions to interfere with the crusade; there was *no* cost too high to free his people from eternal bondage, trapped in a lingering state of oblivion. Nor was there a price to high to release his mate, Elissandera.

"It is my failure!" Thurm screamed to the sky, tears rolling down his face. "No world deserves this, my lord—please, give me more time!"

The olthari was greeted by deafening silence. As he looked to the blood red sky, a crack of thunder exploded and several blotches of nothingness, the chaos that was born of creation, devoured the landscape.

This world contained so much life, Thurm thought, remembering that tens of millions of Therulivan, a humanoid race of reptiles, had once lived and loved on this world. Now what was left of them were spitted on giant stakes spanning across the whole planet. He also remembered the sucking sounds and screams, as those millions were feasted upon by the ferryll, demonic creatures created to do Illenthuul's bidding.

Thurm's iron will begin to falter. He could stop at any time with the certainty that Illenthuul would kill both himself and his mate, who had already endured a thousand deaths at the hands of the Dark God. He knew that with no deity to align himself to, Illenthuul could keep his soul for as long as reality existed, which made the battle-hardened warrior shiver.

The olthari could see what would happen to his entire race should he choose not to go on. Illenthuul was known for his sadistic pleasures, such as destroying the soul and the essence of existence, among other things.

How far I have fallen! At one time he had been the High Protectorate of Starsgalt, the highest ranking non-angel in Heaven, a servant who cherished life above all else. He had been honorable then, battling against demonic angels, upholding Starsgalt's virtue. In the sixth eternity he had even slain the Demon Prince Arviel, First Captain of Illenthuul, before the darkened angel could steal the Godsword.

The rush of memories made Thurm remember the day that his entire race had been banished from Heaven. His god, Starsgalt, had been at the head of the Great Convergence, accusing the Olthari race of betrayal, seeking justice and law without reasoning. The God of Law had been so persuasive that the rest of the gods, who never agreed on anything, had decided to not only close the gates of Heaven to the living Olthari, but those that died as well.

"We did not betray you! We *saved* Heaven, you fools!" The olthari dropped to his knees sobbing. "How could you betray us? Me?" He had survived on the Mortal Plane for over twenty thousand years. The pain was so great that he had tried to end his own life several times, but the curse— the curse did not deem suicide an unnatural way to die.

Finally he had come to accept Illenthuul's holy crusade for what it was. In all of his time spent in torment, not a single god had ever offered to alle- viate the pain of existing without an end.

Until now. This god, a deity of evil and chaos, allowed him a chance at redemption, offering to open the gates of Heaven should he succeed. This god, his immortal nemesis, which he despised above all others, had given him the power to set things right. Thurm wished nothing more than to die with honor and once again be with his people in the Heavenly realms. For that chance, he would do anything, regardless of the cost.

It had taken many days for the olthari to decide what course of action to take. During that time, Illenthuul had forced Thurm to reside in a pocket plane of Hell and witness the suffering of the Olthari race firsthand. Fur- thermore, the god had forced him to watch as his entire race was staked up on giant poles of obsidian, sustained by infernal power even as their entrails spilled out and cries of anguish filled the cosmos.

The olthari could not imagine the torment. At last Illenthuul showed Thurm his mate, nailed against a pair of logs, her eyes glazed over in pain, mumbling incoherently. Thurm could see where her limbs had been cut off and reattached with godly magic, scars left to remind him how much more the god could make her suffer. Under such traumatic strain, the god used the olthari's mind against him, focusing it in a single sharp point: *redemption.*

Elissandera opened her eyes and looked at him, and he was forced to watch yet another of her deaths. In that moment, Thurm's heart sank and his will was broken. He knew that Illenthuul was right. The others had turned their backs on his people! Though this god demanded to be his mas- ter, the olthari knew that Illenthuul would not break his word once the deal was bound.

The rules were simple: Thurm had one year to seek out the unknown source and nurture it. If he could not discover it, he would open a conduit into the world so that the god's minions could scour the world until it was found. If at anytime he unmasked what Illenthuul was seeking, his people would be released into Heaven, curse annulled. However, a world would die each time he failed, along with the souls of his race.

Anything is better than this existence, he thought. With silent resolution the olthari agreed to the terms, not fully understanding the consequences . . . which had led him to this.

The screams of the dying brought him back to the gate crackling in front of him. One last time, he told himself that there was no choice.

Regretfully, Thurm dropped his eyes and stepped into the portal of his fifth world—another world that would die.

Each winter, the Golden Swan Inn brought good business to the small township of Durwin, supplying travelers with warmth and drink. As snow swept across the rough landscape, blowing steadily against the Swan's small wooden shutters, sounds of merriment echoed within.

On this particular night, several middle-aged men relaxed near a blazing fire, their feet outstretched, and telling stories. Though none of them were first-born sons nor could they claim a large portion of power, all were respected members of their families. They were all minor nobles, acting as emissaries or advisors within the Duchy of Calimond and had come to Durwin on their yearly hunting trip.

As the youngest noble, Lord Nolan, finished his tale and dropped a small candle dramatically on the table, the other men erupted in conversation. His tale had been a dark one, a story of murder and betrayal, in which the villain had actually escaped. For the next hour, the noblemen discussed the strengths and weaknesses of the story, coming to the conclusion that such a myth would be hard to top.

When the room quieted, the Baron of Heath picked up the candle and walked to the front of the room. "I have heard a true story much like the one Lord Nolan just told," the baron said. "If there are no objections, I would like to tell my version . . .?"

Cheers greeted the the man. With a brief smile, the noble looked down and let the shadows of the room flicker across his face, hoping it was evil enough to make his friends shiver. Placing the candle on a small pedestal and spreading his hands toward the men with a smile, the baron began to tell his story:

"Legend tells of a man who vanished into the night," the baron said, letting the words linger, "a known murderer, awaiting death at the gallows for his crimes against the town of Brenly; crimes that are unspeakable."

The baron remained quiet as his friends made quick prayers to Starsgalt and symbolic gestures that would protect them against evil. When they looked at him incredulously, he smiled and continued with his story.

"For this, his unwavering faith and loyalty in Balzabuth, the Angel of Evil, the man was given a holy crusade: to search out and destroy a great source of good." The baron trailed off, letting the others spit up their wine at the naming of the Dark Prince.

"In return for the murderer's service, The Dark Prince freed the man of his Bre'Dmorian bonds, offering infinite power upon Aryth . . ." The noble picked up the candle and brought it to his face. "As the Dark Prince's magic flowed through the murderer, darkness split away and shadows swallowed him, letting him pass out of his cage. It is true that in the night the shadows came, concealing the screams of his captors as he cut their throats and walked into the night, never to be heard from again," the baron finished and set the candle down with a mischievous grin.

The eldest noble sat back in his chair, disturbed yet quite intrigued. "Are there no rumors as to the whereabouts of this man?" he asked.

The storyteller flashed bright white teeth and responded. "That is a good question, Count Antoois, a good question. No one knows exactly what happened to the man, or if he even existed. Those that knew the man cannot recall his face . . . or his name. There have been rumors that the man's name changes as he kills his victims. Of course, some say of those same people say that the murderer's vile spirit kills anyone who dare mention this story. I would imagine that some determined research could uncover the truth. But is it worth the chance, if the rumors are true?"

The others glanced at each other than laughed at their self-imposed tension. It was a tall tale, meant for nothing but good times and wine. If the murderer in the tale had existed, the Bre'Dmorian Order would have surely tracked him down and destroyed such evil. As the baron sat down, the room saluted him with a raised cup of wine, asking the origins of such a tale.

As with every story in such company, soon the legend lost its appeal and the next noble moved to the front of the room, recalling a tale about dragons.

When the last storyteller finished, the small company of nobles sat in a drunken stupor which marked the end to a good evening. With a salute, Lord Antoois boasted he had never heard such fine mythology, most of which he would pass on to his grandchildren. The others took the hint and stumbled out after him.

The two nobles who remained, Lord Nolan and the Baron of Heath, sat in the small room, their faces furrowed in thought.

The Baron of Heath broke the silence. "Where did you hear your story?"

"From a bloody beggar in Aresleigh," Lord Nolan laughed. "I am sure the infamous villain in both of our tales was as much a poverty-stricken miscreant as the man who told it to me."

"What makes you say that?" the baron asked.

"You speak as though the tale were true, my lord!" Nolan jested, his smile fading when the baron's face darkened. "There isn't a single murderer that I can think of who is not a flea-infested whoreson. I am sure if the man does exist, he is dead. If not, then he is most likely a coward, who kills people in the night and such."

The Baron of Heath slapped his knee and laughed. "I cannot argue that, Lord Nolan! You are right, either the man never existed or he was a filthy peasant, likely the bastard child of whores."

Lord Nolan chuckled at the fact he had fallen for such dire thoughts. He offered his fellow noble another round of wine and toasted. After another hour of drinking and conversation the pair stood and walked to the door.

Just before Nolan opened it, he felt the impact and spun around. He tried to scream, but other than gurgling no sound came from his mouth.

With a swift motion, the baron, a man named Edelin Selmsy, removed his long dirk from Lord Nolan's throat and drove it into the man's heart. The blow was delivered with such force that several ribs snapped.

Lord Nolan barely felt the pain shoot through his body as blood poured forth. His eyes wide with fear, he looked into the baron's face and saw the man for what he was. Again, Nolan tried to scream but only blood poured forth; the blade had pierced his lung.

Baron Edelin Selmsy looked on impassively, dark eyes gleeful in exultation. He knew he had delivered fatal wounds and so chose not to distribute anymore blows, wanting to cherish the slow death of his companion. It had been several years since God had allowed him to kill anyone for pleasure. However, this man deserved no less for calling him a whoreson.

"I can see you are wondering *why*," Edelin said as Nolan's fingers slipped from the knife hilt. The murderer waited until his friend took his last breath before he added, "Not all rumors are false, my pathetic friend."

12

THE COMPANY of men rode through the northern gatehouse in splendid marching order, sun high above their heads, lending to their aspirations of returning with glory. Their orders were clear: ride hard the first day until the northern road forked southeast towards Stormwind.

For eight hours Areck rode in silence, ashamed of himself. He hardly noticed that the northern road had turned from paved to laid gravel about fifteen miles outside of the city, becoming increasingly ill-kept the further north one traveled. It wasn't until Lord Silvershield called a halt that he saw a series of dark clouds rolling in from the west, driven by the mild coastal winds that often buffeted the Duchy of Aresleigh late into summer.

We must be six miles away from the fork, Areck thought, trying to delineate his surroundings. At the fork the road split and continued either north to the town of Lolindir or veered southeast connecting with the King's Road.

A streak of lighting illuminated the sky, followed by a rumbling of thunder. Areck squinted toward the sky and inhaled, salty air stinging his throat. He could tell by the darkness that an impending downpour, possibly a monsoon, was coming. After a moment of silence another blast of electricity branched out, looking like a giant spider's web, sizzling hot and white. He was surprised that thick raindrops did not follow as another peel of thunder shook the ground.

Starsgalt will not let the rain come, Areck thought, deciding that God was watching him, refusing to wash away the previous night's sins. Areck dreaded the thought of facing Lord Silvershield, although, had his elderly commander wished to strip him of rank, he would have done so at the Academy.

Another rumble jolted Areck from his despair, causing him to look to-wards Knight-Captain Silvershield, conversing with Lords Vinion and Malketh, each studying the sky. Areck assumed that the knights were trying to approximate travel time between Aresleigh and Stormwind in case a storm broke out. Normally the journey took four days, covering one hundred and twenty five miles of both paved road and unpaved roads. Fortunately it had been a dry summer compared to other years, when coastal storms blew in and turned the flat grasslands surrounding Aresleigh into a vast prairie.

Of course, my knowledge is based upon sunny weather, Areck thought. *If we hit a storm this far north, especially with uneven roads, our journey will be extended by one or two days.*

"Squire Areck!" a voice announced. "We are almost there, so stop day-dreaming and move!"

Areck bit his lip and turned red. Could he sink any lower? Sullenly, he gazed downward, issued a verbal command to his steed and once again began moving forward.

† † † † †

The company reached the fork and encountered other travelers, a merchant caravan setting up camp.

The riders paid the caravan little attention as they walked along, stopping only to offer the polite greetings which knightly ethos demanded before moving on.

Areck had spent several years monitoring merchants at the King's gate, learning their capitalistic nature. He found it odd that a caravan of any kind would stop before nightfall, as competition demanded timeliness, oftentimes leading to merchandise being destroyed. He understood the concept well, as Starsgalt regularly recognized those who entered competitions and worked their way to the top.

Areck shrugged his shoulders and looked away. His peripheral vision picked up a guardsman, most likely a bodyguard, dressed in black leather armor, poke his head out of a small coach and watch the company pass by. Though he found it odd that a bodyguard traveled inside with his mistress, it was not Areck's place to question anyone; certainly not now.

When Lord Silvershield finally called for a halt, the small company had traversed three more miles in relative silence. If not for the thunder and lightning, the mounted warriors would have continued until nightfall, which was still an hour away. With several crisp orders from the commander, Areck dismounted and moved the company into a small copse of forest, just off the graveled road.

As Areck prepared to tether the mounts, he saw the knights talking and pointing to the horizon. He heard his name and realized that he was their subject, meaning one thing: it was time to be punished.

The tallest of the trio, Knight-Captain Galwen Vinion, looked angry and deep in discussion with Lord Silvershield as he pointed at Areck. Lord Bowon placed his hand on the man's arm, nodded to the watching squire, and said something that made his second-in-command drop his arm in embarrassment.

Several thoughts cascaded through Areck's mind. First among those was that Lord Vinion was glaring at him as the knight pulled Lord Silvershield deeper into the forest, most likely at the fact Areck's punishment was not severe enough for his taste. Areck tried to calm himself but could not help but envision the repercussions Knight-Captain Vinion would dish out.

"Why are all of you are so bad-tempered about things?" a voice whispered behind him.

Areck stiffened.

How did he sneak up on me? he wondered, realizing that his friend had been standing next to him the entire time. He shook his head in resignation; he had been so absorbed in what was being said that he was not paying enough attention. Areck composed himself and turned around, looking into the pale blue eyes of Arawnn, who was quite cheerful given the circumstances.

"They are discussing me," Areck said.

"Aye, the large one isn't happy that Knight-Captain Silvershield did not remove you from this campaign," replied Arawnn.

"Honestly, I do not know why Lord Silvershield let me stay," Areck said, dropping his head in resignation. "I was sure that my time within the Academy was over."

"Come now, Areck, all you did was stay out one night."

"I have done many things, Arawnn!" Areck listed off the charges that would be named at his sentencing: drinking, sexual contact, betrayal of the ethos, and of course, tardiness.

"But each one of those things was my fault!" the royal courier said. "How can you possibly be in trouble for following up on a given promise?"

Areck considered his words. "You did not *make* me give my word, Arawnn. My arrogance kept me from thinking that you would call me on it, thus leading me to drink the wine, among other things. Plus, I was fooled by that accursed woman."

"You mean that she got you drunk, and you can't hold your liquor?" Arawnn coughed and suppressed a chuckle.

Areck glared at his friend. "Why don't you believe that she did something to me?"

"Sure she did! You could hardly stop drooling," Arawnn retorted, white teeth gleaming.

Areck reddened in mortification. He hoped that his fool friend would not reveal anything before he had the chance to talk to Lord Silvershield privately. It would be a long lecture of how knights behaved themselves, no doubt.

When another squire tripped over the coiled roping, Areck realized that he had not accomplished anything during his time eavesdropping on his superiors. His fellow squire freed his boot and glared at the pair *supposedly* preparing a tether line for the horses. The younger squire didn't say anything, however, since Areck was an officer and beyond reproach. The young man sniffed and mumbled something under his breath before storming off towards a small group of squires who were preparing tents.

As he watched the junior squire go, Areck turned to ask Arawnn for help finding a suitable pair of trees with enough space to secure a tether. His request was silly, as securing the horses was the easiest job in the command, but Areck found it difficult to concentrate even on insignificant things. He knew that eventually his commander would finish talking with the other knights and he would need to atone for his behavior.

Areck placed his boot in a small crevice for leverage and pulled until the thick rope hummed with tension. He then tied off the first part of the tether and signaled for Arawnn to loop around the trees, creating a reinforced line from which the powerful animals would not easily break free. Arawnn maneuvered his body into place, waiting for Areck to place slipknots and tie the rope. Satisfied, Areck pair backed off and regarded their work. The line was not perfect, but quite adequate for his first time securing a tether for an entire company.

In his effort to concentrate, Areck had not noticed Lord Silvershield approach with interest. The older knight looked pleased with the tension and security of the thick ropes, tugging on the knots and walking around the base of each tree. When Bowon was satisfied, he coughed to announce his presence. The noise made Arawnn jump backwards, so that he almost tripped on a thick root poking out of the ground. However, Areck slouched at the sound, lowering his gaze in acceptance.

"Messenger Arawnn, I am sure the men are cooking some fresh stew back at camp. Would you please tell them that the tether is ready for their mounts?" Lord Silvershield asked, though it was not really a question.

With a glance at his friend, Arawnn nodded and gave a small smile to say that everything would work itself out.

Areck nodded, trying not to let his friend see his fear. This would be his last opportunity to show his knightly worth to the courier; after his punishment, he would be a mere civilian, unworthy of following an ethos.

"There is a bond between you," Lord Bowon Silvershield said. "I sense your turmoil in befriending a person who is not like yourself."

The statement caught Areck off guard. He was not expecting a breakdown of his persona by his commander. Considering the statement a weakness, Areck lowered his eyes and hoped that his mentor would not point out other flaws in his character.

"From the looks of it, you feel it too." Lord Silvershield chuckled. "Although, I think you believe such a friendship to be in poor taste?"

"As you pointed out, Lord Silvershield, Arawnn is unlike me," Areck said. "The tension you sense is the reason you are here."

"Always to the point, lad," Silvershield said, pointing towards a small copse of trees. "Let us take a walk and discuss your actions."

As the pair walked in silence, Areck thought of all the time he had spent with his commander. So many of his elders considered the portly knight a fallen warrior, more concerned with wine and women than worshiping God. However, Areck found the old man amusing, with insights into the world that most Bre'Dmorians could not appreciate. He vividly remembered hearing tales of far away places, legends, and of a man who had once been a Champion of God.

Areck had always considered Lord Bowon a particularly good storyteller, mad from creating such fictional tales, until the night he had found several shredded cloaks folded in an unlocked chest. On that night, he began to suspect that the man in the stories might in fact be Lord Silvershield himself, or at least a caricature of the commander who for some reason had fallen into disgrace. Areck listened after that with a newfound wonder, accepting that his commander's stories held more than their share of truth and would most likely lead to a better revelation later in life.

For all of his faults, Areck considered Lord Silvershield a solid person of honor, depth, and compassion. These attributes had always removed the man from the terrible truth: he was a drunkard who solicited sexual acts and often disgraced himself.

It was because of Lord Silvershield's lax attitudes that the knighthood's rules were strictly enforced—an attempt to keep its lines pure and its members untainted. Areck knew this would be the reason they could not allow him to stay—"once impure, always impure," as the saying went. There was a chance Areck's pestilence would spread to others.

"For all that logic, you cannot understand that life is meant to be lived," Lord Silvershield said as small raindrops gently fell from the darkened sky.

Areck looked at him in confusion.

"You are thinking so hard that I can read your thoughts, Areck." the knight-captain chuckled, placing a hand on Areck's shoulder. "You are doing what I did so long ago."

Areck looked at Lord Silvershield and lowered his gaze, unable to look his knight-captain in the eye. He felt ashamed. He was trying to rationalize his actions by considering the source of his past. He tried to explain but no words came forth.

"Areck, I have lived a knight's life for twenty-three seasons. I have traveled the world in search of the unknown," Lord Silvershield explained. "Now it is time for you to learn from my fool's errand, a symbolic measure of our life. We all try to decipher the unknown, hoping for some great answer. The day comes when we realize that we will never find those things. At least, I never did."

"I do not understand, my lord. Why you are telling me this?"

"Let me finish, Squire," Lord Silvershield whispered. "We are taught to live a perfect life, yet none can be perfect save God. The Bre'Dmorian tenets teach faith by servitude. Yet there is no faith in servitude, only blindness and shackles, which ultimately smother men. Think on this, son: we have gotten His message all wrong. Only by living life, by appreciating everything that has been given to us, can a man truly cherish God."

Areck snapped his mouth shut. His commander's words were bordering on blasphemy.

Lord Silvershield sighed when Areck refused to comprehend the meaning behind his words. It was the same way with most knights, all of them blinded by servitude, judgmental to the end. "Before you arrived at the stables, Arawnn pulled me aside and told me everything: you gave your word as his escort, you thought of duty while seeking a cleric, and you were poisoned while seeking information in the bar. He *also* assured me that you denied your manly passions in appreciation of your virtue."

"Arawnn told you that?" Areck's mouth went slack in amazement. He had criticized Arawnn so much, yet Areck knew of no one willing to sacrifice himself for the betterment of a friendship.

"He told me many things," Lord Silvershield said with a small grin. "Unfortunately, my council was not private. Both Lord Vinion and Lord Malketh insisted on being privy to any information concerning your tardiness. They both heard the same story and have both thought on a proper punishment."

"I was told that you were worried that your career in the Academy is done," Lord Silvershield continued. "That is what I meant by my first statement. You will be a fine knight someday soon, lad. But you are so afraid to live your life, like most knights, that you think one misstep is proper reason to remove you from nearly ten years of service." The knight-captain paused, choosing his next words thoughtfully. "Heed this advice before I decide what to do with you. Do not waste your life . . . as I have, lad."

What just happened? Areck thought, struggling with comprehension. "I have come to pay my debt to the Academy and will accept whatever justice you would mete out, my lord," Areck said, still confused. His emotions ran a gamut from thankfulness, to regret, to uncertainty, to anger, and finally back to thankfulness for his friend. He had been ready for the worst kind of punishment: to face the situation alone.

Lord Silvershield saw the mixture of emotions play across his squire's face. He knew that most of his words had not registered, as the boy struggled with what he had been taught to believe. Then again, understanding did not come in a single night, so Bowon gave Areck what he wanted: a reprimand for his actions. There was cause, after all, considering that he knew Arawnn had lied to protect the squire. Originally, Bowon had had not expected to press the matter, as the knight-captain saw the honor and integrity in protecting others when there was no mandatory need for it.

"I never doubted you would, lad. You are a Bre'Dmorian, after all. It is your duty to be responsible," Lord Silvershield told Areck what he needed to hear. "Thus, you can understand my need to maintain command in a strict and orderly fashion."

This Areck understood. He raised his eyes to meet his commanders and prepared to accept a fitting punishment. "Of course, I do, Lord Silvershield!"

"Good. I was serious when I said that the other knights have each considered a fitting punishment for you." Lord Silvershield paused so the words could register. "However, I do not feel that a first time offense merits demotion. Nor do I think that a verbal lashing would be proper in front of the other squires. Therefore, the proper punishment needs to illustrate that a squire, even one of your rank, must take responsibility for his mistakes." The knight-captain paced around the tree, trying to hide his pleasure, pretending to consider his options. "I must also show that the young often misstep and although bad decisions are costly, they are not irreparable."

After a moment's pause in which he nearly smiled, Lord Silvershield made his way back to where Areck stood with his eyes downcast in acceptance.

"It is my duty to punish you, Squire Areck," he began, choosing the proper words. "For being reckless in the field and for giving your word when you are not yet a knight, you will be relegated to digging latrines each night that we setup camp. This will be done after you finish your duties of making tether lines, as well as any other duties your other knight-captains find suitable."

Areck gazed at him with unblinking eyes that betrayed his thoughts. His commander had given him a second chance, sticking with the original punishment but sounding almost angry about it. The fact that he would not be demoted made Areck weak with relief. He understood that Lord Silver-shield was protecting him from harsher penalties. He nodded in agreement.

"I glad you understand, Squire Areck," Lord Silvershield said, wheeling towards the camp without waiting for a reply. "I suggest you to start trench-ing before any rain falls."

"It will be as you command, Lord Silvershield," Areck said.

"One more thing, Areck: make sure you are composed before you come back to camp," The knight-captain's voice carried as he vanished behind a copse of trees.

Areck took a deep breath. He looked to the sky and offered a prayer to Starsgalt, who had chosen to look over him. The next two weeks would be hard; trenching was not for the weak. However, if that was the price he had to pay for his failure, then he would dig all the way to Natalinople!

Taking another deep breath, Areck followed his commander's steps through the trees. He walked to his saddlebags, removed a trenching pick, and went off to pay this night's price. Areck moved quietly past the other men and into a small clearing downwind from the camp's setup. As he placed the small pick in his right hand and struck the ground, lightning branched across the sky. In moments, large drops of rain began to pelt the ground, followed by the boom of thunder.

† † † † †

Var realized that he better make up his mind soon. He had paid hand-somely to ride with a small trading caravan to the north, inconspicuously taking the same route the Bre'Dmorians would use.

As his carriage bounced along, the assassin's horse secured to the back, Var folded his orders and stuffed them in a small pouch. He had thought long and hard on what he was going to do, concluding that to ignore the shadowed man's warnings meant death.

He is going to kill me anyway, Var thought, *so what does it matter? There is still an opportunity to ride hard and get as far away as possible before they realize I have betrayed them.*

Var's carriage lurched to a stop and the boom of thunder split the after-noon air. Var poked his head out. To his surprise, the caravan had made good time, reaching the fork before the Bre'Dmorian riders. He guessed that it was because the knights had not left until after daybreak, while the slow moving caravan had moved out several hours before dawn.

Var sat down with a sigh of resignation. *If I leave now and never come back, I will be running for the rest of my life. However, if I can kill this courier, then I may live long enough to track down my shadowy friend.*

"Damn it!" Var exclaimed, sitting back. With all this self visualization, he knew there was no other choice; he had to continue. There was only one thing that mattered: to kill the man who had defiled him.

Just before dusk the Bre'Dmorians caught up with the caravan. As was their custom they slowed just long enough to offer greetings before moving down the road. Var waited for them to pass, poking his head out of the carriage only when he was sure to have a clear vantage.

Var scanned each knight, looking for any signs that might announce his accomplice. He paid no attention to the young blond knight who turned to look at him, instead concentrating on picking out inconsistencies among the riders.

Var smiled as he saw what he was searching for: a single knight rode without perfect posture. He would track his suspect until the Bre'Dmorians made camp for the night, just to make sure. And when he was ready, Var would kidnap his co-conspirator.

As far as trenching went, latrines were fairly easy, being dug with the intention to be refilled. With determination Areck slammed his pick into the soft ground as thick sheets of rain began to pour down. After twenty minutes of consistent rainfall, the soft soil turned from solid clay to slimy mud. The process of digging in such rain created havoc, as Areck struggled to scoop out more mud than water. Fortunately, none of the men had to use the privies.

Though it took most of the evening, Areck finished his task. With a powerful thrust, he slammed the pick into the ground and looked towards the now-darkened camp, assuming that everyone had called it a night.

It was not until Areck heard a pair of booted feet splashing up behind him that he knew a sentry had come to check on him. As the man approached, Areck pushed himself away from the completed pit in exhaustion.

"Lord Vinion wished to let you know that the privy will be finished in a more timely fashion in forthcoming nights," Squire Redmon said. "He said to tell you that if you cannot be timely in this matter, then maybe he shouldn't leave you to your own devices."

Covered in thick mud, Areck could only gape at the sentry. "Please let Knight-Captain Vinion know that I will heed his warning." Areck lowered his gaze. If he had not poked his head out of the pit, Redmon might have walked past. "It will not happen tomorrow."

Redmon nodded then said, "Lord Silvershield also wishes to let you that know that you have spent enough time digging. He said come back to camp and get some sleep."

Areck could hear the annoyance in Redmon's tone, yet the young man said no more before moving off.

Areck knelt painfully down and picked up his pick in hopes that a tent would be waiting for him along with a ration of thick stew. As he stumbled towards the camp, another streak of lighting illuminated the sky, making the neat rows of command tents seem surreal.

It occurred to him that he should check on his charger, making sure his mount had been fed before he marched off to bed. He barely heard the rustling of the horses as they shuffled and nickered, assuming that his brethren had taken care of them. Looking to the sky, Areck paused to let the rain wash off some of the mud that still caked his face.

When he was satisfied, Areck scouted for his tent, a small one-man triangle built specifically for campaigning, and pulled the flaps. As he ducked down to enter, an aroma of still-warm stew wafted from a wooden bowl. The meal was gritty so late in the evening, but Areck was so hungry that he closed his eyes and savored the food.

Removing his armor, Areck placed the leather and chain hauberk on a small log so it could dry before the morrow. He rubbed his aching arms and removed his shirt, pulling a thick woolen blanket around his shoulders.

Areck knelt and lighted a small candle. He said his nightly prayers to Starsgalt, letting God know that he would offer more thanks in the morning. He blew the candle out and closed his eyes.

As the sky glowed with electricity, a shadow moving through the darkness was visible on Areck's tent wall. It resembled a man, so he shrugged it off.

"A sentry," he mumbled, yawning as pulled the covers over his head.

Var moved without noise. His magic armor allowed him to do such things, making the shadows of the night his ally. Thus, when Var saw an armored sentry scouting the area, he moved off to a better position and decided to wait for his accomplice to present himself at a more opportune time.

The sentry moved away and a streak of lighting branch out, accompanied by a loud clap of thunder. Var had been watching the Bre'Dmorians switch between patrol duties for four hours now and there was still no sign of the knight he was waiting for.

With a sigh of irritation Var moved towards the camp, using his enhanced sight to scan the area. He crept forward, doing his best to stay in the underbrush. He noticed that an astute guard was coming his way and Var fell to the ground, pausing long enough so the pouring rain could cover his movements. It took only a moment for the knight to pass. Satisfied that the sentry was gone, Var pushed himself out of the mud and wiped away the grime.

Var mumbled a curse. This was not going the way he had planned, which had been to track the Bre'Dmorians to their camp so he could kidnap his accomplice. The problem was that the company of knightly riders had traveled only a few miles past the fork, forcing him to improvise.

He fumed at the time he had lost along with the opportunity to scout the area. Most of all, he was frustrated at the fact that by entering the forest so far back, he was forced to hike blindly towards the camp. *I should have known how damn predictable they would be.*

As Var snuck within sight of the camp, a stir of movement caught his eye. He ducked behind a small thorn bush, doing his best to stay out of sight. Though Var had no doubt that he could kill a single knight, this was not the time to press his luck, especially with eleven others so close.

Var's patience paid off. The man he had picked out was moving into the forest. He pulled a dagger, crouched low, and maneuvered his way towards his mark.

When he had moved into striking distance, Var picked up a small stone and ducked just to the man's right. He placed his dagger on the ground within grabbing distance, should he need to kill the knight. Deciding that a direct approach was best Var threw the rock, which struck the knight on the right forearm, and ducked back down.

The man swung towards Var and unsheathed his weapon. Seeing nothing, the knight finished pulling out his blade and made his way in Var's general direction.

Var waited for the knight to pass then stalked the man into the forest—satisfied that no one could hear, he struck.

With a precise kick, Var lashed out at the knight's knee. Though it was only meant to knock the man off balance, the knight was unable to keep his footing in the mud, lost grip of his weapon, and flailed to the ground. Not waiting for the man to rise, Var came forward and speared the knight in the chest, relying on leverage to pin the knight in place. With expert hands Var pinched the man's windpipe.

"If you cry out, Lord Knight, I will slit your throat and bury you in the Devoid," Var hissed. When he felt the knight's form go limp he continued, "Now, there are a few questions I need to ask. If you are the one I seek, then you may yet survive this." Var knew the knight was about to pass out from lack of oxygen, so he let go, placing his dagger under the man's chin.

The knight sputtered and coughed. "How dare you?"

"Now, now, my lord, don't make me kill you before this has even started."

"Who are you? And what do you want?" the knight wheezed.

"That is better," Var said. "I was told that there is a man who thinks that certain messages should never reach our fair capitol. Does anyone in your knightly retinue resemble that man?"

The knight relaxed. "You must be the stinking assassin the Master warned me about. It is about time you contacted me!"

Var raised his dagger and struck the man in the face, causing blood to flow. "The next time you insult me, Lord Knight, I will slice out your tongue. And I was serious about burying you in the Devoid. Now, are you such a man?"

The knight did not answer. His body tensed as he dealt with his bleeding nose. After several minutes of silence and the occasional cough, the man answered. "I am the one you seek! Now get off me so we can discuss how to kill Arawnn of Almassia!"

Var relaxed his blade but did not let the man up, deciding that it was not smart to let such a traitorous bastard see his face. For the next twenty minutes the pair discussed their plan.

13

DARKNESS.

Its thick tendrils suffocated Areck as he glided through the nothingness. There was no sound other than that of the soft whir of air rushing past him. The cold of nonexistence chilled his body to numbness. He was insubstantial in this place, a shade in the boundless realities that bordered the chaos through which he fell. Pandemonium tore at his mind, bringing thoughts of true destruction and the caress of oblivion.

The thought that he no longer existed stimulated an emotion of loss, creating a remembrance of life. It also stirred intervals of memories, those of service and love.

If I can think, I must exist. The thought exploded in his mind. The laws of reality were trying to annul his existence. *I am not obliterated!* He realized that this place was a creation of his subconscious: a place of chaos, but still a tool of order and creation.

Light ripped through the darkness as a single massive eye formed. Life sprang into being. Worlds appeared from the nothingness and the eye receded into non-existence. Somewhere deep in his mind, Areck concluded that the eye was a metaphor—one that wished to be understood. However, his mind could only register a moment amongst true reality before it blinked and became another possibility.

Unable to truly comprehend what he saw, Areck reached for a dissipating fragment of probability. The touch sent shockwaves coursing through all things that were and whisked him to a branch of reality of things that could not be changed. The past opened up and he saw things that would be. History sped by and worlds died, only to be reborn in the massive eye's embrace. Areck saw people being burned by the millions. There was war and death. There was love. These things all circled around into life.

The vastness of it all was too much for his mind to handle. He panicked and began to scream, his voice dismantled by time as soon as it spoke. Areck grabbed on to a single shining vision beckoning him into a reality that *was*. As he clung to that reality, the fragmentation of his mind slowed and a man-sized portal, crackling with blue light, coalescing in front of him.

He was compelled to enter and see what the past held; it beckoned him, its rippling surface offering unlimited possibilities. He had the feeling that to cross over would give him immense power, the ability to run through time.

Areck steeled his resolve. He was letting his imagination wander, and it offered him strange ideas. Fate was calling him to this place for a purpose. It told him that, as he passed through the swirling portal, there might be answers to those questions that had none. He had to know. Bracing himself for the worst, Areck stepped through.

There was creation, which was destroyed and reborn. There was madness. There was darkness. The magnitude of it all made Areck loose consciousness for a moment.

Areck looked down to see the tops of a great forest, mountains in the east, and high peaks covered in glacial snow. He recognized the region as the outskirts of Moonwood Forest which spanned most of the Dragonspine Mountains one hundred miles from west to east. As he flew over the ancient redwoods, he realized that he had been there before. If his assessment was correct, he was once again at Stormwind Keep, where tragedy would soon unfold. Starsgalt was testing his faith. This was a puzzle that he must work out in his mind, since vision seemed to be God's choice of communication.

That Starsgalt was giving him assistance made Areck swell with pride! He closed his eyes to pray, but the divine sickness washed over him and he stopped. He looked to the nothingness and smiled, for the sickness meant he was in a version of his reality.

As Areck crested the mountains, he noticed a ghostly form of light hovering on the summit, overlooking the keep. The phantom had no features but was unmistakably a dragon, one of immeasurable size. Although Areck could feel its wraithlike head snake towards him and follow his position down into the valley, it did not move.

He found it odd that another being had been drawn into this vision but did not question God's logic, as dragons were a lesser servant of the One True God. They collected information and were not for the most part aggressive. Areck looked once more to the phantom dragon before turning his concentration back towards Stormwind.

He found himself in a vaguely familiar scene. He stood upon a road still wet with morning dew. The last vestiges of fog clung to the sides of the valley, which he recognized as Three Sentinel Pass. He smelled the brisk morning air clinging to the sparse vegetation that lined either side of the roadway as morning larks chirruped in the distance. He hardly felt a slight breeze whip around a bend in the road, which seemed to veered off into mountainside.

As he approached the bend, the clash of metal rang off the sides of the canyon. Areck heard shouting and was greeted with the metallic scent of blood. His form sped around the bend to a scene of carnage; three men lay at odd angles, bones protruding in several places. Areck could not discern any facial features but relied on their knightly armor to distinguish their identity: Bre'Dmorians.

Dread washed over him as he knelt to inspect the ground for details. Seeing none of relevance, Areck moved over towards the bodies and looked down at one of the broken men. He was no expert in the sciences but though the man had been killed by a slender blade through the collarbone, possibly ambushed from behind. When he switched subjects, Areck noticed that other knights had similar wounds, except that their cuts seemed surgical, hinting at a fierce battle.

With trembling hands Areck reached down to feel the cuts, deciding that it was time to research the oddity. As he touched a body, all three disappeared in a bright flash of light. Confused, he spun around.

Not far away, a twisted warhorse materialized, limbs at odd angles. When he walked over to the beast he discovered another dead body, one he recognized, with a crossbow bolt protruding from its neck.

This is my friend, he thought. He had seen something like this event before . . . with a different outcome. Arawnn had been killed by a dishonorable knightly assassin!

This is why I have been brought here, he thought, *to see who the killer is!*

Areck slowly made his way over to the broken mount and knelt down to examine the missing foreleg of the charger, which had thrown its rider. From the distance Arawnn had been thrown, Areck concluded that the courier had circled the battle and charged the treacherous knight. He guessed that the traitor had rolled away after making impact with the mount's knee, severing its leg, which drove the war-horse into the ground.

Not wishing to cause more evidence to disappear, Areck circled the beast and noticed a thick crossbow bolt driven into the steed's flank, bearing bright colors. He frowned at the recognition of nobility.

As Areck moved closer to get a better look at his fallen friend, he noticed a dramatic difference in Arawnn and the rest of the nightmare. The face stared back at him with blank, lifeless eyes and a look of remorse and failure so unlike his friend's smile. He longed for that carefree grin, a look he might never see again.

Areck pushed away from the body and looked up to Heaven, realizing that he had been given an answer, albeit a tragic one. His friend, Arawnn of

Almassia, would die by a traitor's hand from a single deadly blow. This was history as it was *going* to happen, seen through God's infallible eyes; a grievous event that could not be changed.

"There is nothing I can do about it . . ." Areck let the words trail off, the first he had spoken upon the dream plane. He was greeted with eternal silence. "If I cannot save my friend, then I must find the traitor!" he said. "Anyone who dishonors the knighthood deserves God's justice, even if I must kill him myself!" The words of vindication felt good to Areck's soul. He would honor his friend by sending the assassin to Hell.

With a last look at his friend, Areck reached out and closed Arawnn's eyes, sending a bright flash of streaks across his vision, blinding him momentarily. When Areck's sight cleared, the body had not disappeared but was changing. The eyes became eerily familiar, then the hair, and mouth, until a new person lay in front of him with the still-lifeless expression.

The hair on Areck's arms stood as a shiver crawled up his spine.

The empty eyes looking back at him were almost like his own! They *were* his own.

Sound stopped. Movement stopped. Time distorted.

Areck flung himself away from the body, not comprehending this change of the future.

The eyes of his other self moved.

An intense jolt of pain plucked Areck from his slumber and sent him flailing to his right, veering his warhorse directly into the rider next to him. As a Bre'Dmorian, he had been taught to sleep-ride over long distances, his steed capable of following in line. Sleep was usually light and required good weather, as a mount's jostling stride forced a rider to continually stay in touch by using random commands.

The weather had not been good since they had left Aresleigh. Though the sun greeted the company of Bre'Dmorians each morning, by dusk, thick sheets of rain soaked the landscape. This made Areck's punishment unbearable; digging trenches in such whether was nigh impossible, forcing him into several hours of hard labor and little rest each night. To make matters worse, sleep deprivation was getting the best of him and Areck was becoming delusional, unable to suppress his nightmarish dreams.

He had hoped that by sleep-riding during daylight, his mind would be too conscious to attract nightmares yet tired enough that he could eke out some rest. He no longer knew what time it was and his exhaustion was magnified by his surroundings.

Areck tried to focus his thoughts, his tired mind unable to register that he had not compensated for his initial flail, and he was pulling his charger in a 360 degree circle, creating havoc among the riders. When Areck looked back to offer an apology, the entire line of squires was trying to control its mounts as chargers grunted in disapproval and bit those who invaded their space.

Nervously, he gazed towards the three knights who watched silently as the line of squires tried to get their mounts back into marching order.

As Lord Vinion began to shout an order, Lord Silvershield put out his armored hand to hush his fellow knight; Vinion looked displeased. Bowon Silvershield turned away from his angry officer and stroked Legion's mane, allowing the squires to handle their mounts with minimal interference from the knights. The company returned to order, pulling their chargers into a line.

Areck felt the heated expressions of his classmates boring into his back. He knew how silly he had made them all look, though weariness numbed his shame a bit. *This was mild in comparison to the others,* Areck thought of his vision, remembering that the latest vision had unfolded well, until the dream had been taken over by a nightmare. *Maybe it is time for me to seek counsel from those who are more schooled than I . . . Those less engulfed in the situation.*

"What in Starsgalt's glory is happening back here?" Lord Vinion asked, his voice tinged with a northern accent and his mouth drawn into an angry scowl.

Areck looked up in time to see the small party of knights ride forward, heading straight for him. Lord Vinion dismounted and walked directly to the person everyone was gazing at. The man's dark grey eyes burned a hole into his mind. Although Vinion addressed the entire unit, his comments were directed at Areck.

"A company of knights should never break from their column unless so ordered!" Lord Vinion said. "I heard no such order! If you men cannot follow military code, maybe you should all be back washing dishes! Now which one of you is responsible for this mess?"

There was no honor in assisting in another squire's demise and the rest of the riders sat at attention, waiting for Areck to admit what happened. With his chin raised high, Areck stepped forward, ready to accept another punishment. If he hid his actions, he would forever be labeled a coward in the face of confrontation, an unspeakable slight against his honor.

"Squire Areck. I should have known." Lord Vinion said without looking at the young man.

"Lord Vinion, I . . ." Areck stammered, struggling to keep his dignity. "I mean . . . this situation was caused by me. I was attempting to sleep-ride, to better fulfill my duties. I have no explanation other than I have been lacking sleep these past two nights."

Lord Vinion regarded the rest of the company then finally brought his dark eyes to meet Areck's. "There is no explanation," Lord Vinion said.

"Since you find this campaign so boring, I think it is fair to assume that you need more to do."

"I understand, my lord."

"I do not think you do, Squire. If you cannot control your mount, it is time you lost it. From here on out you will jog, setting pace for the entire company." Lord Vinion ignored Areck's attempt at some semblance of honor. "Furthermore, we are two nights' ride from Stormwind and if you cannot meditate on your shortcomings, I will make you walk the entire way!"

The thought of slowing the company horrified Areck. Lord Vinion's penalty was quite harsh given the circumstances, but even Lord Silvershield did not question it but merely called for the retrieval of Areck's mount.

As Areck dismounted, he pulled a water skin from his saddlebag and slung it around his neck. He would not be allowed to remove any armor so decided that rather than trying to keep a fast pace over a short distance, a more moderate pace would allow his company to travel longer into the coming dusk.

When Areck was finished preparing himself, he walked to the front of the column. "Squire, if you so much as mention stopping, by Starsgalt, I will strip you of rank and make you crawl, regardless of the time it takes!" Lord Vinion added, mounting his charger.

Areck lowered his eyes in shame as Lord Silvershield issued the command to move out. With a slight nod, Areck sprang away at an intermediate jog, paced by a cadence in his head. With dusk four hours away, Areck would be able to traverse several miles, at least until his stamina failed.

† † † † †

Although the storm was not far behind, the clouds above the company began to thin. Areck's thoughts turned from sheer embarrassment to worry about the rest of the day. His armor, a combination of chain and leather, weighed less than forty pounds but transferred the sun's heat to his body. The armor did equally well at keeping his own body heat from escaping.

Though Areck was accustomed to wearing his knightly attire outside of battle, it was unnatural for traveling over long distances on foot. The heat of the day began to affect the young squire and sweat poured down his face, dripping off his nose and chin.

Lord Vinion was so determined to make an example of Areck that the knight did not allow the company to halt, even to rest the horses. He figured that if Lord Silvershield would not reprimand Areck for his disobedience then, as second-captain, it was his job to make sure Areck served out a series of suitable punishments. Unfortunately for the rest of the company, the ride would be carried out in utter silence, though their journey was extended by half a day.

Areck's peers had thoughts of their own, though none they could share aloud. Areck felt the weight of their angry and disgruntled stares.

They are wondering why a ninth-year squire who lost himself in the pleasures of the night has been allowed to retain his position within this campaign! Areck thought. *Actually, it is more likely they are wondering why I am still a squire!*

Areck had to admit, he did not understand why Lord Silvershield had allowed him to remain the senior squire, a junior officer.

The warmth of the waning evening soon snatched every last drop of Areck's energy. His vision blurred and the road became surreal. Areck was so distracted by the circumstances that he did not notice a divot in the road.

He fell forward, hurtling off the road into slick mud. He could only lay there, out of breath, prostrate in front of his company.

Lord Silvershield called for the men to halt while Lord Vinion rode to Areck's side.

"Get up," Lord Vinion said.

Areck's fall knocked the wind out of him. He tried to breathe, wanting to muster enough energy to push his body from the ground. Traveling by foot was one thing, but falling in mud after running for two hours in forty pounds of armor was something else. With shaking hands Areck tried to push himself up, but Lord Vinion maneuvered his horse to splash a puddle of water into the squire's face. Areck breathed in the muck and choked.

Areck's hand slid away and he landed on his chest with another thud, making his cough worse. He attempted to roll onto his back, forcing his shoulder underneath his body and swiftly jerking one leg over the other. His face and armor were barely recognizable beneath a thick layer of mud.

"I said stand *up*, Squire!" Lord Vinion said. "That means get your lazy carcass off the ground. Let's go, Areck, we have little time to waste!"

Areck continued to cough, attempting to sit up. Seeing that Areck was struggling with his breath, Lord Vinion led his horse in tight circles around the squire.

"If I must dismount, Squire, your penalty will get worse!"

The splashes from the horse kept Areck coughing as he placed one leg underneath himself, then the other, and finally stumbled upright, the weight of his upper body carefully balanced by an elbow on each knee. After a moment he stood straight though his breathing was still uncontrolled.

Areck glanced at his company: up at Lord Vinion, over to Lord Silvershield, back at his fellow squires, then down at the ground. He knew Lord Vinion was ready to get the group back on track, his desire having nothing to do with wasting time and everything to do with making Areck suffer for his waywardness. A quick prayer to Starsgalt lent Areck strength to go on, allowing him to ignore his aching, exhausted body.

As Lord Vinion began to instruct the company to proceed, Areck stumbled past him and again prepared to lead the group. However, Lord Silvershield stepped his horse forward, interrupting the knight mid-order.

"Give the boy a few moments, Galwen," Lord Silvershield boomed, and the knight stiffened with anger. "Whether you think his actions merit such punishment, you are *not* the commanding officer of this company! Now get back in line, you have done enough." Lord Silvershield paused. "Areck, we still have an hour before dusk. When you are ready, let's get going."

Lord Vinion turned red and looked furiously down at Areck. Compressing his mouth into an angry scowl, the knight grunted under his breath, shook his head, and moved back into position. Being overruled did not sit well with him.

† † † † †

As the sun began its final descent behind the Dragonspine Mountains, Lord Silvershield called for Areck to halt. A clearing to the north of the road, still wet from the previous night's rain, bore signs of a recent encampment; it seemed a favored spot among travelers.

"We will camp here tonight," Silvershield said. "Lord Vinion, please find us solid ground so the squires can set up our tents."

When the men had unpacked their gear for the evening, Areck took advantage of the clear skies by attending to his nightly duty of digging. The ground was still slick, so it took him two hours to finish the task. The weather remained in his favor, and Areck gave deep sigh and looked towards Heaven, again giving thanks to Starsgalt. He found his punishment easier to appreciate when pouring rain wasn't turning everything into mud. He closed his eyes and breathed the evening air.

From across the clearing Lord Vinion glared at the squire. Areck knew that the knight thought his punishment was still insufficient in the eyes of God and that forcing the squire to lead the company down miles of unpaved road still wasn't enough.

Lord Vinion fixed his gaze on Areck and halted the first squire his outstretched arm contacted. He leaned close, whispering something into the young man's ear.

Areck felt the hair on the back of his neck raise. He pursed his lips and locked eyes with Lord Galwen Vinion. The knight released his squire upon seeing Areck's gaze and pushed the young man towards Arawnn. Shaking his head, Areck followed the squire's path, watching closely as Arawnn argued with the young man before obeying Lord Vinion's orders.

Arawnn hurried towards Areck. When Arawnn saw Areck's "flight before fight" expression, the courier's frown turned into a forced smile. He chuckled when Areck grabbed his pick and started to dig ungracefully. He would have to tell his unlucky friend not to look so obvious when he'd been caught eavesdropping. He walked over to Areck.

"It seems that by order of the mighty Galwen Vinion, we are to gather wood for the campfires," Arawnn said scornfully.

Areck nodded, pulling himself out of the latrine. Lord Silvershield was nowhere in sight. Areck shifted his eyes towards the forest, indicating to Arawnn that he was ready to get started.

The trees were beautiful as the last rays of sun shone from behind them like a focused flame. The usually subtle auburn shades were bright and brilliant. The pair made their way through a lush outer ring of foliage, thick with thorns and unripe berries that protected the small clearing. A couple of feet past the underbrush, the forest opened up into a lush and healthy scene. The trees were spaced as if someone had planted them in meticulous rows.

Areck glanced about and saw plenty of twigs but nothing large enough to sustain a campfire. He wandered deeper into the forest, trying to find anything larger than brushwood. Looking back at the camp, he knew there were still other tasks to complete.

"We need to hurry, Arawnn. The company will be expecting a fire soon," Areck announced. "Plus, I still must complete the rest of my duties before sundown."

"Should we split up?" Arawnn asked.

"No, that will only take more time . . . especially if one of us gets lost," Areck replied. "Let's move deeper into the forest. It seems whoever else has made camp here has already picked the ground clean."

Arawnn nodded. "I noticed a deer trail to the east, shall we start there?" Arawnn pointed towards a group of trees on the edge of the campsite, illuminated in such a way that it distinguished a deer trail leading deeper in to the forest.

The pair made their way over to the trail. Areck hoped that no one had noticed the trail, allowing him to quickly find some larger, drier pieces of wood. He glanced back in the direction of the company, attempting to keep his bearings, although thick underbrush blocked his view. He would simply have to rely on Arawnn to find their way back to camp.

A shining object caught Areck's attention. Squinting, he decided to research the still-shimmering oddity.

"Hold, Arawnn, I see something over there," Areck called to his comrade, pointing to his right. When Arawnn stopped, Areck moved off the path and begin to search the forest floor and failed to notice a fast approaching branch.

Thwap!

A sharp sting shot through Areck's chest. He staggered backwards and fell to his knees. A sharp pain stung his kneecap and he jumped up, hopping around, trying to keep his balance. Doing his best to remain composed, Areck ran his hand upward from shin to thigh, trying to find source of the pain, and grasped a small metal object lodged in the joint of his armor.

Areck pulled a thick pin from his knee joint and inspected the object in his hand. It was a medallion in the form of a shield, with three golden stripes crisscrossing into a long braid which ended in a long thin spike used to pierce armor.

"Do you recognize this?" Areck asked, raising the medallion for Arawnn to see.

"Though I am not fluent in all noble insignias, I believe that is the crest of the Thewlis Family of Brenly," Arawnn said, indifferent to the fact that it had been found so deep in the woods. "May I see that?"

"Of course," Areck said, handing the metallic pin to his friend. "What do you suppose a coat-of-arms medallion is doing out in the middle of the forest?

Arawnn shrugged his shoulders and studied the item. "This does not belong to an important family," he announced. "You see how there are only two colors? That denotes the rank of a family—the more colorful the badge, the more powerful the family."

Areck was hardly paying attention. This item belonged to a noble from within his hometown of Brenly, how could he *not* recognize such a thing? He wondered why it would be out here. He knew no noble would be gathering firewood, nor would they be hunting so close to the road.

". . . probably means whoever this belonged to was out here hunting," Arawnn finished.

Areck pursed his lips in thought and thanked Arawnn for his information. He retrieved the coat-of-arms, opened a pouch, and pocketed the emblem. Still disoriented, Areck realized how stupid he had looked; raising his eyebrow at the offending branch, he readied to cut his own firewood.

As Areck readied to strike the blow, he noticed a dark shadow lying beneath a thick fern. His heart began to race and he recognized the figure as that of a man. Turning to Arawnn, Areck pointed to the body and slunk forward, holding a hand out for his comrade to stay put. Kneeling to check the man for any sign of life, Areck understood why the pendant had been so deep in the forest: The motionless form was a dead body.

Areck could only imagine what this man had been thinking when a knife was slid across his throat. The ground where the fallen noble lay was covered with the deep-brown stain of blood, his once-blond hair matted and dark.

Did he have a chance to fight back? Areck closed his eyes for a moment and turned his face away. *Did he yell for help?*

Arawnn ignored Areck's gesture and approached the body, moving around his friend to get a better angle, he caught a glimpse of another body hanging in a tree. The fact that it was not more than five paces away sent him stumbling into Areck.

As Areck climbed out from underneath the courier, he saw the second corpse. He walked to where Arawnn pointed. Nausea swept over him and bile formed in the back of his throat. This corpse, another noble of Brenly, had suffered wounds far greater than his comrade. The noble's body was bent backwards over a large branch, skin peeled from the torso. Blood had dried in thick streaks down the man's extremities, pooling around a protruding root to which the body was nailed.

Areck had never seen anything like it before. From the look of his comrade, Arawnn had not either. As Areck tried to move away, Arawnn dry heaved uncontrollably.

Pale as lambs, the two men made their way back to their commander. Thorns tore at their faces as they struggled through the thick layer of brambles that surrounded the campsite. Areck paid little attention to the blood that streaked down his arms and legs as he exploded into the clearing shouting. His vision became red with blood as he crawled onto the trampled grass.

Wiping his eyes and forehead, Areck noticed that he was surrounded by several men with Arawnn prostrate at his side.

"Are you lads alright?" a familiar voice asked. "What happened?"

Lord Silvershield knelt next to Areck handed him a dry cloth. Another squire helped Arawnn to his feet, wiping blood from the courier's face.

"Here you are, lad, wipe the blood out of your eyes and tell me what happened," Lord Silvershield's voice was calm but alarmed. He had rarely seen Areck so distraught. Placing a hand on Areck's shoulder, Lord Silvershield steadied his squire, giving the young man a moment to compose himself.

"Focus, Areck; we need to know what you saw out there," Lord Silvershield said. When Areck was calm enough to talk, Bowon asked again, "Now, what did you see?"

"Nobles . . . dead," Areck gasped, "blood . . . everywhere." Areck sat back on his knees and reached into his pocket, pulling out the medallion. He held it out to his commander, long enough for Lord Silvershield to grasp the coat-of-arms. Areck's arm dropped to the ground in exhaustion. Tears formed in his eyes as he spoke. "We found two nobles of Brenly, my lord, both dead. One was . . . was . . . peeled like an onion and staked to a tree."

Lord Silvershield straightened and looked to the other men for confirmation that he had heard Areck's words correctly. A murder so far from the town of Brenly, especially involving their nobility, meant that the political fiasco was already beginning. It was paramount to discover what evidence he could.

"Areck, can you tell us where we can find the bodies? We will need to scout the area for anything that can lead us to the murderers," Lord Silvershield asked. When Areck pointed a trembling finger in the direction of the trampled vines, the knight-captain continued, "Get back to camp and get yourself clean, I will have food brought to your tent, where we can discuss this further."

Areck nodded and staggered off.

Lords Silvershield and Malketh and two squires followed Areck's directions to collect the bodies and wrapped them gingerly in capes. Two other squires were sent to collect wood for the fires, and Arawnn was taken to his tent by another.

Areck retreated to his tent while the others finished their duties. He felt a bit responsible for having caused such a commotion and waylaying the company's evening meal. As he sat down to collect his thoughts, exhaustion washed over him, causing Areck to rest his eyes.

Areck closed his eyes and fell into a dreamless sleep.

The next morning, Lord Silvershield made his way to Areck's tent with a bowl of breakfast: crushed wheat and bits of dried fruit from the Bre'Dmorian orchards. As he entered the room and saw Areck sleeping, the knight-captain lightly tapped the young man's exposed feet to awaken the slumbering squire. His first attempt was unsuccessful but his second knocked him backwards as Areck flailed and jerked his way to a sitting position. Chuckling, a calm but forced smile spread across the knight's face.

"Here you go, lad, eat this," Bowon said, offering the thick porridge to Areck. "You're doing all right after last night?"

Areck gulped the food and looked up. "It is not something I wish to remember, my lord," he said. "Were you able to deduce the culprit?"

"We found few clues, lad. That is why I am bothering you this dawn; I have several questions I need to ask."

"Of course, my lord," Areck said. "How can I be of assistance?"

For fifteen minutes Lord Silvershield questioned Areck about the circumstances behind finding the bodies. Areck retold his tale verbatim, recounting the branch, stumbling onto the pin, and finally discovering the corpses.

Lord Silvershield listened intently to the tale. When Areck finished, the commander offered to take his bowl. "It is as I figured. This looks to be the work of scheming nobility who thought by dropping the bodies so far out, no one would stumble upon them." Bowon hesitated then patted Areck on the shoulder. As he left the tent he added, "Hurry up and get ready, squire. I have some instructions to impart to the company before we get under-way."

Areck paused as Lord Silvershield stepped away. Just before the commander exited the tent, Areck said, "My lord, may I request your council regarding a matter that has been lying heavy upon my mind?"

"I would be honored, Squire Areck. Please seek me when you are packed and ready." Lord Silvershield exited the tent.

† † † † †

Areck sat in silence, trying to forget the details of the past night's discovery. Reaching for his armor, he retraced the events in his mind and shivered.

I need to forget such morbid thoughts, Areck thought, remembering why he sought his commander's advice: another nightmarish vision. He hoped that the knight-captain, for whom he had great respect, could guide him to un-derstanding.

Areck strapped on his armor. He packed up his things, broke down his tent, and placed everything onto his horse. Rubbing sleep from his eyes, he looked around the barren campsite and noticed something was out of place. Though all eight of his squires were mounted, one was out of formation, carrying a litter which contained the bodies while the rest awaited orders.

The three knight-captains stood near the edge of the road and Areck approached them with hesitation. It appeared that his commanders were discussing how they should handle the day. Lord Silvershield turned and called for three squires.

"You may leave for Brenly," he commanded, pointing at the man carry-ing the bodies. "When you arrive, hand the bodies over to their respective houses and wait for the rest of us to arrive." The squire saluted his com-mander and turned onto the road, towards the noblemen's hometown.

Lord Silvershield turned to Areck, who had stopped outside the knightly circle. He was about to speak when he was cut off by Lord Vinion, who was disgusted that Areck was allowed to sleep for so long.

"Squire, why is it that you are the last to be ready, yet again?" Lord Vin-ion snarled. "I trust you got enough rest to control your horse today?"

Areck reddened with shame, trying his best to ignore Lord Galwen Vin-ion's statement. "My lord, if I could speak to you now . . .?" Areck tried to focus on why he was there.

"Of course, Areck; what is the reason you seek my council this morn-ing?" Lord Silvershield asked. Lord Galwen paled at the insult.

"My lords, I feel that I need guidance for a vision from Starsgalt. It is becoming increasingly sinister, and I am confused about the meaning." Though the other squires were several yards away, Areck spoke softly.

All three knights became serious.

"Go on, Areck," Lord Silvershield said.

"Well, my lords, I feel that something terrible is about to happen," Areck said. "My vision has revealed a traitor among the knighthood, one who will murder Messenger Arawnn. Starsgalt never allows me to see the traitor's face. I am unsure what to do, my lords."

"How do you know it is one of the knighthood, Squire?" inquired Lord Stephen Malketh, whom Areck had heard speak only twice on the entire campaign.

"He wore Bre'Dmorian armor, Lord Malketh," Areck said. "Though I cannot be positive, the man was also carrying a knightly weapon. This has led me to believe that the assassin is a knight."

Areck saw concerned interest cross each of his commanders' faces. "If you could not see any faces, what makes you so sure that Arawnn is the person to be murdered?" Stephen asked.

"I am sorry, Lord Malketh; I misrepresented my information. In fact, Arawnn's face is the *only* discernable visage I can make out," Areck said and explained each nightmare in detail. Lord Silvershield pursed his lips in thought.

"Do you have any idea of the location?" Lord Silvershield asked, breaking the silence that hung over the group.

"Though this is just my best guess, Lord Silvershield, the murder will happen sometime during our visit to Stormwind. However, as you well know, I do not know the region well enough to give you a proper location." Areck looked into the eyes of each knight, searching for clarity. Seeing varied reactions, he explained exactly where each hallucination took him. He finished by telling them that each vision ended with the body turning into himself.

"My lords, I am unsure what to do concerning this information. Can you offer me council?" Areck asked. All knights had visions and interpreted them in their own way.

The first to speak was Lord Malketh. "I, for one, do not believe in taking chances. Although his recent actions wreak insubordination, we cannot judge a carrier of Starsgalt's visions. I have to believe that the boy is telling the truth." He spoke with confidence to Lord Silvershield, who nodded. "The intensity of these visions may indicate that these events may unfold while we are on this mission."

"What's to say that Squire Areck has not conjured up the entire story in order to return to the good graces of the knighthood?" Lord Vinion spoke to his commanding officer but gazed at the squire in front of him.

At this point in the mission, there was little Areck could do to change Lord Vinion's opinion of him. He had never worked closely with the knight and was unfamiliar with the knight's temperament. Dealing with Lord Vinion on this unfortunate occasion had increased Areck's appreciation of his relationship with Lord Silvershield.

His commander responded, directing his comments at Lord Vinion. "Areck is not one to fashion extravagant stories, Lord Vinion. It is my opinion that Starsgalt has chosen to use our young squire here as a tool to give warning that there may be trouble brewing." Lord Silvershield's words came as a surprise to the other knights.

"My lord, since we are in agreement, it might be a good idea to allow two squires to accompany me ahead of the group," Lord Malketh said, suggesting that precautionary measures be taken. "Three of us traveling ahead will not draw undue attention to the company. The goal will be to cause less commotion than a full formation, scout any danger that may hinder the completion of our objective, and if we find anything, send word. As far as I am concerned, the courier's safe arrival at Stormwind Keep is still the priority."

"I am well aware of our priorities, Lord Malketh," Bowon responded. "I do not feel that it is wise for anyone to ride ahead, as it will only weaken our defenses. Our best option will be to ride together and keep a sharp eye out for anything unusual." Areck knew an order when he heard one, but it appeared that Lord Malketh had other ideas.

"It is a matter of honor, Knight-Captain," Malketh stiffened. "So far, we have traveled slowly and done nothing to ensure the safety of our charge. This will set my mind at ease."

Lord Malketh stood, head held high, awaiting approval from the commander. Moments passed without a word. Areck looked over at Knight-Captain Silvershield, trying to discern his thoughts.

"I expect a full report when we arrive at Stormwind, Lord Malketh," the knight-captain finally spoke. "Take your two squires and ride ahead. Alert me immediately if anything suspicious in nature comes up, and I will slow our canter so you may have time to investigate."

Lord Silvershield heaved himself up onto his horse, motioning Areck and Lord Vinion to do the same. Lord Malketh followed suit, riding towards the seven mounted squires, who saluted him.

Areck watched Lord Malketh choose his pair of squires, issue commands, and gallop down the road, ahead of the company.

The company, now consisting of six squires, two knights, and Arawnn, began a slow canter down the road. The collective heartbeat of the group amplified as each of them became alert to potential danger.

They rode in complete silence.

† † † †

Var had followed the Bre'Dmorians closely since his contact with the contact knight. He used the shadows to plod along, observing each armored man's weaknesses. It was common for an assassin to stalk his mark. However, Var had not let the party out of his sight for more than an hour, sometimes riding ahead or falling behind, always sure that killing the courier was within his ability.

Though Var had made contact on the eve of the first night and learned that the company consisted primarily of squires, he did not feel comfortable. Something about the traitorous knight's instructions just didn't feel right. He used the coastal storm as camouflage, sneaking in and out of the Bre'Dmorian's camp until he was satisfied that his accomplice would not betray him.

He was about to leave when something happened. One of the squires, a tall young man with ice blue eyes, had entered the camp with frantic news. It had sent the entire camp into a fast paced frenzy.

Var watched the company roar into action, seeking the source of the squire's paranoia. It turned out that the boy had stumbled upon dead bodies—a pair of noblemen had been murdered. Not for the first time, Var wondered why such a thing even mattered.

It is not like a knight has never seen a dead body before, he mused, following several men into the forest. It wasn't until the commanding knight sent his men back to the camp to fetch a litter that Var stepped out of his hiding and bent down. As he poked one of the mangled corpses, he noticed something interesting: the body had a small mark cut into its face.

Must be the mark of a killer, Var thought. With a curious look, he walked towards the next body, which also bore the mark.

Pursing his lips, Var studied the murder site for several minutes. He was so engrossed with the odd mark that he did not hear the soft footsteps approach him from behind. Var felt a stinging pain cut into his back and a rough hand cover his mouth. Var stiffened, struggling for his weapons.

"Shh, assassin, do not move or I will kill you," the voice of his accomplice whispered into his ear and pushed him deeper into the forest.

As they moved Var relaxed. When he felt the knight loosen his grip, Var grabbed the man's thumb and deftly sidestepped. The result was that the knight flipped over and the assassin took control of the situation.

"What in the name of hell's demons are you grabbing me for?" Var whispered, wrenching the knight's thumb.

"Let go of me, fiend!" the knight said. "I was making sure that if anyone saw me approach you it would not look conspicuous."

"Tell the truth." Var pushed the knight away. "You were trying to pay me back for our late night encounters—you wanted to prove a point."

The knight stood straight but did not reach for his weapon. Instead, the man dropped his gaze and turned red in shame. Var could tell that his assessment was right and took a moment to remind the holy bastard that as an assassin, Var could kill his accomplice at any time.

When he was satisfied, Var turned his attention to inquiring the reason the knight was here.

As it turned out, the knight had been waiting for him to talk about one of the squires who slowed the party down repeatedly.

"Damn it!" Var spat. "This job is getting more complicated by the moment. Does this squire have a name? Just kill him, so we have no more problems to deal with."

"His name is Areck of Brenly, but I do not see him as a threat. In fact, I think I can turn this to our advantage," the knight said.

"How?"

"Leave that to me," the knight said and detailed his idea.

"Isn't that risky? What if your commander doesn't think that wise?" Var asked.

"Once again, allow me to handle that."

Var shrugged. "I will trust you then, sir," he said and moved into the forest. Looking over his shoulder he added, "I will meet you at Stormwind in two nights."

With that Var Surestrike was gone.

14

IT WAS mid-afternoon on the fifth day when the last of the clouds dissipated. The coastal storm that had followed the company a hundred miles inland finally burned itself out at the base of the Dragonspine Mountains. The fresh scent of eastern pines wafted down the steep slopes. Because the surrounding area had become calm, birds chirped happily and hopped from tree to tree, watching the riders make their way down King's Road.

Since entering Moonwood Forest the prior morning, the company had passed several merchant caravans heading west. It was common to see a surplus of traders entering the duchy, seeking the rare imports that came through Aresleigh's grand ports. This time, however, the dour faces on the riders kept the vocal merchants to a quick greeting before moving on their way.

As Areck rode behind the pair of knights, he regarded the paved road with interest. In his history classes, he had learned that one of the major advantages Arsgoth had over other kingdoms was the discovery of paved roadways. Furthermore, during his sixth year at the Academy he had been given the opportunity to watch several teams of prisoners construct such a road, an extension of the road running from Aresleigh to the small southern township of Quall. They had followed the precise instructions of mathematicians and engineers, who had first calculated the amount of material required on such a project before letting the laborers move in. Areck vividly remembered the prisoners slaving away with picks, digging down six to eight inches as they created a trench approximately ten feet wide. When the diggers finished, another crew of prisoners hauled in thousands of yards of gravel, pouring enough to fill one half of the small ditch. Finally, the stonemason's guild had dragged in carts laden with rectangular slabs of stone, chiseled smooth to fit together precisely in various patterns. Every fifth stone was left unsealed for runoff, using a mixture of volcanic ash and water to create a paste that, once dried, secured the stones in place.

The art of making roads had been an Arsgothian specialty for nearly two thousand years, since the formation of the kingdom. It allowed armies to march with outstanding speed in times of war and merchants' quick passage during times of peace. It was the epitome of the age, as more kingdoms secured mercantile contracts of Arsgothian artisans and slaves to build stylized roads.

Areck mused at the thought. No other kingdom in the known world could create the longevity or the usefulness of Arsgothian roads. He marveled at the intricacy of the road. He could see the cracks left for expansion created by heat, and crevices left for water runoff. The King's Road was the second-oldest roadway in all of Arsgoth, created seventeen hundred years ago by whichever king wished to access this region.

Seventeen hundred years . . . the thought gave him a spurt of inspiration. This road was almost as old as the kingdom itself. It was built even before the gates of Stormwind were erected in defense of the second ferryll invasion, sixteen hundred years ago. It had seen the burning of Das'Dalmen, an ancient port which fell during the Second War of Ancient Souls, when most of the western shores were destroyed. To be riding on something so old made him wonder if there was magic involved in its making.

"They must be talking about something important," a voice whispered. "Ever since the commander sent Lord Malketh away, Vinion has kept his distance."

The words drew Areck's attention away from the road. He frowned at Arawnn then up at the pair of knights riding side by side, deep in discussion. He knew what they were speaking about and wanted to explain to Arawnn. Yet he did not. If only they—if *he*—could only figure out the true meaning of the vision.

"I am sure they are discussing why we haven't heard back from our scouting party," Areck responded solemnly. He let his gaze linger past the knights towards the massive outline of Stormwind Keep. He saw the three banners of Stormwind fluttering in the afternoon sun: a brilliant red banner with a poised golden lion, a dark navy banner with a sword and staff crossed and a crown encompassing them, and a white banner split by a blue tower shield. The red banner represented Duke Hawkwind, whose family had ruled Aresleigh in service of the King of Arsgoth since its conception. The blue banner displayed the Bre'Dmorian's presence in the region, and the last was that of Baron Marqel, a local lord who had controlled Stormwind before Duke Edelin Hawkwind had taken his uncle's position. Each banner was situated according to power within the region: the Duke's outnumbering the Bre'Dmorians two to one, who then outnumbered the local lord three to one.

Arawnn considered Areck's comment. "Is it uncommon that no one was sent to relay information back to Lord Silvershield?"

"Yes. That Lord Malketh has not reported is a bad sign," Areck said. "In a worse case scenario, he should have at least sent one of the garrison's soldiers."

He had to admit that it was odd no one had made it back to the company. However, his commanders did not seem concerned about the fact, rather discussing privately how they would approach the vision. But the lack of communication from Malketh worried Areck. It was unlike a knight, especially a knight-captain, to be less than meticulous in his duties. To not hear anything indicated possible trouble.

"Does it concern you?" Arawnn asked, trying to follow the array of emotions that played across Areck's face.

"It is unusual," Areck explained cautiously. "But I do not know Lord Malketh's exact orders. It's possible that his orders were to secure the area before any information was sent."

"You were with the commanders when they left," Arawnn pointed out. "Come man, I can see it on your face. What aren't you telling me?"

Areck sighed, disappointed in his inability to hide his thoughts. "I am not withholding any information that is mine to give, Arawnn," Areck said, noting that his friend was saddened at the news. Trying to change the subject, Areck pointed out that the completion of his quest was nearly at hand.

Taking the hint, Arawnn asked about the architecture of Stormwind Keep. Areck took interest in the subject and explained the various aspects of defense. Stormwind guarded the only pass into the region and was fortified, protected on each side by steep mountains, thick walls, and dense forest. On the eastern side of the pass, the local inhabitants had hired dwarves to extend the wall several hundred feet past the gatehouses, creating a killing field should the keep be attacked from the Aresleighan side. The keep itself was built in tiers, expanding partially into the mountain. Its high towers looked down into the pass and controlled all trade coming in and out of the duchy. In times of military action, Stormwind Keep acted as a focal point of the western armies, with the capacity to garrison nearly three thousand soldiers.

As Areck looked over at his comrade, who looked impressed with the knowledge the young squire had of the military outpost, he smiled in a knowing fashion. It felt good to impress his friend, even with half truths, which was why he was loathe to tell Arawnn that he had never set foot inside Stormwind Keep.

He felt like he knew the place like the back of his hand, though all of his information came directly from his studies, which had progressed through various stages of strategic implications and history.

"When I passed through on the way to Aresleigh, I found it very ominous," Arawnn agreed. "I can't imagine it ever falling under invasion."

"It never has," Areck said. "It was built after the third war, when the ferryll came out of the Great Devoid and sacked much of the old world. It was constructed to keep the western part of the kingdom safe, should it ever be surprised again." He also explained that he was fortunate enough to have seen its layout on several occasions, as Lord Silvershield carried around basic blue prints.

"Have there been many invading forces?"

"It hasn't been used as a military bastion in over six centuries," Areck explained. "During that time the Bre'Dmorians controlled the pass to better protect the duchy. Now it's mainly used as a trading center."

Areck became thoughtful. He had not considered that this information might be against protocol. It was not usual for people to talk of military matters or the history of his society. He knew it was frowned upon to release any information that the knighthood did not deem necessary. His look brought a cheerful grin to Arawnn's face.

"Let me guess: you said something you weren't supposed to?" Arawnn chuckled.

"Protocol," Areck answered with a tight smile. "You have seen how my lack of concentration has gotten me into . . . situations."

Arawnn raised his hands in mock surprise, "I don't suppose they give you a list of proper conversations, eh?" Arawnn whispered through the side of his mouth. "Next time let me know what questions I can and cannot ask."

The comment struck Areck as humorous. He gave Arawnn a wide smile and nodded ahead, to where the pair of knights had turned their horses and were waiting for the squires to catch up. Lord Vinion, per his normal demeanor, stared at the pair with disdain.

"Does that man ever keep his eyes to himself?" Arawnn asked.

"If we don't hurry this line up, I think I will be subjected to more than being looked at," Areck said, noticing that Lord Vinion's dark look was meant for him. Since the day Areck had left Aresleigh, the second-captain had not taken his eyes off of him.

I guess I cannot complain, Areck thought. *I deserve this—and at least I am no longer running.*

Due to the haste now required, Lord Galwen Vinion had returned Areck's steed However, the knight-captain had warned him that if he made a single misstep, regardless of Knight-Captain Silvershield's protection, he would be demoted back to squire for the course of the campaign.

For another hour the Bre'Dmorians traveled in silence, passing several long caravans before coming in full sight of the gates of Stormwind.

Lord Silvershield raised his hand for a halt, signaling that the column would take a quick rest before they entered a large clearing that marked the border of the keep. Several squires dismounted, pulled water skins from their bags, and broke into small groups, talking excitedly.

Areck could not help but marvel at the sight. The shadow of the mountains gave the wall an impregnable look. Coming from a walled city such as Aresleigh with battlements every few hundred feet, he decided that Stormwind's walls lacked length. However, the walls were built into the mountain itself, stretching forty feet from ground to crest. Bordering each side, in tiered magnificence, were two impressive circular battlements, no longer manned by trained archers but awe-inspiring nonetheless.

Areck gazed sideways to see Arawnn chewing on some dried meat, his head tilted, studying the guards standing duty on the walls. Areck smiled. It was good to see the carefree young courier take such a military achievement seriously. The thought made him realize that his time with his friend was almost at an end, that they would soon need to go their separate ways.

What if I am making a mistake by not telling him my vision? Areck thought, remembering each night's vision had come and gone with the same conclusion. His friend would be killed at the hands of a Bre'Dmorian, and when Areck reached for him, the dead body became his own, opened its eyes, and stood up.

These are not visions, he corrected himself. *They are nightmares.* The consultation with his commanding officers had eased his doubts somewhat. They had told him not to reveal the vision to one who could not understand. Without comprehension, one such as Arawnn could cause all manner of complications in time and history by trying to hide. Yet he felt guilty.

Areck had never truly been accepted among the other squires, being common-born and an orphan at that, yet here was a man who befriended him regardless. This man had sacrificed on his behalf and accepted him as he was, and Areck was grateful for his companionship.

And now he was going to let his friend die—without ever giving him the chance to choose. Areck considered the words. How could he live with himself if he didn't say anything? How could he live with the guilt?

Areck tried to convince himself there was no other way, that there was nothing he could do. He told himself that Arawnn's best chance of survival was by telling his superiors, which he had done. He even told himself that Lord Silvershield could handle the situation . . . and that everything would be all right. And still, the guilt persisted.

Areck was jolted out of his thoughts by Knight-Captain Silvershield's command to mount up. Once everyone had mounted their horses, Lord Silvershield gave orders to move back into a riding column. He waited for the commander to position himself at the front of the line, move his hand forward, and issue the order to march.

By all accounts Stormwind Keep was the perfect military staging point. On either side of the mountain pass it protected, the surrounding forest had been clear cut so that it was barren of all plants, trees, and wildlife. If an army marched against Stormwind, it would need to cross a death zone of over three hundred yards in any direction.

It meant that guards could see anyone as soon as they cleared the last shadows of the forest. Areck wondered why the builders had taken such great care on this side of Aresleigh. It was not like the rest of the kingdom needed to be protected from the duchy. Had the dwarves who designed the place ever considered that to all appearances it looked like they were trying to keep the people of the duchy *in*? The thought made him smile. He had only seen rough drawings of the other side. If the builders had taken such care on the fortified side, he wondered what they had done on the opposite.

It did not take long for the small company of Bre'Dmorians to cross the clearing and approach two thick wooden doors. Although the activity of such a gate was nowhere near as concentrated as that of his old position as second customs officer back in Aresleigh, Areck saw several soldiers talking with merchants, looking through materials, and passing over documents. One of the merchants seemed particularly displeased with the usual process of entry, most likely due to the fact that he had never passed this far west before. After a long debate, the merchant threw up his hands in defeat and unloaded several large barrels from his cart.

Areck could see Arawnn had followed his gaze and was grinning.

No wonder the merchant looks so disgusted, Areck thought noticing that the barrels looked a lot like kegs. The man had planned to take the alcohol to the port city of Aresleigh and traffic his goods in trade or sales. However, it looked like the guards had told the man they would either confiscate a large portion of the ale or he could sell it to them at a price far lower than the one he would get in the huge city. The merchant did not really have much of a choice. He was not from the region, and although Baron Marqel was known as a fair man, he would not side with a merchant when a fair price had been offered.

"Lord Silvershield!' A voice cut through the afternoon bustle. "It has been many years since I have seen your face."

"Thomas, lad, I see you are still employed by the baron," the commander chuckled with happiness.

Areck watched as a middle-aged man with grey eyes, salted brown hair, and dressed in sturdy woolen garments overlaid by several pieces of leather walked out of the gate and up to the giant stallion that Lord Bowon so prized.

"I see Legion is still with you," Thomas pointed out, rubbing the horse's muzzle and getting a contented grunt in return. When Thomas was satisfied with Legion's approval, he turned to the knight-captain. "You mean I haven't run the baron through yet?" Thomas continued, bringing a dark scowl from Lord Vinion, whom he ignored.

The comment caused the commander to chuckle. "Hah! He should have kept you washing dishes, boy; would have done more to keep that tongue in check."

"Well, if you must know, Lord Marqel has promoted me to Captain of the Guard, so it would not be much use doing away with the one who pays me," Thomas said.

The friendly banter reminded Areck of his own relationship with Arawnn and the cheerfulness the courier brought when he was around.

"If the two of you are *quite* done, my lord," Lord Vinion interjected, "maybe we should ask the captain if he can lead us to our men."

Lord Silvershield scowled at the younger knight but said, "Thomas, we sent scouts to Stormwind nearly two days ago to investigate some unusual circumstances."

The guard captain regarded Lord Bowon and Lord Vinion with confusion and shook his head. "I can't remember seeing a single knight pass through our gates in over a week, my lord."

"Lord Silvershield, this is what I feared!" Knight-Captain Vinion said. "Knight-Captain Malketh must have had trouble!"

"If he did not make it here, he had more than trouble," Bowon said, a range of emotions crossing his face. "Thomas, I trust you, but is there any chance you could be mistaken . . . maybe there was a time when you were not posted?" he asked, raising his hand for silence when Lord Vinion tried to interrupt again.

Thomas explained that during daylight he roamed the entire keep, making sure both gates were opened and the portcullis was raised. Then he would leave the courtyard to go over various activities with Lord Marqel. Throughout the day and until the gates closed at dusk, Thomas made two visits to the gatehouses, checking logs of who had entered and exited the pass. There was a slim chance that a merchant would go unnoticed by the gate's officers, but to miss a knight would be unlikely.

After several more questions Lord Silvershield nodded in grudging acceptance. Lord Vinion's face was red upon being quieted in front of non-commanders but he also looked thoughtful, as though considering the source of information, and the possibility that one of his sub-commanders had been killed.

"Do you have any more questions for the captain, Lord Vinion?" Lord Bowon asked. Galwen shook his head.

"My lord," Thomas began, "when I saw your company marching down the road, I alerted Baron Marqel of your presence. I am sure he will be to willing assist in whatever way he can—a scouting party, or at least a ranger, will be able to track down your missing party."

Lord Silvershield looked over at Lord Vinion, who moved his horse next to Legion and leaned in. The commander's eyes darkened before he nodded his head, grunted in approval, then issued orders to his men before turning to face Areck and the guard captain.

"Courier Arawnn, Lord Vinion, Squire Areck, and I will be attending the Lord Baron," Bowon said to Captain Thomas. "Let me get my men moving, then we will be ready for you to escort us there."

After finishing orders, Lord Silvershield unpacked his gear, handed Legion over to a groom, and beckoned Areck to follow.

Seeing his superiors step through a nearby door, Areck ordered one of the remaining squires to find the barracks captain, make sure that all the men were situated, and that their situation included some *good* hot stew. For the first time since his departure from Aresleigh, a squire smiled at him. Satisfied with his humor, Areck turned and entered the door.

Once inside, Areck heard the voices of Arawnn, Thomas, and Lord Silvershield chuckling ahead. The hallway smelled of ancient dust and stone but was well kept and lit with torches. He guessed that the passage led deep into the mountain and up into the central keep. He further guessed that at one time this tunnel had been a secret passage used during times of war but was now relegated to servants traveling from the lower areas of the keep to the small town.

Areck wound around and up a set of stairs, which ended with a dull stone wall. It seemed a solid mass of immoveable stone but, as he ran his hands over the smooth surface, Areck felt a draft, meaning it opened into a chamber. He heard the muffled voice of Lord Silvershield. It sounded like the commander was getting ready to send Thomas back into the passage in search of him. Areck quickly felt for a small indentation in the stone, which usually held a small lever, and pulled. With a creak the door swung open and several pairs of eyes watched him walked through.

"There you are, lad," Lord Silvershield exclaimed in relief. "Lord Vinion moved ahead while we waited for you. Please try not to get yourself lost, Areck. This place is a maze."

"I apologize, my lord, I will be more careful," Areck said, quite embarrassed that the group had been forced to wait on his behalf.

Lord Silvershield turned back to Thomas and asked about the "old man's" health. This brought a snort of laughter from Thomas and the guard captain opened a second door which led up another set of steep stairs.

After several minutes the small group of men reached the inner chambers of Stormwind, where Lord Galwen Vinion waited impatiently, his face dark with his usual glower. He nodded to Lord Silvershield and Thomas and stepped away from the gilded doors of the baron's personal chambers.

"If you will excuse me, my lords, I must announce you to his lordship," Thomas said.

"Is there no seneschal, Captain?" Galwen asked.

"The duke no longer funds us as he once did, my lord," Thomas met Lord Vinion's frown. "Had the knighthood not abandoned this post so long ago, maybe they could have helped us with more *purposeful* servants."

"How *dare* . . ." Lord Vinion sputtered.

"That will be *enough*, Galwen," Lord Silvershield said, trying to suppress a smile. He addressed the knight informally to emphasize the man's place. Galwen Vinion nodded grimly, accepting the rebuke with ill grace.

"I hate all this formality," Arawnn whispered in Areck's ear. "You would not believe how many times I have had to be introduced to various lords and ladies."

"But you're a noble, aren't you?" Areck replied in mock surprise. "I thought your kind liked being bowed to."

"And I thought *your* kind had no patience for this sort of thing." Arawnn winked.

Areck grinned and looked back to see the door opened by a large, bald man much older then Lord Silvershield. Lord Vinion watched him with burning eyes and as always, with a look of disgust. Areck sighed but understood that there was nothing he could do outside of earning the man's respect. With resignation, he cast his eyes downward to avoid the glare of the officer.

The silence did not last long as the bald man pushed his way past the doors and lumbered in front of Lord Silvershield. Instead of bowing, the man reached out and cuffed the knight-captain with a friendly blow, bellowing like an enraged bear. "It is about time you return to us, lad!"

"You are addressing a knight-captain, sir," Galwen said. It seemed to Areck that every word the officer heard since arriving at the keep infuriated him. "It is not proper—"

The old man cut off the comment with dangerous laughter. He turned his gaze back to Bowon. "This one has got quite a tongue on him, Bowon. Maybe you should find him something to do, if he cannot stay silent while the *lord baron* of a keep is speaking."

Finally, Areck thought, *someone has put Lord Vinion in his place.*

Lord Silvershield had always warned his charges that the outside world was different than that of the Academy. Lord Vinion quivered with rage. However, he was on a thin precipice: if he offended the baron, he would be punished in more ways than even a squire could imagine.

"I meant no offense, my lord," Galwen said, struggling to contain his anger. "It was not my place to speak out of turn."

"That it was not." The baron shrugged, turning away from Galwen and back to Lord Silvershield.

"As I was saying, Bowon, it is good to see you again!" Baron Marqel said. "I had not expected you to return this way since . . . well, since you wandered off ten years ago."

The knight-captain's face assumed a look of distant sadness and longing. "My days of service to God are waning, I am afraid. However, Lord Light-bringer has decided that a commission would serve his needs well. If I may, my lord?" Lord Silvershield paused for the nod that meant he could formally introduce his companions. "This is Second-Captain Galwen Vinion, Under-Lieutenant Areck of Brenly, and Lord Messenger Arawnn of Almassia, a royal courier of our king."

"This one looks about as old as you, when you first came to Stormwind all those years ago," the baron smiled at Areck. "He is young for an officer, is he not?"

"Areck is my personal squire, my lord, and this is his first campaign out of the Academy," Lord Silvershield beamed at his young apprentice, increasing Lord Vinion's anger.

"Well, I am sure you did not come here to stand in my quarters. Let us make our way to the map room and discuss your mission," Baron Marqel said, letting the door swing shut behind him, passing through the waiting contingent of men.

Lord Silvershield did not seem concerned by the lack of formality on the baron's part. The commander looked quite comfortable with being addressed as a lad, rather than his current rank. Neither did he seem upset over the insults that had been directed at his officer. In fact, Lord Silvershield looked delighted to be back at Stormwind Keep after all these years.

As Baron Marqel led them through another maze of corridors, the conversation sped along in all manner of directions. The baron asked about the knighthood at length, involving Lord Vinion in the conversation when possible, using a noble's polite indifference to dance around the lengthy subject. Areck trailed just behind the discussion, hoping that it would not turn to him. Next to him strode Arawnn, eavesdropping, enjoying the varying subjects, a wide smile etched upon his face.

Baron Marqel stopped in front of another set of inlaid doors, these with various medallions emblazoned on the wooden surface. As the party passed inside, Areck noticed the room looked like an officer's war chamber. The room was lit by four globes that winked into being upon a given command, illuminating ashen desks, chairs, and shelving units containing dozens of ancient texts.

"Still looks like the last time I was here." Lord Silvershield broke the silence with a grim smile. Holding up a plump finger, he traced over one of the tomes. As the knight-captain pulled away his hand, he looked down to see his name written in elder script.

"Not much use for a war-room at the moment, lad," the baron said cheerfully. "Not much use for the library, either, though Thomas still comes to fetch maps for trading disputes."

"Then the rumors are true, my lord?" Bowon asked. "There has been no activity in these last ten years?"

"Who in their right mind would attack this place?" The baron shook his head. "About the only action we get around here these days are tavern brawls!"

"That may change soon enough, Lord Marqel," the knight-captain sighed. "If I may cut our civilian talk short, I would like to discuss why we are here.

"Of course, Bowon, go ahead," the baron said with chagrin at having sidetracked the conversation. "Do not mind an old man's memories; there will be time for that later, I'm sure."

"My lord, what news have you heard out of the east?"

"Boy," the old man retorted, "I do not have time for Bre'Dmorian half-talk. Be out with it, if you have something to say."

"This is a treacherous time," Arawnn blurted out. "I think . . . I mean . . . Lord Silvershield is trying to say . . ." The outburst brought deep scowls from the Bre'Dmorians. Arawnn snapped his mouth shut and added, "Forgive me, sirs. Please continue, Baron."

"Since our fine young friend has put it so bluntly, Bowon, I have heard much by way of Natalinople. The worst being that our king has met an untimely death. However, I am sure you were not sent here to inform me of this."

"I think you underestimate that information, my lord," Lord Vinion said.

"And I think that *I* have spent twenty years overseeing this outpost," Lord Marqel boomed.

"Lord Vinion means no offense, Baron," Lord Silvershield interjected, shooting a meaningful glance at Vinion.

"What he means is that the information this royal courier carries will play a great role in how this our kingdom moves forward," Bowon finished.

After some minutes closely questioning the courier, the baron tapped his forefinger against his chin in thought. "So you fear that there may be trouble brewing, eh?"

"Duke Hawkwind thinks as much—enough to request an escort for this young man." Bowon motioned to Arawnn. "Of course, in times such as these it is very hard to know where a noble's loyalties lie and whom to trust . . . excluding our current company, of course."

"You expect foul play, then?" Lord Marqel asked.

"I don't know. You know our customs; we usually stay out of politics," Bowon explained. "However, it is my duty to make sure this messenger gets to Natalinople alive. I had planned on asking you for a night's shelter in your keep, but it seems we might have a problem. Several nights ago, I sent a small party of my men—"

A guard burst into the room, followed by another man drenched in blood.

Areck barely recognized Lord Malketh. The wounded knight held his right arm limply and had several deep gashes across his forehead that could only be from a bladed weapon. He was alone.

The knight was near collapsing as he tried to speak. Lords Silvershield and Vinion ran to the man's aid, noticing the deep cuts that ran beneath the knight's scaled armor. The baron shouted for the guard to fetch some water and send for his personal physician.

Lords Vinion and Silvershield eased the wounded knight into a chair. The man gulped as much water as he could handle. He looked as if he had suffered from dehydration; his hair was matted from sweat and smeared with blood.

Finally the man spoke, "Baron. Commander," he nodded at the baron and the knight-captain, "I have dire news."

Lord Malketh pulled a small piece of parchment from one of his many pouches and handed it to Lord Silvershield. After giving the knight-captain a moment to open the document, he began. "As you can see, my lord, we have a traitor in our midst."

"Where did you get this, Lord Malketh?" Bowon asked.

"It came from Willim and Kenly, my lord," Malketh responded. "They waited less than half a day's ride before attacking me from behind. Had it not been for Starsgalt's grace, I would not have survived."

"They are dead, then?" Lord Vinion asked.

"It would have been me!" Lord Stephen Malketh cried. "However, the younger squire, Kenly, was unprepared when my mount kicked backward. The blow must have stunned the boy and sent his horse into Willim's. It was by God's grace that I was able to slay the traitorous slime!"

Doing his best not to look, Areck watched Lord Vinion place the note on the nearest table. Sighing, he silently read the words:

Make sure the royal courier does not arrive in Natalinople.
Do whatever is necessary to attain his head.
I expect to see you soon.
D.O.T.

The blood drained from Areck's face. They had found the traitor; or rather, a pair, it seemed. His mouth dry, Areck picked up the letter and handed it to a gaping Arawnn.

15

AFTER HIS last demotion to the lowest rank a veteran of twenty-three seasons could hold, Knight-Captain Bowon Silvershield never planned on leading again. It was not that he lacked the capability, nor was it a lack of faith in the One True God. It was the sweet taste at the end of a bottle which had led him down a sinful path; liquor had become his savior.

After nine long years of public drunkenness, excessive womanizing, insubordination, and several infractions for missing evening prayers, Bowon had never suspected that the High Lightbringer would require his service again. Thus, when he had been asked to lead a small escort of men including Messenger Arawnn to Stormwind Keep and beyond, he was skeptical. Maybe it was that it had been so long, or that he doubted himself, since his fall into disgrace. Then again, maybe it was neither of those reasons. It could have been that he questioned the High Lightbringer's methods. Why would his lordly commander take such a chance?

It made no sense until now.

God is giving me another chance, Bowon thought. He knew that many of his brethren questioned his faith and the information he had brought back from a journey he had made over fifteen years ago, a prophecy that foretold of coming doom. In truth, after being beaten by inquisitors countless times, Bowon had accepted that they were right. He had convinced himself that he was mad and unworthy. It drove him even further into the bottle.

Then, out of nowhere—midway through the first part of their trip—things changed. His personal squire, Areck, had shared a premonition regarding the death of the courier from the blade of one of his own order to his attention. Though Bowon had not realized it at the time, Areck's news was something he had known would happen long before it did. He had just not accepted it until now—and for good reason. It had been years since his last visitation by God, since he, Bowon Silvershield, had seen this exact event take place.

In his visions a lone knight always came through wooden doors, bloodied and betrayed by . . . well, he had never seen the betrayer. However, he had clearly seen the aftermath. No matter the outcome, war would come upon his land, and then he would . . . then he must make the final sacrifice: his own life.

The thought was a terrible one. He realized that it was not the thought of war that had led him off the path, nor the bottle, nor his lack of faith. It was a thing worse than anything he could imagine; worse even than the death of a king. Bowon had been shown the destruction of the order. He could no fathom such a nightmare; yet, here it was. Through all of these years he had held it at bay, burying his divine character in strong dwarven ale and potent apple brandy. He had told himself that the vision was one of several possible futures; not a true foreshadowing of what *would* happen.

Bowon absently heard the gasp of the royal courier and the soft flutter of air as parchment fell softly to the ground. Baron Marqel was speaking anxiously as were his fellow knights. His mouth felt parched and he wished he had a malted beer.

When he looked up to see all eyes upon him, Bowon frowned. There was nothing he could do at the moment. It seemed fate had chosen him once again to follow down a dangerous path

His first duty was to Arawnn, then his men, and finally the campaign. He would stay at Stormwind for the night. In the morning he would address the issue with a clear mind.

† † † † †

Areck was too tactful to state the obvious: If the knight had been attacked from behind by anyone who knew how to use their weapon, why were all of his wounds on up front? He apprised the rest of the room and waited for one of the senior members to point it out. Everyone wore a controlled mask of calm and said nothing.

Areck heard Arawnn's startled gasp at the news that his death had been planned by one of his escorts. He could see the words forming on the royal courier's lips. The parchment implicated D.O.T, whatever that meant.

Although the confirmation of his vision had partially fulfilled itself, Areck's conscience remained burdened. He did not like being so restrained regarding the vision which portrayed his friend's death, but the Code was rigid. It was meant to prevent mortal judgment and fear from guiding action. He knew that discretion had been wise in this instance, proving once again that he was flawed, even in basic understanding. He considered talking to Lord Silvershield again; his inadequate logic needed some closure on the matter. Something just wasn't right about this.

I do not want to be penalized again, Areck thought. *It is better to know my place and keep my mouth shut.*

Areck sighed. There was no honor in staying silent; he needed to consult Lord Silvershield regarding some inconsistencies, to understand the implications of things that had not come to pass.

Areck glanced at Arawnn. The courier stared intently at the baron and the knights, who were caught up in conversation. The look on Arawnn's face bespoke betrayal and disgust.

In all the commotion Areck had not paid attention to Lord Malketh. The knight's right arm hung against his archaic gladius, a weapon rarely used by Bre'Dmorians. Areck had never used such a weapon, but in his studies he had come across history that depicted the accuracy of the gladius' killing blows.

Areck condemned himself for being so cold. He was paying more attention to the man's weapon then he was to the knight's grievous wounds.

Conversation raged for several hours while lodgings were arranged. Lord Silvershield sent Lord Vinion to ensure that a suitable shrine was near Lord Malketh's room so that the knight could find basic healing from God through stringent prayer.

Finally, the baron, looking tired, held up his hand and released the men to their barracks.

Areck followed a staggering Lord Malketh, who had been bandaged and retained during the questioning, out of the room, watching as Arawnn pushed past the knights. Nowhere in the questions had anyone asked what the royal courier thought about the matter. Areck decided that his friend needed space to clear his mind, so that he could cope with being the mark of an assassin.

He considered going after Lord Malketh and then after Arawnn; he knew his friend would have been there in *his* time of need—until Lord Silvershield called for him. As for his friend, he would check on him later and offer whatever support he could.

The crisp morning breeze whipped through the mountain pass, swirling the bright banners attached to all military buildings.

A pair of squires rubbed their eyes and stood in loose ranks, waiting for Squire Areck to rouse the rest of the company. They were not surprised when he exited the barracks followed by three more sleepy-eyed squires.

Areck ordered the young men to form ranks then he counted each man, going down the line making sure that each squire looked appropriate. His morning orders had been to rouse the men at dawn, work out any kinks, and bring them for morning prayers, their first since leaving Aresleigh a week earlier. Satisfied that the five young men were awake enough to begin their morning exercise, Areck ordered them to perform maneuvers to get the blood pumping. Areck then moved the men toward the small chapel located within the courtyard, a task often done after spending more than one night on the road. Beds sapped the will of a man, given the chance.

As he knelt and closed his eyes in prayer, Areck felt exhaustion wash over him. For the sixth straight night he had gotten fewer than four hours of sleep. No nightmares had visited him, yet he felt uneasy. The story of Lord Malketh's return was on everyone's lips. Several of the squires approached Areck with questions about their commander's return. It seemed that news of the traitors had spread from the keep to the small company of riders, which seemed odd since no one outside of nobility had been in the room. More important, none besides Areck had slept outside of the baron's personal wing.

Due to rank and title, Areck, as the junior commanding officer, was expected to stay in the barracks with his men. It was common for a military company, in this case, squires, not to be invited as guests. However, considering that the keep was underutilized by the current garrison, Baron Marqel had given the squires their own wing, dinner, and private chapel.

Areck had expected Arawnn to sleep with his small company of squires, as his friend seemed to prefer the life of those without privilege. Yet, that was not the way it turned out.

Arawnn had asked to be removed from any dealings with those of squire rank. Areck knew the courier wished to sleep with people who had not betrayed him.

He had just finished prayer the following daybreak and was about to start his morning meal when an irritated voice cut through the air.

"It was your duty to make sure the squires were *prepared* before the morning meal, Squire Areck," Lord Vinion snapped, looking at the circle of young men gathered around a large rectangular table, eating dripping sausages. "Most still look like they are half asleep."

"I woke them at dawn, my lord," Areck said, snapping to attention. "My orders were to work the blood and prepare them for the day's journey."

"You were to *organize* them, squire," Vinion growled, "in a way that worked them out and readied them for the next leg of their journey. It will take them another hour to be ready to ride." The man stood and walked away, barking orders. Six squires formed a stoic line, chins held high, eyes straight ahead, but hanging on each word the knight said. Areck stood to the side, taking the brunt of anger directed at the men.

"I refuse to tolerate the lax attitude this company has adopted!" the officer said. "If the under-lieutenant cannot handle his duties, perhaps it is time

I again advise the knight-captain to remove his *rank*." Lord Galwen Vinion walked down the line until he stood in front of Areck. Lord Vinion stated several things not quite insulting but effective enough to initiate the questioning of the Areck's ability to lead. He turned and moved down the line, stopping long enough to point out flaws of each young man. "Since we have left Aresleigh, this entire company has broken from the path of righteousness. You, Anton," he said and pointed at the youngest squire, "look unkempt. Kaadin, you look as if you are still sleeping."

Areck had never seen a knight so angry in all his years of schooling. It looked as if the second-captain had not slept, his anger from the previous evening magnified. Areck guessed that the man was having trouble believing that one of the Bre'Dmorian Order would betray his escort, let alone his country.

"Mark my word, squires, when I return from Natalinople, the High Lightbringer will hear of the unprepared nature of his future knights." Galwen whispered to Areck: "It makes me sick that one of common blood could wear this rank. It is even worse that the knight-captain protects you from proper punishment. If it was me, your rank would be removed and you would be sent to the tables with the rest of the first year squires. If it were up to me, another ten years of service would be required."

Areck's mouth tightened but he remained silent.

"Say it, boy. I can see you wish to confront me in front of these men," Lord Vinion hissed.

With restraint, Areck kept his composure. It had taken six days for the Galwen to admit his problem: Areck was common.

"It is not my place to question you, my lord," Areck whispered, still declining to meet the other's eyes. "If you wish to have me removed, then by all means, bring it to Lord Lightbringer's attention."

"It is not your *actions* that have me concerned," Knight-Captain Vinion said in disgust. "Under-Lieutenant, you will run these men until one sickens," he continued as he walked towards the stables. "It should take you no less than one hour. When you have fulfilled my orders, I want them mounted and ready for today's ride."

It did not take long for the sausage to find its way out of the squires' stomachs but Areck did not stop the exercise until an hour had passed. Seeing the boys exhausted, dripping with sweat and vomit, he allowed them to rest momentarily before issuing orders to return to the barracks. Their workout had attracted several common soldiers, laughing and betting on whether or not the officer in charge would ever end the exercise. When it ended before noonday, several of the soldiers gave cheers as silver coins changed hands.

As Areck followed the squires, a barracks sergeant came over to discuss methods of whipping his own men in shape, which turned cheers into scowls. Areck found it almost amusing. Part of him hoped that those men who had wagered on the morning's punishment would be run into the ground.

I cannot blame them, he thought with resignation. *If I were a soldier watching this ridiculous workout, I might laugh as well.*

He saw the irony; the soldiers thought that because Areck was young, he would be the same rank as their own sergeant. Indeed, if he was being equated to a rank in common terms, an under-lieutenant would have been a master-sergeant. He guessed that these men were worried that their sergeant would swap ideas, increasing the soldier's morning regime. The thought made Areck smile.

It took thirty minutes for all five squires, armored in scale and chain, to mount their steeds in a neat column. The youngest boy looked quite unsteady on his charger. All waited in silence for the knight-captain to bring out his own stallion, Legion.

Lord Silvershield appeared followed by the baron, Messenger Arawnn, Lord Vinion, and Captain Thomas; none looked pleased. Lord Silvershield motioned for Areck to join the party, kicked Legion, and rode forward.

"Areck, we have been talking this morning," the knight-captain began. "You were summoned to join us, where have you been?"

"My lord," Areck said, seeing Lord Vinion's face darken in a scowl. Trying not to anger the second-captain further, Areck stammered, ". . . the men were unprepared this morning. It took me extra conditioning to make sure they were ready for our ride."

The baron peered past the knights and frowned at the condition of the young men. The baron leaned in to Lord Silvershield and whispered. He waved to Thomas, who rode to his side and the pair rode towards the eastern gates.

"Squire Areck," Bowon said. "You are not so inclined to dismiss yourself from orders. I do not understand your recent insubordination. It is time you answer—"

"If I may, my lord," Lord Vinion spurred his mount forward, keeping his eyes on Areck. "I told you this one could not handle the responsibility of leadership. However, I believe there is another capacity he can fulfill."

"What are you suggesting, *Galwen?*" Lord Silvershield asked.

"This boy is a master swordsman, is he not?" Lord Vinion asked, eyes lit with rage. When Lord Bowon nodded, he continued, "Then I can make use of him. If he cannot lead as you had hoped, do not drown your men in his mistakes."

"There is no time for this, Galwen," Lord Silvershield replied, moving Legion closer to the other knight. "If you wish the boy punished, it can wait until we return to Aresleigh."

"He is causing nothing but problems among the men—just look at them, they are exhausted from the morning workout," Galwen retorted. "Our orders were to have two men escort Arawnn back to Natalinople. Obviously you cannot take Lord Malketh's place. Therefore, we only have one option, and that is for Squire Areck to fulfill Lord Malketh's role on the second stage of this journey."

The request shocked everyone. Lord Bowon Silvershield inclined his head and the pair moved several feet away before a heated discussion began. Nothing could have prepared Areck for the situation. The man had set him up, he realized, to look like a fool in front of Lord Silvershield.

But why choose me? Areck wondered. Another thought hit him: if the second-captain wished to get his hands on him, it could only be because the man wanted to teach him life's harsh lessons without interference.

Why did I not say he ordered me to mistreat the men? Areck asked himself. He knew why. He had already caused enough problems within the company. If he had openly defied Lord Vinion, every sin he had ever committed would have been brought to attention.

The conversation did not take long. Lord Silvershield shook his head in disappointment while a smug smile crept across Galwen's face. The two mounts rode next to each other and Areck knew that he would be leaving, most likely never to return.

"Second-Captain Vinion makes a good point, Squire Areck," Bowon began, determined to keep his emotions in check. "Before this morning's insubordination I was going to field promote you to first-lieutenant and give you command of the company while I travel with Lord Vinion to Natalinople. However, I cannot take the chance that you haven't been corrupted through all the infractions you have incurred on this campaign. You have become a liability to our cause. As such I can no longer trust you as a leader," the knight-captain said. "Thus, I will be sending you with Lord Vinion, so he may utilize your skills. Maybe it will also give you time to rethink today's actions."

Areck sat in his saddle, stunned. His greatest ally had turned his back. The man was practically his father, though the knighthood would frown upon such closeness. What had Lord Vinion said to solicit support of such a notion? He felt anger run down his spine. He glared at Knight-Captain Vinion with baleful eyes and noticed the look of disappointment on Arawnn's face.

"My lord," Areck said, choking back the unwept tears he held deep in his gut, "I do not hesitate to accept your decision, but would I really be the best choice to accompany Lords Vinion and Arawnn?"

"You will not question it," Lord Silvershield said, moving his stallion towards the eastern gates, signaling a march. The rest of the company moved in unison when another rider rode forth from the stables. The rider held his arm in a sling yet rode with grace.

Lord Stephen Malketh closed the gap between them quickly. When he rode between Bowon and Galwen with a reddened face, Areck could see that his less-serious wounds had already healed themselves, most puckered scars. Areck had never seen self-healing, a skill that allowed a knight to heal minor wounds via the communion with God. The squire guessed the rarity of the skill meant it was given to only those most faithful to Starsgalt.

"Knight-Captain Silvershield," the man began, his voice tinged with emotion. "You would give my place away?"

"It is not my choice, Lord Malketh," Bowon said. "Your injuries were too severe. I was forced to absolve you of responsibility."

"But, my lord!" Stephen responded, terror etched on his face. "If I am not allowed to continue alongside Messenger Arawnn, there are no injuries greater than those that will be inflicted on my honor."

Knight-Captain Silvershield regarded Lord Malketh with skepticism, concerned at the man's passion. In terms of the Code, if a knight was too injured to continue, there could be no questioning his conviction.

Stephen Malketh saw the question in the commander's posture. "It is a matter of personal honor, Lord Silvershield," the knight said. "I was given this quest from the angels of Starsgalt himself. I will be humiliated by not continuing."

Areck could see the words struck a sentimental cord with the commander.

"You are a good man, Lord Malketh, strong in your faith and conviction. It is a trait I appreciate. However, as I said, this is not my choice." The knight-captain inclined his head towards Vinion.

Lord Vinion had not expected Stephen to return to duty; he had worked hard to make sure Areck was on the ride to Natalinople. To refuse another knight his holy right, furthered by a request of honor, was dangerous. Worse, if Lord Vinion disallowed the fellow knight yet invited a squire instead, Malketh's humiliation would be unbearable.

"It is your wish to travel, wounded, with the courier and I, Lord Malketh?" Vinion asked.

"I have earned that right, Lord Vinion," the other retorted, holy fervor burning beneath the quiet answer.

"If we are attacked, you will be a liability."

"Then I will give my life in protection of the courier and in service of Starsgalt!"

"He is not assuming that your convictions are less than honorable, Lord Malketh," Bowon interrupted, seeing the fragile nature of the second-captain's words. "This entire trip has been rather strange; there is an obvious risk of another ambush since the traitors failed in their attempt."

"That and your right arm is injured. Would it not be more of an honor to bow out to one who is uninjured?" Galwen asked, looking at the wounded limb dangling at the man's side.

"There is no honor in being left behind," Lord Malketh said. "It is my right to decide if I am ready to ride, my lords."

The silence that followed was broken by several shouts of guardsmen as a merchant caravan carrying contraband tried to make its way past the eastern gatehouse.

"He gave his life once, in protection of me," called a voice that thus far had remained silent. "I do not see why a squire should take a knight's place . . . especially when it was a squire who tried to kill me."

Areck knew Arawnn's comment was directed to him.

"You were going to replace me with a mere *squire?*" Lord Malketh looked incredulous.

"No," Knight-Captain Silvershield said. "I was going to replace you with the highest ranking member of this company not named 'me.' Of course, that was under the assumption that you were unable to ride. If you can, well, Arawnn is right—there is no reason a man who has sacrificed his life should be excluded in his due honor."

"You are prepared?" Lord Vinion asked.

"Thank you, my lords!" the crease of worry disappeared, replaced with fervor. "I need only fifteen minutes to be ready to ride."

"We are already off schedule," Lord Silvershield frowned. "However, I can spare fifteen minutes if you need time to situate your gear."

Fifteen minutes later Lord Stephen Malketh walked his steed out of the stables, dressed in battle regalia.

"Are we ready, then?" Lord Silvershield asked.

Everyone in the small group nodded. Although Galwen looked unhappy, there was no way around letting Areck out of his sight. The courier had asked for Lord Malketh as an escort, and the knight had asked for the privilege to continue. In respect of the Code, any answer other than agreement would have been deemed insulting.

The column crossed the protected pass and reached the eastern gates. Although Lord Silvershield marched in front, he was no longer an imposing figure of confidence. His hair was unwashed and unkempt, and the smell of sweat and alcohol dripped from his pores. It had been many years since he had commanded others in such a disheveled state, yet he remained composed and alert, eyes following the sun.

As the commander rode in silence away from the other officers, the pair of remaining knights surrounded the courier's mount and discussed matters.

Areck overheard the conversation. He felt uncomfortable knowing that Arawnn was upset. Lord Malketh appeared unworried over the news that a betrayer had come from their ranks. Lord Vinion looked as though he was sickened at the idea of a traitor, agreeing that two bad apples had existed but there was no possibility of another. By the time the riders reached the gatehouse the conversation was over and Lord Silvershield brought Legion near the baron's dun-colored gelding.

"Commander," the baron said, "if you don't mind, I would feel better about the situation if Thomas and I could accompany you. I wish to say good-bye to our royal friend."

"We are only escorting these three," Silvershield nodded and waved his hand at Arawnn, Galwen, and Stephen, "just beyond Battlement Row."

Areck looked past the nobles to see thick stone walkways carved out of each side of the mountain. Battlement Row was an extension of the keep, high enough that siege ladders were useless in such a narrow pass. After thirty yards each walkway emptied into a circular battlement, readied with a pyre of brush, countless stands of arrows, and narrow gaps in the stone wall; an archer's paradise. At the western end of each battlement the walkway resumed its path to the next battlement, ending three hundred yards away from the gatehouse. Once again Areck found himself admiring the foresight and strategy.

"Shall we, lad?" Baron Marqel asked Lord Silvershield, nodding towards the eastern pass.

The commander nodded and spurred his mount. The baron pulled up next to Bowon, and Thomas fell into order next to Areck.

Stormwind Pass was a rough mountain pass, forty feet wide and a hundred feet high, lined on both sides by Battlement Row. The company of knights and squires did not move with great speed but marched in a formal manner and in silence.

After twenty minutes at a slow canter, the riders reached the final battlement, which allowed the pass to turn sharply to the south. As the column passed it, Lord Silvershield and Baron Marqel split so the three-man party could pass through. Arawnn moved his horse into the middle of the clearing and turned to wait for the knights to follow.

"My lord," both knights uttered simultaneously.

"We have decided that it is no longer safe to dally, nor is there time to be subtle about this journey," Lord Vinion glanced at his counterpart. "Lord Arawnn thinks that if we ride hard through the pass, we would only be several days away from the capital."

"That may very well be true, gentlemen," Lord Silvershield replied, squinting at the sun. He did not address the knights in formal terms. "And I see your point. With the information that Courier Arawnn caries with him, there will be more at stake than just getting the courier to the Lord Constable of Natalinople."

"Keep your voice down, lad!" Marqel hissed. "I do not mean to be presumptuous, but we have no idea if more of these men have been corrupted."

"I refuse to hear such blasphemy!" Lord Vinion said. "For all we know, those boys may have been following the will of Starsgalt—*it* might have been ordained by God!"

"That is absurd," Baron Marqel said. "There is division and possibly corruption in your precious knighthood, Lord Vinion. There is no reason to deny it!"

"I will not argue!" Galwen cried. "How dare you accuse the Bre'Dmorian Knighthood of breaking its ethos? Let me ask you this: how do we know *you* are not a traitor?"

"Why you arrogant little bastard!" roared the baron, reaching for the hilt of his sword.

Lord Silvershield at last reacted, placing his hand across the arm of Baron Marqel and glaring at Vinion. "That is enough, Galwen!"

Lord Vinion looked at him but thought better of speaking. It was obvious he had pushed Knight-Captain Silvershield to his breaking point, and he moved his warhorse over to Arawnn. Silvershield moved his own charger to block Vinion's path.

"This is ridiculous!" the commander's scorned cheeks were red with fury. "We could very well be on the brink of civil war, and here is a baron and knight insulting one another. Lord Malketh," Silvershield continued, "since you seem to be the only one who can stay quiet long enough to think: how long to Natalinople?"

"As Second-Captain Vinion was saying," Lord Malketh replied, "we have been advised that with a hard pace, our party could reach the capital in three to four days."

"Then make it so! I will expect your return in no more than two weeks." Bowon nodded and stared to the east.

"Yes, my lord."

The trio of riders sat in conversation for only a moment. With a last salute to Knight-Captain Silvershield, Lord Vinion mumbled something and gave the order to be off. The three warhorses shot down the road at a hard canter.

"Squire Areck," Silvershield said as he watched the party put spurs to their mounts and break off down the road, "there is no more room for mistakes. This entire journey has gotten out of hand."

"I will do my best, Lord Silvershield," Areck said, turning his gelding and moving with the baron to where the commander had positioned himself.

"I expect more than that, Areck. I need you to be your ever-solid self again—to be *you* again. I need your support from here on out," Lord Silvershield said. "If you can contain yourself, I would like to promote you to my second-in-command."

Areck nodded. "Of . . . of course, Lord Silvershield."

The commander gave a stern smile and motioned for Areck to give the order to move. "We shall talk tonight, Areck, when we stop for rest. I expect a report of the men's morale and a referral of who shall take your place as the junior officer."

Areck was stunned. How were things getting so out of control? Just a moment ago he was being reprimanded, about to be shipped off, and then now he was being field-promoted. He wondered what in the name of Starsgalt was going on. Though he wanted to tell the world he was unworthy, Areck said nothing but motioned for the company to move back to the keep's eastern doors.

Areck watched the men file through the great wooden doors of the eastern gatehouse. The first half of the journey had gone poorly. He had not left his friend on good terms. He was once again in trouble despite promotion. And Lord Malketh's tale of being attacked did not sit well within his mind. It felt as if he was leaving something behind, as if he had seen this in one of his many nightmares. He looked ahead and saw that the column of men was halfway through. He looked up to appraise the high mountain pass.

There was no doubt in his mind that he had been down this passage in the vision, though it did not look so foreboding now in the mid-afternoon sun. There was something he did not understand . . . something nagged at his memory.

Pulling his brows into a scowl, a shimmer of light flashed into his eyes. He shielded the source with his right hand and glanced down to see the uncovered blade of his longsword. The blade must have popped loose from the slow jostling of the horse.

A thought popped into his head about the two traitorous squires. He remembered facing off against two men in mock battle and sword play— Willim had been an outstanding opponent and an excellent wielder of the longsword, while Kenly was a nearly a braggart who preferred a bastard sword.

It was not odd that both boys chose to wield different weapons now. Knights were known to vary their choice: longsword, bastard sword, longsword and shield, or claymores. These kinds of weapons were known for their ability to hack and slash through lighter armor, including most chain. Not that a slashing weapon didn't have its drawbacks. The fact that they were slower weapons and had difficulty piercing plate and scale made them only viable against infantry, unless the wielder found a joint or weak spot in which to strike a mortal blow.

Areck sighed. His observations were going nowhere so he moved into line. He went rigid and began to remember:

It seemed strange that on the eve of their arrival, a wounded knight had miraculously entered the keep just in time to inform the commander of the traitors. That same knight had declared that it was not a true Bre'Dmorian who had been the betrayer, but a pair of unlikely squires. Not only that, but those squires conveniently bore a note with orders to assassinate the man they were escorting.

Realization was swift: the injured knight had been wounded by a *piercing* weapon. Areck yanked on his charger's reins, wheeled his horse, and broke away from the gatehouse. He was so engrossed in his actions that he hardly heard the shouts of Lords Silvershield and Marqel.

I hope they haven't moved through the pass, he thought, knowing that if he were right, the traitorous Lord Malketh would have found an excuse to stop shortly after they had lost sight of the company. The problem with his theory was that without any concrete evidence, he could not condemn an officer, nor could he accuse Lord Malketh of being the traitor.

I always foresaw the death of two squires, Areck thought, digging his spurs into the horse's flanks, coming to a full gallop as he sped past Battlement Row and into the wider passage. *I just didn't know it! The difference is that in my nightmares they died at the event horizon rather than before. What if I am seeing this all wrong? What if the vision is simply telling me they would die, and that though they died in the forest, their deaths were a significant sequence within the event!*

The future cannot be changed. He thought of the passage a philosopher once told him. *Yet, it did change! Well, that is not wholly true—the event foreseen is the death of the courier, which may yet still happen.*

He assessed his thoughts until an option bloomed. *If the future holds the death of the squires, and the squires have already died, then the vision is about to come to pass. Even though the circumstances changed, the conclusion will be the same—the courier will be killed by a traitor.*

Areck knew he was right. The killers were not the squires who had seen their life shortened by Areck's discussion in front of the real assassin. It was Lord Malketh who reeked of treason. Everything made sense. The man had wounds to his right side; piercing wounds made by a piercing weapon. The squires would not have attacked his off hand. They would have attempted to take out Malketh's most dangerous aspect first; plus, a longsword would not have done piercing damage. The fallen warrior must have killed them then turned the gladius on himself, which was why the wounds were all on the right side of his body.

Areck sped through the curvaceous mountain pass, each step taking him closer to what he feared would already be a tragic situation. Thoughts of death swirled in his mind.

As he rounded a sharp corner to the north, he came upon the nightmare he knew so well. In the distance he saw a crumpled form lying awkwardly in a broken position, limbs protruding at different angles. Blood poured from a gaping hole in the man's shoulder, a wound made from a gladius being pushed down toward the lungs. There was no doubt that the body was Lord Vinion; his horse lay just in front of him with its neck twisted, broken in what must have been a terrible fall.

A pair of horses stood impassively next to the fallen knight, nostrils flaring in battle-frenzy, their masters nowhere to be found.

Areck heard mocking laughter and the distinct ring of steel. He spurred his mount again and rounded the corner at full speed. As the clash of steel grew louder, he heard Arawnn's voice cry out for help.

Areck came upon the last stages of what he had seen so many times. The royal courier took a wound to the hand, his blade falling away with a clatter. Lord Malketh grinned, his numerous injuries apparently not affecting him. He walked in a confident strut towards the courier, who backed away, bleeding from multiple wounds to his legs and arms.

Areck started to whoop and holler. The noise of Areck's approach the knight to the oncoming steed. Lord Malketh recognized Areck's tactics and prepared to accept the squire's charge.

Areck knew that he was most effective upon foot regardless of the advantages that being on horseback would give him. He brushed past Malketh and kicked out, catching the knight in the chest just as the man's gladius scraped past Areck's thigh. Doing his best to control his mount, Areck reached around and unsheathed his weapon. The squire leapt from his warhorse and turned to face the duplicitous knight.

It did not take long to close the distance to where Lord Malketh awaited Areck with scorn. The knight had picked himself up after being struck, apparently unharmed. Stephen's face was red with fury, as being touched by a squire was a blow to the man's pride. Areck told himself that he would use the knight's rage to his best advantage.

Lord Malketh circled Areck, looking for an opening to strike, using quick thrusts to measure Areck's style of swordplay.

Areck was unaccustomed to fighting against such a short weapon and circled with the older man, parrying each teasing blow, checking his opponent's defense. He allowed the teasing attacks to continue until he saw an opening that allowed him to stride into a counterattack with multiple strikes to the torso and head.

Although none of the blows landed, the attack drove Stephen Malketh backward. The knight no longer looked smug after the attack; instead, his eyes squinted in assessment of a real bladesman.

After another round of minor thrusts, Lord Stephen began a complex series of strikes, forcing Areck to parry successive blows to his off hand and driving the squire to his right. Areck knew that the knight was waiting for a moment when his opponent would make a mistake and expose a vital area. Areck changed strategies and opened up, letting the other man come in for the kill. Just in time, Areck feigned a parry and spun away as the gladius whirred by his head.

Lord Malketh was frustrated with his much younger opponent. He decided that it would be better to let the opposing swordsman use all of his endurance in short flurries, knowing that such frenzied swordplay sapped strength.

Areck parried and spun away from another round of attacks, this time centered on attacking his extremities. It did not take long before Lord Malketh was breathing heavily. With another flurry the knight dipped his weapon, trying to draw Areck out of his defensive posture. Areck fell for the simple ruse, bringing himself into the gladius's killing zone. Fortunately, when the knight brought his weapon around and impacted Areck, the squire moved with the slashing blow.

Though his chain mail absorbed most of the impact, Areck felt a stream of blood running down his sword arm. Grimacing, he felt the sticky fluid roll down his fingers.

"The next time you won't be so lucky," Lord Malketh chuckled, his sword poised for another round of attacks.

Areck concentrated and slowed his breathing. Only then did he realize that the fallen knight was moving in a pattern of attack styles. High, low, flurry, chest, arms, high, low, flurry . . . the next round would be centered on his chest. Seeing his opportunity to strike, Areck allowed Stephen to get past his defenses, close enough that a single strike would be fatal.

Areck's feigned ineptitude worked. He saw the gleam in the knight's eyes as Lord Malketh moved inside Areck's critical range, gladius in a killing position.

As the blade sped down toward Areck's neck he brought his blade up, parrying the death blow at the last moment then spinning too fast for the overexposed knight to match.

Areck was startled at how fast his longsword whirred past the knight's lowered defenses, and impacted his face with a dull *thud*. Areck saw his sword slice through skin and bone in slow motion, angling as it dug deeper in the knight's skull. He wanted to stop looking, but he couldn't turn away as dark red blood and brain sprayed outward from Stephen's shattered eye.

The sound was almost sickening . . . and the fact he had just killed someone was even worse.

Areck let go of his blade and backed away, slick with gore. He looked down to see the crumpled body of the assassin lying on the ground, blood pooling around his lifeless form. The sight made him gag. He had never killed anyone before.

Areck slumped to the ground. His shock was so profound that he barely heard the hoof beats. It seemed the others had finally come.

Boom!

A sound rocked the mountain pass.

Boom!

Areck looked at the body of Lord Malketh, distorted by massive beams of light, and at his blood-drenched hands. It was as if colorful beams of light were being pulled into a globe of energy, clear as water. Large chunks of rock crashed near Areck, becoming louder as the globe of energy grew.

Areck felt the tingling sensation before he looked down to see his limbs distort; skin peeled away to bone, only to be revitalized by youth. The pain helped to clear his mind. As the globe drew energy to it, movement began to slow. Areck saw imperceptible movements, such as the cracking of rock. He could no longer feel his body.

Reality distorted.

Time stopped.

16

LORD MALKETH had explained the plan to Var in detail. It had been a simple plan, really: Var would meet him in Stormwind Keep within two nights of their last meeting. Var would then travel up into the mountain range and find a perch with a good line of sight. The assassin would wait there until the courier and his escort came into view, and he would kill the messenger while the traitorous knight took care of his brethren.

As usual, the plans did not play out as supposed. Var had waited late into the third day for Lord Malketh to arrive . . . *after* the rest of his company, and severely injured. The problem was that Lord Malketh was supposed to beat the company to the keep so they could go over their plans.

"Damned Bre'Dmorian hotshots." Var mumbled a curse under his breath.

He was unsure what to do. His informant had said that the fallen knight would not be able to ride. If that were true, such circumstances would make Var's job much more difficult, especially if his accomplice was replaced by another knight.

That was when Var had decided, against all stealthy habits, to send a messenger to Lord Malketh and try to figure out a plan of action.

Surprisingly, the knight had returned the notice, explaining that everything was going as planed. The fallen knight also informed Var of the dark passages leading through the mountain, and to a place where Var should be waiting—which was where he currently sat, perched in the shadows of a long crevice, crossbow at the ready.

The thunder of hooves brought Var out of his reverie. He assessed the situation as a trio of riders cantered down the road: two knights and the messenger.

With a deep breath, Var steadied himself and raised his crossbow with a practiced hand. He picked out his target, a lightly-clad young man with light brown hair, a face free from stubble, and haunted eyes. Var held his breath and felt his hand steady.

His finger tensed against the trigger.

A beam of light reflected off metal into the assassin's eyes, making him curse and raise his weapon. He looked down just in time to see Lord Malketh drop back, unsheathe his weapon, and plunge it into his fellow knight's shoulder. It was an amazing feat considering the trio was moving at high speed.

Var winced as the dead man's horse jerked to the side and lost its footing, stumbling into the paved ground. The dreadful scream of the broken knight's mount was so great that it spooked the courier's stallion, which skidded to a halt and threw its rider several feet into the air.

This is as good of time as any to get this over with, Var thought, once again raising the crossbow. However, just as he held his breath, a dismounted Lord Malketh stepped in front of his shot.

Watching his accomplice in action, Var decided to let the knight have some fun while he found a better position.

Instead of killing Arawnn directly, Lord Stephen Malketh kicked the courier, yelling obscenities at the young man. He kicked away Arawnn's sword and commanded the young man to stand and fight.

"Of all the idiotic things," Var hissed, moving to a clear position. Once again, he dropped to a knee and leveled the crossbow. As he was about to pull the trigger, his target stumbled to the side and made it around a corner, blocking his view.

That was when Var heard another mounted warhorse charging upon the scene. To his surprise, the young man who had been reprimanded several time during the trip sped by, oblivious to his presence. Var watched as the squire looked around, heard the clash of steel, and charged around the corner. In the distance, he saw plumes of dust coming from Stormwind.

"*Damn it,*" he muttered, doing his best to maneuver around the sharp rocks.

By the time Var had moved far enough to see the action, both Bre'Dmorians were in heated combat. He tried not to concentrate on the battle raging below, instead looking for the wounded courier. Var saw the young man lying prone, his body mostly protected by a large outcropping of rock. He decided that it was too risky to waste a shot without exposing himself.

Var moved into another position. From this vantage point he saw that the courier was unconscious and that the man's face was deeply gashed— blood poured from the messenger's mouth. Var assumed that if the courier was not killed by a crossbow bolt to the heart, there was a good chance the blood pouring into the man's lungs would drown him long before he regained consciousness, but Var was not a man to take chances.

He was just about to kneel when he saw the younger man, a squire, land a fatal blow on his accomplice. Not willing to take any more chances and with speed born of killing, Var closed his eyes and again leveled his crossbow. This time, his finger twitched in perfect timing with a deadly shot and a bolt sped on its way, aimed at the downed man's chest.

Then he heard the rumbling from the very foundation of the rock.

Boom.

The mountains reverberated. The rock began to shift under his feet. Pieces of mountain broke away and toppled to the ground.

Boom.

Var staggered as the thunderous noise grew louder. To his amazement, the crossbow bolt spun unceremoniously in the air, but no longer moved forward. He tried to brace himself against a thick piece of stone as the mountain itself undulated. The chaotic movements made Var drop his crossbow to the ground and seek cover. However, before Var reached a more stable spot, a chunk of rock cascaded through the air and struck his thigh with a splintering sound.

Var cried out as intense pain shot through his leg. He was sure that the crunch of meant he had snapped his thighbone. With his leg now useless, there wasn't much he could do. He knew the only way to protect himself was to hide with his hands over his head and hope for the best.

Then he caught movement. Var looked down to see the courier lying on his side, still unmoving, surrounded by large fallen rocks strewn around—in what he considered a small miracle. No one had touched the man. He then noticed the corpse of Lord Malketh, face neatly split in two, looked to be disintegrating, as if his corporeal form was being blown away like dust.

The same thing was happening to Var's crossbow bolt.

The sight of the dead did not affect Var; to an assassin, there was nothing odd about the dead. However, the fact that reality—whatever its definition—was distorting made the assassin shiver.

A globe of light coalesced between the fallen courier and the squire and started to change the things closest to it. The young man was the first to distort, his limbs becoming almost translucent. Then both road and the mountains warped, then the sky.

"It is a miracle," Var babbled, unable to turn away.

The glowing ball twisted and pulsed. Each pulse further distorted time and reality. It stopped a bird in mid-air. The next pulse stopped the bird again, turning it into a falcon. The next peeled its flesh and left nothing but ash. And then it was there again, this time a fish. Then it was gone.

The essence of the globe seemed to grow more powerful. Var watched in horror as a wave dissipated just before reaching him. He gritted his teeth and tried to move, noticing that the squire still existed in the middle of such utter chaos. Var saw nightmarish creatures. He saw the burning of thousands of people, of cities. He saw time unraveling, yet it did not affect the squire in the middle of it all.

The next wave hit him in the face and he froze, though his mind never lost consciousness. Var's thoughts receded into the depths of madness. He could not move as his life sped by: choices he had made, choices he had never considered. Each vision had a different outcome. He was about to fade gratefully into nothingness when another wave ripped past him.

A lifetime had passed, yet nothing had changed.

Another wave raced towards Var and he screamed. The pain of eternity was more than he could bear. It felt as if his very essence was being destroyed.

Another wave.

Another. Again and again the globe pulsed, until Var could not take it anymore. He could not see—the whites of his eyes had turned red as blood. He could no longer speak—his tongue had swelled and his teeth were gone. His iron will was the only thing that told him he still existed, that he belonged in this existence.

The last wave had almost ripped him from reality and cast him into nothingness. The next wave would surely destroy him. He closed his eyes and waited to cease being. He had long ago accepted his mortality, but not like this. He was afraid; there were so many things he had yet to do.

Boom.

There was nothing left to do but lay and wait.

Areck stood in horror as time unraveled. He could not understand, but it looked like the very fabric of reality was unraveling around him, changing everything except him and Arawnn.

The globe continued to pulse. Areck could not hear anything but the boom that shook the heavens. He watched in horror as a portion of the mountain collapsed and fell towards the unconscious friend he had tried to protect. Areck could do nothing to save his friend; in fact, he could not move more than a single step in any direction.

Another shockwave pulsed outward, this one changing the body of Lord Malketh into a duck. Another went out which changed the man back, then blew him away. Areck looked on helplessly as each wave that pulsed out changed the dynamics of his world.

However, unlike everything else, the wave did not change Arawnn's corporeal form in drastic measure. Instead each wave offered Arawnn's unconscious form life . . . and new possibilities.

Another pulse sped outward, driving everything else into more and more variations of itself.

Areck noticed that the stone of the mountain no longer fell at full speed but was stopped by the pulsing waves passing through it. He could not be certain, but each time the falling rock was hit by the distortion it seemed to grow less substantial. As it neared Arawnn, it no longer looked like a landslide.

Another wave pulsed, this one standing time on its side.

Areck looked around, noticing that several riders had followed his mad dash. The only rider who mattered was Lord Silvershield who was caught in the middle of a time-altering wave, mouth agape with shock.

The limitless canyon walls looked like dark glass. No wildlife remained. The pulse of the globe had hit a crescendo. Nothing moved. The riders were captured in mid-stride. One had his sword drawn.

The pulsing stopped.

There was an unbearable silence.

As far as Areck could see, nothing moved besides himself. The restraints that had bound him were no longer in effect. It was as if time no longer existed.

Areck walked over to the landslide hovering several feet above Arawnn's unconscious body. He reached out and touched one of the stones. To his amazement, it no longer felt like rock, rather it felt like . . . roast beef. At this thought, the landslide turned into giant haunches of roasted meat.

Areck snatched his hand back and paced around the oddity. With uncertainty, he reached out to touch the savory beef, and once again it transformed, this time into a rubbery stone. Areck took a step backward. Taking no chances, he did his best to avoid the hovering rock, knelt down, and reached for Arawnn. The young man looked in dire condition but breathed; blood no longer flowing into his throat. Areck reached towards the courier but before he made contact, a shiver ran down his spine.

Areck was too logical to just reach out and help the man.

I don't even know what's happening, he thought, looking around at the carnage that had affected everything but him.

What if I kill him? What if he awakes?

Areck scowled. He had changed so much over the course of the last seven days. Even now, as he knelt over his fallen comrade, he envisioned the stupid grin Arawnn would be wearing. In that moment a new thought came to him.

If Arawnn was not meant to survive, I could never have saved him in the first place, Areck deduced, reaching his hand back to the courier.

The instant Areck touched the courier's face, he was struck with a blinding flash that threw him back several yards. When he opened his eyes, Areck stared in horror as an unconscious Arawnn was picked up off the ground, hovering as if an unseen hand held him in place. Areck tried to move but could not.

The divine pain started. First it felt like needles behind his eyes. It spread down through his chest and stomach until it reached the tips of his feet, becoming so bad that Areck nearly lost cognizant thought. He wanted to scream out for it to stop but he couldn't.

As Areck writhed in pain, he never noticed the wounds on Arawnn's limp body close. Nor did he notice that his friend grew an inch and put on several pounds of muscle. He if had been looking, he might have thought that maybe Arawnn was being recreated in a new imagine—a better, more proper courier.

Just as Arawnn's final wound closed, the unseen force which had held Areck in place picked him up and moved him into a standing position. Again another powerful wave of divine sickness rolled over him and he screamed in pain.

Trying to keep from losing his mind, Areck forced his eyes open. What greeted him was something that would forever change him: the ghostly apparition of his soul was climbing out of his body. The pain of it all made him feel like he was about to explode, like his organs wished to burst out of his chest. It was too much for his mind to handle.

Areck passed out but something brought him back, giving him a sense of clarity and calm.

His face contorted in pain Areck tried to snatch at his ghostly phantom but his fingers passed through the incorporeal body as his soul started to move away. It was then that Areck noticed another phantom, the soul of Arawnn, climbing out of its body.

Areck was horrified as the pair of ghostly souls passed through each other, never looking back to their parent bodies.

The force holding both Arawnn and Areck in place vanished, dropping both men roughly to the ground.

With little time to react, Areck scuttled backwards, hands stinging from gravel. He had not noticed the trajectory of either soul as they floated in opposite directions of their bodies. It wasn't until Arawnn's ghostly apparition was nearly upon him that Areck understood that it was coming for him.

Seeing that the apparition wasn't going to stop, he rolled onto his knees and pushed himself up. He took several steps away and the apparition continued floating towards him.

For the first time in his young life, Areck felt truly afraid. He told himself that this was not happening, that he was delusional, under a wizard's spell. However his frantic thoughts did nothing to stop the progress of the ghostly soul's relentless approach.

He looked around to find a route of escape. There was nowhere to run. The apparition moved in unison with him. It was coming for him.

Areck steeled his resolve.

If it is coming for me and I am the only one unaffected, then I may be the reason for all of this, he thought. *This could all be my fault.*

Areck turned around, his face stoic. He did not understand what was happening, but there was no honor in running away from fate. If sacrificing himself meant saving reality, there was no choice; he would die with the honor of a knight.

Areck stood his ground as the apparition floated towards him. Its eyes were pulsing with an eerie reflection of multiple timelines, possibilities of the future.

Areck reached out, inviting the phantom into his arms. He looked over to see his own soul dive into Arawnn.

There was pain.

It only lasted for a moment, however, before he passed out.

Areck's eyes flew open; he sucked in a breath of air. His lungs felt full of water, as though he was half-drowned. His eyes did not recognize the multitude of color that filled his vision. He lay on the ground and something very large was blocking out the afternoon sun. He pushed himself up and squinted, which did not immediately help but he was able to discern that he was under a cliff that was suspended several feet above his head.

Memories came flooding back. Areck remembered the phantom's outstretched arms and its painful touch. He remembered time in its unchanging glory; a great wheel turning, unaltered by events.

Areck closed his eyes. When he opened them, strands of history formed in front of him: that which would happen, that which had happened, that which was plausible, and that which in fact was. History dissipated and several new threads weaved themselves into the vacant space.

This is impossible, he thought, trying to comprehend. *Time is infallible. It was created by God. Nothing can undo the truth.*

Areck looked over to see Arawnn frozen in time, fully awake, terror etched on his chiseled features.

Areck felt an immense pressure build. A sharp pain ran up his spine and spread into his neck, moving into his eyes. The pain was excruciating. Areck thought his head would explode. He reached both hands to his temples. The pain hit a crescendo.

Areck began screaming. Light poured from his mouth, eyes, nostrils, and ears.

Boom.

All energy gathered itself into Areck, creating a loud crackle. He knew he was about to die.

Boom.

The shockwave that was released from Areck's body tore into the rock hovering above him, reducing it to dust. It rippled outward, searing away all chaos that remained of the distortion. The final wave repaired the residual damage of time.

Areck collapsed face down, smoke rising from his body.

Areck's eyes snapped open. He shoved himself up and rubbed his hands over his still smoking body. Seeing that he was still alive, he fell to his knees and looked to Heaven, tears welling in his eyes.

"I have seen your miracle!" he screamed to the skies, his hands outstretched.

Areck barely noticed that Arawnn was alive, hands reaching out in reverence. He hardly felt the touch. He only heard the courier laughing hysterically before tears began to pour.

Areck turned to regard his friend. He wanted to explain that sacrificing oneself in the name of God was blessed. And that any knight would have done the same thing.

"How . . .? How?" Arawnn choked, his face without any trace of the dignity and humor it once held.

"Lord Malketh was the traitor," Areck replied, trying to comfort his friend. "I could not bear the burden of knowing you were riding with the betrayer."

"No . . . you did . . . There were angels! I saw!"

Areck assumed that his friend was talking about the landslide. "We are taught that God will protect those who serve him the most," he said proudly of the miracle.

The words did not have any effect on Arawnn. Areck reached back and gently slapped the courier. Although it did not bring Arawnn out of his maddened state, it seemed to bring some order to his addled mind.

Arawnn reached to touch the squire's face. The touch was gentle, reverent. The royal courier retracted his fingers and held them in front of his own face, eyes wide with wonder.

"Breathe," Areck whispered to his friend. "What do you see?"

Arawnn lifted his eyes. He was looking at something very far off. The soft lines of his friend's face no longer existed; neither did any hint that the man had been injured. The young man looked different, as if he had suffered a tremendous trauma. He trembled in shock.

"I saw my death," Arawnn said. "I saw so many things, things that weren't meant for my eyes."

"Keep breathing," Areck said, knowing that the commander would appear any moment. He turned around to see Lord Silvershield standing next to Thomas and Lord Marqel, watching him with wide eyes.

The silence of the canyon made him uneasy. Everyone was staring at him, and the animals looked at him as well.

"My lords . . . are you okay?" Areck asked.

Lord Silvershield was the first to break out of the trance. He carried his girth down to Arawnn. "Your friend here is going to need a cleric, lad," Lord Silvershield said, doing his best not to look into his squire's eyes.

"What is wrong with him? I . . . killed Lord Malketh before he could do anymore damage."

Then he remembered riding past the fallen Lord Vinion. He bit back another reply, lowering his gaze in shame at not being able to warn Lord Vinion of the danger. It was his fault that this entire thing had happened. He should have figured it out sooner.

Lord Silvershield stared at him with wide eyes.

"My lord?" Silence. "My lord, why are you all staring at me?"

"He . . . is a . . . an angel . . ." Arawnn babbled, again reaching out to touch the squire.

"I'm a *what?*" Areck asked, backing away from the four men.

Lord Silvershield squinted in thought. "I don't know what it was that you did, lad. But you are either a Champion of God or not of this existence."

"What are you talking about?" Areck pleaded, losing all semblance of dignity.

It all seemed like a dream. *This is impossible,* he thought. *There is no way for history to be changed. What have I done?*

"There is no way to explain what we saw," said the baron, clutching his hands. "It was as if time had stopped. Well, except for you. You performed miracles. There was light. Everywhere I looked I saw you, and time was passing in waves, and . . . and there was madness. I thought I would surely perish."

Thomas looked scared. The guard captain looked like he was staring at a ghost. "I saw you rip the spirit from that man," Thomas nodded at Arawnn as he spoke. "You surely must be an angel."

He's looking at me as if I am a demon. Areck thought. *They all are.*

"It is not my place to question God, Areck. You are his tool, there can be no doubt about that now," Lord Silvershield said. "We will report this to no one. I do not know what is about to come, but only bad things can come of spreading this information. Would you all agree with that?"

"I am not even sure if what I just witnessed was real." Baron Marqel looked at his hands. He looked like he was about to cry, clenching his fists as though to check if he were real.

"It was real," Thomas stated, his voice quivering in fear. "However, I do not want this information to leak before the High Lightbringer can be made aware of it. I, for one, won't be saying anything."

"I don't want anything to do with this!" Areck blurted, his face ashen. "I wasn't responsible for this!"

"Calm down, Squire." Lord Silvershield did his best to keep his voice even and stern. "You have been bestowed a great honor."

"We need to get Arawnn to Natalinople," Marqel added. "Or should we send one of my own couriers with the news?"

"No," Silvershield replied. "No disrespect, my lord, but the High Light-bringer would never permit the impending fate of the realm to ride with common couriers."

"Then what do you suggest?" Thomas asked, alight with anger at being called common.

"Send the boy." Marqel nodded at Areck, no emotion in his voice.

Lord Silvershield looked at the squire, lips pursed in thought. "I am thinking about taking Lord Lightbringer's orders myself."

"Who will lead us, then?" Areck asked.

"You will, lad," replied Silvershield, no longer looking like the weathered old man that he was. The smell of beer was gone and his look of sorrow had faded.

"My lord! I hesitate to take such an honor after all of this."

"You have no choice. The company will need a commanding officer; you are the highest ranking member left. I no longer hesitate to appoint you. Neither will I waste time explaining my reasons," Lord Silvershield said.

"Will Arawnn be okay?" Areck asked.

"Like I said before, this young man needs a cleric," Silvershield said of poor Arawnn. "His mind has been seriously addled by our current situation."

"You think it is safe to take the young man with you, Bowon?" Baron Marqel asked.

"I don't see any other choice," Thomas spoke up. "Brother Parley is no longer stationed with us. It will be at least seven days ride back to Aresleigh."

"I agree, captain," Lord Silvershield stated. "There is no avoiding this. Arawnn will have to come with me. It will reduce the speed at which I can travel, but it is the only way to save the young man's mind."

"Give me a hand, Squire," Silvershield said as he reached out to pull Arawnn to his feet.

Areck hurried to the commander's aid. He positioned himself to carry the majority of the mad courier's weight and staggered with Lord Silvershield to the courier's mount. The men pushed Arawnn into the saddle, while Thomas tied the courier into place.

"Lord Marqel," Bowon began as he swung himself into his saddle, "will you do me an honor and send your fastest courier back to Aresleigh and inform both Duke Hawkwind and High Lightbringer Taryon of our struggles?"

The baron nodded.

"Thank you, my old friend." Lord Silvershield nodded back. "Let them know that our company has encountered several casualties, that I have appointed Areck as the first-lieutenant, and that I am continuing out my orders by escorting Arawnn to the lord constable. Make no mention of this miracle."

Lord Silvershield looked to Areck, no longer as a father. He had changed in the moment since his revelation. He looked years younger, and his eyes were clear and thoughtful.

"As for you, Areck, the rest of the company will head to the town of Brenly and wait for my return. You will need this," Silvershield said, pulling the insignia of rank from his cloak. "You are to follow through with these orders and get my men to Brenly. You will also promote a squire whom you see fit to replace your role as under-lieutenant. I will do my best to return to you within two weeks."

Areck gave a resigned sigh. He was not worthy of such attention. He was not an angel. He was *not* a Champion of God. He was just lucky to have been in' the right place at the right time. Look at all the chaos he had caused.

"My lord." Areck took the insignia, and gave a formal bow to his commander.

Lord Silvershield pulled the reigns of Arawnn's mount and gave a sharp whistle. Areck swore he heard him say, "I have finally found it. God, if you are still listening, I think have finally found it."

† † † † †

Silverwing perched high in the Dragonspine Mountains, her sparkling green eyes keen against the backdrop of her mountain home. She had resided in the greatest of the Three Sentinels, Mount Valadon, for nearly twenty years, searching out all ancient information in the region. She had been able to hoard several volumes of ancient text that God would wish translated, though why the All-Knowing would need her assistance was beyond her. Still, she did not question an edict from the All-Mighty. She had been about to began translation on one of the priestly scriptures she had confiscated during her latest travels when her sharp draconic eyes picked up riders traveling down the King's Road toward Natalinople.

Then something happened that defied all belief. Being partly divine, she felt reality tear in the vicinity of the riders.

Silverwing was too curious not to approach. She flew towards the powerful source of divine intervention. It was not common to witness a miracle. In fact, she was seeking miracles. In all of her twelve thousand years of life she had only witnessed a few occasions when the All-Knowing or one of His servants had intervened into the life of mortals.

Silverwing glided to a position high in the eastern hills which overlooked the King's Road. To her surprise a powerful globe of divine power had began to coalesce. What happened next was far beyond anything she could understand. In the middle of it all a human male stood, calling upon such divine energy that it rivaled one of her kind. In fact, the man was doing something far greater than anything outside of God. She watched as powerful waves of heavenly energy poured from the globe, stopped time, and unmade anything it touched.

She could no longer deny the truth; she was witnessing a true miracle.

With a gaze to the man in the middle of it all, Silverwing extended her mighty wings and soared off. She had research to do.

Bowon Silvershield rode toward Natalinople, his mind in turmoil. He had not felt such trepidation in ten years. His faith had been given rebirth, yet fear was mixed in with the joy of possible redemption: fear of himself. He had once been given the prophecy that he was the bringer of death. His sword arm would cause betrayal and the subsequent downfall of the Bre'Dmorians. It was the price of one who had failed in his faith. He knew that.

He could not help but relive the moment. Fifteen years ago a prophet had told him the future; it had caused a redirection to his search.

And it started with a single betrayal. There would be miracles unknown to man. He would see an angel. There would be civil war. His hand would bring down that which had been sought for so long. All the signs were there. After fifteen years the prophecy was about to fulfill itself.

Now it was time. He had fallen from God's grace. He had witnessed a miracle given to a true champion of Starsgalt. There could be no doubt. The prophecy was about to be fulfilled.

A single thought shined through all of his relived anguish. He could not help but to say it out loud: "After all of these years, I have finally found the source!"

Var woke with a start. He had seen amazing things, possibilities, endless possibilities. He could not help but think that his life could have been so much better had he chosen to apply his many talents in different directions. *So much loss,* he thought. *There has been a better way.*

Tears slid down his face as he pushed himself from the ground.

He had remembered being struck with a rock. His right leg had been shattered . . . yet there were no wounds to be seen other than scraped palms and several cuts above his left eye. There could be little doubt that he had been privy to a miracle. He could no longer sustain the belief that the gods did not exist or that they simply did not care.

Var studied his surroundings. He was still on the same perch when the miracle had begun. His crossbow sat on a ledge just under his position. Oddly enough, it was locked and loaded ready to fire into the heart of his mark. Considering that such a thing was impossible, he shivered.

Where is that damn man? he wondered, trying to discern tracks. He remembered seeing the young man in a prone position with scattered rocks surrounding him. He was sure he had fired his crossbow—and he was sure it would be a killing blow. But blood represented his mark's demise. There wasn't even any debris. It just didn't make sense.

Biting his lower lip, Var made his way down the mountain. He had no idea what to do. For most of his life he had been a killer, cold hearted, and mechanical. More important, no one had ever escaped.

He gave a frustrated sigh.

Var couldn't take the chance that Arawnn had lived. He would have to go after him. Then he would find the warrior who performed an act of God. He had not decided if he would kill the man, but there was no doubt that his fate would forever be tied to the man who had changed history.

Var walked off to find a room for the night. He told himself that he could not look back to see what might have been.

PART III: TO BECOME A HERO

17

21st **Eternity (Eternal Timeline)**

THE ANGEL Gabriel marveled at the empty council chambers and the
flawless order that was embodied in the massive law-bound building structure . . . the perfection of the floor, the columns and spherical domes, and
the power that it took to maintain it all.

If only all things were so easy to comprehend, he mused, knowing that order
was related to creation, and to the reality that was.

However, contemplating reality was not why Gabriel had come. He had
come on behalf of Starsgalt to meet with several powerful ambassadors of
the various factions of Heaven—order-bound high seraphim, neutral archon savants, and chaos-bound demon princes—to discuss the repercussions of growing older . . . in the mortal sense. All were of the angelic hierarchy, yet all were vastly different. He knew such a meeting could prove
disastrous should the heavenly population find out.

It was not that the angelical race feared aging so much as its aftermath:
non-existence. Long ago, the gods had come together to create time and
marked it as one of the limitations of the mortal races. This was the problem: angels could not realize the reality of dying, at least not in the mortal
sense. In Heaven, angels could be slain but did not die. They simply ceased
to exist.

Only the gods knew exactly why this happened. It was a secret they had
kept to themselves and something they could not reverse. Even after the
Godsword War which had consumed millions within the Angelic Order,
they had not given their angelic servants transcendent spirits. Instead, after
an eternity of deliberation, they concluded that to allow the angelic race to
transcend would make Heaven less than perfect. This gave rise to the belief
between the gods that transcendence was a falsity, and that by doing so

would destroy their omnipotence, the foundation of the universe. In short, the gods believed that the transcendence of a being who already resided in Heaven would give rise to the belief that there was something *after* one's life in Heaven.

Though Gabriel did not know the gods' reasoning, he did know that he was young by angelical standards, an eternity old when the Godsword War had erupted.

It was then that the gods discovered that angelical beings could not die, but only be winked out of existence upon being slain. This discovery led to the eventual conscription of the god's first creation: the Olthari.

The memory brought back thoughts of Gabriel's past. He could still recall the days when the Olthari, a race of immortals who were created by the gods, resided in Heaven. He had never questioned the fact that the Olthari race was shaped with the sole purpose of being mindless servants to the angelical race—infantry that could be wasted in war.

But that is because I know my purpose, Gabriel thought. In fact, it made a lot of sense to the angel. The gods had created an alternative to angels' dying to make sure the angelic race didn't exterminate itself. It was the proper, orderly, lawful way of things. Just as the Olthari were meant to follow angels, so were angels meant to serve the gods.

"My purpose," he whispered out loud.

After their creation, the Olthari had made up the majority of the gods' troops, and as such the gods threw their omnipotent power around with no regard to reality. In those days angels had watched impassively as the gods slaughtered the Olthari like fodder.

Though he was incapable of mortal emotion, Gabriel had been brought to something like sadness at the aftermath. It seemed that most of the Olthari race had been destroyed in those wars, along with many angelical generals.

"Heaven nearly crumbled," Gabriel mused. "And the universe was nearly undone."

In the waning moments of the war, he remembered that something unexpected had happened: the Olthari race was given sentient thought.

Gabriel vaguely remembered the event—a moment of weakness when the gods had created sentient thought and gave it to the Olthari. The effect of this miracle allowed the gods' personal retainers to steal the coveted Godsword, remove it from the Eternal Timeline, and place it the one place no immortal could go: death.

The gods are infallible, he assured himself, never doubting this history. He just didn't understand how the gods could make such a mistake—why give sentience to those you force to follow? He assumed they had their reasons, but by giving the Olthari sentient thought, the gods had also given the heavenly race the ability to transcend—not to Heaven, but some *other* place the gods had created for Olthari spirits.

Gabriel had always thought such a thing was odd, given the circumstances. For a moment he could feel an unknown presence, shimmering on the edges of what was real.

It almost feels like an olthari, he thought.

Gabriel shook his head, ruffling his angelic wings. He had not felt such a presence since the Olthari's banishment. If he had not been on such an important mission from Starsgalt, he would have investigated such a random thought. However, time was running out.

"I see Gabriel is once again in thought," said a high-pitched, melodic voice. "Did you ask us here to announce more dire news, or are we here to contemplate reality?"

Though no gods deemed this meeting important enough to attend personally, all sent their emissaries to discuss matters.

Gabriel did his best to hide his irritation. He was not accustomed to being addressed so informally, even though rank and title were of no use when the gods met on neutral ground.

"For a moment, I thought . . ." Gabriel paused as he turned his attention to the other twelve angels in the room. He couldn't help but notice the scornful faces of his brethren. Rather than suggesting such an impossible thing, he started the meeting. "For a moment I thought that some of you wouldn't show up."

"I think the gods have no choice, Gabriel. They need us to have this meeting for them," Michael, the archon savant of Illuviel, said in a nonchalant voice. "The last time they all met, you were out discovering something they did not know. None will *take* that chance again."

"The Angel of Understanding is correct," said Raziel, the Archon of Punishment; agreeing with his neutral brother and causing a murmur to run through the council. It was not often that the first archon savant of Lahatiel agreed with anyone.

"I asked for this council," announced Gabriel loudly, trying to calm his fellow angels, "to discuss another problem that we all face."

"What problem?" asked Lokhivel, the Demon of War; by mortal standards, the first demon Prince of Araziel.

"Come, Lokhi," said Gabriel, turning to address the whole council, "let us not pretend that Heaven has not been afflicted with a terrible curse. We are here because the gods are no longer fully capable of omniscience." Gabriel let the words hang for a moment before he continued. "If I am correct, those of you who embrace chaos have it worse."

Again Gabriel let his words sink in before continuing. "The search for the unknown source has revealed nothing . . . nor will it, I am afraid. It is time to come to the realization that the gods are dealing with something greater than they."

"Blasphemer!" the council screamed.

"Impossible!" murmured others, several shaking fists. Still others cried, "Gabriel is speaking blasphemy! The Angel of Mercy's mind has been corrupted!"

"I am speaking the truth!" shouted Gabriel, slamming his hands onto a table made of pure order. The blow shook the foundations of the council chamber. "If something has the power to stop time, it is far greater than even the gods. And they *know* it!"

"What would you have us do?" said Michael, his voice calm.

"There is only one way," said Gabriel. "So far each of us has attempted to seek out the source individually, and each of us has failed—utterly, I might add. The only way to address this issue is to unite against our common goal."

Again the council erupted into chaos.

"And who would lead us?" shouted Lokhi.

"I suppose the God of Law and Order offers himself up!" shouted Mulciber, the Demon of Lies. "You all remember the last time we united!"

"Silence!" shouted the Archon of Punishment, angrily pulling Lokhi by the arm. "We may have no choice," Raziel continued. "Tell them!"

The Demon of War looked nervous, very unbecoming for a demon prince. With as much dignity as he could muster, he began, "The Dark Lord is systematically destroying entire worlds, searching for the source," said Lokhi, his eyes growing desirous of such destruction. "He has figured out a means to allow his corrupted armies into the Mortal Plane of existence."

"And why is this bad? We all feed off the spirits of the faithful," said Caym, the first archon savant of Gabriel, better know as the Archon of Luck.

"Because the gods have not come together to create *anything* for an eternity," finished Gabriel. "Illenthuul is harvesting *every* gods' faithful souls, and Heaven is not united to balance the equation. There *must* be creation for such destruction to take place. The dead are not making it to Lord Raziel's realm. Even Lokhi understands this."

"Do we know how he is doing it?" asked Vendal, high seraphim of Araqael, or the Angel of Love.

"When Gabriel first showed me the information, I scoffed," said Michael. "We have researched the information in a hundred different realities, and our view is blocked. Whatever Lord Illenthuul is doing, he is able to hide his actions from Heaven."

"So what are we to do?" asked Caym.

"There is no choice," said Gabriel. "Unless we stand together, none of us is strong enough to discover such information. That means each god will have to rely on each other . . ." Gabriel let his words trail off.

The council broke into arguments, discussing all the possibilities.

After several moments, Gabriel raised his hands for silence and nodded solemnly to Michael. "Continue, my brother."

"For those of you who doubt the validity of this claim, I will tell of the end of all things," Michael said slowly. "Know this: that unless the source is found and we *all* can convince our lords to stand united, the Dark Lord will control the flow of all souls. *We* are all in danger of this. If Illenthuul succeeds, he can destroy Heaven without ever collecting the Godsword. And if that happens *we* will cease to exist."

18

21st Eternity (Eternal Timeline)

2009 A.D. (After Devoid) (Mortal Timeline)

THE STENCH of dead bodies washed over Thurm Stormrage, a token of the limitless men, women, and children he had sacrificed in his holy crusade. The smell of the deceased was a constant reminder of his role in such a slaughter. His immortal soul was no longer able to escape the guilt.

"I have become a murderer," Thurm whispered and the thought of the innumerable dead that overwhelmed his senses. Gritting he teeth, he place one foot after the other and forced himself to move forward, always forward. Some part of his goodness, or what was left it, refused to look back upon the carnage he had wrought.

Without looking at the portal awaiting him, Thurm focused his gaze on the ground and stepped through towards the next dead world.

It only took a moment before the olthari passed into and out of the nothingness, materializing in his next conquest. However, as his eyes cleared, an unexpected sight greeted him. He was shocked to see that instead of a mortal world, an alternate plane of existence stretched out before him, one he thought he would never see again.

It made Thurm remember what he had once been, and he was wracked with terrible memories.

Thurm was considered prehistoric among his people as the fifth of his divine race to be given life by the gods. They were to be the perfect servants, created with no conscious thought; loyal, subservient, and sacrificial in the grand scheme of things.

Thurm realized that such loyalty and subservience had been his race's downfall. How many times had he seen the mortal races betray each other, their beliefs, their ethical and godly devotions for their sinful nature? Yet *their* punishment was a pittance, a slap on the wrist, their souls redeemable. It frustrated him that mortals were treated like children, with infinite patience and understanding to prepare them for servitude in the afterlife, while his own species had been shown no mercy.

The Olthari had never been children of Heaven; rather they were treated like criminals, punished harshly and absolutely. Furthermore the gods had not given them the ability to think, binding them to meaningless existence. He realized now that the Olthari race had been slaves. The problem was that it had taken him several thousand mortal years, trapped outside of Heaven after his race had betrayed the gods, to realize such a fact.

The slaves were never given a choice. His kind had never realized their loyalty was forced until the end, until they were banished from Heaven and given this wretched curse that had killed off their entire species.

To think that I caused of all of this, he thought. Most of his kind did not understand why they were being punished. And that was a great part of his guilt. Thurm understood why he was the last of his kind. He had been the first to be given sentient thought. Furthermore, *he* had made the choice to realize such a feat, to accept the gift, to accept what must be done to save Heaven.

At the time, all those millennia ago, he had sacrificed his entire race based upon loyalty and what would set everything right. He now knew that he had been wrong.

In the wretched Godsword War, a bloody civil war that had almost ripped Heaven asunder, the Olthari race had served as infantry. He still remembered the screams, the terror. It had not been angels dying over Thallindaviel, the Godsword. It was *his* race. They had been slaughtered by their gods so that their deities could claim the Godsword and rule Heaven.

Then Starsgalt, in his omniscience, brought together a Great Convergence of Heaven. It was there that Thurm's god had convinced all of Heaven to call a treaty, one that put the Godsword in the hands of their servants, a completely neutral, subservient race who would act as guardians until one god could control such power.

Thurm had been such a protectorate, one of twelve grand inquisitors to represent each god in Heaven. He and his served without question, unable to take sides. And for two eternities heaven was at peace.

Eternity crawled by; no god could claim Thallindaviel.

Then something unexpected happened. The Corrupted One, Illenthuul, who had been believed to have been winked out of existence and who created of the Godsword; the one who had demanded the essence of each god to forge the blade; had returned from the nothingness.

The gods recognized the danger before them. If the Corrupted One was successful in conquering Heaven, he would destroy the gods and bind each to the Godsword.

Heaven tried to react but it was too late.

Illenthuul summoned those angels loyal to him and marshaled an army of dark, possessed creatures, unleashing the first real demons, the ferryll, upon existence. He then began to systematically conquer parts of Heaven so that he might retake the Godsword back to his personal plane of existence, Hell.

The Second Godsword War raged.

Again the most lawful, benevolent gods of Heaven started to fight each other, trying to claim the Godsword before Illenthuul.

After countless wars, stalemates, and loss of olthari lives, a damning miracle occurred—Heaven allowed their first-born children sentient thought.

In an instant of clarity, the olthari realized that no deity could resist the ability to mold Heaven to their own will. The Olthari formed a plan regarding the god-forged blade: the servants of the gods would remove Thallindaviel from Heaven and place it safely where no deity could go. They hoped to end the war and unite Heaven long enough to drive Illenthuul out.

The plan had been simple. The Olthari were trusted everywhere. No one in Heaven, even the gods themselves, would question the Grand Inquisitors. They used their authority to travel into the Forge of Creation. It was there, in the bowels of reality, that the eldest olthari inquisitor was sacrificed on top of the Forge. The sword severed his artery and was then placed in his hand. Godsword and Olthari vanished together. With his death, the betrayal was fulfilled. The death shocked Heaven and all the gods transported to the Forge, only to realize that the Godsword had disappeared from their previously omnipotent hands forever.

Thurm dropped to his knees under the weight of the memory. Once again, he was trying to do the right thing, this time aligning himself with the betrayer in hopes of gaining his race's redemption. He would destroy everything for the chance to save his people.

This was the tenth mortal year since he had accepted Illenthuul's proposal and started his crusade. The knowledge made him cold. He had entered and destroyed another thriving metropolis of life, another failure, another dead world devoured by infernal demons. Though he could barely stomach the sight of dying mortals he shrugged it off, allowing himself no room for remorse.

I am the Harbinger of Destruction. The infamous title satiated a hunger that he had never recognized; by destroying all of creation, he was betraying Heaven again, this time out of vengeance.

"Vengeance . . ." The word stroked Thurm's fire. It almost made the pain of being locked away from the gods bearable. Long ago he had accepted that his race would never again sit in service of the gods, but he missed not so much being in a relationship with the gods as being cut off from the divinity that was his birthright. There was no way to explain the pain other than a longing to be next to the loving embrace of all creation.

Thurm's thoughts came crashing down with finality. *I will never again see my home; none of my kind will, not without a miracle!* So walking through the portal and into this particular place stirred such emotion in the immortal: Thurm recognized that he was in a plane of existence that he could not be in . . . the implications were preposterous!

The olthari was standing on the Path of Fate surrounded by the turbulent white waters of each aspect of Heaven. He did not know what to think. Maybe it was the fact that he had been thinking of the tragedy, or maybe it was a hole in the fabric of reality, but whatever had happened, he was sure of it: this was the Divine Plane.

"The Forge of Creation," the olthari clarified, grasping the magnitude of the situation.

The Forge of Creation consisted of thirteen raging rivers, all flowing without regard to who or what they swept away. In between each was a triangular mass which contained each river until they all reached the epicenter, a gaping hole in the middle of this strange plane.

Why am I here? he wondered, standing on the edifice of creation. *For that matter* how *am I here?* His blood raced. Was it possible that after ten years, the God of Chaos had finally discovered that which He so frantically sought? Had Illenthuul summoned him here to reopen the Gates of Heaven?

"I must be dead," Thurm said, "or dreaming. This cannot be real."

The olthari bent down to look into the waters of creation, making sure not to touch the turbulent surface, just in case he was wrong. He did not care to be swept away into oblivion before the crusade was complete. The waters stilled and became so smooth and clear that the olthari's reflection looked back at him.

If this was indeed the Water of Creation then even looking into the pool would cause a ripple, increasing the possibilities of his future a thousand-fold. No one dared look into the water for more than a moment for one's fate changed in an instant, and not always for the best.

Thurm's reflection blinked, moving with the same gestures that the real olthari used. It began to speak in a haunting voice.

Your fate beckons you, the apparition whispered. *You must follow the Path of Fate and once again gaze upon the Great Forge.*

The olthari did his best to keep his composure. There was no other explanation to this madness. It *was* real! He was on the Plane of Creation, and he was being beckoned.

Thurm scrambled to his knees and peered into the water. The smooth plane once again begun to froth and flow towards the epicenter.

If Illenthuul had truly summoned him to this place . . . well, the possibilities were endless. The most significant thought in Thurm's mind was that he could sense no danger, unlike his first meeting with the Dark God. This time there was peace and serenity. This time, there was hope.

Not wishing to waste time and strain the god's good will, the olthari pushed himself up and gazed to the horizon. It was beautiful.

The sky was littered with stars, the whole universe in its chaotic splendor. This was eternity bound to time. This was time tied to multiple realities. This was reality woven through each universe. He was gazing upon true creation. Thurm was overwhelmed.

Reality meant nothing here, as power was assumed through the strength of "self" and "thought."

Thurm was so deep in deliberation that he hardly noticed the great edifice which overlooked all of creation and destruction. For the second time in his eternal life he saw the massive rivers flowing, traveling, and creating as far as the eye could see. He was in the middle of it all, where each river dumped its churning waters, forming thirteen massive waterfalls which poured into a circular pit of nothingness. In the middle of it all was the Forge of Creation, his last memory of Heaven. And his birthplace.

The olthari was hesitant to teleport himself into the center. He would have to rely on a steep staircase that plunged headlong into the eternal dark. It would not hurt to take his time, reveling for a few more sweet minutes in all of creation.

He walked to the staircase and with one last wistful glimpse at the beauty then traversed the Path of Fate. Descent into the darkness only took moments, as time and reality warped, folding upon themselves to distort distance. Existence pulled at him as he passed through the chill of nothingness. Slowly, blindly, he made his way down to the Forge.

Although he heard the rumble of water converging above him, no water touched his material spirit, instead vanishing somewhere into Eternity. With an iron will, the olthari concentrated, parting the blackness and stumbling blindly into the chamber of creation.

"Have you ever wondered why there are thirteen rivers?" a mild voice asked from behind.

Thurm had been so caught up in entering the Forge he hadn't noticed that an elderly human sat cross-legged on the ground.

The gods often assumed the identity of the lesser races, thinking it was easier to relate to their creations.

"I do not recognize your form," said the olthari. "Are you a representative of the gods?"

"You could say that." The old man's colorless eyes met the olthari's. "Some would argue that I represent all of Heaven."

"Why have you brought me here?" The olthari asked.

"Good question," the man said smiling. "But you have not answered mine."

Thurm sighed. It had been long since he had dealt with the stubbornness of an angel; the gods were notoriously worse. "I have never questioned the creators, nor do I care to. Now, have you summoned me here to discuss the Plane of Creation, or is there a more formal reason for breaking Heaven's edicts?"

The old man chuckled. "So you would rush to the point of the matter." He stood, bent with age, hair disheveled. It struck the olthari as odd that a god would take on a form that was frail in comparison to his own and less magnificent. The old man only came to his waist.

"Oh, I have my reasons." The old man read Thurm's mind and stated the obvious. "If you wish me to be blunt, I think I can help you in your search for redemption."

"The Olthari race cannot be helped, nor can I! Anyway, I serve the God of Chaos now, and your kind would never accept me."

"I have always felt the pain you have endured," the old man said. "Unfortunately, it was the only means to prepare you for what I will bring next."

"More lies from the gods," Thurm spat. "Nothing can be worse that what I already endure."

"Believe, son, things will get worse," replied the old man. "You are not the first race I have eradicated over time."

"You have eradicated?" Thurm said, fury boiling up. "I was under the impression that another . . .*You* are the one responsible for our banishment?" He decided that if the answer was wrong, he would kill this malevolent angel.

"I am! However, not in the way you perceive," said the old man. "I am He who gave the Olthari sentient thought. I am He who broke the will of Heaven, allowing your race to hide the Godsword. I am also the one who helped The Dark One hunt your kind down."

"Then you deserve to die, angelic scum!" The olthari screamed in rage. He grasped his giant battle-axe, only to see it turn into a fish. He charged the old man, who moved with blinding speed.

"Think, Thurm Stormrage," said the old man. "Do not let your irrational heart drive you to inconclusive decisions. I did what must be done, as you do now. The choice was beyond moral implications. It was necessary."

The olthari was stunned by the use of his name, which he had not heard spoken in longer than he could remember. He tried to move, but was bound to the spot, frozen in time by the angel's might.

"Are you an angel?" Thurm whispered, as a powerful force crushed the wind from his lungs.

"Unimportant," the old man replied. "Now, if you will not hear me out, how can I offer you the chance to be reaccepted into Heaven?"

"I already have that chance," Thurm gasped, nearly losing consciousness. The pressure subsided.

The old man laughed at Thurm, stroking his hand across the Forge. "Oh, I guarantee you will find what—or rather, *who*—you are looking for, youngling; but there is no saving your kind by finding it. I give you my word that I will open the gates of Heaven should you listen."

"Angelic words mean nothing to me, old man! Anyway, what you offer is not in your power to give!" Thurm charged him again, only to fall flat on his face, grabbing at air.

"Isn't it?" the old man asked. "Yet you do not question the power of the Fallen One. Is it in *his* power to allow your race back into Heaven?"

The statement froze Thurm in mid-stride. If Heaven knew his plans, then they were trying to stop him . . . or were the gods plotting against each other? There was no point in dying for this, at least not without hearing what the old man wanted.

"Who are you?" whispered Thurm, finally feeling the oppressive power of divinity around him.

"Do not worry about who I am," said the man. "I have brought you here because it is time for you to fulfill your purpose, and free your people from bondage. Let's talk, you and I."

† † † † †

Lord Bowon Silvershield paced around the war room of Stormwind Keep, his brow creased in frustration. He had been searching for the chaotic source for ten years. Of those years, this would be the fifth since the knight had found Malacheye in his mountain home; rather, since Malacheye had found him. It was the first of many visits to the peculiar man, a blind prophet who could foresee the future.

The words of prophecy still rang in his head.

"You seek that which cannot be known," the prophet had said. "You will find that which cannot die. You will betray that which you love. In your ignorance, you will begin the downfall of the Bre'Dmorian Order."

Bowon had never questioned the guidance of God. He assumed that Starsgalt had led him to this place and assumed that the creator was ever watchful, assisting him in his holy crusade. The problem was, not finding the source was beginning to wear him down. His young heart was very tired. And it was getting worse.

Starsgalt had certainly allowed him to find the prophet and be cursed with a terrible knowledge of the future. In truth, some part of him concluded that his fate was sealed, his choices grim: He could either seek the source and destroy the Bre'Dmorians, or not seek the source and deny God.

Bowon was becoming frustrated. If his belief in God was true and his faith strong, then he could not question the choice. Yet he felt guilty over what must be done. It bothered him that the Bre'Dmorian Order had to be sacrificed. He tried to tell himself that there was no price too high when serving God.

Bowon grimaced and sat down at a circular table. Though not so fine as that of a high ranking noble, the table was made of long-grained ash and polished to a high gleam. It was only in this chamber that he could reflect upon the vision that anointed him a Champion of God.

It seemed like yesterday that he had set out from Aresleigh, beaming with pride and fanaticism. He had been given a commission from God to find a source of chaos that roamed the land. It was easy to find chaos; he found it everywhere he went. The problem was that God wanted a *specific* chaotic source—an unknown chaotic source that centered around miracles.

God had said only, "*Seek the chaotic source.*" He had never indicated what might be causing such chaos or its whereabouts. It was always left to the knight to seek the unknown source, again and again, by himself.

After ten years of failure, Bowon felt little of his former faithful conviction. He tried to describe what emotion now ran through his heart; the most common was despair. He was failing God.

The knight glared at his reflection. He was only thirty-three seasons old but a perpetual frown marred his once-handsome face. His features had become became gaunt and dark bags hung under his eyes. There was little left of the young man who had burned with holy fervor, the man who had undertaken an impossible quest.

At least God still speaks to me each communion, he thought. *At least He still believes that I am serving His purpose.*

He did not doubt that he was serving God. *But why did God forsake me? What purpose am I serving?* He could not understand why God would not reveal more information.

Bowon had answered this thought a dozen ways: God was teaching him to have faith, regardless of sacrifice. If he truly loved God, then he would trust in the creator's flawless reasoning: a test of true faith.

Bowon's search had taken him through five kingdoms, countless repositories of knowledge, even into the outskirts of the Great Devoid. It had led him to abandon his ethos on several occasions. He had been forced to deal with wild creatures that he normally would have killed on sight. It wasn't until the moment that the prophet told him that he would find what he was seeking, destroy it, and bring down the whole order that doubt had entered his mind.

He always wondered what the High Lightbringer would do if he thought for a moment that the order would be undone by one of his own. Bowon could not help but wonder if the order or Lord Lightbringer would have him killed. Maybe this was the point of his quest: to weed out those not pure enough to be trusted with the divine sanctity of god.

The knight stood and paced. He told himself that it was only a matter of time before he would be presented with knowledge that would help his cause. He needed only to have patience. He had endured for so long, believing that failure was unacceptable, to give up now.

It is not my place to question, Bowon reminded himself. *A prophecy is merely that: words spoken by a flawed mortal, interpreted by another; not the infallible wisdom granted by a minion of Starsgalt. It is my duty to honor the pact I made with God. I will search my entire life, if I have to. I will destroy the usurper. I will even bring down my brothers.*

He realized he was not prepared to deal with the consequence of his actions. If it came down to it, could he really sacrifice everything he stood for? Even if the cause was just, even if it was ordained by God, could he betray those to whom he had given his life in service?

I am a knight! His thoughts raged in conflict. *I will do whatever God demands!* But he could not shake the feeling of despair. Ten years of failure. How long would God accept his blunders? *How can I call myself a warrior of Him?*

An abrupt knock interrupted Bowon's musings. It was not like one of the servants to come so late at night, nor was it likely his good friend, Baron Marqel Colstom.

Bowon wasn't prepared to discuss matters in his present condition; it was most likely a restless servant checking on his hunger. He was about to sit when the knock sounded again, urgent and forceful.

Intrigued at the servant's persistence, the knight did his best to push his thoughts aside. He walked to a small bronze basin and splashed water on his face, then to the wooden doors of his chamber. Slowly, he opened them.

A clean shaven young man with cropped dark brown hair, steel grey eyes, and face bright with eagerness stood before him. It was not his physical appearance that surprised Bowon though, but the fact that he was wearing a suit of scale-mail. The young man was a newly anointed Bre'Dmorian, fresh in the face, most likely graduated less than a fortnight ago. The young man's eyes burned with a holy fire.

It must have been a dire need that sent the young man out in the middle of the night, for he looked exhausted. Bowon guessed that he must have ridden hard for several days to get there. He thought something horrific might have befallen Aresleigh, or the Academy.

"Consulate Bowon Silvershield?" the younger knight asked. When Bowon nodded his head, the young knight continued. "I am Videon Hammerfell. I have ridden several days to get here, my lord, may I enter?"

"Of course, Lord Hammerfell," Bowon replied and stepped aside, sweeping his hand in a gesture of etiquette. He seated himself behind his desk and leaned forward. He noticed that the other man looked down, refusing to meet his eyes.

"I do not mean to seem hasty, Knight Hammerfell, but it is late and I am working on several texts. How may I be of service?" Bowon decided to keep the conversation brief, taking the man's lack of eye contact as an insult.

"My lord," Videon Hammerfell stammered. "I have been sent . . . I mean I have been asked . . . I mean, the High Lightbringer has given . . ."

"Out with it, lad," Bowon relaxed at the knight's obvious nervousness. The fact he was looking down was not an insult but rather the young man's way of dealing with direct emotion.

Videon sighed and met his eyes. "My lord, I have been sent here to remove you from your assignment, upon the request of Lord Taryon Lightbringer. Furthermore, you are to report back to Aresleigh and explain your failure to the high council."

"You are here to *arrest* me, Knight Hammerfell?" Bowon asked. It was a significant slight to his honor that Lord Lightbringer had not delivered the message personally. He was to be put on trial in front of everyone he loved. His ethos would be questioned. There was no greater shame than being recalled from a holy crusade.

"No, my lord," Hammerfell seemed surprised at the question. "I have been given a vision to complete the journey which you started. I am simply here to take your place, and to make sure that the proper instructions were given."

If they had sent a military escort to arrest him, Bowon would have convinced himself that he did not deserve such a fate. He told himself that being brought in forcefully was different than being ordered to face humiliation.

But what can do I do? Bowon thought, his pride stinging. Lowering his gaze in shame, he knew what he would do. He would walk into Aresleigh and face his punishment with grace. He would most likely be reduced in rank, branded a coward. Why hadn't they sent someone to bring him in? He might have died the way he imagined he would: in battle, serving God's purpose. Instead they had sent a newly inducted knight to the deliver the message . . . and expected him to return without protest.

"Were there any other instructions, Knight Hammerfell?" Bowon tried to remain stoic in front of his replacement.

"The High Lightbringer said you would come as commanded, that you would not fight or argue the fact that you had fallen from God's grace," Videon Hammerfell said. The lack of sorrow in the young man's eyes concerned Bowon. "He said only that your trial would commence at the summer solstice."

"I appreciate your candor, Knight Hammerfell," Bowon said. "If I have less than three weeks to arrive in Aresleigh, I must begin to pack. I don't suppose you will stay here?"

"No, my lord; the west calls to me," Videon explained. "I think it would be best for me to start there."

"Then I think our meeting is at an end, and you should be on your way," Bowon stood and extended his arm in formal etiquette.

"Lord Silvershield, I apologize for this . . ." Videon Hammerfell faltered and clasped Bowon's arm. "May Starsgalt shine upon you."

"You too, lad, you too."

Videon Hammerfell nodded and stalked from the room. As the door shut, Bowon sank into his chair in utter despair. His instinct was to pray, but there was no point. He had failed God. He was a fallen knight and deserved this fate. He would walk into Aresleigh with his head held high and pray for death.

"*Yaarrggghhh* . . .!" Bowon yelled, grabbing the desk and with all his strength, throwing it into the air, scattering maps and religious documents. He had never felt pain like this.

He stormed to the side of the room, poured himself a mug apple brandy and drained it. If he was going to face humiliation, at least he no longer needed to feel its pain.

For the first time in his life, Lord Silvershield was introduced to the numbing company of alcohol.

Silverwing soared high in the morning air, which made her feel revitalized compared to the earthy gales that plagued lower travel in the sky and made her elder body tired. More so, she appreciated such heights because they gave her a greater perspective of the world. If only she could travel so high more often!

She was glad of her distance from the ground on this occasion. The Great Devoid looked like a mosaic of ash, coal, and brimstone. It was almost beautiful when one was flying several thousand feet above it, though nothing was further from the truth. She hated the place. There was nothing—no wildlife, no vegetation, not even carrion creatures survived in this place of utter chaos. Even the mountains seemed to cry out in anguish at having been stripped of all life.

For a creature as old as she, it was a tragedy. Though dragons held to firm neutrality, they considered creation beautiful and assisted in the process when they could. Yet there could be no help for this destroyed region; only skeletons of great trees remained, distorted in the agony of a slow death.

Not even dragon fire could purge this land, she thought sadly, remembering it had once been the great Goldenwood Forest. She still remembered that elves had cared for the ancient woods, maintaining and nurturing a balance with nature, over three thousand years ago.

That was before the ferryll destroyed their civilization and the humans waged the First War of Ancient Souls, she thought.

Another thought bloomed in Silverwing's mind. *It is odd that I haven't seen any Vul'd'Kat patrols yet.* She grimaced upon using the true name of the ferryll. The dragon did not say that name lightly. No denizen of the Material Plane did. Most were afraid of drawing the attention of the demonic race—a race known for slaughtering anything that moved, anything in their path.

Silverwing shivered, remembering her first meeting with the ferryll. They had come out of the north, unleashed upon man by the angel Illenthuul, an unholy plague of chaos and destruction. She had been young silver then, full of pride and arrogance, and had almost lost her life. Needless to say, it had been an enlightening experience, changing her view of what lesser creatures were capable of; they destroyed with no regard to balance. Wherever they walked plague followed, reducing entire regions to wastelands in days. Entire kingdoms vanished, races became extinct.

Again she shivered.

For the first time in history, dragonkind was forced to unite with dwarves, elves, and humans, all united under the banner of a human general named Anduin of the Light, a Champion of the angel Starsgalt. For nearly fifty years, the alliance fought the ferryll, to incalculable losses on both sides. Finally, the ferryll were pushed back into the depths of the Devoid where mortals could not easily travel. Although the dragons had been willing to form an invading force to wipe the world clean of the filth, the lesser beings decided to leave the ferryll in the wastelands to rot and rebuild the destruction to the south and west.

We could *have rid the world of such vileness,* Silverwing thought. She had never forgiven the mistake. She had seen countless dragons perish during the war, including most of her brood. *We should have destroyed the Vul'd'Kat when there was a chance!*

Two thousand years later, she remembered the war as if it was yesterday. She recalled fields littered with bodies, as the stench of death was nigh unbearable to dragon senses.

As the thought passed, Silverwing banked hard to the east and the ruins of an ancient city spread across the wasteland coming into sight. Although she would never forgive such ignorance, there would be time to fume over the stupidity of the lesser races later. For now, she needed to concentrate on the task at hand.

Catching a current, she tucked her wings and spiraled downward. With an acrobatic twist of her body, the dragon positioned her wings to allow for maximum speed. At the last moment, she spread her wings and caught a strong draft to slow her descent. The maneuver shot intense pain through her body as wings flexed and rippled, doing their best to decrease the speed of her plummet.

Having her fun for the day, Silverwing circled the ruins twice looking for a proper landing place, which ended up being a partially destroyed court-yard. With the grace of a five ton feline, she set herself down as lightly as she could. The impact shook the ground, reducing a crumbling fountain to shattered stone, dust and lichen clouding the air. Although she was not large for her kind, only twenty-six feet from nose to tail, Silverwing's body took up half of the courtyard and left little room to stretch her wings and maneuver. It was a drawback of being a dragon; as large as she was, it was always a hassle to collect useful information within the confines of the lesser races residencies. She had decided long ago that unless she needed to destroy something of significant size, it would be in her best interest to shift her form into something better suited for human cities.

She had chosen the form of a graceful young woman whom she had watched bathing in a stream fifteen hundred years before. She had modified and sculpted a perfect frame over millennia of using the disguise.

Most dragons refused to shape-shift, insisting that it diluted dragon blood and disrespected the powerful nature of their immortal race. There were even some who thought of shifting from the dragon form into that of a human as blasphemy.

That might be true, she conceded. She had never particularly liked shifting into the form of a human female, but the end justified the means. She was a servant of God first and foremost, and though her methods were unortho-dox, none could question her ability to extract information and record his-tory.

Silverwing released a sigh. Walking as a human no longer bothered her anymore, so she assumed that her blood had indeed become diluted. That she no longer minded being one of the lesser beings scared her, an emotion uncommon for a dragon

But humans can do things even a mighty dragon must envy, she mused. *Being able to go unbothered through ancient repositories of knowledge, actually* experiencing *life, and being limited by time are all positive attributes,* she concluded. To her, the pain was worth the experience.

She began casting in a draconic chant which sounded like thunder rumbling. She could not help but feel exhilarated as she recited the poly-morph spell for the fifth time in a row. A buzz of arcane power danced around her, culminating in a loud rumble that shook the broken walls of a nearby building. The hum grew louder as a soft glow enveloped the dragon. Excruciating pain ran down her spine as her body began to shrink. She did her best not to roar in anguish. If there was a ferryll mage nearby, he or she would feel the powerful spell taking shape; it was best not to alert them *precisely* where she had landed. The spell took several minutes to complete as it snapped bones, stretched skin, and redesigned the pulpish mass of organic material into a lithe female body.

The human female lay naked and panting on the lichen-covered stone, suffering from the shock of such an intense event. She shook with cold in the stale air of mid-morning. The effects of the transformation would leave her numb and addled for nearly twenty minutes before she could regain wits enough to summon clothing that she had stored in a pocket plane of existence.

"I see you have the gift of poly-morphing," commented a voice. "I suppose that is why you are such an effective agent of the All-Knowing One. Your reputation is why I sent you here."

"Who is there?" she gasped, pushing herself up with numb limbs. When she saw a handsome young man dressed in a tailored royal tunic and green hose staring back at her, she collapsed. The man's features were compelling: an angular face, green eyes, and perpetual smile. The vertigo of looking up almost made her vomit.

"You do not recognize this form?" the man teased, sweeping his hand to present himself with a laugh. "Maybe if I gave you a hint, would that help?"

The female said nothing as she slumped to the ground and groaned.

"Well, if you are not going to play along, I will have to just *tell* you who I am. I am he who burned away the last vestiges of time from your soul." The man's tone became serious. "Come, child, as easy as the transformation came, I figured you would be able to shake off the after-effects. Needless to say, we have business."

"How did you find me?" she asked, voice touched with concern. This was the being who had done something that was relegated to God. The entire event was a fresh wound in her mind. It was he who had driven her here. This man, she well knew, was the Shadow Dragon Vulsevandat who had shape-shifted into human form. This was the malevolent being who had driven her and her God to seek this accursed city along with an artifact that it once held.

"Do give me some credit," Vulsevandat said. "I have agents roaming the entire region, seeking the same thing you do. Besides, I am the one who told you of this place."

"You told me of an artifact, not of its residence," the female said. "If you knew its whereabouts, why don't you already have it?"

"Ah, well, finally a legitimate question," the man said. "I told you of an artifact that could foresee the future. I also tried to explain that our entire race is bound to divine subservience. When you accused me of being evil, I said I could prove Illuviel's shortcomings. Do you remember this, Silverwing . . . or whatever human name you choose to go by?"

"You did not answer the question," Silverwing did her best to stand on the wobbly legs of a nearly perfect female.

"Didn't I?" the man arched his eyebrows in a very human reaction to a stupid remark.

Silverwing knew she was being made fun of and remained silent.

"Yes, well, let's look at my statement, shall we? I promised you proof of God's limitations," remarked the man. "Do you not find it odd that God did not know the whereabouts of such an item?"

"I have never questioned God, unlike some who have lost their faith in the One," replied Silverwing.

The man chuckled. "The reason I have never sought out this artifact is because it does not exist. I made it up. It is a figment of my blasphemous imagination. I knew you would come here, because it was I who planted the information you would find."

"That is untrue, heretic! You just want all this knowledge for yourself!" Silverwing stood straight and began casting a spell that would strip her fellow dragon of any magical defenses.

"I would think twice before acting too rashly, child," the man said sternly, as though lecturing a daughter. "I could bind your soul to this body and leave you naked—and quite limited—in this form forever."

"You wouldn't dare!" Silverwing shrieked, ceasing her casting in midspeech. "Answer me! How did you know I would be here?"

The man sighed. "I told you why. Now think. Why would God allow such a thing to exist? If Illuviel knows all things, then he would have already known that such a thing would be flawed, limited, and altogether useless to his cause. If it wasn't, then he would know its whereabouts and already have it in his possession. Instead, he took my information as fact and sent you in search of an artifact that he knew nothing about."

"Illuviel is God! He *is* perfection! Nothing else can be true!" screamed Silverwing in desperation.

"I do not doubt Illuviel's power, or that he is beyond even me, but he *is not* God," the man replied with a firm tone of authority. "You can no longer deny that he has limitations. It is proven daily by the fact that neither he nor *any* in Heaven know what you are searching for."

"Impossible!" Tears streamed down Silverwing's delicate human cheeks, which was impossible for Dragonkind. "He *is* God. You are lying! You are a Shadow Dragon heretic who has turned from the faith!"

"It is only your shackles of servitude that keep you from realizing that I speak the truth. I promised you proof, and you have now seen it for yourself," the man pulled his lips into a thoughtful smile. "Now you must decide what to do with this information."

For the first time Silverwing felt alone. She could no longer deny that God's holy crusade to find something He refused to talk about was indeed quite odd. She had asked herself many times why the All-Knowing One had never revealed exactly *what* was being sought. She had asked herself if an artifact for seeing the future existed, why Heaven hadn't demanded it in the first place. Illuviel had seemed surprised to hear of such a relic. Now, if this Shadow was not lying, her God had sent her on a false assumption.

Sitting in the middle of the ancient city, Karth'Palax, supposed home to an artifact that could see the future, Silverwing brought her unhappy face to meet that of the Shadow Dragon male. She did not attempt to clothe herself. She did not try to get away. Without God looking over her, what was there to live for? But if she was to die, she needed to hear the truth of which her kin spoke.

"If you know so much, then tell me the truth," Silverwing cried.

"I am glad to hear that you are finally willing to listen," the man said, eyes sparkling. "There are truths happening that you cannot even comprehend, child, but, we will get to that later. The first truth you must learn is that of the Shadow Dragons . . ."

In the year 2009 A.D., the City of Aresleigh's future would change forever.

The Duke of Aresleigh grumbled, still partially asleep, as he was led down the palace halls by his retainers. He had been summoned by Lord Orbury, the castle seneschal, with urgent news. The duke could not imagine why his elder statesman had not been more direct. For that matter, what could possibly be so urgent that it needed his personal attention in the middle of the night?

He had *planned* on several weeks of peace and quiet. His sons and nephew, Count Edelin Hawkwind of Vendria, were on an annual hunting vacation in the far north. It was very like his sons to request their father so late in the night for unimportant business. The duke thought himself a patient man; however, if those young men had come back before their very expensive hunting excursion was up . . .

If my three sons are behind this, they will rue the day they were born! the duke fumed. The thought made him vow to send his younger sons away to be merchants, maybe even monks! His humor was short lived when he realized that such a punishment would not be effective for his eldest son, Arturius, the heir to his throne. He would need to think of a fitting punishment that would not undermine the family's position. Maybe he could pick each of his sons a young, healthy and very ugly bride . . . a perfect punishment for annoying young men. The thought almost made the duke smile.

The party walked down the long hallway in silence. It wasn't until he rounded the last corner that he shouldered past his men to personally greet Lord Orbury with a glower.

The portly seneschal was standing in front of the doors that the duke used to greet high ranking noble dignitaries. Lord Orbury looked quite grave as he reached to grasp his old friend's arm in salute.

The duke frowned at the silence. He had known Lord Orbury for thirty-five years. The man had been his closest friend and advisor for nearly twenty-seven of those. It was not like the man to be so formal, nor so quiet.

The duke pulled his friend close. He could see Orbury's brow furrowed in nervous sweat. He noticed the dark circles under his friend's eyes. This was no practical joke.

"Leave us," the duke announced, turning to the captain of the guard.

"Your highness?" the captain asked, surprised at being dismissed after being commissioned to retrieve his liege lord.

"I said leave us, Captain," the duke rounded on the man, eyes dark with warning.

The captain took the hint. With a quick series of orders the small contingent of men allowed their commander past before following him back down the long hallways and back to their previous duties.

"Captain Barret is a good man, your highness," Orbury said, watching the last of the guardsmen disappear. "However, I thank you for dismissing him."

"What is so urgent that you needed to summon me at such a late hour, Lord Orbury?" the duke asked, curious.

The seneschal paused, considering his choice of words. "It is your sons, my lord," Orbury began but was cut off by a royal snort.

"Damn it, Orbury, if you have called me here to tell me that my hellion sons have been gallivanting across the landscape—"

"If your highness would let me continue . . . On their hunting trip, they were come upon by a war-band of bandits. There were . . . casualties."

The duke was overcome by a moment of speechless candor as rage turned to dread. His face lost its reddish hue and became pale. Questions boiled in his mind, and fear of answers. The duke did his best to remain composed.

"Were any of my sons among the dead?"

"I think we better go inside, your highness," Lord Orbury said.

"*Answer my question, seneschal.*"

The seneschal took a deep breath. "Prince Arturius was among the slain," Lord Orbury said, "as was your youngest son, Lord Calvius. If you will enter the room, sire, I will escort you to Lord Davius. He has asked for you."

The duke did not move.

"Your highness." The seneschal placed his hand upon the duke's shoulder. "I can not imagine your pain, but this is not the place to despair. You need to come to come with me; Davius does not have much time left before he too passes into Heaven."

"You said only two of my sons are dead," the duke said, gripping the seneschal in a painful grasp, tears blurring vision.

Lord Orbury did his best to offer comfort. "Lord Davius yet lives, your highness. However, he has suffered many extreme wounds. Please, my lord, come inside."

"Yes, of course," the duke dropped his hands and stumbled into the stench of death.

In the middle of the room, lying on separate tables covered by white sheets trimmed in the royal red of Hawkwind family, was a pair of bodies. Each sheet bore brown stains where the blood of fatal wounds had seeped through.

The duke went straight to the bodies, reaching gingerly out to the first one, rubbing his fingers over the smooth silk, stopping at each blood crusted stain. By the size of the body, he recognized the final resting state of his oldest son, Arturius, heir to the Hawkwind throne.

The duke pulled back the sheet and looked at his son's alabaster skin, blighted by wounds. The fatal wound had been an arrow to the right of the heart, lodging in and collapsing the lung. His son had drowned in his own blood. The thought sickened him. The duke was a grizzled warrior of many battles and he had seen death—was even unafraid of it—but he had never imagined outliving his sons. He caressed the cold face of Arturius.

The seneschal waited patiently as his duke grieved his fallen sons. He tried not to hurry him, but it was likely that Davius would not survive the night. It was imperative that the young man not die before his father could say goodbye. Although Lord Orbury's first duty was to the duke, his second was to the City of Aresleigh; more precisely, to the duchy. If the duke did not escort his son into death's embrace he would never recover, leaving Aresleigh defenseless against political intrigues. It would be the beginning of the end.

Lord Orbury waited another agonizing moment before placing his hand on the duke's arm. "There will be time enough to grieve the fallen, your highness," he said. "But the living still require your attention."

"A man should never outlive his sons," the duke whispered, pulling away from the table. "Starsgalt please grant this old man guidance."

"Please, my lord, come with me," said Orbury. "I am afraid there isn't much time."

"How many?" the duke asked, pushing himself away from his youngest son's corpse. "How many of the sixteen survived?" The duke wiped his eyes. "How many deaths will I need to explain?"

"There were only four survivors, sire. I am afraid that we must hurry to find that number the same."

The duke nodded.

It took several minutes to arrive at the infirmary through the castle's intricate network of tunnels. As the pair entered, several pairs of soldiers snapped to attention. The royal physician glanced up then bent back over his patient.

The duke went to the side of Davius, his middle son, the new heir to his throne. The duke knelt next to the table, massaging his son's hand, easing a cool cloth across the young man's forehead. He did not notice the seneschal dismiss all but two guardsmen and move to his side.

The duke looked up into the weary blue eyes of the young physician. "Have you done everything you can, doctor?" the duke asked, gazing upon his unconscious sons face. "Everything? I will hold you responsible if he dies this night."

"I have done everything that can be done without using divine magic," the physician said cautiously. "Without proper aid, this man has at most, a few hours. However, I recommend two things, if you are serious about saving his life."

"Anything," the duke pleaded, his eyes burning with hope.

"I would start by erecting a shrine in this room, so Starsgalt may look over him . . . and a prayer wouldn't hurt either," the physician began. "I would also advise that you send for a priest. It is said that they can repair damage done to a faithful servant of God."

"Make it so," the duke said to Lord Orbury, giving him his signet ring. "Take this, Orbury, and hand it over to whatever church official it takes to get someone here."

"My lord, the Bre'Dmorians are not likely to come without proper documentation," Lord Orbury offered.

"I do not care how it happens, seneschal, just make sure you get a holy man here," the duke said as he looked upon his dying son's blood-smeared face.

"Yes, my lord," Orbury replied, leaving the pair of guardsman and the physician awaiting orders.

"If you don't mind, your highness, I have been waiting on several healing unguents to assist Lord Davius," said the physician uncomfortably. "It would be a shame if our young lord regains consciousness with nothing to soothe the pain. With your permission . . .?"

"He has been awake?" the duke cut the young man off.

"If you would like to call it that, sire," the physician said, spreading his hands helplessly. "He is in a delirious state. He asks for you but the pain is more than his body can bear, sending him nearer to death's door."

"I will watch over him while you go collect the healing salves," the duke replied. "Please hurry."

The duke watched the physician rush from the room. As the door closed, he laid a damp cloth on his son's forehead, willing himself to remain strong.

The duke knew that it would be awhile before either man returned. He was not a religious man. He had turned from Starsgalt's embrace long ago, upon his wife's death while birthing a stillborn fourth child. Now he counted on the One God's loving nature to save his youngest son. A hand weakly gripped his own, causing him to jump.

"Father," the young prince whispered, eyes closed, his voice rasping.

"Shh, lad, you mustn't speak." He remembered vividly what the doctor had said about his son's life growing shorter each time he awakened.

"Stayed alive . . . long . . . as . . . could," Davius said, his face contorting in a pain. "Needed . . . to . . . warn . . ."

"There is no need greater than your life, son," the duke replied, squeezing his son's hand. "You need to rest, Davius, what you need to tell me can wait."

"No time . . . father . . ." Davius said, his voice weakening, a milky film forming over his green eyes. "We . . . were . . . betrayed . . ." the words trailed off as Davius shuddered with pain. His chest rose unevenly several times, and his heart stilled.

"Get Physician Korl back in here *now*," the duke screamed at the guardsmen, toppling a small table.

Several moments later Korl soon rounded the corner, out of breath, followed by the guardsmen. The duke had positioned himself over the dead prince, trying to resuscitate him. The doctor pushed him off the corpse, deftly trying to find a pulse, checking for any sign of a whisper of life.

Lord Orbury entered the room with a disheveled Bre'Dmorian priest, an elderly man wearing the red robes of a prelate. The man looked quite displeased, but being in a position to gain the kingdom and church's favor he did not speak but approached the body.

The duke watched in horror as the two men tried for an hour to bring his son back from the void. Finally, Lord Orbury placed a hand upon his shoulder.

The duke spun around. "How did this happen, Lord Orbury? I need to talk to the other survivors."

"That can be arranged, my lord," Orbury replied. "However, before you start questioning the men, Lord Edelin also lies severely wounded. You may want to look in on him as well."

The remark stung the duke. The reason the man brought up Lord Edelin was something the duke had already considered but was not ready to admit. In one night his entire line had been decimated, his family destroyed.

Edelin Hawkwind was the next in line for the Hawkwind crown.

19

2021 A.D., Year of the Sword (Mortal Timeline)

THE SMALL company of squires rode in a double file line, following the King's Road west. It had been more than a day since they had left Storm-wind Keep with orders to move towards Brenly where they would await Knight-Captain Bowon's return. The squires were quite morose, as was their commander, a tall squire with blond hair and deep set blue eyes.

Areck did not try to lighten the company's spirits. He needed time to further contemplate his own guilt, guilt over the fact that he was cause of their sour mood. He let the men brood over their personal beliefs, riding for most of the day in quiet recognition of the traitorous events that had preceded them.

Doubt crippled his mind. He could no longer comprehend his place in the grand scheme of things and why, with all of his misconduct and ill luck, Lord Silvershield had made him the commander of his own company of men. It worried Areck. He could hardly keep himself out of trouble. Now, an entire company of squires relied on him, and he did not know what to do.

Areck sighed. Was it the thought of leadership that troubled him, or the fact that Lord Silvershield had called him a Champion of God? He believed that to be a true champion, a man could not be limited by his sins or a personal lack of conviction, which he was. It worried him that he had misrepresented himself so much that Lord Silvershield, Baron Marqel, and Captain Thomas would sacrifice everything with the claim. Areck knew he was a bumbling boy who had done nothing but make mistakes. Why couldn't the others see that?

I am no champion of anything, Areck thought sourly to himself. *I am not even worthy of being a tyro. I must tell everyone that if they insist on giving me such a title, then it should be the Champion of Limitations.*

Areck knew it was be only a matter of time before Lord Silvershield came back and told the High Lightbringer of the event.

How long until they realize their words are a mistake? Areck thought. He knew that although his infractions had been swept away with the death of Lord Vinion, another, more terrifying penalty awaited him should Lord Silvershield's claim prove false. The penalty for impersonating a Champion of God was a severe beating, possibly even banishment. To impersonate a holy warrior when you were nothing more than a heretic would result in the death penalty.

I must make Lord Silvershield believe nothing unusual happened, Areck thought. *I want nothing to do with making myself anything more than I am—a squire.*

That Lord Silvershield was no longer with the company of men only served to increase Areck's worry. The knight-captain had chosen to leave his command in Areck's care with orders for him to carry on as the senior officer.

He groaned, trying to forget how the two riders had flown from Stormwind Pass—one a mad friend, the other his fatherly mentor—but could not. He was, after all, the reason that Arawnn of Almassia was babbling mad with the indecipherable phrases of angels. He was also the reason why everyone thought of him as a . . . a champion!

Areck frowned and tried to think of something else. The first thing that came to mind was the trip to Brenly.

What if there is trouble along the way? he wondered. It would take Lord Silvershield two weeks to make the round trip from Natalinople back to Brenly, assuming no more mishaps occurred during the commander's quest. Could Areck truly to take responsibility of these men?

The distant pounding of hooves brought his attention back to the road as a single armored rider appeared in the distance. He recognized that the rider wore Bre'Dmorian colors, the colors of a fledgling squire. Areck noted that the squire was the man who had been ordered to ride to Brenly and inform the local magistrate of the mutilated bodies.

With a slight squeeze from his knees and a deft maneuver with his hand, Areck brought the column of riders to a halt. His second-in-command, Redmon Thelluvin, a noble-born eighth year squire, appeared on his left and maneuvered his stallion next to Areck's, awaiting instructions.

Areck shivered and his stomach clenched. This was something he had been expecting since the departure of Stormwind Keep—that the young man sent to Brenly would backtrack upon reporting to the town's commanding officer. This was his first chance to act like a commanding officer.

"It looks like Squire Lysen, Under-Lieutenant Redmon," Areck said casually, adjusting the angle of the charger with his knees.

"It would seem likely, sir," Redmon said, his calm voice belied by the excitement burning in his eyes.

Areck shrugged off of the fact his second-in-command referred to him as "sir," rather "captain." He was just happy to be recognized.

Areck peered sideways at Redmon, a tall young man with hazel eyes and short cropped brown hair. Though he had his doubts, Areck had chosen the man based upon his ability to reason out problems, an invaluable tool in an officer. Areck did not doubt the young man's razor sharp mind or the religious zeal with which Redmon fought. The only real issue he had with his under-officer was that he had been under the tutelage of Lord Vinion as the deceased knight's personal squire. Areck could only hope that Redmon would not hold a grudge or use his keen military sense to take over command.

"Are we to rest while the rider approaches, sir?" asked Redmon, turning in his saddle to look at the other four riders lined in a perfect column.

"No, Lieutenant," Areck said, noticing a small animal trail breaking off into the forest. "We have been riding for several hours; this is as good a place as any to take food while we wait for our information to arrive."

Redmon merely nodded, pulled on his charger's reins, and faced the company. Soon, backpacks were undone, canteens were unzipped, and horses were moved off into the shade.

Nodding in satisfaction Areck swung his leg over the charger and dismounted in a single move. He knelt to check the stallion's fetlock where a small sore was forming. Concerned that his injured mount might not make it to Brenly, he moved it into the shade.

After attending to his mount, Areck turned his attention towards the rider, who was now bearing down at a hard gallop and less than a mile away. He could discern that the mount was too long and sleek to be a war-horse and decided that the breed was thoroughbred, meaning speed was paramount.

The rider was upon the small company within five minutes, his mount's nostrils flaring and its sides in a thick lather. Areck frowned at the rider, who kept his mount in stride and apparently did not recognize the Bre'Dmorian company until too late; he galloped past the squires.

The rider shouted commands and yanked on the reins, nearly standing in the saddle. The horse responded by shortening its strides until it circled back around with a gaited walk to where Areck stood.

Wow, Areck thought, admiring the beast as the rider brought it to a halt. *This steed must of cost some noble a lot of gold.*

His initial assumption had been correct. It was a thoroughbred, apparent by the mount's skittish nature. Areck could tell that the beast was a noble stallion, fifteen or so hands tall, with a long sleek body meant for speed. Though he didn't recognize the exact breed, it was most likely imported from the great deserts of the far south where horses were bred for long distance marathons. It was a beautiful horse, superior in looks to even the best charger.

"Sir?" The squire started, recognizing Areck's previous under-officer stature in confusion. "Where is Lord Silvershield?"

"It is a long story, Squire Lysen," Areck said, unfolding a piece of cloth that contained the knight-captain's insignia of rank. "To sum it up, we ran afoul, had casualties, and the commander thought it best if he personally escorted the messenger back to Natalinople."

"You have assumed command, then, sir?" Lysen asked with a small frown, noticing that the company was short two squires.

"As you can see, Lord Silvershield has given me his personal badge of rank until he can meet up with us in Brenly," Areck explained, trying to bite back his irritation.

"Then I am here to deliver dire news, sir," replied Lysen, handing a small piece of parchment to Areck. "Count Gustafson sent me to deliver this."

Areck took the parchment, unsheathed his dagger, and unsealed the note:

Dear Commander,

Thank you for sending the report. It is hard to believe that our Lords Ulwyth and Helwyth have been murdered. However, our town has more severe problems on the horizon. I am sure that you are aware of the reports I have sent Lord Lightbringer? My scouts have reported a large group of orcs who have been burning and pillaging the outlying thorpes.

So far, my best efforts in securing aid have fallen on deaf ears. Or so I thought, until I received a notice stating that a group of Bre'Dmorians would be arriving in our town. For this I am grateful, my lord, but am still concerned. Although I am no military strategist, I do not think one company will be enough. Please request more aid from the Academy, or at the least ask for a small contingent of men from Stormwind.

May your ride be swift and safe.

Count Oslov Gustafson

"Is this accurate?" asked Areck. The note sounded dire, but if the scenario was so bad, Areck wondered why the duke hadn't sent military aid.

"I was only stationed there for two nights, sir," said Lysen. "However, the town is abuzz with talk of farms being stripped down and burned, while entire families have disappeared."

In the Academy, it was standard schooling to study the denizens of Aryth, especially those that opposed the church. Though the list of monstrous creatures extended into several volumes of text, there were five main noted enemies: shadow dragons, ferryll, ogres, dark elves, and orcs.

Areck had studied the orcish race on several occasions, and he knew the tell-tale signs of their presence. Dragons wouldn't have left anything standing, dark elves would have killed everything for sport, ogres would have eaten everything, and there was no way ferryll would be so far south.

Areck handed the note to Redmon who scanned it before handing it back with a grim nod.

"The count is right," Redmon said. "If we encounter orcs, our small contingent of men will be insufficient."

"Lord Silvershield asked that Baron Marqel send a courier back to the Academy to inform the High Lightbringer of our current situation," Areck said, scanning the horizon. "He also asked for reinforcements."

"The fact that we are here means Lord Lightbringer does not see this situation as a threat; nor did Lord Silvershield, sir," Redmon said.

Areck stroked his chin in thought. "Squire Lysen, did you ask why the count sent you east, rather than to Aresleigh?" he asked.

"He seemed to think that the request for aid would be considered more important if a Bre'Dmorian was to initiate it," Lysen explained.

Areck sighed. He knew the answer to his question before he asked it. The count had asked for reinforcements several times and had been met with little success, so the noble lord would attempt to use a Bre'Dmorian knight to achieve what he needed.

So how shall I deal with this situation? Areck asked himself. He knew that if his small company continued to ride towards Brenly, they would be asked to deal with the circumstances. His rag-tag group of squires was not ready to engage such an enemy. *My only goal is to protect my men.*

He looked up to see Redmon looking at him, awaiting orders. Areck did his best to hide his discomfort.

They are looking to me for answers, he thought. *Well, I don't know what to do. What would Lord Silvershield do?*

If he turned them back to Stormwind, he would lose all credibility with his men, though it would be safer. The Code crawled inside his mind: at all costs, protect the kingdom from chaos.

If I recall my men, I disobey another direct order, Areck thought. *Such an order would show my weakness in the face of danger.*

Areck did the first thing he knew every commander would do: he asked for his lieutenant's opinion. "I am not sure the risk is worth it, Lieutenant. Yet, I see our duty plainly calling," Areck said, turning his attention to Redmon.

"I think it would be unwise to recall our company, sir," replied Redmon, taking the hint by answering the masked question. "If we head back, it will be at least another week before we could send word to the Academy."

Areck considered Redmon's reasoning. Though he faced a tough choice, he needed to obey orders and provide what aid he could. Resolve washed over him. If he could not make the tough choices and remove personal feeling, he could never be a true commander.

"That is what I think as well," Areck said. "Judging by this thoroughbred, the count has a stable full of such beasts. We can ride into the town and offer what help we can. We will make sure they are somewhat fortified, and I will prepare a request for reinforcements, detailing the town's status."

His choice was not easy. Areck was taking a gamble with this decision. If the count asked for him to lead a small party of men in search of the marauders, especially without first consulting the High Lightbringer, this would be a dangerous move. Yet Areck felt confident that his men would respect his decision to offer help first and send for aid as a secondary measure.

"You should be aware, sir," Lysen said, turning his mount west, "that the town of Brenly is in a terrible state."

"What do you mean, Squire Lysen?" Areck asked.

"It's just that . . . well . . . *we* have nothing to fear, but the people are . . . sick."

"Sick?" asked Redmon in alarm. "What do you mean, sick?"

"It is hard to explain, sir," Lysen said in grim tones. "I never got a chance to talk to a physician."

"Brenly wasn't a wealthy town when I was accepted into the Academy nine years ago," Areck said, perturbed that the young rider had not offered this information earlier. "Such townships are known to contract the plague or the weeping fever."

After several moments of silence, Areck gazed up to see the rider looking at him in appraisal. It was an uncomfortable feeling, everyone counting on his decisive action.

"Squire Lysen," Areck began, "you are welcome to rejoin our company or ride back and alert the count that we are coming."

"I would prefer to ride under a Bre'Dmorian command," said the young man.

"Take some water, then, and let the others know that we will ride towards Brenly within the hour," Areck replied.

Areck watched the young man dismount and move to sit with the small circle of squires, each greeting him with warmth. He felt his under-lieutenant's eyes boring into him.

"What are you thinking, Redmon?" asked Areck with a sideways glance.

"If his reports are accurate, we have a problem, sir," said Redmon with a shrug. "We have no idea how far this sickness has spread, nor if it has affected the local garrison. If we are dealing with plague, there is nothing we can do outside of quarantining the sick and burning whole portions of the town."

"Do you think we should head back to Stormwind and request aid from there?" Areck asked. It seemed that his second-in-command, though young, was also very practical.

"No, sir," replied Redmon with hesitation. "I think you made the correct decision. If we do not carry out our orders, all of us will be branded cowards in the face of duty, especially us officers."

"What do you think, then?" asked Areck, regarding Redmon with respect.

"I think we should approach Brenly with caution," said Redmon. "I can tell you think the same thing; you are also worried about what will happen. And that even though we are Bre'Dmorians, there is not a true knight among our number." Redmon paused before continuing, "I am not so stout to admit the thought of losing more friends doesn't worry me some. If we continue this path, sir, we will eventually be called upon to track down orcs, and we both know that there will be casualties, if that happens."

"A very candid account, Lieutenant," Areck said. "Since we are in agreement, I will rely on you to get things in order once we reach the town. There is a chance that things will already be so, but just to make sure, you will need to inspect the barracks and give me a report on the garrison."

The lieutenant nodded with respect. With a quick salute, the man marched towards the small circle of squires now deep in conversation. Redmon went to his stallion, unpacked some dried meat, took several swigs of water, and began to dish out orders with authority.

A year younger than me and already a leader, Areck thought. He felt a certain pride that he had done an adequate job of choosing his supporting officer. Moreover, the man supported him.

Areck approached his charger, planted a foot in the stirrup, and pulled himself up. It was time to remove the lethargic aura from his company.

It was time to ride hard into Brenly.

20

THE BRE'DMORIANS rode west out of the forest and into Brenly, the easternmost township between Aresleigh and Stormwind Keep. It was a small town, one that had been set upon by plague, starvation, and madness, which had ravaged the population piecemeal. Though no one alive could remember those days, it had once been the foremost trading outpost between the duchy of Aresleigh and Natalinople, and in those days, very prosperous. Now the town had been reduced to ramshackle brick buildings that stood crookedly against the landscape, all that was left of ancient dwarven masonry.

Areck paid no mind to the fact that he saw no guardsmen or welcome from the count. It was likely that the ranking noble did not expect an answer from Stormwind for several more days, and therefore was not prepared. In a way, Areck preferred it that way. He considered it better that Count Gustafson had not come to greet them; it gave him a chance to see the machinations of the town before he made any decisions regarding its people.

It had been ten years since he had last visited the town of his birth. In truth, he barely recognized the layout, as recurrent raids of bold orcs had laid waste over the last decade, reducing the desire of nobles to serve it and the ability of the municipality to maintain itself. Mysteriously it had never been destroyed but survived each raid with unified grace, relying on the capital to provide what aid it could.

I wonder why they never built walls. Areck thought, looking at several makeshift attempts to fortify the town.

Truth be told, it amazed him that anyone lived here at all—being part of a dying community must wear thin on a man. He tried to remember his days in Brenly, but nothing remained of those years. All that came to mind was tragedy, making him feel numb. He did his best never to think of the brutal murder of his parents at the hands of marauders.

It seemed so long ago that he had been saved by a drunken Bre'Dmorian, Lord Silvershield, who had stumbled on his small unconscious body. That event had led him into the Bre'Dmorian Academy and his continued rapport with the man had who saved his life. The thought of the knight-captain brought a vivid flurry of emotion that nearly ran him into a small group of civilians.

To Areck's surprise, the appearance of knights did little to cheer the gathering. In fact, resentment seemed to form as the riders paraded through the main mud track which the town used for a road. It almost seemed like the people hated them for the life they assumed a Bre'Dmorian led— pampered and easy.

That these people disliked him for his life of servitude made Areck cringe. He could see it on their faces. None would recognize him, yet they imagined his life full of gold, treasure, and power.

Areck felt a hand grab at his leather boot—a young boy was looking at the carved stirrup of his war-saddle and whispering to himself.

It was then that Areck noticed everyone was staring at him, resplendent in his leather and chain armor. Though his leather breastplate held no intricate patterns, the fine craftsmanship was evident and the people accepted him as a knight. He became conscious of the fact that his white cloak held no denotations as a ranking officer, lacking the insignificant clasps that the lower ranking knights and squires wore.

To make matters more confusing, the entire company of riders were clad the same as Areck, although most wore unmatched sets of chain and scale rather than leather and chain.

Areck's mount snorted and picked its way past another group of commoners. As the company of riders passed a rat-faced beggar, he heard whispers about the fact that his white cape lacked rank insignias, as did those of the entire contingent of men that followed him. The average man could be fooled by shining armor and a chivalrous attitude, but even commoners knew that a knight was defined by his cloak. His field-promoted rank of knight-captain should have earned him a golden crown set with a pair of crisscrossing longswords.

Areck did his best to act nonchalant as he glanced to his right. Redmon rode with eyes locked ahead, ignoring the unpleasant crowd.

To anyone untrained in the Bre'Dmorian way, they might have even been a pair of official knights if not for their youthful faces and unmarked cloaks. Both men radiated authority that made people draw their breath and whisper in confusion.

It wasn't until Areck noticed a small congregation of elderly men dressed in tailored linens that he began to breathe. The count had heard of their arrival after all. He took another glance at the crowd and hoped none took his exhalation as arrogance. He almost remembered thinking so long ago that knights were an arrogant breed who thought themselves superior to low-born peasants. It usually bred resentment.

Lord Silvershield had lectured him several times on the use of temperance; young men often falsely believed that since a knight followed the will of God, triumph was a foregone conclusion. It was something Areck had always tried to take to heart.

Areck hoped that as they waited, the expressions of his company would mask their concern. Soon enough the count would find his way through the crowd and learn that he had been sent a company of squires rather than veteran warriors. At that point, all pretenses would fail. It would be up to Areck to persuade the nobleman that he was a capable commander placed in charge by a Bre'Dmorian knight-captain. Areck could only hope that his men would stand by his side; however strong their belief might be that he was unworthy of such an honor, they all would have to assist the count in whatever way he could until he could request reinforcements.

Areck knew that many people, even most knights, saw themselves as heroes; heroes that would be needed to deal with the problems in Brenly. *I need to make show of authority*, he thought. If he was going to try to sell his command as heroic, he knew he needed to plant the seed.

"Squire Lysen, to the front!" Areck shouted to the young man who had rode out of Brenly earlier that afternoon to approach his command for aid.

Areck watched the tall young man come out of line and ride forward. If he was going to play the part of a real commander, he needed to treat his men thus.

The act garnered the results he desired; the entire crowd went silent.

Perhaps I should give an order that will break up this welcome, Areck thought. Though he was still unsure if the squire would follow his lead, Areck knew the man was a Bre'Dmorian. *Actually, it is not what Lysen thinks that bothers me. It is that I think it myself.* The thought came unbidden as he sat deciding what to do.

Areck was about to issue an order for the man to trot ahead and offer a formal escort to the count, when his warhorse stumbled in a muddy divot. Fortunately he had not been wearing a visor, and his numerous saddle bags and weapons rattled against the thick flank of the charger. In his haste to arrive at Brenly, Areck had almost forgotten that his charger's fetlock was wounded. The fact he had forgotten angered him.

Areck rubbed his beardless chin and stroked the neck of the stallion, issuing clicking commands. Once he was sure that the stallion was stable Areck turned his attention back to Squire Lysen.

"The good count will need an escort from his manor," Areck said. "Please ride ahead and clear a way for him."

"It will be so, Captain," Lysen responded with a nod, using Areck's formal title, the first time any man in the company had addressed him with more than a "Yes, sir."

Pleased that his men recognized the situation and were playing along, Areck dismounted, coming face to face with several grimy men, their breath stinking of cheap ale.

He could not help but stare at the dirty, torn clothing of Brenly's men and women. He had been so absorbed with his entrance that he had not even noticed the sickness that Lysen had mentioned. Up close, he could smell it. As he looked into the feverish faces, he could see that the eyes held a yellowish tinge, as did the skin. In fact, most of the onlookers looked feverish, even delirious.

He recognized the weeping fever, the plague that killed one half of those it infected, and passed through unsanitary areas like wildfire. In pity, Areck began to reach out to a small child in the last stages of the virus whose eyes leaked small streams of viscous blood.

He silently cursed himself and withdrew his hand. The child took the action with excitement and dug his head into a young woman's tattered gown, peering out shyly. It was a common saying that the Bre'Dmorians could offer help but not friendship, which only got in the way of duty. His ethos was in conflict. He was to protect the weak at any cost. Though disease could not break its way through a Bre'Dmorian's divine protection, neither could he destroy it. It seemed that protecting the weak meant offering a hand in friendship, a word of comfort, a look of hope.

That rags hung loosely on frail frames unnerved him. He wondered how much food was available, and when—or if—these people ate. Part of him wanted to untie his saddlebags, remove his military rations, and throw it to the crowd. It would probably be the best meal they had in months.

A sudden thought reared in his mind. *How did the duke allow this happen? How can God allow this happen?*

"Out of the way, you," a healthy man growled, shouldering an elderly lady out of the way.

Areck shook himself. He had been very close to giving away his rations. He knew it was wrong, as the Code proclaimed, but still it was a strong desire to right the injustice that these people suffered.

Just another sign of my inadequacies, he thought angrily. *Those that doubt my abilities are right; I should have never been accepted into the Academy.*

His thoughts were interrupted by a commotion as Squire Lysen returned with a group. A short, bald man with sweat beading on his forehead marched past the diseased peasants to the waiting company. Though Areck had never met Count Gustafson, he could recognize an important noble a mile away. The man bore an aura of practical experience and therefore could be considered a commander. The count was followed by several burly guardsmen, all armed and armored to the teeth.

Areck watched as the guardsmen shouted orders at peasants trapped between the company and the count. The rest of the crowd drifted to the side of the road, rediscovering the various tasks they had forgotten during the knights' arrival. It only took a minute for the small procession of nobles to wind its way past the last of the commoners.

Areck waited with an impassive eye, noticing how fast the commoners moved when confronted by the count's guards, likely thinking that to linger would incur the wrath of either the count or the Bre'Dmorian commander. He hardly noticed when the contingent of soldiers stopped, and Lysen dismounted and walked past him to join the Bre'Dmorian ranks.

"Commander." The voice of Count Oslov Gustafson drifted over the crowd. "We were not expecting you so soon!"

Areck bowed as the count approached. The man's small stature did not diminish his vibrant green eyes or the excited smile that stretched across his face.

"Forgive my informal greeting, my lords," said the count, taking the silence from Areck as being aimed at his own breach of protocol. "I am Oslov Gustafson, Count of Brenly. I oversee this town."

"Thank you for the welcome, my lord. I am Field Captain Areck of Brenly," Areck answered, trying to remember the proper etiquette to greet a high ranking noble lord.

"Not much of a welcome, Lord Areck," Gustafson said with a small smile, glancing around. "As you can see, my title has done little to help this town."

"It hasn't changed so much since I left," said Areck, following the count's gaze. "However, I am sure you have more—"

"You come from here?" the count interrupted him.

"A long time ago."

"I do not remember seeing any notice of knightly conscription from this region in over thirty years. How old are you, commander?" Gustafson asked.

"Old enough to be a field captain," Areck responded, annoyed at the questioning.

"I meant no disrespect, Lord Areck," said the count, "but you don't exactly look old enough to be a knight—none of you do."

Areck felt his face flush in anger. The count was questioning his command! Thinking quickly, Areck put on his best face of rage and leaned towards the noble lord. Several guards stepped forward, hands resting on their hilts. If it became known that a young man, not even promoted to the rank of knight, had come to protect the town, none of the local soldiers would follow.

"Stand down!" Count Gustafson said, his face creased with worry.

"I told you I was a field captain, my lord," Areck whispered in the noble's ear, his eyes upon the guardsmen. "You are wise to assume that that none of us are knights. In fact, there isn't a knight among us and I am no lord. However, if you would be so kind as to accept my help and move this procession to your estate, I would be happy to explain myself."

Count Gustafson was about to protest when Areck cut him off.

"Do not press this issue, my lord," he whispered. "We are here to help you. If you show us up now, you will be forced to wait another month for the Academy to respond, if ever."

The count stood in thought, his face flushed in anger. Areck realized too late that by securing his own command, he had unwittingly shown up the count. Even if Count Gustafson agreed to his terms, it would look as if the Bre'Dmorian had said something threatening. Areck realized it would be the gossip of the count's estate long after his command ended.

"My lord?" said the nearest aid, his face pinched in fear.

Finally, Count Gustafson shook his head and turned to face his estate seneschal. "Lord Barton, please hurry ahead and ready my war room for a private audience."

"Are you sure, my lord?"

"Do not question me, Seneschal," said the count. "The commander has explained his plan to me in short and needs a more private setting to make me fully aware of his preparations."

Areck was about to argue; he had said nothing of a plan! He opened his mouth for a retort when Redmon walked up.

"My lord has ever been cautious when considering these dangerous times," said Redmon, nudging Areck in the back. Areck snapped his mouth shut as his second-in-command continued. "By your leave, my lords, I think it would be wise for me to take the men to the barracks and discuss matters with your captain of the guard . . . at least while the two of you discuss operations."

"A fine idea," Lord Gustafson said, turning his attention back to Areck. "However, I am afraid you will find most of the guardsmen infected by this wretched fever."

"How many?" asked Redmon, frowning.

"Enough that we have started to conscript soldiers from outlying hamlets. I do not have an exact number, but Karl here will lead you to Captain Telmouth for details."

"Thank you, Baron," Redmon said with a slight nod, displaying no emotion. "Do I have permission to leave, Captain Areck?"

"When you are finished, please report back, Lieutenant." Areck nodded, seeing his company of men staring straight ahead, following knightly Code to the letter.

"Lord Gustafson, we should get to business before nightfall," Areck continued. He was about to play a dangerous game and he knew it. Fortunately for him, the count seemed willing to listen to the masquerade. It would now be up to him to continue the pretense.

"Of course, Captain," said Count Gustafson, not referring to the knight with proper etiquette. With a flourish the noble turned away and issued orders that sent various aids scrambling.

Areck could tell the count was furious . . . yet stuck. He guessed that the noble was not happy about the current situation, but at the same time was not willing to openly alienate any aid the Academy had sent.

Areck glanced at the sky, which had been perpetually overcast since the day they had left Stormwind. It always seemed about to rain, but never did.

He faintly heard Redmon issue orders to move: "Dismount and break from the column. We are moving to the barracks." When the men assented, Redmon followed the pock-marked Karl, signaling the others to follow him.

Count Gustafson pulled on Areck's arm. "If you will follow me, Captain, preparations have been made." Count Oslov walked close to Areck, hinting at a greater meaning. "And my private chambers await our arrival."

So the count is preparing a room where he can interrogate me, Areck thought with an amused smile. *I should not be surprised—since I did force his hand.* By telling the count he had something significant to say, there would be no way out around it. However, Areck had achieved the most important part of entering the town—securing his power. Now that the tough part was over, he needed only to show his insignia of rank and explain the purpose of his company. It was a long story, one that would no doubt anger Count Gustafson. But it was not Areck's fault that a single company of men, all squires, had been sent as aid. He would also point out that at least his small company would alleviate *some* of the stress. It wasn't much . . . but at least it was something.

Areck could not help but feel that though he had done his job, it seemed so useless. The seeping sickness Brenly harbored should warrant several priests. Even if he could secure the area, there was no way to defend the town without walls and soldiers' units. He just couldn't shake the question: why had Starsgalt not intervened on the behalf of these people?

As he rode in silence, his thought became, *How could Duke Hawkwind and Lord Lightbringer allow this to happen?* He had been taught his entire life to protect the weak. Who was protecting these people? He wondered what other small towns of Arsgoth looked like; and if they were anything like this, no wonder chaos seeded itself in the weak.

Areck clamped his mouth shut. He dared call himself a squire after such blasphemous thoughts!

When the small party reached the first gates of the count's estate, its marble pillars chipped and its vegetation overgrown, Areck realized that this was not a lord who lived regally while his people starved. From a distance visitors might have taken the large estate as a rather extravagant version of a small keep. However, as was common in an unfortified town, there was no central keep or castle built on high ground. Instead the estate was surrounded by short walls, only high enough to keep out onlookers, a single entrance guarded by a pair of guard towers, and a weak iron gate.

As the party approached, a pair of bedraggled guardsmen leapt to their feet and saluted Count Gustafson. The short man dismissed the guard's formality with a quick wave of his hand. Both guards took the hint and barked orders inside, where Areck could hear the cranking and creaking of a chain opening the gate.

Waiting for the count to march in, Areck saw a hopeful glint in the young guardsmen's eyes, and noticed that they were several years younger than him, younger than fifth year tyros. They looked at him with eyes that burned with sickness, and something else he had seen so often: knightly respect and admiration. He nodded at each young man and moved on, disguising his pity. It was unfortunate that they had been conscripted at such a young age. It was something he would bring to the count's attention, as the law stated that no male under the age of sixteen was allowed to serve in the military.

Though the military age of young men was the least of Areck's concerns, the law was the law, and Count Gustafson should respect it.

As Areck followed the count up a set of stairs and into a small room, he noted for the first time that there was more to the count than politics. As they entered the room, he saw aged parchments: maps of the duchy, ancient military outposts, and various geographic locations of natural landscape dotting the walls and floor.

Areck reappraised the count. Though the noble had obviously been born to privilege, what Areck saw indicated that the tiny man was more of a military man than a spoiled noble. It also meant the count knew the goings on of the rest of the realm.

The count walked over to a desk made of a dark brown wood, moved around behind it, and scribbled on a piece of parchment. He rose and extended the document to one of the guardsman blocking the door. Satisfied that everything was in motion, he closed the door, mindful to lock it. Finally, the noble lord sat back down and waved at Areck to take a seat.

Areck would have felt more in control had he remained standing, yet to do so would be a slight to the noble's honor, something he couldn't afford.

"So tell me, Captain Areck," Count Gustafson began, eyeing the young man with skepticism, "why shouldn't I tell everyone our little secret?"

"I think your question might answer itself, my lord," Areck retorted, gesturing towards the small city. "However, if you will hear my story, maybe you can find a better reason."

"Yes, yes," the count said, his voice crackling in emotion. "I suppose it would be a good idea to hear more Bre'Dmorian words—words meant to cover up the shit I smell every day! You know the ones I speak of, Squire: the shit that goes by the name of roses."

Areck was too stunned to be appalled. His jaw dropped open at the savageness of the words.

"I am not sure what words you are speaking of, my lord," Areck finally said. "However, I assure you my company has come to offer our services."

"You are *squires*, damn it!" the count slammed his hand down. "I asked for reinforcements from Duke Hawkwind and your precious Academy, and look what they sent me!"

"If you are referring to the squires who have been through a great deal to get here, or the ones who notified you of your fallen comrades, or the ones who rode east to assist in transferring information, then I think we have been of great use," Areck looked into the count's eyes, his tone firm and unforgiving.

Areck's manner gave Count Gustafson pause; his eyes grew dark and more reserved. They were on thin ice.

"Do tell me, Captain, what use do you think seven young men are against an entire band of marauding orcs? What good can you do for my poor, sick people?" Lord Oslov said, fighting the rage that burned behind his eyes.

Areck gave a frustrated sigh. He needed to give a practical answer but there wasn't one. "Regardless of my age I have been field-promoted to knight-captain," Areck said. "You have already seen for yourself that my second, Squire Redmon, has begun to assess your manpower. It may be that we can do nothing against these orcs, but—"

"Where is your proof?" interrupted the count.

"My what?"

"Your proof, *Captain*," Count Gustafson said, drawing out the words as if Areck were daft. "Where are the papers, signed and dated, that have given you a field command?"

"There are no papers," Areck said, pulling Lord Silvershield's signet ring from a pouch, along with the insignia of a captain and handing them over to Gustafson. "However, I do have these."

Count Gustafson took both pieces and rolled them over thoughtfully, his eyes still dark with anger. "How do I know you did not take them from your dead commander's fingers?"

The comment was absurd, and Areck tried to remain patient, his eyes locked on the count. "What would be the purpose of killing a knight-captain, removing his ring, insignia, and orders, then riding into a town surrounded by orcs and disease?"

"Granted, that question was a bit of a stretch," the count relented. "But I do want to know how you got these."

"I told you we have come to offer aid," said Areck, leaning forward so his hands were folded across the table. "Are you now willing to listen to me?"

"It is going to have to be a great tale." Count Gustafson snorted in contempt. "I still do not see how a single company of men, even if you *were* knights, could assist in our plight."

"To start, these two items belong to Knight-Captain Bowon Silvershield, the commanding officer of this company," Areck said, ignoring Lord Oslov Gustafson's snort. "And this was to be a select group of squires' first campaign, a training exercise."

"How dare they . . .! You are here on a *training* mission?"

"We were sent here to offer aid for a small disturbance. By all reports, we were told that you had requested aid for missing persons and possibly a small group of bandits," Areck replied. "The reports of orcish activity and sickness are unexpected dilemmas which we are now forced to deal with."

The count opened his mouth, but Areck continued, "One of *many* unexpected events that we have been forced to adapt to."

"What do you mean?" asked Count Gustafson, his rosy complexion piqued with curiosity.

"Well, to start, we have suffered casualties: two of the three knights our company carried," Areck explained. "That is the reason Lord Silvershield is not here, as he was forced to continue on to Natalinople. It is also why Knight-Captain Silvershield promoted me, his personal squire, before continuing."

"What could have possibly caused casualties to an armed party of Bre'Dmorians . . .?" Count Gustafson was cut off mid-sentence, as Areck raised his hand for silence.

"I mean no disrespect, my lord, but that information is private," Areck said. "What is important now is the fact that when I received news of your jeopardy, I decided to continue on with my orders, rather than turning back to Stormwind. Those orders were to report here to you, awaiting Lord Silvershield and possible reinforcements."

The count's eyes sparkled at this news. "Reinforcements?"

"Baron Marqel was asked to send a pair of writs to both the ducal palace and the Bre'Dmorian Academy for assistance. I saw the couriers leave with my own eyes," Areck explained. "However, looking at your township, I would guess that neither the church nor Duke Hawkwind consider our 'training exercise' important enough to send more men, even with the unexpected events."

"So say it straight, Captain, what do you want of me?" asked the count, realizing that Areck was indeed trying to assist.

"I need you to embrace my command, my lord," Areck said, tapping his leg in nervousness. He was finally to the crux of the matter. "I will send a writ to Lord Lightbringer, relaying my personal interpretation of the situation. After that, all we can do is hope that it will be enough to draw reinforcements."

"It is my only option, isn't it?" sighed Lord Gustafson. "And what will we do in the meantime?"

"To start, we need to quarantine the sick and possibly burn the infected parts of town for the sake of containing the sickness," Areck replied. "Then we must begin to fortify this location, sending scouting parties into the outskirts of the forest. Orcs are cowardly beasts. If we can show them enough military activity in the area, they may move on to easier prey. And finally, we wait."

The conversation took several more hours to complete, as the men discussed various strategies. The new Captain of Brenly learned all he could about the landscape, defensibility, and the layout of the region. When Areck finally left the room, it was dark and streaks of moonlight pierced the ever-shifting cloud cover.

Well, he thought to himself, *the first part of my plan has taken effect. Now if I can only convince myself that this is a good idea.*

Areck lingered only a moment before he moved off into the darkness. His next stop would be the barracks, where his men would be fast asleep.

21

ARECK'S SECOND day in Brenly kept him at the count's estate, away from his men. He was so busy writing greetings and petitions for knightly aid that he had no time to visit with Lieutenant Redmon. He wondered if every other commander spent most of their days processing paperwork. Shrugging, he put his head back down and went to work.

It wasn't until late in the evening of the third night, as he was studying maps, that a solid knock sounded on his chamber door. Areck looked up from the maps, hoping whoever was knocking would either think him gone or let themselves in. He was about to pull an architectural map of the town layout from the bottom of the pile, when the knock came again.

Areck grumbled, stood, and moved to the door. He had specifically asked for a night of peace; if this was a servant, or another aid from the count, he would show his ire and dismiss them at once.

With a sigh he opened the door. To Areck's surprise his second-in-command stood outside in an informal stance. Turning sideways, Areck gave the proper gesture and invited Squire Redmon in. He closed the door and moved behind his desk.

"Take a seat, Squire Redmon."

"I prefer to stand, sir," Redmon replied, but his stance relaxed. "Are you enjoying playing captain?"

"Busy, very busy," Areck said, nearly smiling. "After a night of explaining who we are and why we are here, Count Gustafson has kept me running from one aid to the next. Everyone wishes action, but they won't give me time to plan anything."

"That is to be expected, sir," Redmon said, a small smile cracking his face. "If I were the count, the arrival of a mere seven men would be insulting. He is most likely testing your resolve, using your charisma to raise morale."

"Did you see how these people looked at us when we rode in? How can I possibly help their morale?" Areck asked, face relaxed but betraying desperation.

"I know my late Lord Vinion despised what he viewed as your shortcomings," Redmon said after a moment, "but he also saw a man who would accept punishment and demand a certain respect. Count Gustafson is obviously using those same strengths to his advantage, hoping that you are willing to play the role and charismatic enough to pull it off—which will give him time to make his own plans."

Areck mulled the information over. It was bold of Redmon to admit that Lord Vinion had despised him. That Redmon had been the knight-captain's personal squire made the words more significant: Redmon was establishing rapport, and offering his support.

Areck knew his lieutenant was correct. If he was in Count Gustafson's place, he would use the same advantage. It was risky, but the count was playing on Areck's own need for secrecy.

"Let us hope that I can continue to play the part, then, until a refreshment of forces arrives," Areck said.

"You have sent the writ, then, sir?" Redmon asked.

"Unfortunately, no. As I said, the count has not let me out of his sight long enough to take any action."

"The writ needs to be sent *as soon as possible*, sir," Redmon said, his voice low. It seemed this was the reason he had come to Areck so late in the night.

"I was finishing it as you knocked on my door," Areck offered.

"I do not mean to pressure you, sir. However, I have nearly finished my investigation; if we are forced into action, our situation will turn from bad to dire."

"You have ascertained the health of the garrison, then?" Areck leaned forward with interest. This was the piece of information for which he had been waiting. This would nudge Lord Taryon into sending a proper column of knights into the town. Everything depended on this number.

"Indeed, sir. Captain Telmouth has been helpful, if a little condescending. Each time he looks at me, I can see him calculating a way to use my authority to his benefit." Redmon described the shenanigans of the amiable captain.

"That is all fine, Lieutenant, but what of the numbers?" Areck said to curtail the tangent.

Redmon's face flushed and his body stiffened. "I apologize for the small talk, sir," Redmon said. "The town holds a garrison of approximately one hundred soldiers and several dozen guardsmen. However, Count Gustafson has employed several conscripts due to illness. Quite honestly, the count has done a remarkable job keeping the town as safe as it is."

Areck listened to Redmon's report on the military deployment of Brenly and a thought came to him of the boys used as guardsmen at the count's estate. Though he had not mentioned the younger men being posted as guardsmen, he had not forgotten the fact. Clearly, the boys had been accepted as guardsmen in lieu of healthy conscripts.

The town was commissioned with only a single regiment of men, or one hundred and forty soldiers, with a single captain as the commander. Though the captain would have several lieutenants and sergeants, it really was a small, ill-prepared garrison meant only for protection.

Areck sighed. He had hoped the numbers would be much higher, or at least more veteran, better equipped to bring the fight to the enemy.

"The numbers are weaker than they seem, sir," Redmon paused, his face splitting in a frown. "Over seventy percent of the men have the weeping fever; a dozen of those have entered the last stage of the sickness. I am no doctor, but I guess that most of the infected will not last more than a week."

Areck did his best to detach himself. The disease was lethal and he had to look objectively at their situation. He also needed to figure out how many men would be healthy enough to use, should any problems arise. He dreaded to think what his next problem would be—quarantining the sick into two camps: those who might still shake the sickness, and those who were beyond help.

"That leaves us roughly forty-two healthy men," Redmon droned on in an analytical manner. "The good news is that Captain Telmouth is unaffected by the sickness, as are most of his commanders. Like I said earlier, each officer is willing to do whatever it takes . . . to save themselves."

Areck sorted through the information. This was grave news. Out of one hundred and forty total men, only forty-two were healthy. He could almost guarantee that half of those men would be of actual use.

How can I be so unfeeling? I am about to insist that the count quarantine his own people. I am about to send hundreds of men, women, and children to untimely deaths! And here am I thinking only of military strategy!

He did his best to maintain his composure as his stomach rolled in knots. He knew this would be the only way to save the town. The thought of sentencing men to their deaths by lack of medicinal aid almost made him second guess his decision.

"Have you been able to track down the source of the disease?" Areck managed.

"Two of the three barracks account for nearly all of the sickness, the same with several quarters of the township," Redmon replied.

Areck wanted to scream. He wanted no part in this game. *Why did I not turn back to Stormwind and allow someone better to deal with this situation?*

"Because we are following the will of God," said Redmon, as if he had been wondering the same thing. "I saw the look in your eyes the day we rode into Brenly. You want to help these people. We all do. That is our purpose."

Areck looked up with the realization that he had said his last thought out loud. "Tomorrow we begin," Areck said through clenched teeth, his frustration showing. "At daybreak, gather the sick and quarantine them in one of the infected quarters."

"There are not enough of us to carry out such an order," Redmon said.

"Gather whatever resources you need. You said the captain is willing to help us. If so, then he will know that this is a necessary action and should be willing to sacrifice enough men to accomplish this task."

Redmon nodded. Areck saw that his second-in-command had been waiting for this, and though he was reserved, it looked like the man's pulse had quickened. Areck took it as a good sign that the man did not take killing lightly, whatever the justification; even in this situation where they would be saving thousands of lives, it would still be hard.

As the lieutenant turned to go, Areck spoke another thought that gripped him. "Make sure each family gathers their belongings; this relocation will leave many people bereft."

"What do you plan to do, sir?"

"The following daybreak, I will burn the infected areas to the ground," Areck said, dropping his eyes. He had finally said what had been eating at his soul. The end would justify the means. To save thousands, he would need to purge the sickness—something that the count had refused to do.

"It will be done, my lord," Redmon said as he walked from the room and shut the door.

That Redmon had referred to him with a knightly title did not go unnoticed. Areck's eyes lingered on the door, then he pulled a quill from atop a shelf and began to pen a letter. There would be no turning back after tonight. From here on out, he would no longer be acting.

A line of people followed several squads of escorting guardsmen to the eastern district of the town. A large stone building, once known as the Lawlian Fortress, had once quartered a column of Bre'Dmorian knights and now loomed menacingly in the morning sky, made more ominous by the fact that it had once been a jail.

Areck noticed that the people were sullen, accepting their fate with quiet dignity. As he looked back, he could see that the line trailed off to the town center, where his company of squires sorted out the sick and those still unaffected by the disease. He felt the trepidation of each person. Their eyes were cast downward, and many held weeping children with a yellowish tinge to their skin.

Areck could not help but think that the line looked a lot like a criminals being marched off to their death. The thought made him shiver.

He was so deep in self-loathing that he did not hear the slow plodding of hooves approaching from the town center.

"How *dare* you issue these orders without consulting me, Commander?" Count Gustafson hissed, his face contorted in rage. The man sat on a thin stallion who danced around Areck's charger. The commotion caused the line to stop, and the creaking of the carts holding the terminally ill to come to a halt. All eyes turned towards the hostile count.

"I told you this town needed to be quarantined, my lord," Areck held his hand up before the count could respond. "If you had not kept me so busy with your local dignitaries, I would have started this task the day after we talked. Even now, it may be too late."

"Does the Bre'Dmorian Order now condone killing innocent people?" said the count through clenched teeth, his voice catching.

"My lord, if you can not keep your voice down, you will have to leave," Areck said. Did Lord Gustafson not understand? Areck hated this as much he did.

Count Gustafson looked taken aback by the comment and his eyes were wide with uncontrollable rage.

He is asking himself how I have the gall to call him out, Areck thought. *He is trying to show me up and remove his mistake.* He wanted to tell the count that inaction had cost many lives. This was the only way. The town had to be purged.

The count moved his horse next to Areck and leaned in. "You are killing my people!"

"I am doing what must be done!" Areck shot an accusing glare at the count. "This decision should have never fallen to me! It should have been done *weeks* ago, when your people were in the beginning stages. Only by God's mercy has most of your town been lucky enough to stay unaffected."

The words had the desired effect. Count Gustafson shut his mouth, his hands shaking. Areck had not wanted a struggle of power and had intentionally left the man with few options. He knew that if the count tried to publicly embarrass him, it would be a rebuke to the Church. If Count Gustafson did that, *all* aid would be cut off to his town.

"I should have never hoped," Lord Oslov Gustafson whispered, his face draining of its color. The man looked old, as if the event had sucked out ten years of his life. "How can you be so unfeeling under these circumstances? You are ordering the death of my people!"

Areck looked at the count. He wanted to tell the noble that duty came first. However, first he needed to get things moving again. He gave several orders and the carts began to heave and the line began to move.

"I am not as unfeeling as you might think, my lord," Areck whispered. "I will have my men make sure that we offer as many comforts as possible to the sick. We will save as many as we can. This is not my preference, but there is no choice here. The disease is running rampant in your poorer quarters and the barracks. I am afraid this is only the first part of what must be done."

"What else do you plan?"

"You know what must come next," Areck said. "I will collect every diseased person in the town, move them to this section, and light it on fire."

"You will burn the town to the ground, then? The duke will be infuriated with the cost," Count Oslov announced. "He will never allow it. There is no way we can rebuild."

"I would never slander a lord, but the duke has allowed . . . *this* to exist. If it becomes an issue, I am sure can explain that you thought this was the only way to save his loyal subjects."

"There is no way I can go to the duke with this," the count whispered furiously. "I don't agree with it. I will—"

"Then give the order for it to end, and it will," said Areck his face flushing in embarrassment. He knew the other man was being selfish, tucking his own guilt neatly away.

Count Gustafson turned away. His red face told Areck that he was right. "Is there anything else you need from me, Commander?"

"Tell your men to offer as much help as they can and be ready for action. Once we start the fires, there is a chance that your orc tribe will see the flames and come closer," Areck explained, turning to look at the forest where the first sighting of the orc tribe had been. "If we are lucky, they won't come until we have built some fortifications around the perimeter of the town."

"I will do as you ask," Count Gustafson said, with his back to Areck. "You sent the writ to Aresleigh?"

"I did," replied Areck. "That is why we must hurry, in case we get no reply and are driven into more severe actions."

The count was silent for a moment. "You will let me know if any word comes in, Commander." It was not a question.

Areck watched the nobleman as he rode away. He couldn't help but notice the man's shoulders were shaking, as though he was crying.

For three days Areck met with Count Gustafson before dawn, discussing the logistics for gathering the people of Brenly. With the backing of the count, whom the people trusted and respected, the procedure had gone over without a riot. However, Areck feared that as the sickness began to claim more lives of those in the hospital, people would panic. He did not want to suppress such an outcry with force but could not allow those already dying of the disease to further spread it.

Early the first morning Areck set the poorest district within the town aflame, his men managing the flames with an alchemical liquid that suppressed the fire's spread.

For the most part Count Gustafson had lain low for Areck's benefit. If Gustafson had shown up in the same state as he had the first morning, people would begin to ask questions. However, the man had been busy inside his own household and did not waste time explaining the tough decision to purge the city. Areck did not mind that the count had embellished the story by adding that this had been the duke's plan from the beginning, to be carried out by God's knights as a reward for the town's piety.

Around mid-day, as Areck watched the wandering billows of smoke rise from the western portion of the town where the buildings lay smoldering, Redmon trotted up.

"My lord," Redmon began, his calm voice belying nothing, "Captain Telmouth and I have sent a group of woodcutters into the forest. We have charged them with felling enough trees to begin fortification of the perimeter."

"Have we gathered the rest of the sick, then?" Areck asked, grateful for Redmon's ability to follow orders without question.

"It will be complete by nightfall," said Redmon. "The people are dignified in their unhappy fate. I think those truly sick know they are going to die regardless."

The voice was filled with the emotionless candor of a Bre'Dmorian doing his duty. Areck knew this is how he must have sounded to the count, and even to his own men.

"We still have a good day before us, Lieutenant," Areck said. "When you have stripped each quarter and moved the last of the people, burn the last contaminated sections of the town. I want it purged by nightfall tomorrow."

"What of the sick?"

"You know as well as I that there is nothing we can do for them," Areck replied, "but save all that you can."

"And for those that are in the last stages?"

"Place them away from the others and send word for Count Gustafson. He seems to be under the impression that we do not care . . . so let him give the order to save the rest of his town," Areck explained. "Personally, I will offer God prayers so that our Shepherd may lead them into His embrace."

"I will do as you command, my lord," Redmon said, his eyes bright at the mention of God. "And, I will also offer a prayer for their souls."

Areck nodded and turned back to the plume of smoke rising high. He was surprised that the fires had not brought any undue attention and did not want to press his chances. He would send several men to douse the flames with buckets of water or a viscous retardant. The last thing the town needed was to be scouted by a band of curious marauders, especially in their current condition.

He was just about to issue the order when he heard the pounding of hoof beats, as did Redmon. The noise made the pair turn to meet the incoming riders.

Areck could tell that the riders were not couriers, but rode mounts with steel-shod hooves. His first thought was that the High Lightbringer had already responded to his writ, but the thought did not last long. The riders, their uniforms soiled and faces creased in determination, rounded a small cluster of ramshackle houses.

Areck noticed that the horses trailing the party carried several figures slumped over and laying across saddles.

What are they doing outside of the town? Areck thought, then remembered Redmon's words. These were the lieutenant's wood-gatherers and scouts

With a pull on the reins and a soft squeeze of his knees, Areck's stallion trotted to the town's courtyard. He felt Redmon's mount approach from behind, pace to the right, and then stand next to him. Redmon was pale at having sent men to their deaths.

The leader, a man in his middle years with a beak nose and salted black hair, held up his hand. The riders halted, dismounted in a swift movement, and knelt before Areck's stallion.

"My lord," said the man. The three golden bands on his right arm indicated he was a sergeant in the royal army.

"Rise, Sergeant," Areck replied, his stomach once again rolling, his eyes drifting to the bodies hanging over the horses. "What happened?"

The sergeant stood as did the rest, though their eyes remained on the ground. "As we were scouting out the area, we were ambushed by orcs. I tried to form ranks and fight, my lord, but when men started dying . . . well, I issued the order to fall back. We heard drums and I figured it wouldn't be proper to be killed without first warning you."

"Thank you, Sergeant," Areck said with understanding. He wondered if he would have done the same thing—to lose men, and then recognize that a retreat was his best option. It was something that the great generals of the past had done.

"You said there were drums?" Redmon asked.

"Yes, my lord," said the sergeant. "The force we encountered was skirmishers. It wasn't until we stood to fight that the drumming began. It sounded as if it was coming from several locations."

Areck grimaced. It seemed his instinct had been correct: the orcs had sent scouts upon seeing plumes of smoke. The question was, what would they do next? By all accounts the race was fractured, cowardly, and loved to plunder weak targets. However, drummers indicated that there was more than one orcish tribe within the surrounding forests; each tribe contained thirty to a hundred orcs.

"We'd better double the guard posts, my lord," said Redmon, his hazel eyes burning. "If there are drummers in the forest, more than a small marauding party sits out there, waiting for an opportunity to attack."

A deep silence followed. Areck sat atop his stallion with his eyes closed, head tilted in consternation. The entire town was in danger. If a tribe of orcs waited in the forest, then his small force would be hard pressed. And with the town ready to be burned and no fortifications, there were just too many attack points for his few men to cover. There would be no way to stop this orc attack. What if they lost a granary? Or if there were multiple tribes wandering about . . . wouldn't that make them bold enough to try to sack the town itself? They would completely raze the village, killing whomever they couldn't take for food. He could see only one option, and it was another gamble.

Are you a fool? He screamed at himself. *I sit here on my horse, acting like some sort of hero out of the Tome of Anduin!*

Areck calmed the furious thoughts in his mind. He told himself that he was now a commander and that he needed to act like it. All these things he had done and would continue to do, were because he was a Bre'Dmorian, and sometimes a leader needed to make decisions that cost some lives to save others. This had been his philosophy when quarantining the town.

However, this was different.

His plan was to fight in the forest. He would use surprise against the orcish forces. That he had never fought in a true battle made the decision even harder. None of his company had ever killed another sentient being, and now they would be expected to fight for their lives against a race of ravenous destroyers. Worse, he would lead men to their deaths. If he chose this course, there would be significant casualties in the best of scenarios, a fact the town could hardly bear.

What if your plan fails? What if the entire garrison is destroyed? Who will protect the rest?

"Well, from the looks of it, our small army has been decreased by several soldiers," Redmon broke the silence. "I don't think we have enough left to defend the town. We could . . ."

Areck raised his hand, politely gesturing for silence. "How many men have cavalry experience?"

The question surprised the lieutenant. "Fewer than twenty, my lord," Redmon said. "I would need to confirm the number with Captain Telmouth."

"Do that, Lieutenant."

"You have a plan?" asked Redmon with a frown.

"I would attack these orcs preemptively, but first I need those numbers," replied Areck, looking across the hazy valley to the estate. He needed to talk to Count Gustafson, and time was running out.

Redmon murmured as he left, "A wise choice, my lord; the men will follow you."

To their deaths, Areck thought in resignation. This outpost was now in his hands. He considered his choices: fight or flee. He wondered if it was even in him to retreat.

Areck decided then that taking the offense was the only choice. He would sacrifice some of his men, though the greatest casualties would come from the common soldiers.

Maybe I will be one of those who perish. He pursed his lips in thought. If he died, no one could say that he had been a fake, a coward, and worst of all, poor in his decision-making.

With a last hopeful gesture, he dismissed all the men standing in front of him. They needed to find a bath and some food. He prayed that his writ was in Aresleigh by now, and that Lord Taryon would send reinforcements. Last, he prayed that Lord Silvershield was hurrying out of Natalinople and back towards his command.

Areck wished that he had never been given command, that someone would step up and relieve him of the burden. In a moment of clarity, he knew that his soul would be forever changed. He felt the momentary derailing of the fate that followed a warrior through life. If he survived this, if his men survived this, maybe they would only court-martial him. And if he died, it would be with honor.

Areck turned his horse and spurred himself towards the count's estate. He hoped that the information had preceded him, making his explanation easier. Maybe Count Gustafson would embrace this action simply in hopes that Areck would die and he would no longer have to submit to the demanding squire.

The count is a good man, Areck thought. *He is only trying to do what is best for his people. Let us hope we see eye to eye on this matter . . .*

Even if Gustafson didn't, Areck knew that his destiny was to lead his men into the forest. With a resigned sigh he passed through the gates.

On the morrow, the town of Brenly would rise up.

22

WHEN ARECK awoke the next morning, he heard the smatter of rain drops against the stone of his windowsill. He had not slept well; visions of his atrocities swam in his mind. The last nightmare had woken him in the middle of the night, sweat pouring from his face, cold chills running down his spine. That he awoke to a downpour made him apprehensive. Rain on the eve of battle was a bad omen. It took all of his strength to swing his legs over his bed, stand up, and move to a small water basin that had been filled for his use.

Areck cupped his hands and splashed cool water on his face. When he looked into the small mirror, he saw someone else looking back at him. His eyes bore dark circles and his once-soft features looked hard, as if the innocence had been burnt away, leaving only determination and duty. His stomach clenched in nervousness.

Why shouldn't *I be nervous?* He whispered to himself, drying off his face. *You are about to gather all military within the town and kill them.*

He knew his doubts were getting the better of him. The others had readily agreed that this was a good choice. He had spent several hours in council with Count Gustafson, Squire Redmon, and Captain Telmouth. Each man admitted that the venture was risky but necessary.

Areck appreciated the count's acceptance and understanding. In fact, upon mentioning that he would lead the men, Lord Oslov had looked at him with . . . respect? Areck shook away any thoughts of camaraderie. It would only be a matter of time before the count turned him in for fraudulent actions; that was, if he lived long enough to see reinforcements arrive.

Areck pulled down on his eye, revealing the soft pink flesh underneath. The whites of his eyes were streaked with small veins.

A lack of sleep, he thought. *I can't wait to be back in a bed with no responsibilities.* The thought seemed almost alien to him. He had gone down a forbidden road and he knew he could never recover. When the dying started he would forever be changed, either given the responsibility of blame in which he would be court marshaled, or responsible for a victory in which he deserved no recognition.

As he strapped on his armor, his mind turned back to the night's conversation with Count Gustafson. Areck was glad he had not gotten another verbal lashing from the man. He had expected the count to corner him, call him a fool, and denounce him as a traitorous fraud. However, Oslov had actually agreed with the plan, though he did not condone attacking an orc tribe. The noble had seen Areck's point: there was no way to defend the town with so few men and no fortifications. The noble had even been adamant about using haste and secrecy when leaving the town, using hunting trails to enter the forest from the north rather than marching directly off to war.

Areck agreed with many of the count's suggestions, trusting him and Captain Telmouth to provide accurate details of the terrain. He had listened attentively, writing down details, as the men strategized.

The plan was solid. His full contingent of men would consist of only twenty-four riders, a single column, seven of whom were Bre'Dmorian squires. Though none of the soldiers besides Captain Telmouth and his officers was expert horsemen, each man bore the marks of lifelong soldiers. That was to say, all had been blooded. Areck had been unyielding in his request: only those soldiers who had been in battle, excluding his group of squires, would be brought along for the expedition. That decision had cut their numbers in half.

His four advisors shook their heads against his logic. Yet in the end they had all succumbed to his will, understanding that untrained cavalry would only get in the way, and the point was to bring back as many men as possible.

Areck would send out a pair of scouts to report back each hour or upon seeing any signs of the orcs. He hoped that his scouts would find some skirmishing units before the main force came upon an encampment, hopefully cutting off reinforcements and catching the orcs by surprise.

If his plan succeeded, they stood a chance. Amazingly enough, everyone agreed—and none looked concerned; or if they were, they hid it well. He knew *he* was concerned!

They all think I actually know what I am doing, he thought as he tied the last of his straps. He walked outside to find a pair of soldiers waiting for him, hands held in salute. He wished the nervousness would go away. The men had come to escort him to the stables. They would all expect his nerves to be made of steel, hard as iron, with the grace of the silver.

He dismissed the men's salutes, doing his best to stay formal but polite. He assessed that both looked excited and ready for battle. However, he had business to see to before heading off to his stallion. He turned to the men and invited them to the chapel for a morning prayer. They squinted uncomfortably and asked to attend the horses instead. Areck smiled.

Though he assumed that each man in the town believed in Starsgalt, only the most pious would give thanks before entering battle. For him it was a way of life. He prayed each morning for a glorious day in service. He prayed each evening in thanks for the day's blessing. He prayed when he was conflicted. He had not fallen into a communion with God nor did he feel the sickness that accompanied divine magic, but this did not worry him. It was a test of faith. He might be unworthy of God's attention, but his men and this town certainly deserved God's consideration.

Areck cleared his mind as he moved past the dining hall and into a small chapel with red candles burning.

"Praying for a glorious battle, Commander?" Count Oslov Gustafson shuffled up behind him.

"I am praying that I bring each man back alive," Areck said, dropping to his knees in a reverent position. He pulled one of the candles to the floor and lit his own.

The count grunted in a satisfied tone and said that he would be waiting at the stables.

Areck ignored the words and closed his eyes. Instantly he felt the warmth of God's embrace and the divine sickness which followed it.

Starsgalt, I bask in your light, he began. *I have come so many times in the last few days seeking solace that I doubt you even care. However, this morning I come not for myself but for my men. They believe me, your servant, to be something I am not. Please give me the strength to see them through this. If you desire a sacrifice be made, take me instead of any man. I offer my life willingly to you and to them.*

Areck let the silence in his soul linger. It felt so good to say those words. It nearly relieved the guilt of his predicament. He saw his candle flicker. His prayers were heard.

Thank you, God, for this lesson in humility. I forever bask in your glory; he continued to recite the Code to which each knight adhered. It took almost an hour before Areck of Brenly was done.

The rain fell without mercy as Areck entered the stables, his face lit with a fervent smile. He perceived God's presence as a blessing. For the first time in weeks he felt as if he would no longer have to bear the burden of these choices, that God would keep his word and look over the column. It made him wonder if God would participate when they engaged the enemy.

Though he had never led such an exercise, each man looked alert. He hoped that they maintained such faith in him—rather, in God—to lead them all into the woods and out again.

Before he was ready to give the order, Areck turned around trying to find the count. He wanted to let the man know that he would bring his men back alive. As his eyes adjusted to the dim light of the stable, he noticed Count Gustafson near the doors, waiting for him.

Areck looked at each officer and four eyes stared proudly back, their faith unwavering in the face of duty. He respected these men. They meant to follow him to the end. He hoped he could serve them well.

Count Oslov approached Areck and offered several final pieces of advice—places where soldiers could find high ground and tactical observations—before bowing his head and stepping back. Areck thanked the count for his input then pulled himself onto his warhorse.

"Knight-Lieutenant Redmon, I think it is time we ride out and take a look at our column," Areck said, turning the mount towards the stable doors. He hardly recognized the breach in protocol he had just committed—it was custom to ask the captain of the guard to lead them out—and most of the men in this column were the captains.

He was about to say something, when Redmon cut him off.

"If you would permit us, my lord, we would like to ride out prior to your exit of the stables, and to take positions amongst our company." Redmon brought his hand across his chest in a salute.

Areck nearly smiled. He could see the question in each officer's eyes. They wanted to show their men that they would lead them into battle as equals, willingly following their commander's orders. It was a custom that knights used when of the same rank and traveling in the same company. He thought it very poetic and wondered whose idea this had been. If the soldiers knew the customs of the Bre'Dmorians, they also knew that each man here did not hold the title of knight. He shrugged it off. It didn't matter why they followed him; each man had embraced his leadership.

With a firm salute he nodded in acquiescence. The three officers walked their stallions outside the stables and Areck heard cheering. When the cheers faded, Areck pressured his warhorse to move at a walk outside the stables.

The column of soldiers was split into two smaller companies of twelve men, each led by their senior officer. At the head of the first company rode Areck, followed by Squire Redmon. The other would be led by Captain Telmouth, a lieutenant poised behind him.

When his officers had first met, Areck had been prepared to split the Bre'Dmorian squires between both companies. However, Telmouth had been against such an idea, saying that he knew his own men's capabilities, as Areck knew his, better than the other. Areck did not argue the point. The plan would depend on each company's ability to work together. He had conceded that the captain knew what he was talking about, as the man was a veteran of several military campaigns to the north.

Areck pulled on his reins and stopped the charger. He looked on without expression other than the sparkle of his blue eyes as fat rain drops splashed on his armor. He tried to be methodical in his approach, trying to look like a strategist and deserving of the respect he was being shown. The thought chilled part of his soul; he knew that some of these men gazing back at him might not return.

"Lord Gustafson has asked that we defend our homes," Areck said, looking at the plumes of smoke that still rose. Why had his life seemed so perpetually overcast since he left Aresleigh? "Brenly suffers, and now marauders in your forests seek to plunder your town and take your women and children for their unholy purposes."

The men stared ahead, faces stoic.

"You have heard the reports that orcs roam the wilderness, destroying whole hamlets, burning and pillaging the land! And now they come for us," Areck's voice rose in a crescendo. "Today is our chance to fight back and do a great service to the land we have all sworn to protect! This is your chance to rid the Aresleigh of these foul beasts that bring plague and destruction!"

The men began to chant a battle hymn, releasing their frenzy before they left town. They would count on silence afterward, and there would be no chance to do it later.

"Today we will become the aggressors—the hunters, rather than the hunted. Today we will purge our lands of evil!" Areck finished, surprised at his own sincerity. Men shouted his praise. The Bre'Dmorians shouted praise to Starsgalt.

It was time.

† † † † †

Areck sat atop a small rise, waiting for the fourth report from his scouts. His company had entered the forest several miles to the north and had followed a well traveled hunting trail, hoping to catch wind of the orcish skirmishers. Though his plans were predicated on the column of riders detecting signs of the vile beasts, so far none of his scouts had reported anything.

Could it be that I am wrong? he thought, grimacing. He had backtracked all the way back to where the initial ambush had occurred, sending scouts to patrol the area, while he hid the rest of the column behind the rise. They had been searching for orcs for over six hours to no avail. *It all seems so useless. On horseback we make too much noise . . . they are probably reporting back to their own commanders and waiting for us to venture closer.*

Areck did not betray the fact that he was worried. He did not want to continue this search in the dark. The creatures he was hunting were renowned for being able to see in total darkness, while his own men would be severely limited. This near to the town, if the orcs spotted his column they could choose their dying grounds, or simply skip a fight altogether and go right to the town. The thought made his skin crawl. He decided that this hunt would be a singular try: they would either succeed before darkness, or they would head back and try again upon the morrow.

As Areck looked out towards where his scouts had begun tracking the beasts, he could not help but notice the vibrant trees, standing as silent sentinels. In another time they might have stood for the beauty of the forest. From a distance, he could see the different species of trees fighting for light and precious space, a vicious cycle of competition where only the fit, and the first to evolve, survived.

A man appeared out of the dense foliage, his helm the conical shape of a royal soldier. One of his scouts. It was not yet time to report back to the column, so Areck assumed that the man had found something useful. One of his scouts had reported orc tracks that looked months old. That piece of useless information had cost them several hours of valuable time.

He tried to contain his excitement, telling himself that this would just be another piece of worthless information. Typical of his newfound habits, his face became an emotionless mask that hid the hope that he was wrong.

For what seemed like an eternity the man climbed the small hill that hid the Brenly forces. The scout's back was exposed, as the woods seemed to have decided not to grow on the hillside. Areck wondered how he would see this land if he were not trying to hunt down those that were trying to ravage it.

He saw for a moment the vibrant energy of the forest's essence. With such vile creatures residing in it, the aura was almost sinister.

His vision blurred and he was taken to another place:

The forest was on fire! Black husks lay twisted and smoking. Areck heard a roar overhead. He felt the heat of the fire scorching his skin.

When he looked up he saw hundreds of dragons. They were circling him.

† † † † †

Areck rocked, his breath coming quickly as he teetered in the saddle. Redmon rode up with concern on his face. Areck brought his hand up to his nose and saw blood smeared on the dark gauntlet.

"My lord?" Redmon placed a hand on Areck's mount. "Bring us some water," the lieutenant ordered, seeing the blood pouring from Areck's nose.

"What happened?" he whispered to Redmon. "I remember . . . I saw the forest burning . . ."

"One moment you were staring down at Corporal Taurine, the next your eyes were vacant and you became unsteady," Redmon replied. "You almost fell out of your saddle."

"Must be from the heat," Areck said unconvincingly.

"Is my lord all right?" Captain Telmouth asked as he rode up.

Areck nodded and the captain did not press the matter. The solider handed a skin of water to Captain Telmouth who grimaced at his commander's bloody hands and passed it on to Areck.

"Thank you, Captain," Areck stammered. His head spun but his senses remained acute. "I think all the heat over the last few days finally got to me."

"Aye, my lord, I have been involved in plague burnings before," the captain said. "They tend to have this effect on people who are near the source."

Before another word could be uttered, the scout crested the ridge.

Areck could sense the man's nervousness. His eyes darted here and there, in tense gestures. This was the man who had reported the last set of signs. Areck knew the man was afraid that another error would cost him his life as a soldier; Bre'Dmorians were not known to be forgiving of inaccurate information, especially of common born suppliers.

Clutching his hands, the man gave a brief description: he had followed tracks southward when a motion had caught his eye. Passing through dense brush, he had come upon a clearing with several sentries posted.

"What can you tell us about the surroundings?" Redmon asked. "Were you able to spot a more *reliable* source . . .?"

"I saw the encampment, Lord Redmon. However, I could not get close enough to see their numbers," said the man, his eyes turning to Areck in apology.

"Any information is better than none," Captain Telmouth clapped the young man on the shoulder. "Can you give us an estimate based on the camps size?"

"At least forty creatures, including their sentries," the man replied. "From what I could see, there are at least three attack points."

"Thank you, Corporal Taurine," Areck said, dismissing the man.

"I think we should have the corporal lead us to this encampment," said Redmon. "If he is right, the creatures do not know we are here."

"I agree," said Telmouth. "It won't do us any good to charge blind. We might be able to attack from multiple locations. That could give us a great advantage."

Areck did not argue with his officers but tried to clear his head from his blackout. He felt blood soak the small rag. For a moment he remembered how real the blackout had seemed. Sensing no divine touch, he knew it was not a vision. He pushed away his absurd thoughts.

"So be it," Areck said and motioned his men forward to show he was steady.

The column followed Corporal Taurine, who trotted with trepidation past foliage and into the underbrush.

For thirty minutes the column ducked around low branches, their nerves raw, every man seeking foes behind the thick trunks. Finally Taurine held up a gloved hand, calling the procession to a halt. He brought his hand to his mouth to indicate silence and pointed at a small ridge.

Areck and his officers dismounted. He hesitated to speak. Areck motioned for Redmon and Telmouth to follow him. He left the master sergeant behind in case something went wrong.

The men pushed their way through several dense copses of underbrush and up the small hill, one of the few in the area. If orcs lurked nearby, they would be here. Taurine pointed to his eyes then up ahead to a small clearing, indicating they had arrived at the encampment.

Areck motioned his men forward while Taurine moved back down to stand guard. The trio crawled up to the ridge and peered anxiously at a thriving encampment buzzing with orcs.

There must be sixty of them! Areck thought, risking a peek into the small valley to see several grunting orcs fighting over their meal. He had heard many tales of their heathen ways and brutality, but watching them eat was more chilling than he had anticipated.

He concentrated on finding the camp's weaknesses. As he took another peek he smiled at the question. These were orcs! They would not have any fortifications, nor would they choose a defensible place for a camp. Areck moved to a better vantage point.

His assumption had been right. There were no fortifications that he could see. The scout's information had also proven somewhat accurate: there were two entrances into the valley, both guarded by sentries who would shout an alarm upon attack.

Hearing Redmon sigh, Areck turned to his officers and motioned downward. He guessed that his second-in-command had been mentally prepared for this moment, however, now death loomed several feet away, he had reservations.

Areck could not help that. All he could do was ask both officers what they thought and show no sign of weakness. He recognized that each man would be scared and need to draw on his strength.

Reaching the bottom of the clearing, Areck motioned Taurine to lead them back to the column. The four men snuck through underbrush, met their company, and mounted their horses.

"Well?" Areck whispered.

Telmouth spoke. "There are at least five dozen orcs in that valley; it's much too large to be a skirmish unit. If we can successfully attack from both ends of the valley, it will be like crushing wheat into flour."

Redmon nodded in concurrence. "I believe, Captain Telmouth's assessment of the orcs is correct, my lord. It looks like we have struck a wandering tribe of the ugly creatures—nothing we cannot handle."

Areck looked into each man's eyes and saw conviction. He also saw pride and hope. "Are both you in agreement that this is a wise decision?" Areck asked, knowing the answer but wanting to hear his men believed in him.

Both men nodded in agreement.

Each held a certain fire in his eyes. He had seen it before when fighting in blade master tournaments. He had felt the same feeling many times; first fear, then calm, then acceptance of one's fate, and finally a cool fire that burned to do battle.

When Areck looked back to the column and saw the nervous glances and the fire in each man's eyes, he knew they were ready. They were scared, but ready to lay down their lives.

A poetic moment, Areck thought.

Areck pointed to Telmouth. "Take your company around the right side. I will take mine to the left. When you hear an owl, charge the valley and engage the enemy in combat. I plan to crush these beasts as a hammer crushes a walnut. When I know you have their attention, I will take my group around, seal off the valley, and flank them from behind."

"It shall be as you request, my lord." The captain saluted. "May Starsgalt show you the way." Telmouth turned his warhorse and moved over to his men, waiting for Areck to give the signal.

Satisfied, Areck turned to his second-in-command. "Redmon, you are responsible for taking two men from each company and getting to that ridge. I want you to start the attack by signaling the captain and then raining arrows down upon orcish heads," Areck continued. "When the combat becomes too involved to fire arrows, kill stragglers one-on-one. We cannot have any escapees."

Redmon shifted uneasily but did not argue. Areck knew his concern. His lieutenant had planned on being in the midst of fighting, shouting battle cries, fighting back to back with his men. However, Areck needed Redmon on high ground to cover each company.

Areck looked into Redmon's eyes with a pleading look. At once, he saw his second-in-command understand that this was a necessity. Areck felt a tingle of relief to know that Redmon understood and accepted his orders.

Some of the column shifted but no one made a sound. Areck shifted his gaze back to the captain who was issuing orders to his master sergeant.

He looked at his own men, trying to read their feelings. He wondered what they were thinking and how they could follow him, a mere squire. He shook his head in frustration and told himself that self-doubt should not be going through his mind so close to battle, that he was better than this. He was a commander. The self-praise had little effect.

Kicking the sides of his warhorse, Areck moved over to his men. He whispered their orders as Redmon picked out one of his men and two of the captains. Satisfied that everyone was in place, Areck nodded to Telmouth and gave the order to move out. Telmouth led his men away, as did Redmon.

Areck knew that the pair would do their jobs flawlessly. He wondered why he had ever doubted them. Then again, he had not expected to find an ally in the personal squire of Lord Vinion, a man he could almost call a friend . . . not like Arawnn, but a loyal companion nonetheless.

With a last look, Areck saw Redmon lead four men, bows slung over their shoulders, into the copse and disappear.

Areck motioned forward and led his men into position.

The ride was short. Orcs were creatures who thrived by sheer numbers. They were a sloppy race, having few leaders and less military strategy. However, he couldn't take the chance that an enterprising leader might patrol the fringes of the camp. The race survived through plunder, meaning they had little, if any, true skill with weapons. When fighting, orcs relied on numbers to pull down foes. This made him uneasy; in this fight his men would be outnumbered three to one.

Areck positioned his men and rode until the orc camp was in sight. He saw a pair of sentries arguing, neither paying attention to their surroundings. Most of the camp seemed to be broken into groups of five or six, all sitting around cauldrons.

To say they were ugly would be an understatement. Their skin ranged from dark green to mottled grey, tusks protruded from their lower lips, and many had large piercings. He had read that they were very strong; many stood seven feet in height and weighed several hundred pounds. Areck felt so fragile in comparison. He tried to look for their eyes, which must have been mere slits for he could not see them in the dimming light. He felt the chaos and malevolence the creatures bore. These were the antithesis to the human race, a plague on Aryth, and a race toward which Starsgalt showed mercy; none could be killed unless preceding violence was imminent. Areck wondered if that was the reason God had never intervened for this community, if He was waiting for the orcs to turn hostile.

It doesn't matter now, he thought. *I have ordered their slaughter. In my eyes, they are a threat to this region.* He would deal with the consequences later.

As Areck stood mesmerized by the sentries whose argument had become a lethal duel, an orc rushed in from the far side of the valley, yelling and waving its arms. Areck's heart skipped a beat. He noticed the largest orc raise his head from his food and motion the smaller orc to him. The leader stiffened and shouted an order as its compatriot whispered something into its ear.

"May Starsgalt guide my hand," he whispered as he realized what was happening. Either the newcomer had been a guard posted farther out or a wandering hunter looking for food, but either way the orc had stumbled upon Captain Telmouth's men approaching from the other side of the valley.

Their plan was hinged on a surprise attack. If the orcs had time to prepare for an attack, they would be ready, and it would be fifty versus ten. He hoped that Redmon was already drawing bows which might at least scatter the orcs, who had started to gather themselves into an attack formation, forming two lines on either side of the road, spears extended, awaiting a cavalry charge.

Damn it! The entire camp had taken up positions, several with bows, all aimed towards the right side of the valley. *With the element of surprise gone, Telmouth will easily be struck down.*

Areck could not hesitate. He had not heard the owl's hoot from Redmon, so there was a chance the lieutenant had already been compromised.

He pulled his helmet from a strap on his saddle and unhooked his sword and shield.

"*Charge!*" he screamed, kicking his mount forward. His order was followed by the ancient battle yell of the Bre'Dmorian Order. "*May Starsgalt guide my hand!*"

† † † † †

Squire Redmon Thalluvian was the first one to see an orcish scout charge into the enemy encampment, its arms flailing. He watched helplessly as the creature seemed to explain something to what must be considered the chieftain. He watched as the camp exploded into action and seemed to prepare for an attack.

Pulling his mouth into a tight line, he considered giving the signal for Captain Telmouth's riders to attack. The problem, of course, was that he knew neither of his small army's companies would be in position. If he called it out now, it would give his own position away and most likely not help the riders. His situation made him curse. What choice did he have? He could send a runner to Areck's side of the valley . . .

But what will that solve? he wondered. *It would take too long, and we can ill afford to lose another body. I wonder if we can distract them enough to break their concentration.* In his studies he had learned that orcs, though extremely strong, were stupid. Again he wondered if he should give the signal.

Hollering won't be enough to break them out of rank, he thought. It only left him with one alternative: break Areck's orders and start firing below before the attack commenced.

Redmon motioned for the three men accompanying him to come closer.

"It looks like Captain Telmouth's forces have been detected, sirs," he said. "And I just don't know if we can get to either force and warn them." He paused for the proper words then continued, "I think our only chance is to spread out along this ridge, pick out the front ranks of their defenders, and kill a few. That might shock them enough to throw them into a disorganized frenzy."

"I think I can reach that ledge over there, my lord—" Corporal Taurine was cut off when a distant yell broke their silence.

"Charge!" Redmond heard the muted call followed by a Bre'Dmorian battle yell.

Who in Starsgalt's name is making so much noise? he wondered, drawing his bow and scrambling up the ridge. What greeted him was a shocking sight.

It seemed Areck had also been in position to see the enemy scout stumble back into camp and rather than wait had called for his men to charge. Redmon thought the move brilliant except for one problem: Areck was the only rider charging the fifty or so waiting orcs.

Redmon bit his lip and turned around. He tried to calm his mind, knowing he needed to act fast. "Stay calm, gentlemen and get your hides into position! As soon as you see a single orc react toward the knight-captain, rain down hell upon their ugly heads. Take out archers first."

None of the men said a word as they all gave small salutes and skittered off.

† † † † †

Areck's warhorse sprung into action, nostrils flaring. As it charged for a line of archers the rest of his men were still slamming down their visors.

As an orc turned to face this new threat, Areck heard a loud whooping sound. He was shocked to realize he had left his company standing in the forest, a bold but unbelievably foolish move. He had been too excited to think. His inexperience and haste might cost him his life.

Thirty yards away, the first orc recovered its wits, drew back its bow and others followed suit. Areck saw a blur from his right as the closest orc grasped at its throat and choked on its own blood, then fell silent.

The distraction was enough to keep the rest of the orc archers from firing and forced more than several to jump out of formation and into cover. More arrows flew into the fray, but Areck's only thought was to save his men.

His horse charged into the midst of orcs and Areck's sword whistled through the air, severing an orc's head. He swung again as an archer tried to raise his bow and cleaved through the creature's weapon and arm. Another rushed forward and placed its spear on the ground, foot on the end, forming a makeshift pike. Areck shouted a signal that made the warhorse lash out with his front hooves. The orc was drilled in the chest and temple.

Redmon had been the first soldier to draw his bow and fire it, hitting an orc archer in the neck and killing the creature just before it had fired at his commander. With silent determination he pulled another arrow and notched it, this time aiming for an orc carrying a spear. Drawing the bow back, he let the arrow fly, but overshot to the left.

The war-chief shouted orders to his tribe and pointed into the hills. Several of their archers broke away from the main group and took cover behind the cauldrons.

He hardly noticed that Areck had reached the first ranks of the orcish forces or that several more arrows were being notched and fired next to him.

Redmon ducked back behind the ridge and cursed. Hands shaking, he pulled another arrow from his quiver. It struck him then that he had killed another sentient being and his battle lust faltered. He closed his eyes and tried to calm his mind. He told himself that though he was no expert with the bow, he was still a Bre'Dmorian squire, proficient enough to use the weapon with accuracy. This proficiency, he knew, came from God and though these were sacred creatures, he needed to protect his commander and men.

Steeling his resolve, Redmon poked back up, drew his bow, and fired, this time hitting the leg of an orc who was charging Areck. The creature stumbled headlong into Areck's charge, and he swept down his sword and decapitated the creature.

Then the scene became chaotic as the orc war-chief rallied its troops and reset them into a proper formation to meet Areck's charge. Redmon watched his commander hack and slash another pair of orcs in the arm and face. He was about to fire another arrow at an oncoming pikeman when Areck ordered his warhorse to become a weapon. He dropped his shot as the creature was pummeled times by iron-shod hooves and teeth.

Redmon heard the pound of hooves, followed the battle cries of "Stars-galt!" and "Brenly!" It seemed that the captain and Areck's forces had fi-nally arrived!

The only thing Areck could concentrate on was fighting long enough to allow Telmouth to join the fray. He felt a sting in his right arm. His sword lashed out again and another orc fell to its knees.

An arrow whizzed by his ear and he raised his shield in time to deflect a battle axe meant for his chest. The orcs reformed their lines and headed for him while archers found cover and pulled their bows taut. In that moment, Areck saw his own death. He had offered his life for his men's, and God seemed ready to accept.

An arrow sailed through the air and landed in his warhorse's flank. The beast went into a wild frenzy that Areck could not control. More arrows buried themselves in the charger and a blow struck Areck across the chest, knocking him from the saddle. As he fell back his foot caught in the stirrup and Areck slammed face first to the ground. His horse bolted out of the area, dragging Areck by one leg.

Just before blackness took him, Areck saw his men pouring from all sides, slaughtering the orcs.

He felt peace. He would die in battle, for his men and for the cause. And, more important, he would die a knight.

Redmon drew another shot, this one aimed for the war-chief of the orcs. At first the beast had been protected by its troops but with archers raining down arrows from above, Areck charging in from the west, and another force charging in from the east, the orcs had began to break.

With great effort he steadied his hand and looked down the sight of his left forefinger. He was about to let loose the arrow when the orc com-mander was spun sideways by a pair of arrows, one impacting its forearm the other hitting him just below the shoulder. The creature gurgled and pulled itself along the ground, trying to reach cover.

Redmon tried to get an open shot, but the creature never offered itself up. Grunting, he turned around just in time to see a massive orc charge Areck. He drew his bow taught, steadied his breathing and let fly.

Unfortunately for the orc, who was running full speed with its mace held high, Redmon's aim was true and the arrow impacted the back of the creature's skull. Its head snapped sideways and its sprint turned into a stumble.

The creature did not drop its weapon; rather, its arms gave out and its stumbling inertia sent it falling towards the unseeing captain.

"Lord Areck, look out . . .!" was all Redmon had time to say before Areck was struck in the chest by the creature and its heavy weapon.

Though he was more than fifty yards away, Redmon heard the dull thump before he saw Areck driven backwards off his horse. More so, with Areck's foot caught in a stirrup, the commander couldn't move and several orcs, seeing an advantage, had started to charge.

Redmon drew his bow back, targeting the first of several orcs trying to flee the oncoming riders and reach the commander. He let fly just in time to hit the creature in the thigh, sending it stumbling into its brethren.

He called out to the riders below but was not heard over the clash of metal and wood. Redmon slung his bow over his shoulder and slid down the ridge to reach the commander.

He vowed that if Areck was still alive, he would personally salute him in Starsgalt's name for his courage and valor.

He never got that chance.

Another arrow, this one from an orc, struck the commander's warhorse in the front shoulder, making the stallion rear in anger and bolt. Redmon stopped in mid-stride, his mouth open in fear. He watched as Lord Areck's body was dragged behind the beast into the forest.

As he reached the bottom of the hill Redmon unslung his bow and dropped it to the ground. He pulled his bastard sword, let out a Bre'Dmorian battle chant, and charged into battle.

He did not notice that only five his men lay dying or that the battle was over. From all accounts, Brenly's army had won!

23

IT WAS dark when Areck returned to consciousness. For a moment he thought he had died and undergone the transition of the spirit to immortal resting place. He had heard several theories regarding utter darkness. There was always darkness before everlasting light.

He heard a noise and an owl's hoot. He tried to push himself up but felt a great weight pinning his right leg to the ground. The soft patter of raindrops echoed in the night.

If it is raining, I am still alive, he thought, bringing his hand to his temple to inspect the throbbing that interrupted his thoughts. Pain stabbed through his eyes, making his vision blur. He tried to remember.

I was in a battle, he thought. He had obviously suffered a blow to the head. He moved his fingers to his face and began probing his eye sockets, nose, and cheeks, finding deep lacerations before noticing that the right side of his mouth stood out in swollen pain.

He must not have fared well if he was alone in the dark, pinned to the ground. He was parched and fumbled for a canteen. His fingers recognized a saddle and fumbled through several packs, pulling out jerky and a water skin. As he raised the cool water to his lips, he realized that he was not riding the mount but his leg was trapped beneath the saddle.

He probed the area around the saddle, finding several arrows and a sticky substance he assumed to be blood. His horse lay on top him, its neck twisted.

Memories flooded his mind.

He saw his own death approach as orcish archers fired arrows. No arrows had struck him, however, but buried instead into the horse which became uncontrollable. Then he had heard shouts . . . but that had been before he was struck in the chest by a hammer, which knocked him from his horse and his foot tangled in the stirrup. He shivered as he remembered the impact of landing face first into the ground and his charger bolting from the area.

He thought he had died to save his men. Anger ran through his soul. His mount had probably hit a rut and dove to the ground, breaking its neck. He guessed it was a fate better than bleeding to death. That he was alive surprised him. *Am I so quick to desire my own death? I do not deserve to be a knight!*

With his back against a tree trunk, Areck place his left leg on his saddle and pushed. Though he could barely move the heavy horse, he was able to free his right leg. The pain made vomit run up his throat.

He waited until his head cleared and his eyes adjusted to the night before looking around. Though he could not make out the terrain, he heard the soft trickle of water. He wracked his brain, trying to recall the maps of Brenly and its surrounding areas that he had spent hours studying.

He turned onto his stomach and pulled himself away from the fallen steed. Though his sight was limited, he could vaguely make out dark shadows of the forest.

Judging by the cool air and the mossy ground beneath him, Areck figured that the stream was wide with a quick current. With a grunt he moved into the clearing, to the bank of the stream as rain splashed on his face. If his mind was clear enough to think, it was clear enough to walk.

He recalled the name of the only fresh water source in the region, Eagle Creek, a mountain stream that erupted into a small lake, the local reservoir.

As he knelt down and splashed water across his swollen face, he felt oddly satisfied at discovering his whereabouts. If memory served him, the creek wound itself over fifty miles from the mountains to the Emmonds Lake, coming no closer than five miles from the grasslands that spread at the heart of Aresleigh. He could not be precise, but he was at least seven or eight miles into the woods and lost until he could see the morning sky.

Areck tried again to stand. He found that the pounding in his head subsided to a mere annoyance if he did not move his neck, turn his head, or make quick movement. With so much armor, his pace would be jostling—not good for a concussion.

"I wonder which way the stallion took me," he whispered, wondering for the first time how close he was to enemy territory. He wondered if the others thought him dead, or perhaps they had realized he was a coward, stupid enough to charge fifty orcs, get knocked off his horse, and run like a weeping child.

A sliver of moonlight danced on the rushing water revealing a wide riverbed with fast, shallow water. The rain subsided to a drizzle. If the cloud cover cleared and if no mist pushed its way down from the mountains, moving with soft feathery fingers out into the forest, he would be able to move.

Areck pursed his lips. He could wait out the night and begin his trek in the morning, which would be safer. However, if he was in orcish territory, he would stand out. Or, he could try to find his way by night and hope the darkness would help conceal him from the Orcs' keen vision. Neither prospect pleased him.

Bringing his hands to his head and rubbing his temples gently, he made his decision. He did not like the thought of traveling blind in the night, but he liked traveling alone in unfamiliar territory in plain sight even less.

Going back to his fallen steed, Areck realized that he would be without sword or shield. However, he was not unarmed and retrieved a small dagger from his belt, sliced away the straps that tied his saddle into place, and unwrapped a small rectangular shape swathed in fine cloth. The dull gleam of a gladius shone in the moonlight. He had brought Lord Malketh's blade with him so he might present it as evidence to the High Lightbringer. It looked like God had shown him some mercy. He fumbled through his saddle bags and retrieved a small pouch containing dried meat and a canteen.

For a moment he doubted himself then turned towards the river bank, and followed it.

† † † † †

Due to random spurts of rain and clear sky, the mist never settled. Areck's eyes swam in vertical lines and his stomach knotted, leaving a wave of nausea to pass over him. Unfortunately for his eyes, due to the shifting moonlight he had trouble identifying objects further than ten feet away.

Areck took a deep swallow of cool water and rubbed his right temple gingerly. This was his fifth stop. The change in illumination caused his sensitive eyes to hallucinate things that could not possibly exist. Great shadows stalked him. His nerves made each crashing near and unpredictable.

This has *to stop,* he said, squinting at the shadowed features of his extended hand. *I wish the moon would either stay in the sky or allow the cloud cover to take hold making it rain all night.*

While his eyes readjusted to the dimness and soft rain thrumming steadily, Areck considered his circumstances. He knew that he would be hard pressed to move even if he wanted to. With this light, it was hard to discern detail. It was like a dark shroud was trying to blot out the light.

Areck fumbled his hands over the hilt of his sword, making sure for the umpteenth time that it was attached in a makeshift scabbard and ready to be drawn upon in need. He had to admit that wandering in the utter darkness was unsettling, especially without a shield, which had been destroyed in the horse's flight.

After thirty minutes the rain ceased and a few clouds parted, revealing rays of light.

Areck closed his eyes and utter blackness enveloped him. A stab of pain shot through his eye socket, subsided, and his vision cleared. He thought he heard a movement and tightened his grip on the sword.

God knows what is watching me right now, he thought. The moonlight shifted the shadows again. Areck locked his waterskin around his shoulder and pushed himself off of the stump. He began to take step, and stopped. He sensed something different, a warrior's survival skill.

He closed his eyes. There was a feeling out there, something strange. He couldn't say what it was, though a feeling of nausea swept through his body. It almost felt like . . . divinity.

Impossible! His nerves were playing tricks on him, while his feet were following a path he could not see.

He convinced himself that this was the path God had chosen for him, a sign that a divine spirit had come to rescue him.

He traveled for two hours. The new path took him deep into the forest where his definition of darkness was redefined. In the middle of the forest, with no light to guide him, there was little he could do to avoid low hanging branches and thick wiry bushes that tore at his bruised flesh. He knew he was lost within moments of losing the trail that had shone so brightly near the bank of the creek.

As he walked along, grumbling, arms flailing, his feet snagged on a thick root and he stumbled.

What in Starsgalt's name made me pick this route? His hand passed through a thorn bush, lacerating the skin. He snatched it back and flopped on the ground, pressing the bleeding wound to his lips.

I must be out of my mind! I know my wits are playing tricks on me . . . and so I decide to follow my intuition into the darkness? What did I hope to find out here, a cleric and a horse to take me back? Fool! You would have been better off—

Snap.

That was not the wind, nor branches high overhead. Again Areck heard the snap of branches followed by the harsh, guttural jabber of orcs.

Areck's heart raced as he cursed silently and crawled away from the harsh voices that drew near. He was about to duck behind a tree when he noticed a silhouette. He shifted his hand to his sword fearing to draw the blade for the sound it would make and inched backwards, peeking at the figure.

There was no doubt it was an orc.

Its stench wafted downwind and its guttural breath was deep and menacing. The creature was looking at the ground, its hands full of earth. It was looking for him. He could not let it raise a call for help. In his condition, he might be able to handle one of the creatures, but not a band. He straightened to step behind his prey when another orc stepped out of the blackness, waving its hands in the air.

They talked loudly, one pointing in his direction. The other cackled in its grating voice, slapping his compatriot across the back. The other staggered from the blow, turned, and swung at its tormentor, catching only air as the second orc moved off with staggering speed into the forest.

Areck sighed. His heart raced and pounded with a thunderous beat. Why would God save him from battle only to have him killed by an orc? He made a mental note to pray once he reached a safe haven.

Another feeling washed over him, the same irrational feeling that had possessed him to wander into the nothingness of night. He could not help but feel foolish about the entire matter. He told himself that he needed to stay near the riverbed if he was to find civilization. It was a certainty, an absolute. He would backtrack to the stream and try to make his way back to Brenly.

Without another thought, he set off in the direction of the orcs.

As he strode, he realized that he had turned around and was heading the foolish direction. He had been sure his mind had said that the *creek* was the wise choice. Deciding that his mind was addled and needed explanation, he reminded himself that the orcs were bad news. He concluded that he was right and stepped off again in the direction of the orcs.

What in Starsgalt is happening to me? he thought, realizing that once again he was traveling counter to his warrior's intuition. Picking up his foot, he tried to turn towards the creek but was compelled to right himself. Again he tried to turn towards the creek, but this time he began to shake, each step making his body tremble. He threw up his hands and stopped. He felt like he was being ripped apart. He wanted to scream but thought better of it.

If Starsgalt's leading me, who am I to disobey? God made sure those monsters didn't see me; maybe there is something he wants me to see. Maybe these orcs are my destiny.

He could not argue. There was no doubt that he was being divinely inspired to continue on his current course. There was only one being who would call him to service: God. It would be unwise to not heed a calling.

Areck accepted that his fate was not in the direction he wanted to go, but along a more treacherous path.

Once he stopped struggling, his head cleared and another sickness intensified. He could feel the divine sickness washing over him like an oily film.

He took a drink of water and poured some on his bleeding hand. When he was satisfied, he lowered his head and walked in the direction his feet, rather than his mind, told him to go.

Areck struggled on in the dark for an hour before he saw the soft glow of fire, a stark contrast to the nothingness of night. He picked his way through dense brush and thick trees to where the forest opened into a small clearing. The clearing looked much like the place where he had chosen to attack the marauders. However, Areck could see no chokepoints or ridges that cut across the landscape; one side rose high into the night while the other emptied into the forest. *This would be a much harder battle,* he conceded.

As Areck studied the camp, he saw countless orcs milling about, some metal-smithing, others tending animals, others moving in and out of make-shift shelters.

They have made barracks, his brows lifted in amazement. The creatures were not known to use any military procedure other than killing, pillaging, and destruction. This was a major achievement for the entire race, one that made them all the more dangerous. The implications of what he was wit-nessing sent a shiver through his body. If this race learned organization, they were a threat to the entire region.

This is what God has brought me here to see! Now I must get back to Brenly and warn the others.

Areck noticed a hulking figure sitting on its haunches, wrapped in what looked to be chains as thick as a man's wrist. The sight of the creature in-tensified the divine sickness and he pursed his lips.

Wondering what sort of creature could radiate such power, he decided to get a better look, his vision poor from the current angle. What he could see of the creature was massive. The prisoner seemed literally to be chained to the mountainside. He could see at least a dozen orcs stationed near it, their feet shuffling uneasily. Areck could tell by their posture that the ugly creatures were terrified.

A prisoner of some sort?

The figure was large enough to be an ogre, which were uncommon in the region; a brutal race with intelligence comparable to a man . . . but ogres didn't slouch, as this creature did. He wondered if it might be a giant, though it had been decades since one was last reported in this area.

Although a part of him wished to turn away and slip into the night, Areck's knightly conscience demanded that he lend whatever aid he could to that of his enemy's captive. He decided that he could kill it if it proved a chaotically evil creature. He reprimanded himself for the thought: *How high and mighty I have become, to talk of killing like a trivial matter.* He decided that even if he was allowed to stay in the knighthood, severe atonement was needed.

Areck sighed as his noble side won out. With deliberate movements, do-ing his best to stay inconspicuous, he slipped closer to study the encamp-ment. As he approached, the first thing he noticed was that an argument had broken out, sending several orcs into a frenzy. He used the distraction to inch closer to the camp, using the orcs' makeshift wood buildings to conceal himself. Sure that no one had seen him, he held his breath and poked his head around a building to get a better look.

Satisfied that the orcs were still preoccupied, Areck pulled his blade and slunk into the open, seeing a small outcropping of rock that would act as a better shelter. He was about half way when he heard a guttural voice rasping in the distance. As he continued toward shelter, he attempted to understand what was being said—which was nothing. It dawned on him that it would have been wise to pay attention during his classes on languages of the world; another sign of his lack of knightly demeanor. It irked him that he could not understand.

Pushing away from the mountain wall, he peeked around the outcropping. He could see dim shafts of firelight extending between the buildings. He could barely make out the guards sitting around a fire, poking at some poor creature.

Something large moved off to his right, the rattling of chains clinking in the night. He held his breath to see the reaction of those sitting around the fire. Only one orc looked back towards the noise before shrugging and poking the creature again.

Areck scanned the wall for another outcropping he could hide behind. Seeing a large rock that protruded from the mountain, he pressed his back to the wall and sidestepped over to it. As he reached his next target he released his breath. He was in the middle of an orcish camp following another fool's errand. The thought reminded him of how young and foolish he really was.

Another sound of movement made Areck's heart stop in his throat. He pressed himself into the shadows of the rock as chains rattled just beyond his sight. Again, the divine sickness washed over him and his eyesight blurred.

There is still time to turn back, he thought, as pain shot through his mind and nausea swept over him.

Without thinking, as if compelled to move again, he snuck around the corner of a hut and into a semi-circle of open space. There was the prisoner. The beast was covered in chains, and odd shadows blotted out its features. Though he could not get a good look at its face, Areck squinted his eyes, and tried to discern something about the beast. He decided that the thing had to weigh at least six hundred pounds, maybe more.

The pain of his sickness made him stumble.

A guard rounded the corner, unaware of his presence. It made him wonder what he would do if he made it all the way over to the prisoner. The beast was covered in chains, shackled into place, and Areck was no locksmith. Unless he could find the keys, there would be no way to release the prisoner.

Areck allowed the orc to stroll past him. He fell in step behind the ugly creature and did his best to mask the noise of his armor, using the creature's guttural breathing to mask the clinking of metal. With soft confident steps, he strode behind the orc, blade in his right hand like a dagger.

When he was sure that the creature had passed out of its fellows' line of sight, Areck took a deep breath and with a powerful thrust slammed the blade into the orc's neck. With a quiet grunt the creature tried to yell but only gurgled in rasping tones. It staggered to the side and keeled over. Areck guided the dead guard to the ground then pulled it backwards, slamming his blade into its chest several times.

The smell of death wafted up, as did a rotten metallic smell of orcish blood. This was the first time he had ever killed anything that did not fight back—a sin. By law he should have challenged the creature, or at least came from its front. He felt like a coward.

With a grim sigh, Areck decided that he needed to focus on the situation rather than think about his own inadequacies. He almost felt as if he were becoming a monster, lacking those chivalrous emotions that had once made him so knightly.

Correction, he thought as he pulled the body into to a large shadow and removed its keys, *I have never been knightly. I have been sinful, prideful, a cold hearted murderer, and now a cowardly heathen.*

Areck to wipe the rotten smell from his hands. Wondering if the smell would ever come off, he gave up and looked toward his goal. Something struck him as odd: what were the chances that an orc would wander away from the camp? He tried to calculate the probability that an orc would patrol an area, carrying keys, alone, at the very moment he required it. Starsgalt was truly shining on him . . . but why?

It was a coincidence, he mused, *nothing more.*

Areck bolted from his position and perched less than ten yards away from the giant creature. He heard chortling and realized that the orcs were making so much noise they could never hear his armor, but it would only be a matter of time until they realized that a comrade was missing.

He spotted another small outcropping of rocks barely large enough to conceal his frame next to the creature and darted toward it.

As Areck approached the creature he saw it stiffen and mumble incoherent words; he was sure it knew he was there. Another wave of divine power radiated out from it. Areck grunted in pain. The divine presence was so strong that the pain was unbearable. This was the most powerful godly magic he had ever experienced. Not even the High Lightbringer exuded power like this.

Areck clenched his teeth, peered around the rock, and grasped the immense stature of his target. It was larger than anything he had ever read about; even an ogre.

Not a giant? he thought, clenching his teeth as he examined the creature. It still sat hunched in a ball, its head lowered into its massive hands. An orc stood up. Areck's time was running out.

Whatever this prisoner was, it was smart enough not to move. Areck crept from around the rock and another pulse of energy greeted him. Vomit caught in his throat as he approached.

"I do not know if you understand Arsgothian Common, but I am here to rescue you," Areck whispered, feeling the massive body tense. Incoherent rumbling greeted him. It sounded like the creature was . . . crying.

"Go away," a deep baritone whispered and a massive head lifting up out of the darkness and swiveled around to stare at him.

Areck gasped. In the dim light, a pair of florescent red eyes burned within a smooth face, surrounded by a massive head with two small horns. The face, rimmed with fine hair that wrapped under the creature's chin, was tied into two neat braids. Areck was at a loss for words.

"I am here to free you," Areck moved closer, extending the keys to show friendship.

"I said leave me be, mortal. You cannot save me," the creature replied, laying his head back into its hands. "Anyway, you cannot free me." The creature lifted its hands to show Areck that although countless chains still adorned the beast, he had destroyed the shackles. There was nothing holding this creature to the mountain.

"Are you a criminal?" Areck asked.

"I am the destroyer of your world," the creature said the low grumble began again.

Areck was now sure the creature was crying.

Whatever the beast was, it suffered from the same human conditions as he did: lack of sleep and nourishment. Areck guessed that it was partially insane from whatever trauma it suffered.

Areck reached out his hand and touched the creature. A bright light flashed and enveloped him. His vision began to blur and he screamed.

The world was burning. He saw an entire race of creatures he did not recognize being hunted down and exterminated by their creators. He knew that he was beholding the last of a magnificent race. A dying race. The pain was terrible. It felt as if God had forsaken him. It was an agony far beyond mortal conception.

He saw dragons breathing fire. They were scouring the world looking, looking for something with no face. He could almost see it.

Then the world was burning. He was burning. The end was upon him.

Areck and the creature were catapulted ten yards into the air and landed against the mountain. The ground shook. An explosion of light illuminated the area.

As Areck opened his eyes and saw spots, he vomited. He did not notice that his nose was again bleeding profusely. He tried to move but could not. He nearly lost consciousness, but fought it off with sheer will.

It took Areck a moment to realize that the noise had been real. His ears were still ringing. Somewhere beyond his shattered hearing he could make out the grunting of several dozen orcs, who were gathering their spears and moving towards him.

Shaking his head, he tried to rise but the shock of being slammed into the mountain with so much force caused him to retch for a second time. Lifting his head, he gazed over at the motionless creature, whose body was enshrouded by rising smoke then at his hand.

"What in Starsgalt's name is it?" he asked, still dazed by the ordeal. He concluded that the being was not a mortal but neither was it an angel. Whatever it was, it was ancient, and God has chosen *him* to see it.

The thought somehow summoned his mind to him, and he involuntarily stood. It felt like something was guiding him to move.

The first orc round the corner. It seemed as if time slowed, and the figures were moving at him in slow motion.

"Is dawn already approaching?" he asked the oncoming orcs. He guessed that the question stemmed from the fact that he was suffering from a severe concussion. Or maybe it was that the night sky had lightened and dawn was in fact approaching.

Areck reached down and picked up his blade, turning it over to inspect the shiny surface. He had risked so much by coming here, and now God had shown him a miracle before he was to die. This would be his final stand. He wondered at his own daring and his utter foolishness. The Code stood for something. It meant that his duty was to follow where Starsgalt led, to protect his men and to save the innocent.

His enemy still moved in slow motion, was still only half way to him— except now there were seven of the creatures. He laughed as he closed his eyes. The situation seemed so surreal, like a dream.

Somewhere deep inside his mind, Areck let his subconscious thoughts take him in a new direction. He released the blademaster reflexes etched deep inside every master swordsman. Time caught up then, and the pair of orcs ran toward him.

With blinding mortal speed he parried the first blows with the grace of a master, swinging his blade in a wide arc to keep both orcs at bay. The first orc screamed and brought its wicked axe around in a blow that would cleave a man in two. Areck ducked to the side and heard the blade whistle past his head, then moved inside the overextended orcs reach, and sliced its stomach, releasing its entrails. He gagged and his eyes blurred for a moment. The other orc charged. When it reached Areck and pulled back for a two-handed blow, he grabbed the orc's swing in one hand, using the inertia to overbalance it. With a quick down stroke, Areck slashed at the beast's skull.

Areck looked up in time to see four more orcs charge him and thirty more come into sight. He readied his short blade in defense. If it was his time to go, he would take as many with him as he could.

"*For the glory of God,*" he screamed at the first creature to attack and leaned to the side before it struck. With a perfect counter attack he dropped into a forward roll and, sweeping his sword as he passed, severed its leg at the knee, using the maneuver to get some distance from the other three.

Taking the offensive, he charged the stunned orcs and yelled another chant. His mind began to wonder what in the hell was guiding him. It told him that he should be dead from several blows to the head . . . that what he was doing was impossible.

He let out a savage scream and speared an orc who had raised its axe over its head. He recognized how foolish the move was as he picked it off the ground and drove it into the mountain. There was a loud *thwack*. When he backed away, the creature slumped to the ground, its skull crushed on a protruding stone.

Areck turned around, but not fast enough. One of the remaining orcs, this one using a rusty shortsword, made it past his defenses and scored a hit to his side; not enough to pierce an organ, but painful nonetheless. He lashed out and spun away from the blow, moving into another orc, this one already on his downswing with a two hand mace. Areck decided that it was better to be injured than dead and stepped into the blow, taking a shaft to the shoulder rather than a maul to the head.

The great thump sent Areck staggering into the mountain and almost to his knees. He raised his sword arm in defense of another blow.

He realized too late that his parry was not enough. Areck of Brenly could see his death coming.

A great shadow blocked out the morning light and was followed by a deafening roar. After several moments, he realized the blow never came.

The several dozen orcs approaching him stood with their mouths agape, looking at the sky. Hesitantly, he followed their gaze. What greeted him was another miracle. Soaring through the sky was a creature the size of the small mountain. Though he had just had a hallucination about such a creature, he had assumed that they did not exist except as legend. Not so. Less than fifty feet above him, wings stretched far into the dawn, was a white dragon. It was the most beautiful, terrifying sight he had ever seen.

He again heard the thunder of its roar. He felt boulders of rock break away from the mountain and topple down. Then there was terrible chaos, as orcs in the area split in all directions and the dragon attacked.

Areck watched in amazement as the dragon dove into the middle of the orcs, gouging mounds of soil, flinging bodies in the air. Just like in his vision, it destroyed with no mercy. It dove again, leaving behind a grisly aftermath of corpses.

The orcs screamed and some even heaved spears at the massive winged legend. Their uncoordinated effort proved futile, as it flexed its wings outward and it inhaled. This time it unleashed a fiery fury upon a giant swath of earth. The smell of burnt flesh wafted through the air and waves of heat extended into the woods, setting the trees ablaze.

Areck, bleeding and battered, lifted himself off the ground and tried to make it to the forest. Though divine sickness washed through him as did a major concussion, he was still clear minded and able to move.

Stumbling out of the way, he just missed a blast of heat that blazed over his shoulder that singed the hair above his right ear and left him gasping for clean air. Smoke surrounded him making his eyes water and his vision waver. He knew he couldn't last long here.

He turned to where the prisoner had lain. It did not surprise him that there was nothing there. He had been sure that the beast would be smoldering, burnt from their contact. He staggered over to the area shielding his eyes from the smoke. It must have crawled off.

Areck searched franticly for the beast, stepping over the scorched ground where smoldering corpses lay. He could not find it and moved off into the forest where he guessed it had crawled away.

It proved to be a poor decision. A fleeing orc crossed his path, this one wielding a great sword. He was forced once again into battle. Areck raised his arm but realized that he no longer held his sword. He prepared to fight. Seeing that its opponent was injured and unarmed, the orc charged Areck, its sword held in an offensive posture.

Areck tried to steady himself and waited for the orc to arrive so he could time its attack with precision. They were just about to collide when another blast of fire exploded to their left. The explosion sent the orc flying directly at him, its sword tipped like a lance. Areck swept his arm in an arc instinctively to deflect the blow.

He felt more than heard the resounding thump as his hand connected with the flat of the creature's blade. It was followed by a terrible stinging pain in his thigh.

Areck tried to lift his head. He did not know how he was still alive. He was pinned to the ground. The blade had not only penetrated his armor, but the weight of the orc had driven the hilt deep through his leg. He struggled to stay awake. Deep in his mind, his subconscious whispered that he needed to quit. It was his time to die. He had seen in the last thirty minutes all the wonders that life could offer. Yet his will would not let eternal sleep take him.

He was about to close his eyes when he felt a sudden impact, as if several tons had been dropped to the ground. He heard orcs screaming in pain as the ground trembled with massive blows. He grew faint. He saw trees parting like water before the dragon. It was looking for him.

Only then did the darkness take him.

The last thought thing he saw was the creature's face through blurred eyes. It was a face of magnificence. It was the face of God.

Areck of Brenly passed out.

24

SILVERWING AND Thurm stared at each other, each unsure of what to do. They stood over the body of a young human male with a gaping wound in his leg, several deep gashes to his body and a face like meat from a grinder. Both were surprised the young man still lived.

The olthari broke the silence, kneeling down to examine the boy's wounds. "This is a remarkable mortal," he announced, still feeling the buzz from the human's touch, a sign of volatile magic. It was so volatile that it had fed off Thurm's own divine spirit and caused great pain and discomfort for the both of them.

"Indeed he is." The dragon eyed him with skepticism, not believing for one moment that a servant of Heaven would find a mortal the least bit interesting. She had been tracking this particular human since she had witnessed a miraculous event in Three Sentinel Pass. But that was not what bothered her. *What*, she wondered, *in the name of Illuviel was an Olthari, one of the cursed race, doing here?*

"Can you help him?" Silverwing asked, trying to hide her interest. One could never tell what the traitorous race was up to.

"His wounds are extensive. I cannot understand how he still lives," Thurm answered.

Looking up at the dragon, he felt that the beast was nearly as powerful as he was. That fact should have infuriated him, but he just shrugged. "I think I can staunch the bleeding," Thurm finally said. "As you might guess, my powers have diminished over the last several eternities."

He no longer cared, not anymore. In fact, he had been trying to die when the mortal interfered. But the orcs, who had at first thought him a demon and an ally, had then feared him to much too actually slay him. He had been contemplating his life when this human tried to rescue him.

By Illenthuul's edict, this world would be obliterated unless he could find the unknown source that drove the evil god onward. He estimated that the world had around sixteen full moons, or eight months, left of existence. Guilt washed over him. This would be the twenty-first world to be destroyed in the Dark God's name, and Thurm had been at the center of them all.

"Are you going to cast the spell or shall I?" Silverwing asked impatiently, regarding the olthari with a scowl.

"One would figure that as long as you have been around, your race would have learned patience," snorted Thurm, disliking the dragon's insolent tone. He sensed that she was hiding something. "Do you care about this human?"

"You are dealing with a human, is all," said Silverwing. "They are a fragile race. If you do not cease the flow of blood, he will die. And to be honest, even your diminished powers are greater than mine."

Giving the dragon a grunt of disapproval, Thurm closed his eyes and drew upon the vastness of eternity, molding it into his mind. He sought creation, the source of all healing magic. His hands glowed blue and he extended them down to the young man. Upon touching the human, his power tripled, sending an uncontrollable backlash up his arms and pushing him backward.

The olthari sat back up and frowned; his magic had had very little effect on the human. He almost reached back out for the human, but paused.

He sighed. These were very odd circumstances. He wondered if he should look more into it, due to the fact that his master had told him to look for miracles. He pinched his lips into a frown.

I owe this human a debt of gratitude, he thought. *Even if he were the one, which is nigh impossible, I cannot possibly take him now.*

Sensing that the dragon was watching him with interest, Thurm looked up. He did not see the devout follower that he assumed all dragons were. A shroud of shadow crossed its soul. He was about to comment when she interrupted him.

"This human's settlement is close. If you can place him in my foreclaw, I would like to take him back," said Silverwing.

"Why?" asked Thurm, his bushy eyebrows drawing into a scowl. He wondered what the dragon wasn't telling him.

"I don't know," Silverwing admitted. "But this one is destined for great things. I can feel it."

There it was. This human was a pawn in some dragon game of chess. Thurm was disgusted, yet he would watch this dragon and her pet human. His previous thought about the young man as his possible mark faded.

Nodding, Thurm picked up the human and laid the fragile body inside the dragon's foreclaw. He closed his eyes and sent a spark of eternity into the dragon, searing a small mark in her leg, a soul-link, which would allow him to track her at any time.

Silverwing flinched as though she knew what Thurm had done, but made no aggressive move. Instead, she drew her massive maw into a giant scowl and nodded. With that, she took three massive strides, flapped her wings in a giant sweeping motion, and leapt into the air.

As the dragon flew off into the dawn, Thurm rubbed his chin. "A very unusual human," he mused, recalling the nights events in crystal clear detail.

And a very strange day, he thought. Could it be that the dragon was right? Could it be that he had just met a special human, one who was worth watching?

"Maybe it is time I start paying closer attention . . . maybe *this* is the world that will end my great crusade," he said. He turned into the forest thoughtfully and disappeared into the world of Aryth.

† † † † †

The world burned as demons poured forth from the void. There was so much death, horror, and damnation, on such a grand scale, that Areck's mortal mind thought reality was being undone.

It was almost unbearable for the squire. He had never imagined a nightmare could be so vivid, so real, so unsettling. His subconscious mind called to him. It whispered that this was not a nightmare; this was prophecy, given by God.

Areck refused to listen, believing that God would never allow something so tragic to happen. This vision predicted the end of the world. It sent a shiver down his incorporeal spine.

What if this is truth? his subconscious asked. *Maybe God is giving me a glimpse of the future.*

For the briefest of moments Areck glimpsed God, in all of His ever-shimmering glory, calling out to him, welcoming him into Heaven. It made his heart soar and his sickness rose up. It hurt so good. For so long he had thought that he was a failure to the order, to Starsgalt. However, if his Lord was accepting him into Heaven, he had gotten it all wrong. At that moment he knew he could go in peace, his soul clean.

Areck looked to the sky and opened his arms in acceptance. He was greeted with a beautiful starburst of divine power. The sky split open and he saw eternity. He glimpsed Heaven, or rather, what his limited mind wished to see.

He stopped. Something else beckoned. Though he couldn't fathom why, the sounds of his dying world called out to Areck. He looked around, looked at the carnage that was about to happen.

He no longer saw the world die but was instead standing in the middle of a great battlefield littered with corpses. He heard the distant echo of steel ringing all around him, as spiritual combatants danced in and out of his vision. He felt a ghostly apparition brush against his skin and vivid memories of the battle flooded into his mind. He became aware of the pain, of the suffering, of the tragic downfall of . . . of Arsgoth!

"What are you *telling* me?" Areck screamed. "Why are you telling me this?" He began to cry. He knew that he was dying or dead, and that God was trying to show him the future. The question was, *Why*? Why would God show him this then offer him the chance to ascend to Heaven?

Understand. An angelic voice teased his mind. The divine voice sent a thousand possibilities scattering across Areck's vision. He saw himself being killed again and again until a single reality opened, a reality where he did not die and the world was saved. Not by him, he hastened to add, for he was unworthy of such honor, but because he chose *not* to heed God's welcome.

Areck looked to the sky one more time. He was sure that the ghostly apparitions had stopped and were now staring at him, waiting for him to make his choice.

Once again, Starsgalt beckoned him. *God is asking me to come home*, Areck cried. *How can I refuse him?*

An explosion in the distance rumbled the nightmare. The screams of the dying flooded his senses. Lowering his gaze, Areck knew he could not end his life like this, not with such a threat looming, not knowing that he had failed the knighthood, ignorant of what God was trying to show him!

"I do not know what you want of me, my Lord, but as ever, I shall serve my purpose!" Areck shouted. With all of his resolve he turned away from the call. Images exploded, the ground rumbled, and there was darkness.

† † † † †

"He is alive," someone said from very far away.

Areck felt gentle hands search for his pulse. He tried to open his eyes but they did not work. He was sure that he was blind.

"Praise Starsgalt, Lieutenant Redmon! His chest, it moves!" said another.

"Wha . . . happened?" Areck croaked.

"Do not speak, my lord, you are terribly wounded." Squire Redmon knelt next to Areck, doing his best to keep his voice calm. "During the battle you were struck in the chest and knocked from your warhorse, only to be dragged into the forest by the beast. I ordered our best trackers to search the area, hoping to recover you from the fiends. They found your dead horse but not you, and reported that your tracks had, ahem . . . vanished."

Areck felt Redmon's hand squeeze his shoulder in comfort. He tried to speak again, but only incoherent babbling came out. He wished that he could see his comrade's face before he died . . . or was he already dead?

Is this Heaven? he wondered. *No. I refused God's offer, refused Heaven's call. I must warn Lord Lightbringer.*

Areck groaned and his mind became numb from the pain. He shivered.

Redmon yelled, "He is going in to shock! Get back to Brenly and ask the count to prepare whatever medical aid he can spare. If he is going to survive this, we need to get him back to Brenly . . . now!"

Areck passed out.

"Can you save him?" The familiar voice of Squire Redmon woke Areck up again.

"I do not know," said a female voice. "He is in terrible shape. It looks like he has lost a lot of blood and suffers from internal wounds as well. Honestly, I do not know how he is alive."

"It is a miracle, my lady," said Redmon. "Starsgalt is truly merciful and compassionate toward His commanders. My point is proven just by looking at this leg wound. Look at it . . . it was already beginning to scar when we found him. How is that possible? Then you show up, led by The Merciful, to *this* town, at *this* time, to seek out a long forgotten temple in this region. What are the chances of that, my lady? I mean, this *has* to be God's handiwork."

"I have to admit that either God or His servants intervened on this young man's behalf," said the female. "Where did you say you found him, Lord Redmon?"

"Another miracle, Lady Elyana," Redmon replied. "The scout said that he saw a white dragon land in field and decided to investigate the area. Commander Areck was lying on the ground, covered in orcish blood. From the report, Areck was dead until the moment I arrived."

"Can you confirm that there was indeed a dragon?" Elyana asked.

"No, my lady," replied Redmon. "I was penning a note to Lord Lightbringer about Commander Areck's death when the news came. He was barely alive when I got to him and seemed unaware of his surroundings. In fact, *he* asked *me* what had happened to him!"

There was silence.

Areck tried to turn his head and groaned. Though he could not be sure, he knew the name of Lady Elyana. But . . . if it was the woman he remembered, why was she here?

"Squire Redmon, will you order one of the servants to bring me some fresh water?" Elyana asked, seeing Areck's eyes flutter.

"Of course, my lady," Redmon replied and raced from the room.

When Redmon was gone, Elyana peeked around the corner to make sure no one was near. She strolled to Areck and placed a hand upon his head, casting a simple healing incantation.

The healing magic instantly started working, closing several small wounds before it fizzled and made Areck heave. The woman simply turned his heard to the side and put a small piece of wood in his mouth, keeping it open should any vomit leak out. After a moment, she recast the healing spell, only to be met with the same results—a bout of coughing and throw up.

For what seemed like an eternity, Lady Elyana stood over Areck casting the same healing spell time after time. On her last attempt she grunted with effort and almost fell onto him.

The shock of the blow was enough to make Areck open his eyes to see a familiar face staring down at him. It was her! The woman who had poisoned him. But why, how . . .? He had so many questions he wanted to ask, but his tongue did not work.

She smiled at his struggles, put a trembling hand on his face, and righted herself.

"Rest, Sir Areck, so that I may heal your wounds," she said, her perfect brow covered in perspiration.

Areck mumbled incoherent wounds and tried to pull away, spitting up more vomit.

"Shh," she said. "Didn't I tell you that we would meet again? Now close your eyes so that I may fully heal you." Elyana began to chant again, this time with a trembling voice. It sounded as if she was under a great deal of discomfort.

Areck thought that she had to be an angel. He felt another powerful wave of divinity wash over him, this one wracking his body and mind. As quickly as the power had come, the exhausted voice ceased and it dissipated.

Areck stumbled out of consciousness. If he survived, he would have to ask her why he had been chosen. He was so young and so unworthy of God's embrace! These were all things he would ask . . . but not now, not until he was sure of himself.

Areck let his mind slip away.

Darkness overcame him.

25

"... PLEASE, FATHER, hear the plea of your faithful servant," Knight-Captain Bowon Silvershield muttered, trying to hide his grief. "I am in need of ... of you, God, now more than ever."

Silence.

Bowon raised his red-rimmed eyes to the alabaster statue of God, the One God, Starsgalt the Just, The All-Knowing, He Who Is, as tears streaked down his face. Once again, he was greeted with silence. This was the eighth hour of his communion and still the One God had not responded. He felt great humiliation at the thought that God no longer wished to hear what he had to say.

He felt a great weight press down on his lungs, as if the world was upon his shoulders. For the first time in eleven years, pent up anguish and guilt burst forth.

"My God, Starsgalt, please, Father, your faithful servant comes to you in time of his greatest need ...!"

Bowon continued, uncaring that once again there was no response, no divine presence in the chamber. Words spilled incoherently from his mouth. "... the source! I think ... I may have found it at after all these years. But I cannot destroy it ... you cannot ask me to do this thing!"

Bowon rocked back and forth, his gauntleted hands clasped in prayer, and utter silence descended upon the room.

"... give me strength, Father, please," he choked, "give your faithful servant strength! I cannot do this alone!"

"He cannot hear you, my son," a gentle voice whispered as softly as a gentle breeze. "But, I have heard your call and have come to offer aid."

The voice caught Bowon by surprise, freezing him in fetal position, his scaled mail clicking into place. He told himself many things in that moment, thinking God had answered his prayers. Starsgalt must have found it in his heart to forgive a broken old knight for his sins . . . He became aware that he was curled in a ball, crying like a newborn babe, acting like a squire who had just been punished.

Bowon pushed himself into a kneeling position, inhaling to slow the caustic phlegm of his sobs from working its way up his throat. He decided that it was best not to open his eyes, especially without composure, for fear of insulting the celestial being.

Or is *it a celestial being?* He thought. *What if God has sent a . . . a—*

"I am not an angel, child."

Bowon went rigid, realizing that the being had read his thoughts. Furthermore, he might have insulted the divine messenger by not knowing what it was. Fear surged down Bowon's spine

What if I just called God an angel? Bowon close his eyes tight. He felt the shame of his failure constrict his heart.

"Oh, come, boy, we do not have time for this," the voice snapped. "I am not insulted by your premonitions. Anyway, if you would just open your eyes, you will see who stands before you."

The indifferent tone of the voice and lack of command startled Bowon. Although he had not communed with a servant of God for many years, he remembered what it was like. An angel had a superior demeanor about it, a powerful aura of law which made the room prickle with divine energy. Yet he felt nothing except perfect silence.

"Come, come, stop trying to divine who I am and just open your eyes," the voice said with irritation.

Puzzled, Bowon raised his chin and cracked his eyes, still blurred by tears. The sight before him caused his eyes to snap shut and his body shifted nervously. He told himself it was an illusion. There was no way the old man of his nightmares could be standing in front of him so casually, leaning upon a small oak cane, black eyes frowning at him.

This is a figment of my imagination, Bowon thought, remembering his last visit with the blind prophet Malacheye. *This cannot be real!*

"I assure you, young man, I am very real," Malacheye said, puffing his chest out and tapping the ground.

Bowon let his thoughts fade away as fear and confusion surrounded his soul. "How can you be here, old man?"

The prophet laughed heartily at the question. "Why son, I am everywhere, I am all things. Some would say I am existence."

The comment stung Bowon. The old man had in one comment had denounced everything his religion cherished. "You lie, old man!" he screamed and stood.

"An observation for another time," Malacheye responded, his mouth turning into a slight smile.

"Do not mock me, sir!" yelled Bowon. "I am of the Bre'Dmorian Order, a servant to the One True God and should you continue down this blasphemous path, I shall judge you treasonous!"

Again the old man laughed.

Bowon let his fear slip away, focusing his wrath upon the old man. He drew his sword and stalked forward, intent on destroying the nightmare that had led him down this path.

Malacheye's smile never faltered. Instead the old man watched despite sightless eyes as Bowon approached and just before he set foot upon the altar, an unseen force coalesced around the man. Another step forward and the force unleashed itself upon the knight, picking him up off the ground, hurtling him through the air, and slamming him against the marbled walls of the chapel.

Bowon's body cracked against the wall as bones snapped and metal rang out against stone. It was followed by an anguished grunt. He felt conscious thought slip from his mind, as the pain of broken limbs exploded throughout his body. As he slid down the wall, his sight blurred and a trickle of blood ran from his ears.

"Why does everyone think himself a hero?" Malacheye shook his head in frustration, hobbling down the altar towards the broken form of Bowon.

The knight lay on his side coughing and blood poured from his mouth. As Malacheye approached, Bowon's vision began to slip away, his mind receding into the depths of unconsciousness.

". . . failed you, God . . . forgiveness . . . please . . . let .me . . . .come home." Bowon's breath became jagged.

"Young one, I am sorry I had to show, rather than tell you," Malacheye said, dropping the cane and standing straight. He began to grow, increasing his size to that of a full grown ogre, his features becoming handsome, that of a god.

Bowon's mind was fading fast, unable to understand the perfection that exuded from the god-like being. He could only lay there and look up into the fathomless eyes, his life ebbing away into eternity.

"What *are* you?" Bowon asked with his last breath. His body went limp and his eyes glazed over in death.

New consciousness awoke Bowon as his spirit shed its shell and began to pull away from its mortal coil, longing for Heaven.

The creature, once the prophet Malacheye, smiled at Bowon's corpse, infinite pity in its features. It said nothing as Bowon's spirit pulled away and holy light from heaven spilled forth to envelope the pair. It heard the angels preparing to gather the spirit so that the gods of heaven might feed.

The creature began to chant. It was calling forth pure existence. At its bidding unbridled energy gathered around the godly being, and a new light, pure and unaltered balance, exploded in a massive shockwave, changing everything in its path. The angels shrieked as the portal to Heaven collapsed and they were forced to recede into eternity or be winked out of existence.

Releasing the power, the creature gathered Bowon's wandering, confused soul. It cradled it in its caressing hands and looked down upon such an insignificant thing.

"It is not your time yet, my son," the creature whispered to the soul. "There are things you must still do."

Bowon's soul was held immobile by the creature yet soothed by the explanation.

"Once long ago, I told you that you would find the source that Heaven seeks. I told you that once found, you would destroy it and bring down the Bre'Dmorian Order, destroying those that cherish law and order. Now, young one, now that time has come. You must now slay that which cannot be killed, my son. It is your destiny to do this, to change reality."

The soul of Bowon intensified at the request, becoming restless in the creature's grasp.

"I understand your failures, son," said the being. "I am He who sent you down this path. However, you are the one who can do what needs to be done, the only one with love strong enough to make this happen."

Again the soul buzzed in the creatures hands.

"Do not fret," smiled the creature with sadness. "I am here for you. I know what I ask of you and though I cannot truly empathize, I sympathize with your loss. But this must come to pass. Something beyond your understanding is about to come into existence."

Bowon's soul winked in and out in with more questions. It asked the divine being when such a thing needed to unfold.

"You will know when the time is right, son," explained the celestial creature. "Until then, embrace the miracle that has been sent to man . . . for it still needs time to grow."

Bowon's soul became quiet and trembled with loss and understanding.

The creature nodded. It breathed understanding into the soul of Bowon, purpose and resolve. It added a touch of sadness, forged of love. Finally, it added one last thing: justice.

With a flick of its wrist the creature released Bowon's soul, and chanting softly, used its infinite power to rebind the soul to its mortal body. As the soul found its way home, the creature dissolved, and the silence lifted.

As the soul struggled to find its way back to existence, it heard the fleeting words: "And so begins the Apocalypse."

ABOUT THE AUTHOR

ERIC FOGLE is the Vice President of Sales and Marketing at Sunmark Seeds, Intl. in Portland Oregon. He began his writing career in 1994 after reading an extraordinary novel, *The Magician's Apprentice*, by Raymond Feist. At the time, he was unaware how awesomely vivid settings and deep characters would inspire him to write. As such, he has not stopped reading nor writing since; collecting over 200 novels from various fantasy writers.

In 2004, Eric finished the first book in the Forge of the Gods series, *The Last Knight*.

Now, he lives with his wife, Kristy, in Troutdale, Oregon. His life is filled with days of writing, nights of playing computer games, and weekends filled with softball and basketball. However, it can only get better now that he is living his dream—writing compelling novels for the world to read.

He can be reached via e-mail at eric@ericfogle.com. Or you can visit his website at: www.ericfogle.com.

ALSO AVAILABLE FROM BREAKNECK BOOKS

By Jeremy Robinson
". . . a rollicking Arctic adventure that explores the origins of the human species." -- James Rollins, bestselling author of *Black Order* and *The Judas Strain*

www.breakneckbooks.com/rtp.html

By James Somers
". . . a nice read of battle, honor, and spirituality . . . that left me wanting more." -- Fantasy Book Spot

www.breakneckbooks.com/soone.html

By Sean Young
". . . captures the imagination and transports you to another time, another way of life and makes it real." -- Jeremy Robinson, author of *Raising the Past* and *The Didymus Contingency*

www.breakneckbooks.com/sands.html

BREAKNECK BOOKS
PUBLISHING COMPANY

COMING IN 2007 FROM
BREAKNECK BOOKS

ANTARKTOS RISING

By Jeremy Robinson
"A new dark continent of terror. Trespass at your own risk." – James Rollins, bestselling author of Black Order and The Judas Strain

www.breakneckbooks.com/antarktos.html

By Michael G. Cornelius
"...a dark and dangerous book with suspense and surprises aplenty" – A.J. Matthews, author of Follow and Unbroken

www.breakneckbooks.com/ascension.html

THE NINEVEH PROJECT

By Craig Alexander
". . . an action packed race against time and terrorists. Absolutely riveting." – Jeremy Robinson, bestselling author of The Didymus Contingency and Raising the Past.

www.breakneckbooks.com/nineveh.html

BREAKNECK BOOKS
PUBLISHING COMPANY

Printed in the United States
102115LV00004B/29/A